THE ICE-SHIRT

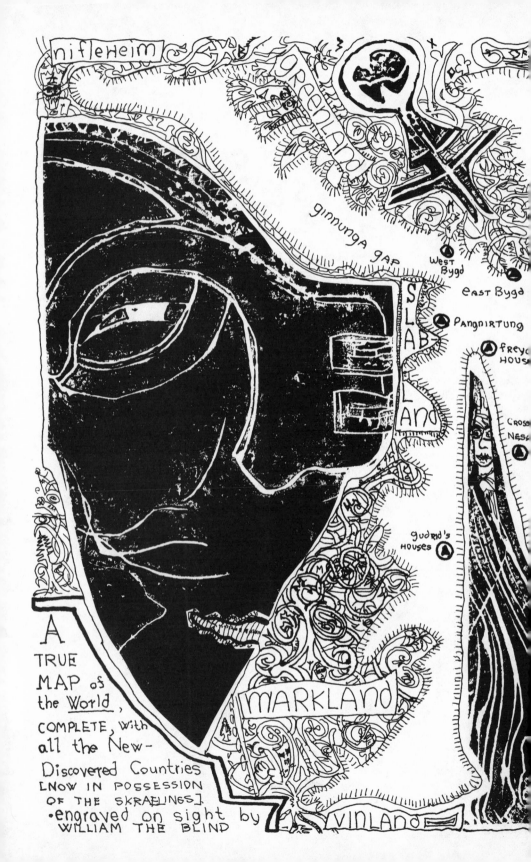

nifleHeim

GREENLAND

ginnunga gap

West Bygd

East Bygd

Pangnirtung

freya House

S L A B L A n d

Crossa Ness

gudrid's Houses

A
TRUE
MAP of
the World,
COMPLETE, with
all the New-
Discovered Countries
[NOW IN POSSESSION
OF THE SKRAELINGS]
·engraved on sight by
WILLIAM THE BLIND

MARKLAND

VINLAND

SEVEN DREAMS
A Book of North American Landscapes

THE ICE-SHIRT

by

WILLIAM T. VOLLMANN

VIKING

SEVEN DREAMS

ABOUT OUR CONTINENT IN THE DAYS OF THE SUN

making Explicit
many ★ REVELATIONS ★
concerning Trees and Rivers,
Ancestors,
ETERNITIES
Vikings, Crow-Fathers,
TRESPASSES, EXECUTIONS, ASSASSINATIONS,
MASSACRES,

Whirlpool – Lives;

Love-Souls and Monster-Souls,

Dead Worlds

Wherein we made
FOUNTAINS OUT OF PROLEHILLS;

Voyages Across the Frozen Sea

Told COMPLETE with Accounts of
Various *TREACHEROUS ESCAPES,*

White Sweet Clover,

GOLDENROD
&
★ The Fern Gang ★

As Gathered From DIVERSE SOURCES

by

WILLIAM T. VOLLMANN

(Known in This World as
"WILLIAM THE BLIND")

VIKING
Published by the Penguin Group
Viking Penguin, a division of Penguin Books USA Inc.,
375 Hudson Street, New York, New York 10014, U.S.A.
Penguin Books Ltd, 27 Wrights Lane,
London W8 5TZ, England
Penguin Books Australia Ltd, Ringwood,
Victoria, Australia
Penguin Books Canada Ltd, 2801 John Street,
Markham, Ontario, Canada L3R 1B4
Penguin Books (N.Z.) Ltd, 182–190 Wairau Road,
Auckland 10, New Zealand

Penguin Books Ltd, Registered Offices:
Harmondsworth, Middlesex, England

First American Edition
Published in 1990 by Viking Penguin,
a division of Penguin Books USA Inc.

Illustrations by the author

LIBRARY OF CONGRESS CATALOGING IN PUBLICATION DATA
Vollmann, William T.
The ice-shirt/by William T. Vollmann.
p.   cm. — (Seven dreams)
ISBN 0-670-83239-1
1. America — Discovery and exploration — Norse — Fiction.
2. Greenland — Discovery and exploration — Fiction.   I. Title.
II. Series: Vollmann, William T.   Seven dreams.
PS3572.O395I27   1990
813'.54 — dc20   90-50051

Printed in the United States of America
Set in Bembo

For
Janice Kong-Ja Ryu
and
Patti Simmons R.I.P.
Veronica Compton #276077

. . . just as Europe and Asia received in days gone by their names from Women.

Cosmographiæ Introductio (1507)

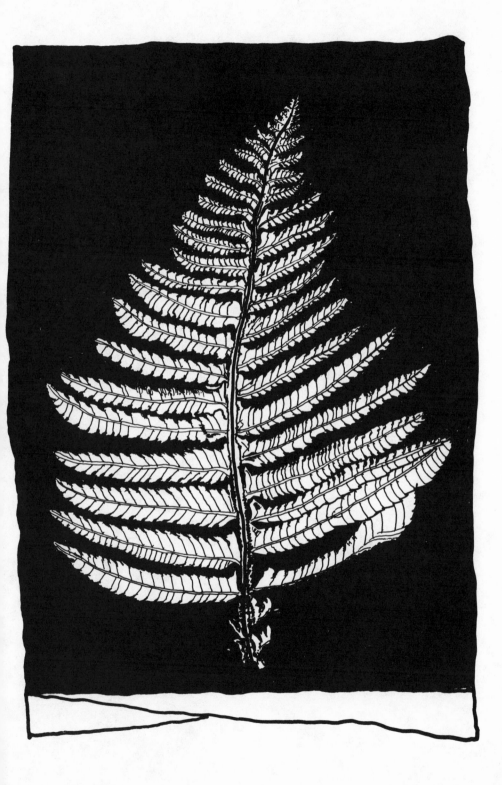

Preface

SHOULD I dream one dream or seven? – Anyone would prefer a single afternoon fancy to grease his heels, so that easy wings might flower there, and then he could play between blue skies and rooftops, but as I could never fly, having put on the **Ice-Shirt,** the **Crow-Shirt** and the **Poison-Shirt,** there is no hope in frivolous ambition. Any shirt, be it of ever so many colors, is but a straitjacket, which is why I see no beauty, nor hear of any, except among the naked. The clouds are as hard as stones, and we all dream one black dream. – I, however, will now dream seven, to which correspond the Seven Ages of WINELAND THE GOOD. Each Age was worse than the one before, because we thought we must amend whatever we found, nothing of what *was* being reflected in the ice-mirrors of our ideas. Yet we were scarcely blameworthy, any more than the bacilli which attack and overcome a living body; for if history has a purpose,* then our undermining of trees and tribes must have been good for something. – Be it so.

—>•••←—

Readers are warned that the sketch-maps and boundaries here are provisional, approximate, unreliable and wrong. Nonetheless, I have furnished them, for as my text is no more than a pack of lies they can do no harm.

WILLIAM THE BLIND
San Francisco

---

* If not, then there is nothing wrong with inventing one.

I am grieved that the book and many other writings on these subjects have, I don't know how, come sadly to ruin; for, being but a child when they fell into my hands, I, not knowing what they were, tore them in pieces, as children will do, and sent them all to ruin, a circumstance which I cannot now recall without the greatest sorrow . . .

NICOLÒ THE YOUNGER, *The Discovery of the Islands of Frislanda, Eslanda, Engroenlanda, Estotilanda, & Icaria; made by Two Brothers of the Zeno Family: viz.: Messire Nicolò The Chevalier, and Messire Antonio* (Venice, 1558)

FIRST DREAM
The Ice-Shirt

Contents

The Glossaries and Chronology are conveniences, to be used if needed. The Glossaries define and give the origin of any word which might be unfamiliar. (A list of characters and cultures will also be found here.) The Chronology serves as a mnemonic for all important Kings, dates and historical or mythological events referred to in the text. As for the Source Notes, they may be ignored or skimmed; their function is to record my starting points, which may interest travelers in other directions.

List of Maps

Ice-Text

The Book of Flatey 1382
A Historical Note

T he story of the demon Blue-Shirt (known in His native land as AMORTORTAK) is hinted at in a variety of codices, being revealed nowhere and everywhere, like cabalistic doctrine. Explication, therefore, remains a task of almost celestial difficulty – a pity for me, as I could otherwise be drumming my fingers and peering admiringly through my window-bars at the driveway. But I must do my best. – In but two sources, then, has anyone found direct mention of this LORD of our secret worship: the *Grænlendinga Saga*, known in English as the *Tale of the Greenlanders* (*ca.* 1190), and its companion *Eirik's Saga* (*ca.* 1260) – and in both of these He appears in the form of a great glacier-mountain, which some are disposed to equate with Gunnbjorn's Peak (at 12,500 feet the highest point in Greenland), and others with the lesser glacier-tower of Ingolfsfjeld, near Angmagssalik. No traces of demonic origin were reported by the expedition that first scaled the former's summit in 1935; nor is Ingolfsfjeld anything more than a sky-colored eye of ice, gazing dully out upon the sea. – Where then is Blue-Shirt? – Why, nowhere and everywhere. – History being nothing more than a long list of regrettable actions, such equivocation should not surprise us. But where corpses were buried secretly, there the grass grows thick; such signs (and there are ever so many others!) may be read by those to whom truth is more important than beauty.

———>•◆•<———

But what if, as in our case, it is winter, so that the Sun has gone away and the grass lies deep beneath the ice?

———>•◆•<———

Well, as on a darkly moonless night the sensible course may be to become a part of the darkness; so here we may learn to conceive Nothing from nothing. Proceeding gropingly upwards, then, against a frozen night-cliff of twelfth- and thirteenth-century words, we must ascend many dark chimneys to attain the greater darkness; here the two sagas brace each other; for they are our climbing-legs, left and right, Freydis and Gudrid, Bjarni and Leif; and so up the Ice-Mountain we dully trudge, as if we did not even know that the eyes decompose first, that arsenic is almost tasteless, that younger bodies take longer to putrefy! – But central to our preoccupations must be Freydis's axe, and though, being double-bladed, it lies gleamingly across both accounts, only in the *Grænlendinga Saga* does it take white lives as well as red. And the *Grænlendinga Saga* appears in that great graveyard of tales, the *Book of Flatey*.

———>•••<———

The *Flateyjarbók* is so named because it was commissioned by Jón Finnsson, a wealthy farmer on the isle of Flatey, in Breidafjord. (The name of the scribe who did the work is, of course, lost.) The first page was begun in 1382; the last was finished thirteen years later. – In the meantime, Blue-Shirt's weather became more severe in Greenland, and two troll-children died there for love of Bjorn the Crusader, as will be told. – Jón Finnsson's descendants cherished the book and kept it in the family for nearly three hundred years, until one of them (moved, no doubt, not by coercion, but rather by piety and true regard) presented it to the Bishop at Skalholt – a place which, though ice-green on the atlas-page, must in reality have been as garden-green as the grass over corpses, for RELIGION grew there, and it had become a most flourishing diocese, as Leif the Lucky's lover foreknew at the turn of the millennium when she asked to be buried there between its river-bends. (Poor Thorgunna! Though she was a Hebridean witch, still she could not make Leif's heart bleed, for it was impervious in its Blue Shirt. Her tale too I will tell.) – When the Danes acquired Iceland in 1380, they necessarily, by the rule of metonymy, acquired the unwritten *Flateyjarbók* as well, and so in due time the Bishop sent the manuscript on to the Royal Library in Copenhagen. There it stayed for another three centuries, unmolested by the Danish Kings, who, between the gold crowns that encumbered their heads and the gold crowns that stuffed their purses, found their lives to be quite full enough. (They had annexed Greenland, too, but they cared not a whit about Blue-Shirt.) So the Kings ate smoked fish and prayed. – In 1944, when Denmark was distracted by German troubles, the Icelanders helped themselves to their sovereignty, and so the decaying mass of vellum of which we speak returned across the sea. It is now under glass in Reykjavík.

———>•••<———

What is there to say about this talisman? Well, it is happily not so decomposed as the original *Njal's Saga*, whose greasy tissue of black leaves most resembles a squashed crow's carcass. We read that one hundred and thirteen calfskins were required to make it – a fact singular in its uselessness, but certainly believable, for the page-height of this book is from my wrist to my elbow, and the margins are sumptuous. Each vellum sheet is brown with age, and upon this brownness is a sea of brown ink, stained with islands of darker decay, like Flatey itself, which is a flat island of grass and orange lichens and stones, where hunks of sheep-wool lie on the grass like clouds, and the sheep themselves are so thick with it as to resemble haystacks. The lambs crunch grass very watchfully, but the old ewes and rams do not look up at your approach because nobody has ever hurt them and they do not understand the meaning of the sheep-skulls that lie in the grass they graze on. – The birds, on the other hand, await the worst with hysterical foreknowledge, so that if you venture into their nesting-fields, where the grass is green and then white, as if frosted, thousands of them begin to swoop and scream and flap until their gull-cousins on the rocks offshore are infected with alarm, and sob like babies. (Would you, reader, rather be a sheep or a bird? *I* say that the sweet sheep have no cares, and for that reason their stupidity is to be prized.) – But these catastrophes are strictly local. The grey sea protects the separate fears and pains from each other. After all, there are so many islands in Breidafjord! Close upon the isle of Flatey, for instance, is gathered a constellation of little isles whose rocky tails wander into the sea; these skerries are sometimes white with birds, who hear not, or care not (I cannot say which) when the Flatey-birds begin to scream of broken eggs. Black-and-white ducks drift serenely around the perimeters of those isles – all *low* isles, by the way, formed of parallel slabs of rock piled upon each other at a steep angle to the sea; and their ridge-tops are nothing but rocks on rock, with grey and yellow lichens, so that your eye goes less frequently across the water to other low islands than down the mossy, rocky slope you stand on and across the rolling grass to the flowers, so many flowers, more flowers than islands! – for in the spring months of Sowing-Tide and Egg-Tide, Iceland is golden with Arctic poppies in their different races of *Melasól* and *Steindórssól* and *Stefánssol* with yellow milksap and white milksap spilling down your fingers like liquid sunlight; and pink sandworts blossom by the water, and white orchids grow in the mire, and the stones are softly velveted by the little purple moss campions; and in the moss-chapters of the *Flateyjarbók* rise the spring-shoots of initial letters with their long tails and handles; from their cliff-ledges among the words they send down fertile runners, like the Þ that goes far down into the margin to sprout a red flower pillowed against little delicate white leaves, just as a woman's vagina is lovingly pillowed by secret fragrant hairs; and a white-and-green bone-blossom swells its ruffles inside the head of that Þ that begins the story of how Freydis and Blue-Shirt brought the frost to Vinland; and the words themselves are flower-silhouettes with wriggling dark roots; so that every story-isle is a flower-isle carpeted with ease . . . and every flower-isle is peculiar to itself, although, as I have said, there are uncountable numbers of them in Breidafjord; and the tide comes in and the tide goes out, but the isles remain on the sea-page like all the different stories that crawl letter by perfect letter in the two-column sheets of the *Flateyjarbók*.

———>•••‹———

Among these stories, for the reasons given above, I have trapped myself in the *Grænlendinga Saga*, which rises like a column of rock in the grey sea between the *Saga of King Olaf Trygvesson*, among whose skull-cliffs scream gulls and Christian ghosts; and the *Saga of King Olaf the Saint*, a softer, mossier story generally, although not without eye-gougings or mutilations of hands and feet; by divine right I now command these story-isles to burst into flower! – and if they do not, no matter, for I will seed them with my own imagination: – Upon the rockiest chapters I will plant the moss of my speculations; through the moss my asphodels and orchids will rise, fertilized by that poor dead bundle of a hundred and thirteen calfskins . . .

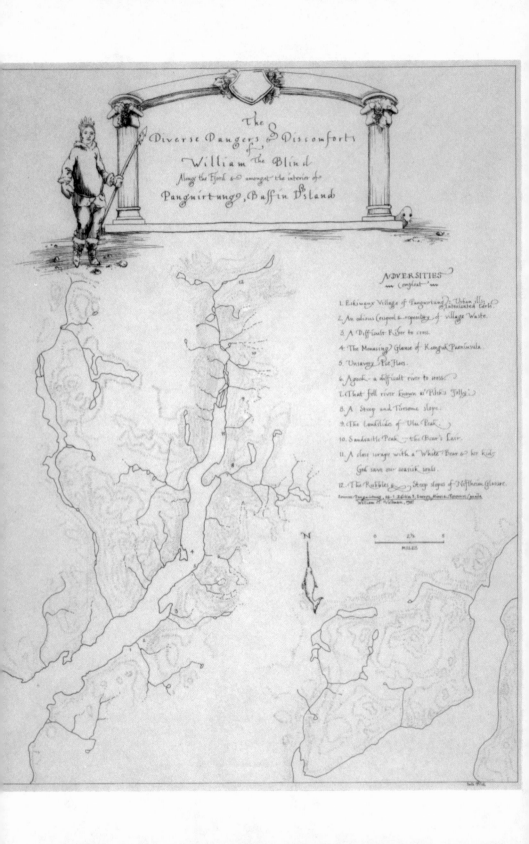

The
Diverse Dangers & Discomforts
of
William the Blind
Along the Fjord & amongst the interior of
Pangnirtung, Baffin Island

ADVERSITIES
~ Compleat ~

1. Eskimaux Village of Pangnirtung & its Urban Ally: Intoxicated Girls.

2. An odious Cesspool & repository of village Waste.

3. A Difficult River to cross.

4. The Menacing Glance of Kingnuk Paeninsula

5. Unsavory Ice Floes.

6. Agook – a difficult river to cross.

7. That fell river known as Pitik's Folly.

8. A Steep and Tiresome slope.

9. The Landslides of Ulu Peak.

10. Sandcastle Peak ~ the Bear's Lair.

11. A close scrape with a White Bear & her kids
    God save our seasick souls.

12. The Rubbles & Steep slopes of Niftheim Glacier.

Sources: Pangnirtung, 46-1 Edition 3, Energy, Mines & Resources Canada
William H. Vollmann, 1991

0   2½   5
MILES

N

The Ice-Shirt

In a geographical tradition of northern Europe Vinland came to be located among the mists and ice of the Northern Ocean in Arctic latitudes.

Professor of Maps, 1965

The ice is like a mean dog. He always waits for you to stop watching him and then he tries to get you.

Wainwright Eskimo, *ca.* 1964

1

The Changers,
or,

How the Bear-Shirt was lost,
and the Ice-Shirt was found

Wearing the Bear-Shirt
ca. 200 – ca. 940

Towards the east . . . there is a place called the Ice Pass. Through it,
they say, there is a way towards Greenland, but I was never there . . .

JAN WELZL, *The Quest for Polar
Treasures* (1933)

J ust as incipient dizziness may be proclaimed by a change in the cadence
of running water, so Greenland, being too hard a fact to fall all at once upon
the world's endurance, first presented itself by means of secret signs – or so
I *should* write to please you, for what 𝕳𝖎𝖘𝖙𝖔𝖗𝖞 𝖔𝖋 𝕺𝖚𝖗 𝕮𝖔𝖓𝖙𝖎𝖓𝖊𝖓𝖙 could be of
interest that did not deal in secrets? – or at least with INTIMATIONS across the
sea-bights which none of our northern fathers could readily interpret, being
preoccupied of themselves by ungreen pursuits even in summer when the
birds sang to the sun for all the long green moss-days; for grandfather-weather
was grey weather, cloud-walled tight against the sun's golden tears so that
wherever men came, came the thunder of grey armor, the screaming of grey
warhorses, "the war-shower of grey arrows" (Thord Kolbeinsson); while in
winter men were coldbound, greybound, watching grey snow sifting down
between grey branches, as silver-grey icicles grew long from the roofs of their
houses. Snow-mists hemmed the farmsteads in; snow fell grey in the black
forests, and north and east the mountains were greyly snowclad. Where the
frost-seeds had sprouted grew new trees of ice, whose branches were harder
than iron. But there was one tree that gave life, though it rose so high into winter
darkness and summery afternoons that we could not understand it: Yggdrasil,
the World-Ash, whose third root covered us (the first roofing HEL, the Queen
of the Dead, and the second affording Frost Giants sky in Jötunheim). This

tree was always green, dew-crowned; in its boughs the birds sang to the sun
for the long green moss-days. This tree stood green above the Well of Weird.
Yet even here there was no peace, for rabbits gnawed at its leaves and branches,
and fat serpents gnawed at its roots beneath the earth.

The Bear-Shirt

This appears to me quite natural, but why the condition of our ancestors was
so miserably perilous I cannot say, for they were wise enough: – ODIN could
call the dead from the earth, and King Dag, between whom and the god FREY
were only seven generations, knew the language of the birds. Surely it was not
greed; nor could it have been selfish jealousy, for if our ancestors were selfish
then what hope is there for us, when we cannot call the dead or converse
with birds? – It must have been the witchcraft of the Finns, whom everybody
blamed for everything in those days. – Lives sought to rule lives; Kings burned
Kings sleeping in their houses. What glory there would have been in it, if only
they had not been forbidden long since to be Lords of Rainbows and Angels!
– They could still, of course, be Kings of Trees if they chose; or Fen-Kings,
Snow-Kings, Bear-Kings; in the sagas we read that they were Bear-Kings.
Although they did such wickedness that their victims' groans became moss,
and their victims' tears became black seeds in the moss that sprouted into
blood-slicked saplings, and the saplings grappled into the earth with their
claw-roots, and thickened and grew into great pain-trees whose black shafts
rose to heaven, the Kings, too, suffered, because on becoming bears their
hairy shoulders grew so wide that they spanned the narrow forest-avenues, so
that jagged pain-leaves and grief-leaves tore their flesh as they ran bellowing
towards each other, and every leaf was green and fragrant and the light swirled
around them. When they stood sniffing in the tree-shadows their faces ran
like pigment down a canvas, in correspondence with their liquid desires, so
that sometimes they sprouted yellow bear-fangs beneath their beards, and
the hair thickened on their cheeks, and then a moment later their skin was
grey-green-scaled like tree-bark, and they wept tears of sap; at times they were
even men, ruddy-faced with full lips, looking abstractedly at their mismatched
hands (one unclawed, the other still velvet-spotted with great black bearpads
in which the talons gently curled . . .) In those times a man might be born a
"wolf of evening," as the Icelanders called him – a bearsark. When his fit came
upon him, he howled like a wild beast, foamed at the mouth and gnawed at the
iron rim of his shield. Arrows could not kill him; fire could not burn him. So,

too, the Changing-fit came upon the Kings; and they made themselves bears; then, having overborne each other, they knew not how to be discreet, and charged on down their bear-roads, so intoxicated by *metamorphosis* that they were sure they grew bigger each time they changed their skins. Being heedless of the habits of their serpent-brothers and lobster-cousins, who hide under stones until they are surely hardened in new forms, the Bear-Kings gloated in contemplated cross-sweeps of their great arms across their enemies' faces, gashing and ripping; and as they gloated they lay in the sunlight that shouted so brassily through the trees, and the sun-music rolled from golden horns and lulled the bears to sleep head on paw; then by murder and trickery they were easily undone by others. – Sometimes they undid each other simultaneously, as was the case with the brother-Kings Alric and Eric, each of whom wanted to engorge his twin, and, so nourished, grow for himself a bright double kingship-skin. They went riding, and at the same moment smashed each other's skulls in with their bridles.

The Shirt of Perpetuity

Oh, that game of Changing! The players did not really want to be anything; they only wanted to be what they were not. Nobody saw that change came of its own, unfolding as was ordained, so that one would be as ungracious to rush it as to stay it – which latter in his anxiety did King On, Jorund's son, who did not want to die, and so offered up nine of his ten sons to ODIN for longer life, one by one, and longer life ODIN gave him, although in time he could not walk, and then he could not sit, and then he could not eat; and still he wanted to sacrifice his tenth son, but the Swedes would not allow it, and so King On died. – Imagine the terror that kept him from seeing that most corpses close their eyes so peacefully! How his skull gaped, before he was dead, the flesh around it hardly more than a worn habit! – and all along he had *known* that it must someday be so; he knew it before his father was hanged by the King of Halogaland; he knew it when he fled from two Kings of Denmark; he knew it when his wife died and was buried in the ground, with a horrible empty space beside her that waited for *him*, and must be filled by his dead body someday, and then his dead wife's skull would kiss his skull in a great hard clack of bone; but his knowing the inevitability of it did not at all help him, so he mummified himself alive for his second sixty years, taking only mummy-amusements that made his mummy-mouth grin and grin in the coolness of his palace vaults where he sat to be safe from drafts and wars and angry sons; so he preserved his bones as if they were Turkish glass; but finally he had to change just the same; he had to put on the Mold-Shirt.

Old Blood

Thus went the game, down the long dynasty of the Yngling Kings, which no one yet saw an end of; – as if those Changers would never run out of carven pieces to play! as if the world-circle could possibly continue to give birth to new seas and islands of itself! – although it was true, as the Changers well knew, that King Dag's sparrow had one day leapt up from his shoulder to spread wings and claws and swoop through the tower window to see the news and never returned; it was true that King On was dead; – and men agreed that in earlier days nine sons would have bought nine centuries, but now scarce nine decades could be expected; nor could sons change as easily as they ought: so On's last son Egil, who was now King after him, called his son Ottar before him and said, "Become a bear!" and little Ottar slavered and shook himself and ground his teeth and the yellow fangs sprouted from his lip; and King Egil said, "Become a wolf!" and Ottar fell on all fours growling softly and working the corners of his mouth and he slunk into the corner watching his father over his shoulder and clothed himself with grey dog-hair, so that Egil knelt down and stroked his head between the warily lifted ears and the little wolf-prince licked his teeth in delicate modesty as Egil said, "Well done, my son!", but later, when he had transformed himself into a boy again, Egil saw how much effort it had cost him, and felt misgiving. After King Egil was killed by a bull, and Ottar succeeded him, he ruled justly, ravaging the lands of the Danes and giving booty always to his men, so that he was well loved and supported, but one day the Danes came upon him in the woods and though he sought to change himself and his right arm had already become hairy they killed him just the same. – Hearing what had befallen, his son King Adils said to himself, "Indeed this would never have happened to my grandfather, King Egil!" and he went into a dark tree-grove to see how he might fare at the practice. The black leaves whispered about him like secrets, and his father's howe cast a shadow upon shadows (inside, his father lay amidst his dearest treasures, but the serpents crawled in his beard). Now King Adils climbed up upon the mound and prayed to ODIN, saying: "My race has always been Were-Kings, dear Raven – so I ask you: guard our Changing-blood so that it does not bleed out of us!" and then he clambered down and parted the black thorn-branches beyond the mound and stood between two ash-trees that rose into each other's darkness and King Adils began to pant like a bear and said, "ODIN, help me!" and it was very dark and shady like the Hall of HEL where men's ribs lay scattered among the grave-timbers, and the branches creaked about King Adils's head and he was afraid, but he curled his left hand into a claw and talons flowered, and he curled his right hand and again the fingernails grew, and he growled and glutted himself with great breaths to make his chest swell into a bear's chest, but nothing happened. Though he strove with himself, beating his chest until it was covered with welts and bruises, he could not become a bear. With an oath, he clapped his hands together and let his breath out, and his claws shrank back into flaccid fingers again, and he flung himself down into the leaves exhausted. "Our blood has been weakened by women!" he cried in dismay. But neither FREYJA nor FRIGG was there anymore for him to take. He married Yrsa, a yellow-haired girl from Saxland, and had sons by her, but it is said that in fear for the future he privily consulted the Lapps. They stirred their hearth-fires as they listened; they offered him reindeer milk. – "But you are cold!" they said with ironic tenderness. "*That* is why you shiver in the Changing – you must put on your serk!" When he had paid in cattle, thralls and good red gold, they revealed to him certain magics and stratagems by which the game might be played out awhile longer; for although indeed the god-blood was failing with the new generations, yet sufficient powers remained in the hearts of animals to help, if eaten at those times when the sun dripped down like blood into the marshes and the wind smelled like ice. So as yet all remained well with the Ynglings, and after that blood-festival to FREYJA when King Adils was killed in a fall from his horse, his son King Eystein ruled over Sweden, and though his mother Yrsa had been carried off by King Helge of Leidre, the son of that rape fell in battle, being unable to change himself, and King Eystein lived knowingly on, eating the hearts of wolves and bears as prescribed by the Lapps, and he fought the other Bear-Kings in a great clamor of shields until they burned him asleep in his house, at which his son Yngvar became King; and perhaps it was Yngvar who, considering what he had to have no longer as an attribute of himself, but only as a *thing* like his axe, persuaded the Lapps to sew him a special Bear-Shirt that he could carry with him whenever he needed it, or perhaps it was Yngvar's son, King Onund Road-Clearer, who did it; we know only that Halfdan the Black, a King in later times, reckoned back with his fingers through the thickets of his ancestors and said that it was not much after King Adils that the iron chests of Bear-Shirts became common among highborn men, to be passed down from father to son. The stuff of these shirts was matted hair, stinking of grease and blood; men pulled them down over their heads with hot voluptuousness; claws sprouted from the sleeves almost as rapidly as in the days of old King Egil, and the shirts began to pound with the heartbeats of the bears beneath . . . Even these, however, gradually became rare or lost their virtue with age, so that within a couple of hundred years there were not so many; but meanwhile the Changers changed with more ease than ever, and battle-suns clanged against battle-moons* as the treetops whipped in war-winds to show the rushing clouds of night, and many a winter there was when the red eye of fire glared through the bare trees so that pink tongues of light rippled on the snow and then there came shouts and terrible screams and the crashing down of burned timbers, at which the burners loped away with their chins low between their shoulders, grunting with happiness to see their enemies sent to join King On, King Egil, King Adils, King Eystein; and the Bear-Kings fished for treasure in Norway's streams and wandered among the trees seething with pride-lust and striving one with the other for gold and goods; many a summer field was marked by the swaggering prints of the usurping bears, and then other Changers trampled the soil, as if runes and words had been written one upon the other on a single page, so that the whiteness of the evening fields was dark with bear-hordes growling and tearing each other to pieces in mad rages, while the Wolf-Kings skulked on the outskirts, waiting for their chance. But the Yngling dynasty came to its end at last with Onund's son, King Ingjald the Evil-Worker.

The Wolf-Shirt

Like all of us, Ingjald was born naked; it was not immediately that he put on the shirt that he was destined to wear. A pretty blue-eyed baby, he made his mother happy every hour, but when his clumsy little hands let go the spear-haft that was placed in them, then his father, King Onund Road-Builder, turned his face away. When Ingjald was a lad of six, there was a great Yule-feast in Upsal, where the Swedes held their sacrifices, and Ingjald played at war with Alf, King Yngvar's son, each of them leading an army of imagined boy-specters who offered perfect loyalty but had no strength, so that Alf and Ingjald were themselves compelled to lay hands on each other, no matter how ringingly they cried to vaporous spear-guards to conquer for them; and Alf knocked Ingjald down, saying, "Death to you, wicked Estlander!" – for it was in far

---

* Both kennings for shields. On kennings see Glossary IV.

Estland that Ingjald's father had gone a-ravaging; then young Ingjald jumped up flushing and marshaled his air-bearsarks and cried, "Pierce him, you men!", but the bearsarks were no stronger than air and Ingjald was vanquished by Alf a second time, so that he fell and his head hit the hard ice and blood trickled through his hair; then Alf stood leaning over him and gloating, so little Ingjald stood again and raised high his shield, Bloody-Back (which was, however, but a sheet of bark), and he gripped his spear (which was an ash-twig) and drew up his air-soldiers in the proper order of battle and advanced on Alf with awful resolution; but no matter how fiercely he strove with him in the snow he was thrown down with all his army, while the Bear-Kings gathered around in a circle and jeered. At last Ingjald was almost in tears. Pitying him, his foster-brother Gautvid led him in to his foster-father Svipdag the Blind, who ruled over Upsal, and now sat where it was warm, exchanging news with the cracklings and sap-pops of green wood in the fire; and Gautvid cried: "Listen, father, and you will hear Ingjald sniffling like a whipped girl! Pass your knowing hands across his face, and you will find it wet with his unmanly tears! How may we expect this calf to be a King?" – "Oh, yes," sighed King Svipdag the Blind, "it is a great shame, a great shame indeed. Gautvid, go hunt down a wolf and bring me his heart." – Laughing, Gautvid snatched up his spear and ran from the hall, while old King Svipdag rocked himself in front of the fire, muttering, "A great shame; oh, yes," and Ingjald King Onund's-Son stood wishing that he had never been born, as Alf marched round and round outside the hall, breaking off icicles and smashing them against the gables and calling, "Come fight again, Ingjald, if you dare!" – "Oh, he'll fight again *tomorrow*, hee-hee!" snickered old Svipdag to himself. "Poor little Alf!" – Gautvid for his part ran swiftly and silently through the forest. The north wind blew furiously against him, and the trees creaked in groaning suspense as he took his way among the dark mountains where the wolves lived. Save for the snow-glare at his feet, it was pitch-black in the long winding tree-tunnels through which he threaded his way, and the roof-branches scraped hideously against his head, as if they wished to pluck his hair. The snow grew deeper, and the forest yet more dreary and gruesome, until presently he saw the darkness around him beset by triangular amber gleams. Gautvid knew well that these were wolves' eyes. He searched about until he spied a tree which he could readily climb, and there he waited with his back against it so that the wolves could not spring on him from behind. The night was black and dismal except for the snow's sick glare. At last he heard a howl very close to him, and another, and then the wolves came rushing upon him. How many of them there were he could not tell, for some lurked back among the trees, with their ears pressed cautiously against their heads; while the bolder ones crowded him, snarling, and their fang-teeth shone like the snow. – Brave Gautvid laughed aloud. He jabbed at them with his spear until they gave him a little peace, and then he leaped up into his tree. Seeing him escape, the animals hurled themselves into the air, but their teeth snicked together harmlessly in midair by his heels, and he swung himself up into the tree-crotch and howled mockingly back at the wolves until they were maddened. The most ferocious of them, a great black she, scrabbled her claws against the tree-trunk again and again in her vain attempts to climb the tree and be at him, until the bark was torn off in a great ring; and even then she raked the smooth wood with gashes. Never did she cease glaring at him with her horrible amber eyes. Leaning low from the tree-branch, Gautvid said, "Necklace tree,* allow me to pluck your queenly heart!" He leaned lower still, as if he were falling; she sprang high to meet him; then with all his might Gautvid rammed his spear down her dark throat. She snapped the haft through with her teeth, but then fell howling upon the snow with the point still inside her. Gautvid jumped down upon her; he stamped once on her heaving belly; he stamped twice, and then the she-wolf coughed and died, with black gore dripping from her black beard. Seeing her companions sneaking close upon him, with their snouts upon the snow, Gautvid pulled the carcass back into the tree and set about the work that his father had commanded, parting the skin of that dark and hairy breast with his knife, and slicing through the ribs so that blood rained down upon the snow, and her brothers snuffed it up and keened. So he cut out the steaming heart. He threw the rest of her to the other wolves, who retired wretched and discomfited, and went away upon the tree-tops. – Surely he was not wicked who brought his foster-brother that evil heart, which beat yet in his hands and seared him with its venom, for he but obeyed his father. – In the morning, when the heart had finally ceased to quiver, Svipdag the Blind washed it and roasted it upon a stick, touching it often and licking his fingers, for he had eaten many such in his time. The black blood dripped hissing in the fire. When the meat was ready, Gautvid brought in little Ingjald, saying, "Eat, brother, and you will become strong!" Almost at once as the boy began to chew, his eyes shone like a wolf's eyes. He bolted his meal in snatches and gobbets; he licked the burned blood on the cinders. His nails and teeth grew long; his body grew hairy, and he became a person of the most ferocious disposition. He rushed in upon his rival Alf as he lay sleeping, and almost killed him. – "I do not know you!" cried his father Onund when he heard of this. "You are not my son." – "Oh, I'm your son,

---

* Kenning for a woman.

all right," said Ingjald sullenly. "And I remember now how once you turned your face away from me. If you do it a second time, I'll burn you out!" At this, Onund embraced him.

When Ingjald had grown into his lust-age, King Onund applied to King Algaut of Gotland for his daughter, Gauthild, so poor Gauthild was sent to Sweden to be married. Before the wedding had even been concluded, Ingjald threw himself upon her and ravished her. Not many autumns after, Onund was killed in a landslide, and Ingjald became King. He grinned for joy; he threw the embers about with his hairy black hands so that his followers must rush about with pails of water to extinguish every blaze. – "Have no fear," shouted Ingjald, "now that I'm King, I'll give you plenty of roast meat to eat!" – He invited seven Kings to his heritage-feast in Upsal. The hall that he built to receive them was called *Hall of the Seven Kings*, and we read that it was equal in splendor to *God-Hall* in the sacrificial grove where wooden ODIN, wooden THOR and wooden FREY stood gold-crowned in the darkness. Ingjald's hall had seven high-seats for the seven Kings and Earls' seats innumerable, for he had invited every man of consequence in Sweden to be his guest. Six Kings came to the hall, among them his father-in-law King Algaut, and when they were stupid with ale King Ingjald burned them all up. So he enlarged his dominions by half.

But the seventh King, Granmar of Södermanland, had not attended, knowing better than to exchange the shirt he wore for any garment of a more glowing character. When it was known to him that King Hjorvard-Viking lay off the Swedish coast with a stout war-fleet, King Granmar invited Hjorvard to a feast, and had his daughter Hildigunn serve him ale. Soon those two were plighted, and Granmar felt himself more secure. When the awaited Ingjald landed with his war-force, Granmar and Hjorvard stood against him where only Granmar had been expected, and Ingjald was forced to retire snapping and snarling, with many wounds, and kinsmen left dead on the shore behind him, like discarded clothing. Men lay groaning, with spears sprouting from their breast-bones like saplings, and their mouths were fountains of blood. As Ingjald fled, he snuffled at his bleeding places, howling so loud that he did not hear his foster-brother Gautvid calling to him for aid – nor would he have aided him if he had heard, for Ingjald's ambition exceeded his generosity. So Gautvid was left to fight alone beside a mossy little brook, whose waters ran pink with blood; and ODIN's ravens flew about his head, waiting for him to die so that they could eat his eyes. Beside him stood his father, Svipdag the Blind, now a man of the most ancient years, who fought ludicrously, because he could not see, his sword sweeping empty air (for no one bothered with him yet; he was poor sport) – but no man's life is ludicrous to him who must defend it. – At last Gautvid was exhausted, and must lean on his sword to rest. At this, Hjorvard's bearsarks grinned with all their teeth, and struck at him, so that Gautvid was compelled to lift his sword again, before he had caught his breath. – "Well, father," said he, "it seems that Wolf-Heart has abandoned us." – "Oh, he has, has he?" quavered old Svipdag. "Maybe I did not make him eat enough of the meat. It was so long ago!" And he laid about him stupidly with his sword. – But now King Granmar saw Gautvid and rushed upon him, crying, "All men know that you and your blind father created that monster; go make HEL your wife and sire monsters on her!" – and so saying, Granmar pierced him deep in the belly with his sword, twisting it and leaning upon it with all his might until Gautvid's guts burst out and he died. – "Is my son dead?" cried Svipdag the Blind. "Did I hear him die? Speak! Will no one answer or avenge?" – "I will answer," said Viking-King Hjorvard, strolling up with easy steps, and whirling his axe in the sun. Then in one stroke he made of Svipdag a headless man. Thus perished the wolf-makers, and whether they were good or evil only the reader can say. – When Ingjald's wounds had healed, and his temper somewhat abated, he concluded peace with his enemies. This peace was to endure as long as the three Kings lived. – "Well," said King Hjorvard, who did not know him, "we've drawn that young wolf's teeth." – "Perhaps," said Granmar. – On a summer night not long after, Ingjald burned them both up like cordwood. So his domains increased, and he capered laughing and alone in the forest.

In time, the saga goes, he had killed a dozen Kings under the cloak of peace, for which he was called Ingjald the Evil-Worker. And yet it was not his fault, for he would never have worn the Wolf-Shirt had it not been for Svipdag. Now he went his wicked way, although, truth to tell, he could easily have eaten a dove's heart and become mild; or he could have gone a-Viking to Africa to get the heart of a crocodile, so that at least he'd be able to shed tears over his victims – but, being a wolf, he was but driven mad by thoughts of doves; and that, too, was not his fault. – By his weeping wife Gauthild he had a daughter named Aasa, who was as wicked as he. When she came out of her mother's womb, she was already covered with coarse dark hair, and she snapped her teeth and glared. – "How perfect she is!" cried Ingjald, smacking his lips over the infant. "She is meant to be my playmate, and by ODIN I swear that I will marry her when she is big enough. As for that old bitch she came from, to the kennel with her!" He let the child run naked in summer and winter to harden her. "Hurry, Aasa my girl," he'd say, "grow up and burn out the world! Then it will never turn its face from you." – But by the time she was of marriageable age King Ingjald was growing grey, and Aasa showed a disposition to hunt afield. For gain he married her to Gudrod King of Skaane. She soon enticed her husband to murder his brother Halfdan, the father of Ivar Vidfavne; then she did Gudrod to death also, and breathlessly returned to her father, who kissed her full in the lips, with his wolf-fangs fastened on her mouth. – "I suppose you know me better than my Gudrod did," she said. Her arm was about his neck. – "Let us have ale!" cried old King Ingjald. "I now take my daughter to wife!" When Ivar's army came upon that incestuous pair in their feast-hall, they, seeing doom, burned themselves and their followers alive as they had burned so many others – a deed for which they were highly praised. Ivar's men, raking through the ashes in hopes of booty, presently came upon two skeletons breast to breast, and inside each one a frantically beating wolf's heart.

King Harald Fairhair ca. 870 – ca. 940

After the Yngling Kings were broken, their descendants fled the country for fear of King Ivar, and so came to Norway, trading white birch-forests for fields of white corn. The Changers raged everywhere. Their lives grieved them now, so that their purpose became to grieve all others, except the young sons who kissed their hands. Between King Ingjald and King Harald Fairhair now passed seven generations, in which Bear-Kings were spear-thrust, Wolf-Kings went a-Viking, and the ringing of shields told the hour more reliably than bells, for these had not yet been invented. Yet everything was congealing. The Bear-Shirts were wearing out, and the Changers were only men. – One day as he sat in his high-seat in Vermeland, King Olaf Tree-Feller, the son of Ingjald, heard a skald sing of the times of King Egil, who could change himself into a grizzly without any shirt, and the skald finished his song and said, "Reward me for my labor, O great King!", but Tree-Feller stood up impatiently and cried, "Out of my house, you liar! No one but ODIN could do the deeds you claim!" – The skald looked at him with mildness. – "It does seem so in these times," he said, and then he took his leave. Tree-Feller sat down again with his chin in his hand and his house-carles were silent, he thought at first because they were not certain of his temper; they heard the skald close the gate behind him and his steps died away in the forest. Tree-Feller said, "Men, could it have been as he said in the old days?" and the men remained silent. Tree-Feller said, "Men, was I unjust then in refusing him payment?" and an old carle said, "Yes, Lord, you ought to have given him something," at which Tree-Feller took a piece of silver from his pouch and said to a messenger, "Run, boy, and bring him this!" and they sat listening

THE DOMINIONS
of the
BEAR-KINGS
IN THE DAYS BEFORE BLUE-SHIRT

The boundary
between Norway
and Sweden
is vague, and
disputed by
Bear-Kings
whose King hanged
King On's father.

HALOGALAND

JÖTUNHE
Where Frost-Giants
live.

BEARLAND
Where Eric
Bloody-Axe
plundered

LAPLAND
Where Harald Fairhair
absconded with a
Yule-Feast.

ALSO CALLED
BY MEN

ICELAND

NORWAY

BREIDAFJORD
Where Eirik
the Red married
Thjodhild after
being outlawed
from Norway.

NAUMADAL
ORKEDAL

DRONTHEIM

(Where
Herlaug
and
Rollaug
met
King
Harald.)

VIKEN

FINNMARK
Where Eric
Bloody-Axe
took Gunnhild,
where Queen
Snaefrid
was born.

UPLAND

HORDALAND

HADELAND
Where the Yule-Feast
should have been.

SWEDEN

UPPSALA
Where King
On sacrificed
his sons
to Odin.

SÖDERMANLAND
GOTLAND

VSTAD
Where ships
sail west to
new lands.

SKAANE
Where Ingjald's
daughter was
married.

DENMARK

FRIESLAND

SAXLAND

ESTLAND
Where King Ingjald's
father went a-
Viking.

NORTHEAST OF THESE KINGDOMS
LIE VANAHEIM AND THE GREAT
SWITHIOD. SOME MEN SAY
THAT AASGAARD ALSO LIES EASTWARD.

as the gate opened and closed and the boy's rapid footfalls were swallowed up by the wind in the leaves; then Tree-Feller said heavily, "Yes, I suppose they were better than we, those old Kings." – After him, six generations passed; for Tree-Feller was burned by the Swedes as a sacrifice to ODIN, and after him came Halfdan White-Leg, and then Halfdan's son Eystein, and then Eystein's son Halfdan the Mild, a warrior who never took his Bear-Serk off, even at night, so that his wife, Queen Liv, was in great fear of him, as he foamed and growled in his sleep; when he died at last on a bed of sickness, his son King Gudrod the Hunter stripped that shirt off with such great avidity that it was still hot with father-heat as he pulled it over his head; and the ribs stood out quite pitifully on his father's despoiled corpse so that for a moment King Gudrod felt almost ashamed, but he said, "After all, *I* did not kill you!" Now the good bear-feeling rushed through his blood and he forgot everything but himself, as he lumbered into the forest and snuffled up honey and fishes until he came into the meadow of many flowers where the virgins crowned him and bedecked him with flowers. He sat in his high-seat; he read the runes of his bench-boards; he stood up roaring, at which his house-carles rattled their spears with a gladsome shout. Soon thereafter he went a-Viking against the other Kings, but in battle he found that the shirt did not fulfill all his expectations, perhaps because his father had worn out much of its virtue. In any event, he was manly just the same, and carried away his second wife against the wishes of her father, King Harald Redbeard, so that Redbeard strove against him but fell; then men called him Gudrod the Magnificent; and he said, "I suppose I must cherish my Bear-Shirt after all!" When the new Queen murdered him to avenge her father, came the sixth generation, and that was the reign of King Halfdan the Black. It was Halfdan's son, King Harald Fairhair, who was to subdue the entire country under him, so that the shield-clangs ceased at last. So doing, he overreached the limits of law and doomed ODIN Himself, for gods raise men up for the most temporary of triumphs, in order that from their dead mold other men may grow to fame. When a man's conquest endures forever, how can the Gods satisfy others, who sacrifice without result? – Because King Harald's triumph was more permanent than he, ODIN could no longer be.*

---

* Norway was Christianized not much more than a half-century after his reign.

Hiding the Bear-Shirt

It must be recorded of Harald that even as a boy he consorted with Laplanders, and it may have been for this that he was unbeloved by his father Halfdan; then again, it might have been that Halfdan hated him almost as soon as he was born, for in that moment when the screaming baby was raised before him, with Queen Ragnhild and the guards and the midwife awaiting his pleasure as to whether the infant would live or die, Halfdan saw the Queen's weakly anxious face looking up into his from the bed, and he thought upon the Bear-King enemies who waited for him in the gloomy woods; then he said to himself, "I will teach him how to become a great war-bear!" so he water-sprinkled the boy and named him so that he could not be exposed and left to die as a being without a soul, but as soon as Halfdan had done the thing he regretted it, for it dawned upon him, as it does on all fathers, that his true enemy was this son of his, who, if he lived, must certainly conquer him; so he turned away, feeling the full wretchedness of the expended seed-bag. In his anguish he plucked out great handfuls of his great black beard. He rushed out, and paced among the trees. Then he swore that he would never allow his son to learn how to transform himself. – "By FREY, I wish I had not water-sprinkled him!" So said Halfdan, groaning and chewing on his beard. And he kept his Bear-Shirt under lock and key. Queen Ragnhild had never seen it, being a woman (nor, for that matter, had *he* seen the many cunning serks which she kept hidden in her bridal chest); but he could not trust her not to discover it out of love for her son, so he took his magic trunk, which was wrought of thickest iron, and oiled it and buried it secretly in the forest. – "Ha, ha!" he laughed. "That man-whelp will never best me now!" – The boy was quick to understand his father's hatred, and returned it.

The Dream of the Bears

As long as Harald could remember, a sentry had stood outside the door of the hall, waiting among those moonlit trees for something evil to happen, and once when the hall was smoky and he wanted to go out his mother grabbed him by the shoulder so tightly that it hurt and said, "Stay by the hearth-fire, for there are bad fires outside tonight!"; and peering beneath her arm the boy saw an orange glow in the sky, and he smelled burning from across the forest, and his mother said bitterly, "The Kings have learned their lessons from old Ingjald Fire-Wolf!" – and that night Harald was afraid to dream, but he dreamed that it was spring, the forest thus being wide and open so that he could run away from his father; joyously he sped across a carpet of golden caribou moss that he could throw himself down on whenever he wanted to rest, and the trees were so widely spaced that he almost forgot that he was taking flight, and thought he wandered through some endless golden orchard where he would never want for anything; and the trees cast their long shadows on the moss, so that it was striped black by them like a warm and sunny tiger-skin, into which he sank to the ankles as he ran, farther and farther away until he thought his father could never find him. But in the moss he left deep footprints that widened effortlessly to mark his trail, like ink-spots in blotting-paper. Presently the trees tightened around him, and then there were trees and trees and trees, rising dark and high as he came into the realms of the other Bear-Kings, where the tree-shadows, from having been merely refreshing, became mellow, then melancholy, then anxious, and at last rushed together into one grim darkness through which Prince Harald must run, trembling with the sensitivity of an animal. He heard chilling silences behind the inky tree-crowds; he felt watched from every clammy root-cave; he screamed when he ran through spiderwebs. Gradually the conviction came upon him that something wicked was scanning him with its eyes, then (such is the foreplay of fear) he began believing and not believing (as his life beat trembling in his veins) that he heard steps behind him. As in lightless depths a grave-beetle beset by moles scuttles through forests of mildewed bone, so Harald sped his weary frightened way among the grey trees trying not to hear, but hearing, trying not to think of the wretched moment not too far ahead when he could run no more. Nor did he look over his shoulder, because if he saw the Face of his fear in darkness he would be lost. (He did not know whether matters would be worse if the pursuer were his father or *not* his father.) The fat, pale leaves shuddered on the trees like moths. – The moment came when he heard more than one pair of steps behind him. Now striving in his fright to run faster than his eyes could see, he threw himself among the mountains where stream-courses foamed down narrow gorges over which he must leap, because he could hear the padding of paws behind him; so he panted through steep ravines overgrown with birch trees and a horn sounded and the Bear-Kings came after, and he ran terrified through the grey gloomy fir-forests, and the Bear-Kings came roaring after, and glaciers sparkled upon the flat-tops of mountains, and reindeer moss clothed the trees in grey shirts, and he struggled through spruce-bogs, desperately trampling purple lupine flowers whose hair-leaves and hair-stalks were so silvery with water-droplets as to seem frosted; and he forced his way through crackling brushwood and the Bear-Kings came easily after, swiping dead shrubs aside with their claws, until at last he came upon a wide river from which a crowned Bear-King had just finished drinking, his fur still wet, his brown head raised, his eyes like darkly glowing jewels; and this Bear-King scooped a fish out of the stream and ate it and blinked at the sun; and then he rose so slowly, slowly up on two legs, the wide murderous forepaws stiffly at his sides until he chose to strike Harald down; and this Bear-King (which of his two natures was the greater Being inside him?) snorted and sniffed disdainfully, and his ears rose until they stood straight up upon his head; and leisurely he turned his very serious whiskered face upon Harald and opened his maw to growl and Harald saw the yellow teeth there; and now the other Bear-Kings came out of the trees and they all advanced on him, striding upon their hind legs; and every one of them wore a crown of gold, and their claws were studded with gold rings, by which their dignity was maintained; but, uniform as were these emblems of their estate, they were very different in appearance, their fur being the hue of their hair when they were men, so that Harald recognized the black pelt of his father, King Halfdan the Black, who was bent now on soothing his anguish in Harald's blood; there stood growling also great King Eystein with his yellow mane-shock – he had fought King Halfdan on Helgöen Island and later made alliance with him, so that now he must join Halfdan in destroying his son; a little behind the others stood an elderly Bear-King with silver fur and shaking claws, who snapped his jaws sidewise in a cunning bite, showing thereby his greed to drink deeper of blood-guilt – he was King Gorm the Old, who ruled Denmark, and made it his habit to support the other Bear-Kings in everything that did not threaten his own tyranny; and now a granite slab rolled crashing down the hill, disclosing a fetid cave from which a fearsome bear-skeleton emerged, shaking its massive skull from side to side and clacking its teeth; it too was gold-crowned, and there was an arrow rattling in its ribs by its left foreleg, so that Harald knew this Skull-Bear to be dead King Sigtryg, whom his father had killed, and who now came forth from the tomb to vent his enmity on the son; and the bears all grinned scornfully upon him, living and dead, and raised their claws against him. Would they tear his head off with their claws or would they hug him to death? – If only Harald could become one of them and fight them! He strained and strained, but no hair burst out on his palms; no fangs blossomed in his mouth . . . "Ho, ho, ho!" laughed the bears.

King Halfdan's Yule-Feast

When Prince Harald was nine years old, a Lapp stole away the entire contents of a Yule-feast by magic, leaving nothing on the table but gently rattling spoons, so that the guests must return home hungry as King Halfdan leaned upon the end of the banquet table, disgraced and dumbfounded. The long-fires burned as brightly as they had before, and smoke rose to the sooty ceiling-rafters, bearing with it the smell of meat that no longer existed; Ragnhild still stood beside the ale-cask, in which was nothing but a few rattling pebbles; and trenchers of venison lay in convenient reach by the men's benches and the women's cross-bench, but they were empty, and so were the benches now that the guests had risen muttering and departed; and the thralls stood stupidly with their arms still full of wood – oh, the futility of it! – Which Lapp could it be?, so Halfdan interrogated himself (for there were several of them in his hall). Well, there was one, a little dark man in a hairy reindeer-shirt, who seemed so "particularly knowing" that Halfdan tortured him repeatedly to get his secret; and the Lapp screamed upon the fire until his eyes were only whites, and Harald begged his father to stop, but Halfdan would not, so in the night Harald freed the Lapp and ran away with him into the snow-roofed woods, for he knew better than to trust to Halfdan's forgiveness. – The night was very dark and cold. The black trees rose straight and tall, like bars. – "I'm afraid!" Harald cried, remembering his dream (and yet at the same time this seemed nothing like his dream), so the broad-faced Lapp bemused him with conjuring tricks as they went deeper into the darkness, so that candles budded from every tree-branch and lit the way, although they did not warm the shivering boy, and then the Lapp raised his arm and a thousand grinning trolls peeped around the trees and contorted their faces to make Harald laugh (but what Harald never saw was that other trolls loped doggishly behind them in the darkness, sweeping away their footprints in the snow); and snow fell from the dull dark sky as they went north to Lapland, and it got darker and colder and a wind sprang up and blew sleet down Harald's back, and Harald cried, "I'm cold!", so the Lapp clapped his little brown hands, and a shower of snow fell down on Harald's shoulders and piled up around his face, and it seemed to him that he was wearing a fine white cloak lined with fur, although really he was no warmer than before; and for hours they kept walking through that dark snow-forest as the wind sang songs among the trees and the snow fell deeper and deeper until the boy began to tire, and it seemed to him that the Lapp was taking longer and longer steps and he was afraid that he would be left behind to die and so cried out, "I'm tired!", but the Lapp only smiled and shut one brown eye, and at once Harald fell into a deep sleep and thought that he was dreaming comfortably in a bed of white feathers when he was actually walking toward Lapland with his eyes open, getting more exhausted with every step, so that in his dream it appeared to him that he was ascending the white

slopes of some immense Ice-Mountain in a shiver of dreamy fear; higher and
higher, treading stairs of stone so thick with ice as to be glass-smooth; and
he staggered on, his dream no worse than his waking, since he still trudged
unknowingly behind the Laplander, but he thought he saw before him a great
blue wall of ice! – ice far higher than ever rose in Norway; and until his dying
day Harald never learned the meaning of that dream. (But a hundred years
later people knew.) – Harald walked on that night and all the next dark day
and late into the following night, for the Lapp did not dare to let him stop,
for fear that the boy would be frostbitten; and the wind grew fiercely cold,
so that he looked at Harald sadly and shook his head; and colder still, until
he himself was compelled to pull his furry hood tight around his face. But it
was the will of the Gods that Harald come to no harm. When he awoke they
were still in the forest, but the trees were somewhat lower, and the sky was
like a great white plate of frost above him. Seeing that plate reminded him
of food, and he cried to the Lapp, "I'm hungry!" At this the wizard laughed
very kindly and said, "Well, we can feast as we go!" – and suddenly a great
hot joint of roast meat appeared in the air! Harald seized it and gnawed it
to the bone as he walked beside the Lapp. How good it tasted! When it was
gone, another appeared. But his companion never ate anything. At last the
boy said, "Are you kin to your trolls, that you need no food?" – "Harald,"
said the Lapp, "never mind about me. This feast is yours." Then Harald, being
only a boy, troubled not at all for his friend and ate his fill. Steaming meat fell
into his hands whenever he wanted it, and the hot grease sizzled down into the
snow. He ate and ate. The meat was done to a turn. How the wizard laughed
to see him try to lick the salt juice from his chin! And so it went until he was
full – and though falsely warmed and falsely rested, he really *was* full, this
being Halfdan's Yule-feast, the only patrimony that the boy ever got (aside
from a title which he had to make good himself and enlarge by cunning);
so north he went with the Lapp, eating all the venison, drinking all the ale
he wanted.

They arrived at last in treeless Lapland; and all winter Harald lived with the
Lapps among the snows of that country, where every camp was pockmarked
with reindeer-burrows, it being the habit of these animals to dig themselves
into deep graves in the snow with their antler-spades, where they could munch
grey moss-browse. Too stupid to put on the Bear-Shirt or the Ice-Shirt, they
lived their lives in peaceful chewing. As for Harald, *he* was too stupid to envy
them. He stood watching their breath-steam ascending from these holes, and
pretended that he was surrounded by hot geysers. – Around the camp rose
smooth low snow-hills like bubbles, white against the low white sky; between

them the wind came shrieking day and night, shaking the Lappish skin-tents until Harald thought that surely they must be blown away, but that never happened, because the Lapps were great wizards and magicians. The women wore blue dresses with red borders, and red kerchiefs on their heads. They had broad short faces; their noses were flat between their eyes. Harald thought them very pretty. Day and night they sat weaving blue shirts in their tents, singing and laughing and shaking their heads so that their long black braids flew, and wolf-dogs crouched beside them, following the motion of those enticing hair-tassels with gleaming eyes. As for the men, they amused themselves in conjuring visions in the air: sometimes Norwegian women, at which their wives became angry, and spat at the mirage to dissolve it, sometimes suns so gold and real that Harald almost thought he was warm; and occasionally they made imaginary landscapes of ice, at which the boy gazed with a dull sadness which he could not explain. – "Oh!" the women laughed. "You *still* don't know about the Blue-Shirt, and why it is really red? You don't know about the King with BLACK HANDS? Oh, you poor little Norwegian! – But see, sisters, he has blue eyes!" – At this, Harald was somewhat uneasy in his mind, but as the Lapps were always friendly to him he let it pass. They ate nothing but snow and ice, which with their witchery they made into steaming meat-pastries. But Harald lived upon his father's feast all winter. He ate beef, and pork, and venison, and grouse, and sacrificial horse-flesh; he drank as much ale as he wanted. In the spring the Laplanders rewarded him with news, saying, "Your father Halfdan died riding on treacherous ice, and his body was divided into four parts, for the fertility of the four great districts of Norway. You may return home now and claim your kingdom." And the Lappish wizard who had brought him hence guided him south through the fens.

The Bear-Hunter *ca. 880 – ca. 890*

King Harald was but ten when he succeeded to his father's power. Five Upland Kings came upon him, but he fought them in many battles and slew them; three he burned like birchwood as they slept. But he did not stop there. – "Since I cannot be a bear like them," he said to himself, "let me destroy them all!" But his mother's brother Guttorm, who served as regent, considered these idle words. And in truth Harald had no idea how he should fulfill them. Although he wore rings and bracelets of gold, he was still no more than a boy. And no one could find dead Halfdan's bear-chest, which rusted and rusted somewhere in the woods. – The story says that when King Harald was older

he wanted a concubine,* so in the autumn he sent his messengers to Gyda
King-Ericsdaughter, a handsome girl but somewhat proud, for, combing her
hair while she received them, she replied, "King Harald and I both know that
I am pretty, but I know something that Harald doesn't – that I will not wed an
insignificant King!" – Laughing, Gyda tilted back her head, so that her yellow
hair licked against her smooth young face. Oh, how red her lips were! Her
face had an inexpressible freshness; her arms were white as milk. – Enraged
though they were by her refusal, they gazed at her nonetheless, imagining
how she must look unrobed. – "Well, Gyda," said the oldest messenger, "what
good do you think will come of your answer? If King Harald's invitation
does not suffice for you, do you intend to wait for King ODIN? You might
meet *us* again before then!" – and he rose, saying to the others, "Let us get a
larger force. Then we can take her away." And he spat into the fire. – Rising
also, Gyda followed them out. "I do not mean to be unkind," she said, "but
only to be particular. Now tell King Harald these words: I do believe him
to be an untrue Bear-King, for such I have heard from a serving-maid of
his mother Ragnhild. Why should I mate with a man who cannot give me
strong bear-sons? But no doubt I am a silly girl who understands nothing.
In that case, it will be easy for King Harald to slay my fears. Gorm the Old
conquered all Denmark; Eric did the same in Sweden. Let Harald give me
all Norway as a wedding-gift!" – When King Harald had heard these words,
he sat very stiff and silent in his high-seat, and the messengers, deeming him
angry, cried, "O King, surely she deserves some great disgrace! Let us bring her
to you; then you can do to her as you will!" – But Harald was not angry; he was
more afraid than he had ever been. Knowing now that his inability to be ursine
was already common gossip, he understood that he must act to falsely prove
it false; else he would be scornfully crushed by some bear-blow. Therefore he
rose, and stood looking out the doorway of his hallway at the water rippling
on the fjord, and the dark trees beyond, where the other Bear-Kings reigned,
and the messengers followed at his shoulder and said, "Shall we take her,
Sire?" and Harald turned to them with his blue eyes all mildness and said,
"No, I think this girl is right." Thereupon he solemnly swore that he would
not cut his hair until he was King of all Norway, and then he pulled his
Bear-Shirt on.†

The red leaves blew down from the trees, and winter came. King Harald
crewed his war-ships with bearsarks; he filled his army with them. He prayed

---

* The Norse word is *frilla*, a pretty word which contains in it the swish of frilly skirts.

† Of course it was not a real Bear-Shirt. His father's was hidden so well that he could never
have it. But the imitation was, as the saying goes, "good enough for government work."

to THOR, and promised to feed Him with blood. Then the horns blew, and Harald rode his white horse across the snow at a canter, pulling back the reins so that it reared and neighed and pawed with its front hoof, and Harald cried, "Become BEARS, all of you!" and rushed on at the head of his army faster and faster until the trees were but a blurred wall of evergreen; and he heard his bearsarks roaring and snarling behind him with the Changing-fit upon them as they rode; looking back, Harald saw not a man remaining; they were all bears, ice-bears and black bears and grizzlies on horseback, with their spears aloft in their claws! – and their teeth grinned as they roared; and King Harald's heart was joyous with cruel lust. Night and day they rode. The snow-trees rose white and thin upon the mountains, and the sky was bluish-orange. Harald led the army along frozen river-roads paved with snow. He went north through the trees, until, says his saga, he came to inhabited lands. He ordered his bearsarks to kill every man they found, and to clothe every farm and town in the Flame-Shirt. Then he led his army north to Orkedal. Here he defeated King Gryting in battle, and made him his prisoner. He killed two Kings in Guldal; then he killed six more. When the whole of Drontheim* was his, he captured Naumadal. Then he sailed south in his war-ships to Möre and slew two Kings. King after King he subdued; if they swore to become his loyal vassal he reduced them to Earls and let them live to rule their lands in his name; otherwise he killed them. And the lands and districts fell steadily to King Harald, winter and summer.

Herlaug and Rollaug

Now I remember the story of the brother-Kings Herlaug and Rollaug. For three summers they had been at work raising a mound of wood, stone and lime, and just as they finished, the news was brought to them that Harald was coming upon them with all his army, and there was no hope, but they waited until they could see the trembling of the trees, and then they waited until they could hear the tramping, tramping of Harald's bearsarks, and then they waited until they could see the spear-heads rising around them like narrow silver flames; and then they bade each other farewell, and King Herlaug went into the mound with eleven others, and meat and ale were brought inside, and then Herlaug ordered that the mound be sealed up, and they feasted their way to death in that moist earthy darkness. King Rollaug for his part ascended the

* Trondheim.

mound and commanded that his throne be erected there. He seated himself upon that highest of seats, there in the sky where he would never be again, and he looked into the sky-horizon, which was bluish-white and curved with the curvature of the earth, above which the sky was a blue of indescribable lightness, and below which the clouds floated like icebergs, while below them, upon the farm-seas and the forest-seas, ponds gleamed like lost pennies in the sun; and then he threw himself and his kingship down the mound, so that he rolled into the bench called the Earls' Seat (which he had previously had his retainers strew with feather beds, for, since he had already sacrificed his dignity to his body, there was no reason to injure that, too), and he called himself an Earl. – A dusty Earl he must have been. – Now he met King Harald meekly beside the mound of his still living brother, and King Harald fastened a sword to his belt, bound a shield to his neck, and led him back to his Earl's seat, naming him his faithful Earl. (Would you, reader, have rather been a Herlaug or a Rollaug?) Then Rollaug served two sovereigns, for Harald was his King, and his Queen was Queen Misery, who ruled inside his chest as Herlaug did inside the mound; and when after three days the noises inside the mound died away, then at night Queen Misery invited those dead mound-dwellers to visit her and feast on Rollaug's heart, so until he died Rollaug dreamed of black skeletons and grey-green skeletons dancing inside him, working their sharp bone-fingers in his head; and his brother-skull opened his jaws in a sharp-toothed laugh at the pleasantries of Queen Misery, and poor Rollaug ached in his chest at that laugh. – It was no surprise to men that he administered Harald's territories faithfully, for had he not become an Earl of his own accord? Equally faithful was he to Queen Misery, walking at nights round and round his brother's forest-mound, from which sometimes came a blue glow of brother-light, treasure-light, corpse-light to light his way, and though the mound was shunned by others, Earl Rollaug wore a wide path around it, until at last he was named the Earl of Sadness. – Never now could he become anything else. In Norway the King-Shirts and Bear-Shirts were ruined, and he *knew* of nothing else.

Gyda's Reward

After ten years, ruddy-faced Harald conquered all Norway, and wore a brown bear-cloak. His shaggy locks were like a curtain drawn upon his face, which made men fear him the more, and King Harald knew this and made use of it, but now that he had plucked the golden fruit of kingship he became vain, and wished men to admire his golden hair as well. At a feast given him by one of his tame Earls in Möre he had his hair clipped, so that his sycophants rushed to call him Harald Fairhair. – "Oh, yes!" men cried, trembling with hope that he might smile upon them. "There is the greatest truth in that surname." – It is written that he took Gyda to him then, with his weapons-carles all around him, but he took also a number of Queens before and after her, so, like many a youthful inspiration, she found herself but pinned between the pages of his woman-album.* At this time he was also married to Swanhild Eysteinsdaughter, Aashild Ringsdaughter, and Ragnhild the Mighty. (This last was a Queen of especially fine blood, as was proved when she bore him his favorite son, Eric Bloody-Axe. – Yes, she had a rare shape! When he married her, he put nine other wives out of doors. As it proved, this was needless trouble, for she lived but three years.) Later he even took to himself the Lappish witch Snæfrid, for by her art she made the lust-fires burn in him when he touched her hand. – Was proud Gyda happy among that crew of Queens? King Harald's saga does not say. It might have been best if, like Ragnhild the Mighty, she died young. As for him, not having the ambition to conquer the world, he sat in peace, his sons not yet grown to quarrelling-age, and all through his kingdom the crops grew.

The Flight of the Earls ca. 890

Of course, because King Harald did what each would have liked to do, his rule was perceived by some as harsh. – Too bad. – (No doubt the dissatisfaction has been exaggerated in the historical accounts, since spoilsports cry out loudly, while on the other side good losers are silent, being dead.) Highborn men longed to oppose him, for they had been Kings, and now must be content with earldoms if they stayed. Their bear-swords lay idle in their white hands. So they fled the country under cover of cloud and darkness, bringing their multitudes with them. It was their intention to people the uninhabited† lands to the west, of which there had lately been much discussion; for now that the old pages of the *Flateyjarbók* were written dark and dense with Harald's stories that the Earls did not care to read, how whitely wonderful seemed the sand-pages of virgin beaches! Islands – so many islands! – lay upon the waves unwritten-on, in reams and realms and quires. Rocky skerries offered

---

* Being a vigorous man, he set her to much bed-work under his belly, and so had by her Aalaf, Rörek, Sigtryg, Frode and Torgils.

† Except by Irishmen, who did not count.

opportunities for hunted men to eke out; then westward stretched many ells
of ocean, in which was no one knew what. (But ever since King Harald had
had the first Ice-Dream on his way to Lapland, men had been dreaming that
pale white dream.) – "In the Faroes," the Earls said to one another, "or in
the Hebrides, or in Iceland we can wear the King-Shirt again!" (They did not
know that what they sought was GREENLAND.) – So they set sail in their great
dragon-ships and their snake-ships, surrounded by the flotsam of their tame
rabble that went anxiously a-bobbing in every available rowboat or ale-cask,
worrying about monsters and whirlpools. To soothe and enthrall them the
Earls pretended that this migration was for a short time only, crying, "We
shall bring the Bear-Shirt back to Norway!", and all the thralls and slave-carles
cheered in the leaky little boats, a hurrah's tiny comfort filling their tiny heads,
and they bobbled on over the grey waves like a fleeing log-jam, with only the
Earls' great ships to give them dignity. – "Death to King Harald!" they cried
(and when Harald's spies reported this to him, he laughed and laughed). But
the Earls knew that they were leaving Norway forever. They did not look
back at the fjords in which they had once ruled subject only to the Laws of
Claws, and the coastline dwindled and vanished in a fog and still the Earls
would not look back, because, being great men, they were expected to set
a high example. With fair winds they swept west over the black water, their
living dragon-prows hissing and flickering their tongues to taste the wind,
and the Earls stood high between the row-seats so that their followers could
take heart in them and their yellow Earl-locks streamed behind them in the
wind (for, being of equal birth with Harald, they *must* be equally fairhaired),
and their square sails fluttered like wings, and they flew and flew upon the
swan-field★ until the hissing prow-dragons arched their necks backward to
gape upon the Earls in astonishment, at which the Earls knew to placate them
with many bull-sacrifices, giving the dragons cups of blood to sip so that
they became resolute again and turned forward to spy out rocks and Swedes
and other dangers; and they sped westward in a freshening breeze until at
last great green-topped pillars of rock arose, with misty mountains behind
them, and so the keels of the Earls' ships made crunching furrows in the
blue shell-sand of the Orkneys . . .

★ Kenning for the ocean.

The War of the Islands

They wintered in the Orkneys; in summer they turned their shield-hung dragon-ships against the land of their birth, ravaging the coast at their pleasure. Up the tree-walled rivers they sailed, burning farms, raping, robbing and slaughtering; they dyed their white hands red in Norway's blood-reek. The Earls split the skulls of those who had dispossessed them, so that teeth scattered from jawbones like seeds, spilling down across the hearthstones where they would never take root. – "That was man's work!" they shouted to each other. But they were answered only by the sound of trickling blood.

In the islands that they had settled, they thought themselves secure, and wooed long slumbers for themselves (dreaming of something white, so that they thought they dreamed of themselves). Wherever the pillars of their high-seats washed ashore, there they built their homes. They built again the close-packed houses they had known, whose wood-roofs and thatch-roofs rose in peaks. Later they built of peat and stone. They cut the turf and made cornfields out of buttercups. (Never had they seen such giant buttercups.) Hiding their towns between headlands, they gathered eels and shellfish from the mouths of rivers. The weather was damp, but mild. The grass was green. – But of course King Harald had not forgotten them. – "Everyone must be thinking by now," cried shrill Queen Gyda, "that you haven't any hair on your chest. But you'll teach them otherwise, my Lord, won't you? Won't you?" In the Shetlands, as the horn sounded and King Harald's men launched fire-arrows into every roof, the people came running out in a throng, expecting to be rallied by their Earls, but, perceiving these lords to be chalky-pale, the people determined to defend themselves against Harald of their own accord; but then, seeing that every street was already walled in flame, they hoped only to retain jurisdiction over their lives, their bundles, their horses and sheep and donkeys; so they went rushing along the log-roads, thinking to escape; few did. "Then," says the saga, "King Harald sailed southwards, to the Orkney Islands, and cleared them all of Vikings." – Thus it went also in the Hebrides, on the Isle of Man, and even on the coasts of Scotland. Many times he sailed against them with his fleet, and slew all who did not take to the open sea. Harald destroyed the Earls' men in every quarter. So the *Heimskringla* tells it; and yet the truth is that the great game of those islands was to last centuries. The Hebrides, the Faroes, the Orkneys, Iceland and even GREENLAND* all fell into Norway's power at

* Greenland was annexed in 1261.

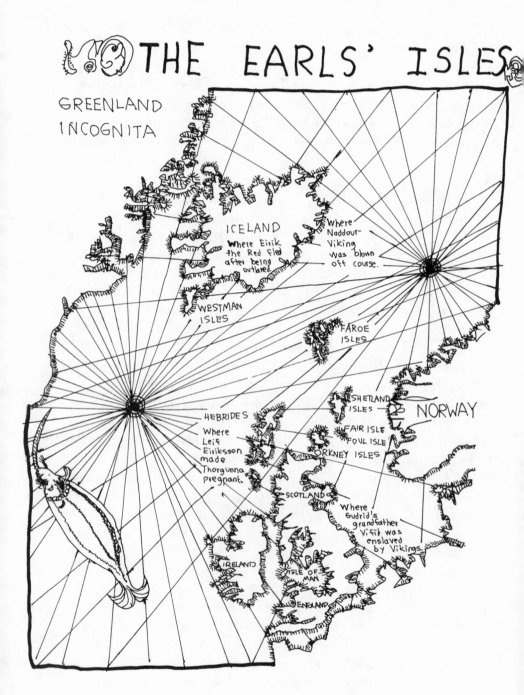

THE EARLS' ISLES

GREENLAND
INCOGNITA

ICELAND
Where Eirik
the Red fled
after being
outlawed.

Where
Naddour-
Viking
was blown
off course.

WESTMAN
ISLES

FAROE
ISLES

SHETLAND
ISLES

NORWAY

HEBRIDES
Where
Leif
Eiriksson
made
Thorgunna
pregnant.

FAIR ISLE
FOUL ISLE
ORKNEY ISLES

SCOTLAND

Where
Gudrid's
grandfather
Vifil was
enslaved
by Vikings.

IRELAND

ISLE OF
MAN

ENGLAND

long last. But in those years there was still time and space on the islands, so the Earl-kin, well aware that they could expect no mercy from King Harald, went west.

The New Lands

Midway between the Shetlands and the Orkneys lay Fair Isle, which had its corresponding Foul Isle; both of these were settled. Midway between Iceland and Norway were the Westman Islands – little more than green cliff-rocks, but even these had a few low flat places by the sea, and men built their houses there. West and west again they went, finding water-girt lands whose doubtful existence became sure forever when they waded onto them, as flocks of gulls took wing astonished, screaming and retreating west. For awhile they had an abundance of new lands: low green sheep-islands and towering sea-cliffs, green hills and grey water, grey hills and green water . . . Islands waxed like clouds upon the sea-sky all the way to Iceland.* When new land came in sight, they jumped from their boats to reach it, with loud and joyous shouts. Often they found stranded whales, and the rivers were black with salmon. Then they praised their prow-dragons and gave them mead to drink; and they offered thanks to HEIMDALL, ODIN and THOR. There were islands as numerous as stars, so that men went dreaming from archipelago to constellation, wind-blown and wave-tossed to flowery little coasts where they were deafened by the booming of waterfalls that no one had ever heard before. When King Harald came looking for them, they hid their ships; they spread moss over themselves. Then they went again in pursuit of islands. – So this confusion of islands became substantial and mapped. But becoming distinct, they remained separate nonetheless, for those were lonely, suspicious days; every island was its own kingdom, with its own laws. Between them sailed the dragons – but since even kingdoms must exchange commercial kisses, there passed also the stout trading-boats. From Iceland to the Faroes was a day's sail; from Iceland to the Shetlands was only two. Islands exported wool, cheese and tallow in exchange for timber, malt and

* Which the Viking Naddour discovered in the year 860, being blown off course on a voyage from Norway to the Faroes. He landed on the east coast, and everything was white with snow. For this reason he wanted to call it Snowland, but history overruled him, for no particular reason. The first settlers came fourteen years later. – It is written that the new country was so thick with birch-woods that the colonists had to hack their way through them. (Now, it seems, the land is mainly grey and orange with volcanoes.)

linen. And the Earls and their descendants worked their windy fields, and birds flew westward over their heads, and at night they tossed in their beds, dreaming of the blue Ice-Mountain. As for Greenland, that stepping-stone to VINLAND THE GOOD, that country was first sighted a decade later.

The Death of King Harald Fairhair *ca.* 940

As he aged, King Harald became niggardly in some respects. He lived only in his dwindling ice-self, as I said; he had not the ambition to conquer the world. At banquets he ate quickly, and then knocked on the table with his knife so that his house-carles must clear away the dishes, no matter whether the guests might still be hungry. Yet he himself ate his fill of hazelnuts and raspberries. After dinner his concubines rubbed the soles of his feet until he fell asleep. – Once, it is said, Queen Gyda, in a transparent attempt to rearouse his interest in her, asked him if he took pleasure in ruling the country, "for without me," she said, "it would never have come about." – "Yes, I have what I want," said Harald gloomily; "now I can sit on it until my life and authority go rotten." – His fair hair became white hair. Once again he let it grow long, so that it tangled itself around his crown like a field of frosted sedges. He had developed a mania for digging, and set many of his carles to spade-work in the forests of Hadeland – yet he would not tell them what he looked for, save that it lay inside a rusty iron trunk. "Look where the trees are dark!" he insisted, slyly wagging his head. – They found skulls and beads, it is true, and once they uncovered a great hoard of Viking gold, but when this was brought to King Harald he only sifted the coins through his fingers and said, "The wizard spoke truly when he told me that I have eaten ice!" And nobody knew what he meant. – When he was forty his sons grew restive; when he was fifty he divided the kingdom with them; when he was seventy he took his serving-woman Tora Mosterstang to bed and had a son by her (she was somewhat hairy of person – a fact in which the King took comfort); when he was eighty he became very fat, and could no longer ride a horse. Then he brought his son Eric Bloody-Axe to the high-seat, and made him Sovereign King of Norway. He lived for three years after that, marrying off his daughters to his Earls, and died in his sick-bed, beset by a vision of Skull-Bears. In his delirium he called for the iron trunk, and when his followers said they knew not where it was, he cried, "Dig in the forest! Hurry! Bring it to me!", but then he had a fit and died.

Gunhild Joins the Family

And so King Harald was succeeded by Eric Bloody-Axe, whom he had always loved best. Of Eric it is written that his father gave him five long-ships when he was twelve. He plundered in Denmark, Friesland, Saxland, Finnmark, and all the way north to Bearland, on the White Sea. In Finnmark his men came upon a girl preening herself in a Lappish hut, who was more beautiful than any of the ones they had raped. Her name was Gunhild, she said, and she had come to the forest to learn witchcraft from two Lappish wizards. – "Hide under the bed," she told Eric's men, "and we will see if we can kill them." When the Lapps returned to the hut, Gunhild let them lie beside her and put her loving arms around their necks. Being rivals for her favors, they were exhausted with jealously watching each other, and soon fell asleep, at which clever Gunhild popped their heads into two sealskin bags. Then she winked like a whore at Eric's men, and they sprang out from under the bed to slice through the Laplanders' necks – a task which, being Norwegians, they undoubtedly performed with diligence. The next day they brought the girl to Eric's ship, and presented her to him. – And so Prince Eric and Gunhild were married, and returned to Norway. Gunhild was a very cruel witch and a poisoner, who used her art to bring her husband some success, although his life was short. – Eric's character becomes clear when we read that at King Harald's bidding he hastened to burn his brother Rognvald for witchcraft, along with eighty other warlocks. "Eric," says his saga, "was a stout handsome man, strong and very manly – a great and fortunate man of war; but hot-headed, harsh, unfriendly, and silent." – His successors were much the same.

Denial of the Bear-Shirt

By then, nobody in Norway believed in the Bear-Shirt. While he lived, King Harald had denied its existence to his sons; they in turn, having never known it, derided it. A few of the Earls still wore it, but they were the ones who had fled to the new lands. What had been easy for grandfathers, possible for fathers, was scarcely to be met with anymore. Men remained men, except by accident, as when, for instance, according to the *Book of Settlements*, "an arrow struck the intestine of Eilif Grisly, and he became a shape-changer."

Dreams of the Ice-Mountain

Greenland, then, what was Greenland? And yet, north and west, the name GREENLAND was written in the ink of poisonous green icicles, water-clear and thereby illegible until the death of the readers, who must first die as green leaves died in the frost; only then were they permitted to put on the Ice-Shirt and sack Wineland the Good. – In Sweden, men woke from nightmares of some far white island; in their dreams they exhausted themselves wandering among the lesser peaks of the Ice-Mountain; and there was neither day nor night, but only a radiant white darkness in which they saw each other as silhouettes. (Can you understand your own dreams, which arise with mushrooms' rank richness in the night-forests within your skull?) Sailors spoke of skerries in the direction of the setting sun, and immense flocks of land-birds winging westward. – What could it all mean? It was only that most desperate tribe of language-crackers, the cartographers, that dared to decipher this alphabet of symbols, and what they wrote they disguised in picture-writing. Some of them drew Greenland as a peninsula extending to northern countries; others made it an icy horn of Africa, but what they were writing (every word a wave, a feather, a pebble) was an interpretation of dream-hopes and dream-rumors.

According to the great Macrobius, the world is divided into five zones, two alone of which are inhabited by men, for at either pole is a zone of fatal cold, and at the equator is a zone of burning and torridness, so that only two rings of temperate clemency, separated from each other by that hot mid-girdle, can be possible to dwell upon. It was clear that Greenland must ascend far into the northern polar death-zone, perhaps all the way to Jötunheim, Land of the Frost Giants. Obviously it required a desperate distracted ambition to make anyone go there. But there are always to be found dreamers who will do anything.

Greenland Dreams Recalled on a Sunny Swedish Morning

In the spring, when the birds sang like green water and the first bees hummed over sunny bushes, there remained shadowed snow-drifts in which saplings lurched like the masts of drowning ships; and even though the foundations of the great pines were green moss-islands in the snow, even though the trees were green, the bark-moss was new-green, yet those grey-trunked and

white-trunked trees spread their hemlock-hued fans of needles in chilly
silence, and a chill seeped up from the ground, so that every dreamer
expected to round a pine-tree hill-crest and come upon some great white
Mountain-shoulder, beautiful and shockingly high. Sometimes the dreamer
thought that he could glimpse the Mountain rising far above the highest
trees, but it was only a cloud, a bleached white wood-corpse entombed in

CLOUDS AROUND MT. ODIN, BAFFIN ISLAND

branches, or the snow-capped crown of some great ash-tree. – At first his
dreams led him onto wide sunny snow-meadows, and he felt very warm. The
Ice-Mountain was grey and white ahead. The tree-branches were bent down
and trapped in the snow, so that they looked like roots. Then everything
became colder and clearer, for, as that thirteenth-century macropedia, the
Speculum Regale, remarks, "it is in the nature of the glacier to emit a cold
and continuous breath which drives the storm clouds away from its face
so that the sky above is usually clear." – As the dreamer proceeded up
a ridge toward the lesser crest, the bluish-white wall before him became
more and more sheer. As the ridge steepened, it became a high broad way,
grandly adorned with trees. The trees had livid grey bark. They extended
widely-spaced branches, as if they were ferns. Then after awhile the ridge
fell away; the trees fell away, and the other mountains fell away; and he

was ascending a vast and featureless slope of white – not impossibly steep yet, but very high and grand and dangerous, so that he became vertiginous if he looked down. The snow was glittering and granular, and there were deep round craters where the sun had melted the snow (for the dreamer was not really climbing the Ice-Mountain; he still stood in the Swedish forest where tree-shadows fell upon the snow, which was sprinkled with dead pine needles, and the trees were cool and black and quiet, so despite himself he brought spring up the mountain with him). There were grey stones and orange lava pebbles on an occasional ridge where the sun had struck in full force, melting snow away, down to the grey spiny shrubs that lived in the sand – for now the dreamer's sunny imagination was beginning to drag him down; and though he strove through the melting dream-snow he sank deeper and deeper into it with every step, and for a moment he thought he saw the summit of the Ice-Mountain above him like a snowy shoulder upon which a hand of rocky ice pressed cruel fingers, but then spring burst forth in an explosion of birds and crickets, and the branches, having been pressed down under the snow, sprang up from the moldy ice and grew heart-cutting spears of green leaves, and the last patches of snow became steam and left the ground black and warm, and it was a hot Swedish afternoon in summer and there might perhaps have been snow somewhere deeper in the forest but by now it would be riddled with tiny air-bubbles; and the war-bears would be yawning and coming out of their caves.

The League of the Ice-Dreamers

Some lives were disturbed in wide but short-lived ways thereby, being crossed by the vacuously perfect ripples of yearning, while others became whirlpool-lives, devouring and spewing not only those who crossed them, but any in their reach. But those lives too have become as mirror-seas, for nothing is left of them save the old stories. It is that way even with cartography. In our new Greenland we cannot find the Ice-Mountain anymore, nor Karsöe, the Island of the White Bears, nor Berefjord, where a Whale's Whirlpool is reported to have lain beyond the sand-ribs (the water is a mere mirror now), and that endless fjord, Longest-of-All, went inland among the mountains, its banks grass-green long past the islands of uncounted birds. – As for Vinland the Good, who knows where it is now? If continents are free to contract and elongate themselves at will, if islands may sail anywhere upon the great Ocean Sea, then how may we pronounce upon dreams, which not even dreamers can find again? We can only say that Greenland had appeared in our dreams for ages – in any event a statement without utility, as dreams come true only for him who sleeps in the pre-moral position.

Queen Gunhild and her Murder-Burners

ca. 962

A lady sits upon her throne,
And many a craft she knows;
Reads the books of well-writ runes
And sews her silken clothes.

Kvaeði af Loga i Vallarahlið (ca. 900)

In those days Norway was ruled by the sons of King Eric Bloody-Axe. These were their names: Harald Greycloak, Ragnfröd, Erling, Gudröd and Sigurd Sleva. They dwelled mainly in the middle of the country, for in Drontheim and Viken they had enemies. They hid their money in the ground. In many ways they were laughable fellows. Their mother Gunhild was still as much a witch as she had been in Lapland. She called herself the King-Mother, and meddled much in her sons' affairs. It was she who counseled them to tax the country more heavily, "for otherwise," said she, "how could you get more gold pieces to bury?" And she smiled at them lovingly.

Harald Greycloak was the eldest of the brothers. It was he, therefore, who had the supreme dignity. – "Mother, it is not so easy as that to get gold," he said. "You must remember that we cannot tax everywhere. Earl Sigurd rules in Drontheim, and Trygve and Gudrod in the east. You know the people hate us! We do not have sufficient strength to march against them all."

"Oh!" said Gunhild dryly. "Strength is a fine quality. Don't think I don't enjoy it when I feel a strong man between my legs! – But if I decided not to enjoy it, what good would his strength do against two drops of poison? – Remember, my sons, that craft is better than strength. Your father was both strong and bold; his boldness brought about his death in England. You were only boys then, who could not whirl your axes around your heads. When I heard that Eric had fallen in battle, I knew that we would not be safe in Northumberland. Of course it was but my woman's cowardice that made me gather our booty and our thralls to set sail for the Orkneys. But if I

had not done it, then you would not have lived to overthrow your uncle
Hakon. Probably it was my lust that brought King Harald Gormsson to my
bed. But after that he fostered you, my own son Harald, on his knee. He
gave you great fiefs in Denmark, and Danish men-at-arms to attack Hakon.
– My sons, when you plundered in Viken, and Hakon cut down your brother
Guttorm, I counseled you to row away, and you were ashamed and angry
at me for so doing, but I comforted you; I knew you would come back.
And you did. When you sailed to Agder I paid a thrall to do what you
denounced as a scurvy trick: – remember? – to kill the man who ran to
light Hakon's war-beacon. And the end of it was that we got as far as
Stad that time. And then Hakon himself used craft to defeat us, for he had
his men raise standards from behind a ridge, so that you thought he had a
great army and fled. Oh, you were gullible, my sons! That gave Hakon the
time to assemble more men together, and the result was that your brother
Gamle – my prettiest little son – died in the water. Once again I advised
you to return to Denmark, although as ever you abused me and called me a
cowardly old whore, but you followed that advice, and we returned to attack
Hakon again. That time, my sons, you thought to stand in battle-lines and
use that strength you boast about. My own brothers, Eyvind and Alv, came
charging boldly at King Hakon's golden helmet, and for their trouble they
were slain. At that you feared, my sons, and so to save you I whispered into the
ear of my shoe-boy and he shot an arrow with many fishhooks into Hakon's
arm, from which he bled to death very slowly. Now, I ask you: Who killed
King Hakon? Was it you, or your Danish Vikings? Was it my shoe-boy? (I
am sure you heard him running through the spears, crying, 'Make way for
the King-killer!' It was for that I had *him* killed.) Was it his arrow? – No, it
was my craft, and my whispered words. Am I not right, my sons?"

For a moment the sons of Eric said nothing. But at length King Erling
nodded his head and said, "Yes, mother, it is exactly as you say."

At this, Queen Gunhild smiled sweetly, for she was charming when she
was not crossed. "Very well, my Golden-Hair," she said. "We will begin by
burning Earl Sigurd in his house."

They lured Earl Sigurd's brother Grjotgaard into their plot, and one night
when Earl Sigurd was in Oglo at a feast, King Harald and King Erling sailed
there by starlight and did what they had come to do.

"Well," men said when they heard the news, "these sons of Bloody-Axe
are not like old King On, who hoped to live forever. But it seems they will
be a nuisance to highborn lords throughout their short lives."

Freydis's Father *ca. 945 – ca. 1006*

There was a man called Eirik the Red, who lived in Jæderen, not far from the sea. People called him well-born, for his father was Thorvald, the son of Asvald, the son of Leif, the son of Oxen-Thori. Thorvald was a man of considerable distinction, devout in his duty to his namesake THOR; in his youth he had fought against Harald Fairhair, but was later forgiven on account of his deeds against the Shetland Vikings. When, at the instigation of Queen Gyda, the King began to reduce the highborn men to vassals, Thorvald said, "Well, this Harald will not live forever. We can weather this out." But when the King was laid in his mound, Thorvald thought his successors even worse.

As for Eirik the Red, he was unproven at this time, being not much above fourteen years of age. Of course, as the Queen never tired of reminding everybody at court, her husband had won both her and much plunder besides when he was only twelve, but then Bloody-Axe had had a fairhaired King-Father to give him ships, whereas Red Eirik's father Thorvald had little left to him excepting his honor and a few house-carles, a fact which gleamed ever balefully in the young man's mind like a lake of ice that must be crossed. When he heard a carline say that Bloody-Axe had once been given a bear's heart cooked in a certain way by the Lappish witches of the court, then Eirik was joyous, for he thought that while he might not have multitudes of men-at-arms, yet *this* should be easy enough to match! – so in the spring he went into the forest and killed himself a young bear, whose heart he roasted and ate; yet he felt no appreciation in his strength, and after this he resolved not to listen to fairytales. But he stood still for a long time, hoping; his eyes were cast down, and at last his shoulders shook.

"Red-Hair, you will surely do great deeds before long," said his grandfather Asvald, who lay dying on a bed of sickness, but Thorvald, who heard this, said, "If there are deeds to be done, no doubt our Eirik will do them, but he is rash and poor of understanding. I would rather he lived his life a deedless coward. Then at least I could be certain he would outlive me." – And Eirik scowled and thought this a very ill saying. Old Asvald saw the expression on the stripling's face and laughed his weak laugh that sounded like the creaking of marsh-reeds in the wind, and Eirik went out and Asvald said, "My son, why do you humiliate the boy?" and Thorvald said, "He is no coward and never will be, but I want him to be prudent, as all must be in these bad times."

When Asvald had died and been laid in howe, Thorvald called the young man in to him and said, "Look you, Eirik, these carven bench-boards by my high-seat have been in our family for many generations, and I believe there is luck in them. Your grandfather once told me that every one of our men who has been or will ever be is carven here. Do you see these grape-vines traced at the border of the wood? There is a hand plucking them, and a man stands behind him. Asvald told me that you are that man."

"He was *fey*,★ then, on his deathbed?"

"No, no. This is knowledge that my father always had. Where he got it from I cannot say."

"That's as may be," said Eirik. "But I fancy there are no wild grapes here in Norway."

"I have told you all that I know," said Thorvald shortly.

Eirik thanked his father and left the room. Thorvald had expected him to pore over his likeness in the bench-boards, as he himself had done at a like time, but it seemed that the boy took little interest in what he had been told. Thorvald sighed, and traced his forefinger through the grooves that outlined a wolf's shape . . .

In those days men believed that power lay in the things carved and dedicated to families. ODIN had learned the art of rune-carving at great cost; sacrifice to Himself He had hung on the Tree of Yggdrasil, suffering all the agonies of the gallows until Something beyond Him let Him see and understand all the arts which He later bequeathed to us. So, although rune-carving was most magical, yet carving itself had still some sacredness, as on Thorvald's bench-boards, where the wood-rings and ring-spirals met each other in splendid confusion upon a plain of wooden darkness, so that each bench-board seemed to depict a night-lit boneyard: – the unsprung wood-bones of Eirik's grandfathers, frozen in their clatter even though snakes and hoops and vertebrae pierced each other through; and these bones were loam for the new, as figures of birds and warriors sprouted from the wood. Thorvald could never run his eyes over the bench-boards without a feeling of satisfaction; they were bound up with the family luck.

As for the son, he went into the fields and ploughed, and the house-carles who helped him said to one another, "It is going as usual, that none can do half as much as Eirik," but as the day went on they saw that their master was setting a much harder pace than ever before, and as the sweat-rain flew from their heaving shoulders and their breath began to come short they thought to plead, but looking into Eirik's face they saw a hardness about his mouth

★ Experiencing a revelation of an ominous and inevitable future.

that they had never seen. – "Has someone done him an injury?" they asked each other when the day was done. But no one could find explanation for his behavior. The next morning he was up long before Rising-Hour, and the thralls saw him ploughing in the dark. But when Thorvald came in among them in his nightshirt, blinking and holding his candle high, they held their peace.

"So he is working, is he?" he said.

"Yes, Lord," said a thrall girl, spooning out some porridge.

"Has he eaten?"

"No, Lord."

"I suppose he is preparing his mind for something," said Thorvald at last. Then he said no more, for while he wished to know his son's intentions, he was growing old, and no longer felt that he had first place.

Among the teeming figures (each no larger than a single finger-joint) fixed so hopelessly on the bench-boards, until the gracious woodworms should free them at last from their shapes, there was one that pictured Thorvald himself – or that his father had said pictured him. It was a man shielding his face with his hands. This had always shamed him, which was why he never spoke of the matter to Eirik. Thorvald knew full well that the tale of his life told little of honor; for he had never resisted Greycloak, nor Bloody-Axe before him; but now that he was old he remembered as the one great failure that devoured other failures the moment when he came of age and his father first showed him the figure with the hands over its eyes, and said grimly, "You see, in all your years you will effect nothing" – but what *could* he have done at that moment? Should he have taken up a chisel and gouged out a bald spot on the wood where Hiding-Eyes had been? Should he have carved in the shape of a grinning bear, and said, "No, father, *this* is I!" and then done whatever the bear would have him do? – No, there had never been anything to do. Once his father's finger had come down on that place, Thorvald saw his fate before him. – And yet his silence had disconcerted his father. Had this in fact been a challenge which Thorvald had failed, as he believed increasingly in the dark-moon years of his age? – But then perhaps the look of strange emotion that had appeared so fleetingly upon Asvald's face before the eye-doors were shut had been a different thing entirely. – So ever he wondered whether his coward-likeness truly *was* his likeness through the seeing of that uncanny craftsman, or whether it was only the likeness of his father's malice; if so, Asvald had certainly prepared it as carefully as a snake nursing its venom, for he gave his son very plausible answers concerning various other line-men, including the ones at the bottom that were neither bears *nor* men (Asvald said he believed that these were the ancient bearsark Kings of greatest dignity, who were so brave and ferocious in battle that the carver sought to pay them tribute in this way); in any event, Thorvald often puzzled over the bench-boards when his father was not there, seeking to know if by any possible chance he might feel a sudden leap of kinship with some other – that crowned one, for instance, who was offering up nine boys to be hanged, or that man who listened as a sparrow whispered in his ear; or that wolf-man who danced in a meadow of flames; but only when he pored over the man with the hands over his eyes did the heart of recognition leap up in him; so at last he said to himself: "Such must be my fate."

How Hall Fared, *or,* The Lappish Gold

It was Grjotgaard Brother-Burner who came one day to visit Thorvald, and invite him to join the men behind Erling. – "I suppose you know that he will be King someday," said Grjotgaard. "He is not the eldest, but eldest sons seldom fare well."

"Oh, so now you plot against Greycloak, do you?" said Thorvald. "One murder wasn't enough for you, I see. Well, I want no part of it. And my advice to you is to leave the country before they turn on you as you turned on Earl Sigurd – may ODIN cherish his shade! Go to Iceland. You will be far away from us there, and perhaps they will even kill you; Greycloak is popular with the Icelanders."*

At this, Grjotgaard stood up and left the house. They never saw him again. But it was not long after that they heard that he had been killed by Earl Hakon in a battle fought by order of Gunhild's sons; as is written in the *Flateyjarbók*, "There was great friendship between Hacon the Jarl and Gunnhilde, but sometimes they laid sly traps for each other."

"That was nicely done," said Thorvald at the news. "And now who will cut Queen Witch-Bitch down?"

---

* King Harald Greycloak got his name in the following wise: The captain of a certain merchant-ship from Iceland, having long exerted himself in vain to interest the Norwegians in his cargo of grey woolen cloaks, appealed at last to King Harald in his despair. – "Will you make me a present of one?" the King asked genially. – "With all my heart!" replied the captain. *He* knew enough to make presents to Kings! – As for Harald, he pulled the cloak around him smiling, and whirled round on his heels to show himself to his fawners and serving-men. At once a murmur of admiration arose to Heaven like incense, and men rushed to buy grey cloaks. (So it had been with the Bear-Cloak; so it would be with the Cloak of Ice.) But Thorvald and his son Eirik bought none, and this was remembered against them.

"Earl Hakon has the arms and men, I hear," said Eirik. "I tell you now that when I see my chance I will go to him."

"You are unproven for such manly talk," said the father. "But we shall see."

Now, among the thralls and cupbearers at Thorvald's house was a man named Hall, who was greedy for gold. Hearing what had been said, he waited until nightfall, and slipped into the forest where King Harald Greycloak lay uneasy in his tent. Though a most politic man, Harald was never as free of spirit as it was his habit to appear to others, so he was often troubled by nightmares. Presently he heard a noise in the darkness. – "Father, is that you scratching at the door?" he whispered. "Is there so little strength in your fingernails now? Is it hard to be buried in English ground?" – Thus he spoke to appease Bloody-Axe's ghost, for he feared him dead as he had feared him living, being now King in his place.

"It's no ghost you hear, Sire, but a mere tale-bearer." – So Hall replied through the tent-wall. – "I bring tidings of treasonous talk at Thorvald Asvaldsson's. Both Thorvald and that redhaired whelp of his spoke ill of you this very day, and the whelp good as threatened to take up arms against you."

"Then burn them out," said Greycloak softly. "Burn them out, and I'll give you thirty pieces of gold."

"Oh, no, Sire!" cried Hall. "I am not man enough to dare such a deed. If I were, would I be talking to you like this, huddled against your tent in the forest at night, so that none may see? To burn them would be a cowardly deed, but still too brave for me! I am a coward, and want but the wages of cowards."

"So I thought," said Greycloak. "Then return you home, friend Hall, without your gold."

Wearing the Grey Shirt

The next day, nonetheless, Greyskin reported the words of Hall to his mother Gunhild. She listened with attention, and in her own good time sent spies to see how things stood with Thorvald and his son. When they returned, they told her that those two showed themselves to be no more oath-fast to the King than before.

"Well," said the King-Mother, "let us try that young lad Eirik's temper. Harald, do you send him a grey cloak by way of one of your toy Earls, with a request that he come to serve you as your house-man. If he accepts, then he is our creature; if not, then I well imagine there may be some convenient manslaughter."

When Earl Torbrand came knocking at the door, his errand was all too clear. Eirik asked his father for advice.

"Do as you see fit," said Thorvald. "You are a man now; advise yourself."

"Very well," said Eirik. He stepped out, and ran the Earl through with his spear.

The First Outlawry ca. 963

And so Eirik and his father Thorvald were outlawed.* – I once read in the *Heimskringla* about Eyvind Kellda, the Norwegian sorcerer, who came on the night of Easter Saturday to Kormt Island, where King Olaf was feasting; and every man on Eyvind's long-ship was a dealer in evil spirits. He clothed his crew with caps of darkness, so that King Olaf could not see them, but when they neared the feast-house the darkness suddenly fell upon their own eyes, and lifted from the eyes of the King's men, so that they were easily seized in their blind wanderings and bound to a skerry which fell underwater at the high tide. So Eyvind Kellda perished, but why the darkness turned against him I cannot say. As to whether the darkness of GREENLAND later turned against Eirik, I leave that for you to judge.

---

* How happy must Gunhild and Greycloak have been in their triumph! – for they could not see the future. It was the King's destiny soon to be killed by another Harald, called Gold Harald, his name signifying his purpose. Of Gunhild's grief it is impossible to have any conception. She called together an army to avenge him, but few came. So she went west to the Orkneys with Ragnfröd and Gudröd (Erling having been slain by his own men, and Sigurd Sleva already sword-pierced for the rape of a noble's wife), and once again she took up her game of harrying what she could not have, for the sake of those two sons remaining. – But Queen Gunhild outlived them, too. Then she sat rocking herself and singing wind-songs. In her young-ripe days the Lapps had killed each other to kiss her mouth and her long hair spread itself wide on her shoulders like a blue cloak and shrouded her pale face when she cast her gaze so steadily downward; but once she was King-Mother she had kept it hidden under a shawl as was becoming to an older woman, knowing that when she squeezed her fist and crooked her arm at her sons they still saw that blue-black color in her eyes that glowed and raged at them to inspire them as they leaned together over their mead-cups, and at night they all took turns combing out her magic hair; but later still, when Ragnfröd and Gudröd were separately destroyed by their predestined spears, there was no one left to be defeated by her, and her hair became the color of ashes. – To the throne of Norway now came King Olaf Trygvesson, whom she had spied upon and persecuted; as we will learn, he proved more relentless than she.

Wearing the Blue Shirt
ca. 981 – ca. 1500

It is their lot that follow Kings that they enjoy great honours, and are
more respected than other men, but stand often in danger of their lives:
and they must understand how to bear both parts of their lot.

SNORRI STURLUSSON,
Heimskringla (*ca.* 1235)

Banished, banished, banished, Eirik set sail forever. His father was already
ailing. Beneath the cloud-sea was the ocean-sea, which seemed blue through
the clouds but was actually blue-grey, a coldly lovely color; wrinkled like
gooseflesh, with comet-like whitecaps which decayed like shooting stars.
The end of this sea could not be seen. Iceland was all alone in it, with the
exception of a single tall narrow iceberg, itself an island or lost column. In
the south, Iceland was flat, and brown-green, with long tongues of white
wave-froth lapping at it; and sea-birds screamed, and to the north rose
reddish-brown volcanoes. The plains were banded of many different-hued
earths. Sometimes they were grassy, but pierced by upward-pointed stones;
ahead lay a long low knife of mountains. This land had already been settled,
so Eirik sailed on as the plain rolled on, its flatness strewn now with little
black piles of lava, upon which a thin layer of whitish vegetation grew, like
mold on dried meat. – Where was he to live? Being an outlawed man, he
took note of the little hiding-gulleys, some richly greened, others white-lined
as if by mildew, while the country undulated northwards, a true paradise
for ambush and treachery. It was not his intention to be outlawed again
in Iceland, but having been thrown down already, he owned nothing but
a quickness not only of strength but also of anxiety in his blood, anxiety
hammering endlessly in his neck-veins, so that for cool survival's sake he

must sometimes stop and press upon his throat. When he left Norway he had sworn never to end his self-defense against any proud villain who might in future lay claim to his head and land. – But though he had the first, he had not the second as yet, for there were other men's farms everywhere. He sailed north. – Ahead were snow-spotted buttes. When the tide was low, white gulls waded in the mud of the broad firths. They crowded upon the little mossy islets just offshore; when his ship sailed by they shrieked. In the best places, where the land was flat and green by the sea, there were always farms. There did not seem to be any place for him.

Red and Blue

Oh, what shirt could he wear? It is impossible that he could have known then the significance of the Blue-Shirt which he was to put on for all time, although had he known it then, he must have taken it to him just the same. – A more interesting question is whether he knew of the *Skrælings*, for that world-wise chronicle the *Landnámabók* does not hesitate to describe certain "Cave-Men" in Iceland whom the settlers killed. Most likely these were anchorites of Irish origin, though there is also mention of trolls. I conclude that of the Skrælings he did not know, either. And again, had he known, how could he have acted differently? There were few opportunities for choice in Eirik's life.

Between Fjord and Ocean

His father was silent, and traced the carved grooves in the bench-boards with his fingers. Eirik sailed north and west, ducking in and out of firths bounded by dirt buttes and lava knife-ridges. Ahead lay grey mountains crowned with snow. There now rose rolling green hill-shoulders, then lava scarps whose banding resembled terracing (but these were steps that only a Frost-Giant might easily climb). Here were three snowy peaks, all in a row above a single sheep-farm – which seeing, Eirik went his way with a bitter smile – and here were grey-dusted walls of volcanic ash, mockingly green-swept at their bases; and then suddenly came many more sharp snowy mountains. Wide shallow streams made their rushing rapids down lava stairs. The steep hillsides, green and pebble-grey, bore deep landslide-tracks. Caves gazed out beneath their ragged cliff-foreheads. – Here there were no settlements, because farming

(HORN-
STRANDS)

DRANGAR
Where Eirik's
father Thorvald
died.

NORTHWEST
ICELAND
in the days of
EIRIK THE RED

VALTHJOF-
STEAD
Where Eirik's
rival lived.

FLATEY
ISLE
Where the tale
of Vinland was
written on calf-
skin.

BREIÐAFJÖRÐUR

BROKEY ISLAND
OXNEY ISLAND

BREIÐABOLSTEAD
Where Eirik fought
Thorgest.

HAUKADALE
Where Eirik
married Thjod-
hild.

FRODIS-WATER
Where Leif's
concubine
Thorgunna
died.

LAUGARBREKKA
Where Gudrid
was born; where
her father Thor-
bjorn guested Eirik.

VIFILSDALE
Where
Gudrid's grand-
father was
given land.

SNAEFELLSNESS
GLACIER
(SNAEFELLSJÖKULL)
Which lighted the way to
Greenland.

SNAEFELLSNESS PENINSULA

THORGEIRSFELL
Where Gudrid's suitor Einar lived.

ARNARSTAPI
Where Gudrid was
fostered.

TRAÐIR
Where Eirik
wintered after
the second out-
lawry.

FAXAFLÓI

SKALHOLT
Where Thorgunna
was buried.

was impossible. He sailed on. – The world had become green and grey and snowy-white under a leaden sky. The streams were grey, and so was the almost lifeless dirt. Waterfalls smashed through shelves of stale ice. Eirik shaded his eyes against the grey-glare and stood looking upward into that waste: a yellow waste of grass beneath grizzled hills, a waste of dead stone plateaux and rusty ridges wandering down to the milky blue sea, a waste of canted lava dragon-heads. Then he cleared the long promontory between Faxaflói and Breidafjord, and swung in west to Snæfellsness.

Snæfellsness

In olden times, one Floxi from Sodor exclaimed, upon first seeing Snæfellsness, "This must be a great land which we have discovered, and here are mighty rivers!" – But what Eirik first took note of was the long blue broken back of Snæfellsness Peninsula, snow-capped at every mountain-joint, and at its terminus the great white dome of Snæfells Glacier, whose blaze and glare pierced Eirik with dazzle-arrows right through his shield-hopes of peace so that he thought to himself, "If ever I must lurk west of here, I can watch this glacier from farther out than my enemies can see," and this thought made Eirik happy, but for now he forgot it. In the interior of the peninsula were other lesser snow-domes, and crowds of lava pyramids. The cliffs were purplish-grey, and banded by strata which marked the sad slow recession of the Muspel-Sea. Slide washes narrowed and widened on their faces like hourglasses.

Drangar

The farming was excellent there along the margin of Breidafjord, but because Eirik had no connections he could not obtain land. The names of the steadings and districts were like jewels: Haukadale, Breidabolstead, Vatnshorn, Laugarbrekka. His father stood beside him and said, "Never mind, son. At least we are out of Greycloak's hands." – Eirik said nothing. – They went north to Hornstrands, where the stony, mossy land was scarcely fit for sheep-foraging. In the bare places nothing grew but purple flowers. Closer to the sea, there was more grass, but not much more grass. – They built their farmstead at Drangar – or rather, Eirik did, for the old man soon caught a sickness from the cold and the labor, to which he was no longer equal. It was a coughing-sickness; both he and Eirik knew that it would be his last.

Eirik often wondered whether his father reproached him in his heart for having slain Earl Torbrand – and yet when he thought upon it and studied his father's face, hoping to catch out a cloud-glint in his eyes, he never saw that, and they never spoke of it. – He roofed the stead with turf and turned the cattle out. He put the precious bench-boards in place. And with that, Drangar became his home. – The mountains rose very steeply behind him. In their corridors the cold wind was always rushing, because a fat blue glacier hid behind them like a spider and breathed down at the sea with its frost-breath, so that the grass froze early, and Eirik's cattle remained lean. Sometimes he came across some little meadow where the farming would have been good, but then came another shoulder of lava-clinkers, and then the mountains, slate-blue and snow-capped under low bars of cloud. – Presently his father lay dying, and Eirik asked him what plans he should make.

"You should not stay here," said Thorvald. "This place will not bring any profit to you. When I die, let the glacier creep down over this house."

"Is there anywhere I can go that seems particularly good to your mind?" said the son. "For it seems to me that we searched over half Iceland."

"Eirik, I imagine that you will have to try yourself in a number of places," said the old man. "You will often have to defend yourself."

"I want to be on good terms with everyone," said Eirik, but old Thorvald laughed at this and raised himself up on one elbow. "You would never be on good terms with everyone unless you were King," he said, "and then not everyone would be on good terms with you. You're brave, son, and I'm proud of you, but life is easier for cowards."

"Well, the way I am can't be changed," said Eirik.

"Not true," said his father. "You are now a lone bear. If you marry well, you could be a man of consequence, with many friends and a purse bursting with gold."

"I think it best," said Eirik, "to be guided by your advice."

Then Thorvald coughed and died, and the black blood burst from his mouth.

Thjodhild Jorund's-Daughter

We're Rich in Viking Heritage, We're Uncommon Good Fun and . . .
We're Very Affordable.

Iceland Vacation Planner
brochure (1987)

At the inner elbow of Breidafjord, in the district of Haukadale, there lived
a man named Thorbjorn, now somewhat gone in years, who was married
to Thorbjorg Ship-Breast, the widow of Jorund Ulfsson. (What Jorund died
of I cannot tell, for there is a wormhole in that part of the manuscript.)
Thorbjorg and Jorund had had a daughter, Thjodhild, whom Thorbjorg
brought with her to Haukadale. This girl was now of marriageable age.
The *Flateyjarbók* does not say that she was lovely, from which I infer that
she was plain: – all the more likely, then, that Eirik could have her. – "I will
not aim at yonder Ice-Mountain just yet," he said to himself, sailing south
towards Snæfellsness. "But let me see what I can do." Surely Thorbjorn of
Haukadale must be more willing to let the girl go to a deedless man than he
would any of his own daughters, and she was more than marriage-ripe, so
he decided to pay a visit to Haukadale. The farming was excellent there.

Now when his house-carles gave him word that a guest waited at the door
of his hall, Thorbjorn came out to give Eirik good greeting as custom
required, and led him to the hearth and bade him sit beside him at
his high-seat. Eirik was somewhat downcast by the wealth that he saw
everywhere about him – for riches are a curse to those who have none –
but he counted on his luck to help him. To fight the golden gleaming of
so many polished spears, to conquer the little blue troll-folk who grinned
at him in the thread-forests of Thorbjorn's tapestries, he had brought a
bracelet of his father's, well-worked from that good red gold that comforts
men in their sorrows better than ever a cool beloved hand can soothe
a fevered forehead. – For this gift Thorbjorn thanked him cordially. But
still he cherished some reserve, for he thought he could tell what errand
brought Eirik here. – "Still," thought Eirik, "the deed must be tried."

"I will not hide what is in my mind," he said to Thorbjorn. "I want to
marry your stepdaughter Thjodhild."

"Well," said Thorbjorn, "she's a good girl, and needs to be married, but I
can't say I know much about you. You're the Thorvaldsson that came from
Norway?"

"Yes, Lord," said Eirik proudly. "My father was of high account in
Norway."

"In Norway he was, no doubt," said Thorbjorn. "And you have a farm in
Hornstrands? The pastures are stony there, aren't they?"

"They could be stonier," said Eirik.

"In Jötunheim they could, no doubt," said Thorbjorn smoothly. "Well, let
me talk it over with my kinsmen."

Eirik bit his lip, but said nothing. If Thorbjorn became his kinsman, such affronting words as he had meted out would no longer require atonement; if not, well, Eirik could easily send him to HEL. So thinking, he waited patiently, and felt no fear.

The next day Thorbjorn and Eirik discussed the terms of the betrothal, and reached agreement. Although he did not say as much, Eirik's high birth had weighed heavily with Thorbjorn. When he told Thjodhild she raised no objection; for she had begun to feel herself a bit of a burden to her foster-father, and certainly she could not become of any account by staying at home. – Eirik and Thorbjorn shook hands, and Eirik paid the bride-price: thirteen *örers* of silver, counted out from the sack at his belt. – "The bench-gift will be another five *örers*," said Thorbjorn quietly. For his part, he agreed to give his stepdaughter a good dower of gold and silver, as well as land in Haukadale, near Vatnshorn, where roseroot grew in profusion and moonwort rose green and yellow-green in the fields, its leaves like racks of double-bladed axeheads; and the grass was soft and springy beneath his feet, and later, as Eirik gazed upon the land, he saw all his fat white dream-cows grazing there, for this must be the vortex of his whirlpool-life; the cold black waters had whirled him down and down to green deeps, the bright green fields of Haukadale ... Eirik pronounced himself well satisfied with their wedding-bargain. Then Thorbjorn summoned his stepdaughter into the room, and placed Eirik's hand in hers. "I now pronounce you betrothed," he said.

Thjodhild had black hair and greenish-grey eyes. Her smooth young face was lightly freckled.

Happiness

Bright candles burned at the wedding feast. The bride sat on the cross-bench, linen-bound, and Eirik's household keys hung from her belt. Her eyes were wide and sad, but Eirik could not see them because by custom she wore the wedding headdress that hung low over her face, so that it seemed to Eirik as if he were marrying not a woman, but a bale of clothing. But he laughed and drank his ale, and soon put this peculiar notion out of his mind. Of late the trolls had been troubling him while he slept. He sat with his friends Eyjolf, Slayer-Styr and Thorbrand of Alptafjord, while on the other long-bench sat his father-in-law and his men. – "He seems to me a wild, tangle-haired sort of fellow," said Thorbjorn to his kinsmen in low tones. "I hope we are doing right by this match." – But they told him to be easy in his mind, for it was patent,

they said, that all Eirik wanted to do was to settle down on some good land
and increase his fortunes. Some day the family might have need of him, they
said. – "If it is a good match," said Thorbjorn, "we will need him more than
he needs us." – But at this, his kinsmen told him to stop saying words of ill
omen at such a time. Then Thorbjorn drank heavily, and stared into his cup.
– The wedding-toasts were drunk, the solemn prayers were made to FREY and
FREYJA, who watch over the fertility of man and wife, and then Thorbjorn
conducted the pair to their marriage-bed and left, shutting the door behind
him. – Thjodhild stood in the center of the room, listening to the guests
shouting and laughing in the hall outside. She felt rather dreary. As for Eirik,
his emotion was relief that he had got Thjodhild at last, and with her a measure
of security against his poverty and friendlessness. – Thjodhild's *slœdur*-dress fell
very narrow and straight around her body. After a long time, in which Eirik
neither touched her nor said a word to her, for he did not want to disrespect
her person, she flushed and turned away from him abruptly. She began to take
her dress off. She pulled it over her head. Beneath it she was wearing a light
wool tunic. She hesitated for a moment. She unfastened her headdress and
let her long dark hair down. Then very shyly she undid the buttons of her
tunic, one by one. – Still Eirik did not say anything. But she looked into
his face and thought she saw desire there and began to feel pleasure in her
anticipated delight with him; and she undid the last gold button of her tunic
and slipped it down her shoulders. Beneath this she wore her white linen
night-serk against her skin. – Now in those days, although highborn women
loved to preen themselves with bright colors for their outer garments, the
custom for all women was to wear a white under-serk, the whiter the better,
and as Thjodhild was a very cleanly woman and it was her wedding night
she had taken particular care with this, so that her night-serk glittered and
sparkled with its whiteness; and as Eirik looked upon her his eyes were drawn
away from her face, which though plain was by no means unpleasing (and,
moreover, was fixed rather anxiously on his) and away from the shape of
her breast, which certainly ought to have pleased him, and his eye lost itself
in that whiteness, so that to Eirik it seemed once again that he was marrying
not a woman, but a bundle of clothes; and as he stood there so bewildered
and bedazzled as to be for the moment not right in his mind, the white
glitter mastered him as Thjodhild stood so straight and stiff (for she could
see that he was occupied with other thoughts than those of her); and the
folds of that white, white night-serk seemed to become the tongues and
fjords of a horrible white cliff of ice that reached higher than the sky; and
Eirik threw himself upon his knee and prayed to his patron-god THOR to

send the awful vision away; while Thjodhild stood looking down upon him in astonishment and anger.

On the morning after the wedding night, Eirik crossed the floor and gave Thjodhild her linen-fee and her bench-gift as she sat on the cross-bench. But she did not raise her head.

Haukadale

Now suddenly Eirik had friends and kin and slaves, for he had married well. His land brought forth blueberries of its own accord; and on Yule-days they drank the sacrificial blood. The turf-roofed houses of his farm stood watchful in a thicket of birch-trees behind the outhouses. There Thjodhild sat, working at the great loom in the corner, with porridge bubbling on the hearth-fire for her husband when he came home from the fields. Every chest was locked; at Thjodhild's belt was every key. But she was always weary. She milked the cows early on dark mornings, when there was ice in the byre, and her breath and the cows' breath rose as steam, and sometimes when she was finished she sat on in the darkness, letting thoughts of her husband rack her. What was he? What was he? Her spirit was numb and snow-choked; the wind blew from the cold, cold hills.

The Children

By Thjodhild had Eirik the Red three sons: Leif, Thorstein and Thorvald. They were all water-sprinkled. Much later, in another country, he also acknowledged a bastard daughter, Freydis. She was clever, with much knowledge, but false. – All of these children were destined to reach for new lands.

The Eldest Son

Very occasionally Eirik played chess with his wife, and then young Leif sat down and folded his arms upon the table with bowed head, watching the board. His face was delicate, his lower lip somewhat too full. His father considered him a disappointment, for he took no notice of the fact that the boy always won at chess no matter how carelessly he played, that he never injured himself at his chores, that, in sum, he seemed to live a life of almost indolent ease. Though Leif was the eldest son, Eirik did not want to acknowledge that he had inherited the family luck – probably because it did not seem to him that he had any luck to speak of. Within a few winters of his settlement in Haukadale, he was outlawed again.

The Second Outlawry *ca.* 979

Eirik lived at Eirikstead, and his neighbor Valthjof lived at Valthjofstead. They saw little of each other, and both were content that that was so. Eirik knew well that Valthjof despised him for an interloper and a wolf's head;* indeed, he could not but wonder why Thjodhild's foster-father had given him land so close to such a man, for Thorbjorn had considerable land to give; and in the end, by the nature of things, Eirik and Valthjof must become enemies. – In this belief Eirik was not deceived. There presently came a terrible famine to Iceland, in the course of which many were forced to eat ravens; and it was said that men sometimes killed their grandfathers to escape the necessity of feeding them. A cattle-plague made matters much worse. The Haukadale-dwellers were not so badly touched; and Eirik was proud that neither Thjodhild nor the children ever had to go hungry, although the portions were sometimes small indeed. Their herd had been touched by the plague, and they had but three beasts left, a dappled heifer, a bull and a stout red cow by which the family set great store, for she gave milk in abundance, so that at least there could be something to put on the porridge. Thjodhild guarded what food they had carefully, and doled it out in the most economical way. It was wonderful also to see how well the children bore it; even Thorvald, the youngest, who was only an infant still unweaned, scarcely cried; in large measure this was due to Thjodhild, who acted always cheerfully with the boys, despite her own mournful nature; and even when she was spinning or milking she nourished them with stories. One warm evening in Sun-Month† the door was open as Eirik came home to his stead with a great load of fish, which he was very thankful to have caught, and as he stopped on the threshold he heard Thorstein say: "Mother, am I lucky?" and Thjodhild said, "Of course you are, sweet boy, but there is only so much luck to go around," and Thorstein said, "Who has the most?" and Thjodhild said very gently, "Your father has it now, for he needs it to feed us," and

---

* Outlaw.
    † The Norse months were as follows: Harvest-Month (fall), Gore-Month (when cattle were slaughtered), Frost-Month, Ram's-Month, Winter's Wane, Sowing-Tide, Egg-Tide, Sun-Month, Haymaking-Month, Grain-Reaping Month.

Eirik listened, and Leif said, "But I'm luckier than Thorstein, I know!" – There was a haughty fierceness in the lad that repelled Eirik. But he strode into the house and said nothing. – Thorstein meanwhile had begun to cry at Leif's taunts (it was then that Eirik realized how seldom the boys cried or complained), and Thjodhild said, "Hush, and I will tell you a story about luck. As for you, Leif, you may listen, too, if you are good and apologize to your brother." – But Leif would not, and shouted, "Truly I have more luck than Thorstein!" and he ran out into the fields. – "Perhaps he does," said Eirik wearily, "for tonight I have no patience to chase him and punish him." – He sat down in his high-seat, watching the flame-flickers reflected in the polish of those carven bench-boards, which he had just recently greased with a little seal-fat; and Thjodhild sighingly desisted from her spinning for the moment and sat Thorstein on her lap to tell him the story of King Harald Fairhair, the luckiest man in the world, who could turn into a bear whenever he chose and best the other bears in battle, so that all feared him; and Thorstein's eyes were wide and he said, "Where did the King find such luck?", and Thjodhild said, "His father gave it to him," and Thorstein said, "But if his father had it, why didn't he chase away the bears himself?", and Thjodhild said, "Silly boy! If he had done that, what would there have been left for his son to do?", and Thorstein said, "Mother, I wish that King Harald Fairhair were my friend," and he burst into tears again, so that Thjodhild grew quite vexed. – "Stop it," she said. "All of us admire King Harald for his luck, but he used it evilly, to strip other Kings of their dignity. Anyhow, he is dead." – Just then Leif came running in, crying, "I cannot find the red cow!" – Eirik leaped up and followed his son into the pasture. They searched until the late darkness fell, and the little boy began sniffling in the damp, so Eirik was forced to bring him home. – "I cannot think what could have happened to her," said Eirik. He could not sleep. – "Perhaps she strayed," said Thjodhild, to console him. "You must go to Valthjofstead tomorrow, and ask for her."

Eirik lay beside her with open eyes until Rising-Hour. Then he was on his way.

"Your red cow?" said Valthjof. "No, I have not seen her. You may be sure that I would have told you if I had, for I have no meadows to spare for my neighbors' strays."

Eirik answered not a word. He swung himself onto his horse and rode home.

The cow was never found, and presently the famine lifted. A year went by; and one day Valthjof let his cows graze on Eirik's grass. Eirik said nothing, but had his slaves drive the cattle back into Valthjof's pastures. The next day the cows were back again. Eirik went in and told Thjodhild about it. – "Will your kinsmen support us if I give Valthjof what he deserves?" he asked her. – Thjodhild was churning butter. She did not look up at him. "You do what seems best," she said. – Eirik stood gazing at her for a moment. "I see no reason why I should endure this slight to my reputation," he said at last. He had his slaves drive the cows back to Valthjof's stead again, and this time he gave instructions that they were to whip them. That evening Valthjof met Eirik at the boundary between their property. – "Well, Eirik," said Valthjof, "I see you have been disturbing my cattle as they graze. Since you have few friends in this district, I advise you to suffer whatever fate intends." – Red Eirik leaned upon a fence-stone very thoughtfully. "Well, Valthjof," said he, "the world holds nothing that can be had without a struggle." – The next day Eirik's slaves started a landslide that destroyed Valthjof's farm. Valthjof was killed. His kinsman Eyjolf Saur, being honor-bound to take revenge, killed Eirik's slaves at Skeidsbrekkur, so Eirik killed Eyjolf Saur and his oath-brother, Hrafn the Dueller. – It is, alas, the way of the world that the more people one kills, the more kinsmen become exercised. Eyjolf Saur's kinsmen set a case against Eirik and got him outlawed from all Haukadale. – "Anyhow," said Eirik carelessly, "I have no wish to stay here."

The Dream of the Black Hands

When he left the district, he had no idea where he should go. His kinsmen must support him against his enemies, that was their obligation; but he had strained their patience. His father-in-law did not come to see him away. – Slayer-Styr, at least, was there; he slapped Eirik on the shoulder and said, "Come now, Glumgrim, it is no great matter to be outlawed, as you know from old experience!" at which Eirik smiled somewhat, and Thjodhild laughed, saying, "You are crazy, Styr!", and Styr had even made a little wooden sword for Leif to distract him from his parents' troubles, for he was a very considerate man despite his name. – The child was delighted with his toy. He rushed hither and thither with it uplifted, shouting, "I'm going to kill my enemies, like you, father!", and Eirik shook his head and said, "Well, it seems the lad has some heart in him." – "So you have enemies already, do you, little man?" said Styr indulgently. "And who might they be?" – "I'm sure I don't know," Thjodhild answered cuttingly before Leif could say anything. "We never see anyone." – After that, no words were spoken until the horses and oxen were loaded.

That night, Eirik and his family were guested by their friend Thorbjorn Vifilsson, who owned a farm in Laugarbrekka. There was plenty of room at Thorbjornstead, since his wife Hallveig had recently died in childbirth; the infant, a girl named Gudrid, had lived and been sent out to be fostered. Eirik had been a witness to her water-sprinkling, and thought her a promising baby. He asked his host how she did, and was told that she thrived. – "It may well be that I could be a good foster-father to one of your sons," said Thorbjorn. – "Yes, that may be," said Eirik, a little shortly.

The boys were put to bed; and for once they did not fight among themselves, but made no noise, for which Eirik was grateful. He sat up late into the night talking with Thorbjorn about what he should do, while Thjodhild gazed dully into the fire. – "No one has taken possession of all the islands in Breidafjord," said Thorbjorn. "There you will find good pasturage, as I know, for I have fished thereabouts. I think you should lay claim to an isle or two." – "You had best do it, Eirik," said Thjodhild. – "Well," said Eirik, "since you are both united in your plans for me, so shall it be." – They lay down by the fire and slept, but everyone in the room was soon awakened by Eirik's groaning in a dream. – "Let him sleep," said Thjodhild. "However difficult his dreams, he will not thank us for waking him now."

Tradir

Eirik was a man who trusted to islands. On islands he would not be surprised by his enemies. Considering Thorbjorn Vifilsson's advice to be sound, he sailed down Breidafjord and took possession of Brokney Island and Öxney Island. He burned the fires of consecration; he made a little temple to THOR. Because the autumn was too far advanced for him to raise his house, however, he took his family south to Tradir for the winter. Tradir was far away, beyond the mountains, past the silver geysers and the yellow sulphur-springs that trickled from the volcanoes down through the yellow grass, behind the snow and lava and ice; and since he must ride there quickly, Eirik left behind everything that he would not immediately need. – In Tradir they lived with Thjodhild's kin, and though Eirik worked with a will at any chore to be done, he felt unhappy in his mind that he must always be indebted to them, it seemed, for his living.

"Yes, we have served your turn well enough," said Thjodhild with a laugh of anger.

"What would you have me do?" cried Eirik.

"Perhaps I would have you divorce me," replied Thjodhild, "and take up kinship with the trolls." Such was the bitterness in her face that for a moment he could not look at it. He was silent, and stood twisting his fist in his palm. He might have struck her, but he could not; he remembered only too well how she had stood stiff above him that night in the bridal chamber, when he had been lost in his dream of snow and ice.

In the spring they returned north to Breidafjord, and Eirik built a stone house on the isle of Öxney.

Öxney Island 1987

Those who worship symbols will be titillated by the fact that Oxen Island appears at first to be E-shaped, E for Eirik, but it is not, and Oxen Island did not quite fit Eirik. – Puffins bob in the inlets. The island is very green. It smells of sheep manure. A cormorant cries petulantly. All around, the sheep, who have inherited the island from the oxen, bleat, but their bleats are as faint and far away as the hummings of flies. The sea is so grey as almost to be white beneath the clouds. From a high rock can be seen a little white house, with a dilapidated shed beside it. The path goes past the kitchen window, in which stands a bottle of vodka, and then across a series of rotten foot-bridges over bogs and streams and pawed-up mud. Then one can leave the trail, and strike out across the hard grass-hummocks until, on a sloping field that ends in a low sea-cliff, one comes across the stone foundation of Eirik's sheep-pen (all grass-grown now). The stone wall that Eirik built begins there, running down in the direction of the white house, and then left. It seems longer than it is, because Oxen Island's edge has become a spurious horizon for it to pretend to stretch to. Brown and black horses graze by this wall, and purple flowers grow on the stones of it. One horse mounts another, and then they both graze again. After awhile, the horse-herd raises its half-dozen heads and canters away, over Eirik's wall. A chilly breeze blows. Birds call faint and querulous against a cloud. A semicircle of pink moss campion smiles from a stone.

The Bench-Boards ca. 980

Eirik meanwhile had begun to puzzle over the bench-boards as his dead father Thorvald had done. One night he cleaned them so that he might see them better, and Thjodhild got a cloth to help him, and later brought a bit of tallow and polished them, for which he was grateful, and she said, "Are you homesick for the place where you were born?", which startled Eirik, for she was not wont to ask him such questions, and he answered, "Somewhat, I suppose. But little enough; it is no matter." – Seeing that he was in no mood for talk, she left him. He brought a candle closer and studied the figures. Something was not right. He knew very well the place where he was pictured, for since his father had pointed it out to him it seemed that his eyes most often wandered to it. There was the man standing behind Grape-Plucker, drawing his cloak tightly about him with one hand, and reaching with the other for some treasure that would never be known, because the cruel Carver had hidden that arm from the wrist downwards behind Grape-Plucker's shoulder (and with a very strange stirring Eirik realized that Grape-Plucker must be his son Leif); but beside his own image was something that Eirik was certain had not been there before, not even at Haukadale. For one thing, it was at least twice as tall as any of the other figures; surely he would have noticed it before. In outline it seemed less a man than a mountain, for it was very broad up to the shoulders, narrowing abruptly into a sort of peak of darkness or blankness; for it had no face. In one hand it held a knife; in the other, a sword whose blade widened outward from the handle, so that it almost appeared to be a great icicle gripped by the point. The knife-hand was drawn in to guard the figure's left side, the haft snug against its cloak. The sword-arm crossed the breast, though what there was to guard there was a mystery, for the very heart of this strange being was exposed in a cave of rune-bones like latticework. Or perhaps there was no heart, but simply a jewel or crystal; what it was was difficult to discern. – Eirik liked this figure exceedingly ill.

He went and roused his wife, who had lain down, and made her inspect his discovery, which she did in no good temper. – "Have you seen this before?" he asked her.

Thjodhild curled her lip. "I have little time to be straining my eyes over half-rotten wood," she said. "There is enough for me to do with making a home in all these places that you bring us."

Eirik would have replied to this, but just then the boy Leif, who had been awakened by his parents' talk, came out from his bed and peeped at Eirik from behind his mother. With a sudden pang, Eirik wondered if his son were afraid of him.

"Come here," he said.

Thjodhild looked at him in surprise. "You know that he should be sleeping, Eirik," she said.

"Yes," he said. "But I want to show him something first. – Leif, do you see this carving, here, the man picking grapes?"

"Yes, father."

"You will be that man when you are older. You will help me, if I fail, and gain our rights. Do you understand? You are the eldest son."

The boy's face flushed. "I understand," he said. And he kissed his father's hand.

These things had happened at Haukadale. When he was outlawed, and had to take his wife and children south to Tradir as quickly as he could, travelling light, he left the bench-boards with his neighbor Thorgest for the winter. – "The workmanship on these is very fine," said old Thorgest fussily. "Yes, I will keep them for you." – But when Eirik returned to Öxney Island, Thorgest did not return them, and he rode over to Thorgest's farm to see about the matter and Thorgest asked to keep them just a little longer, for he had found that they became the farmstead; he was often complimented on them, he said. The summer went by, and still Thorgest would not return them.

Once when Thorgest was drunk he started boasting about all the fine possessions he had. "My farm-house is the envy of my neighbors," he said (this was true). "My cow-byres and grain-houses are full. My wife is the best *hús-freyja* of any. My sons are my strong arms. And I will keep my luck! In fact, I have even more of it, for the bench-boards of that young Eirik Wolf's-Head now belong to me."

"A wolf's-head I am, am I?" said Eirik. "A Valhalla you have, do you? Well, remember the hour when ODIN will meet the Wolf."

Thorgest flushed with rage at this, and began to rise, but men restrained him, saying that after all he had been in the wrong to say what he had said in front of Eirik. And Eirik took to his horse, and rode away to where his skiff awaited him on the coast of Breidafjord. And he returned home.

He ate his meat in silence, so that Thjodhild stared at him, and his children also were anxiously silent, and presently he went out past the sheep-pen and up the grassy hill, until he came to the edge of the island. He stood there for a long time looking to the southeast, where Breidabolstead was a low field of ochre-green, underlining that blue-grey wall of snowy mountains that Eirik so often set his gaze to, following them, peak to peak, until his eye came to the great white shining of Snæfellsjökul, beyond which nobody had gone; but now he turned his eyes to the line of ochre-green where old Thorgest the Yeller had his farm. – "It is certainly unendurable to bear such insult," he said to himself, "and a man of no reputation is doomed. If I go and take my bench-boards back, my honor will be increased." – At length Thjodhild

came out of the house to see what ailed his mind, and when he told her of
his resolve, she used dissuading words, but Eirik said, "I hear your warning,
but no weeping, by which I deduce that you can be convinced. Convince
yourself, then, and leave off troubling me." For, after all, they had scarcely
married for love.

The Dead Dream

That night, Eirik dreamed that he had a hairy bear-face with long narrow
jaws full of teeth, and he sniffed the air with his wet black nostrils and scented
Breidabolstead and came at a lumbering run and smashed the house in with
a single blow of his claw – but when he awoke he was not a bear anymore;
the age of the Bear-Kings was long past, and no man would ever become
a bear again.

Wearing the Blue Shirt *

He was wearing blue clothing and carrying an axe in his hand . . .

Hrafnkel's Saga (ca. 1260)

Eirik jumped on his horse and rode towards Breidabolstead. He had fifteen men
with him, all resolutely armed. Slayer-Styr was there, and so was Thorbjorn
Vifilsson, who was very fierce and imposing (although, as they all knew, he
was but the son of a freed slave). Thorbrand and Eyjolf and all the others
were there with their thralls, waiting on his word. It was his intention to take
Thorgest by surprise. Because Thorgest was old, he often slept until after
Rising-Hour, but his sons were men in the height of their strength, and saw
to most matters. For this reason Eirik set out when the moon was still rising
in the sky, and when they came near the farmstead he led his riders a cunning
course between ridges and grassy mounds, so that they were usually hidden in
the cold moonshade. When they came in sight of the farmstead, Eirik reined

---

* "It should be noted," says an authority, "that the Icelandic word for blue (*blá-r*) had
a much wider range of meaning than its English cognate and counterpart. It denoted every
shade of blue and black, and was used to describe not only the colour of the clear sky,
but also of the raven. This was the colour particularly associated with Hel, the Goddess of
Death, which may partly account for the literary convention of dressing killers in blue."

in his horse and said, "I don't intend to harm Thorgest or any of his people. I won't support any of you who kill unprovoked. If possible, we should simply take the bench-boards. That will be the most elegant humiliation we can inflict. If they choose to follow us, however, let us kill as many as we can." – They dismounted, and crept through the grass. It was still long before Rising-Hour. When Eirik raised his hand, they smashed the door with a log-ram and rushed inside.

The Outcome

Eirik killed two of Thorgest's sons.

The Supporters of Thorgest

After this, the two enemies were forced to maintain bands of armed men at home, for each feared the other. The men sat polishing their axes; they walked about in the wet field-stubble, never alone and never easy in their minds; they stroked the hot necks of their horses. – Thorgest was supported, so we read, by Thorgeir of Hitardale, Aslak of Langadale and his son Illugi, and the sons of Thord the Yeller. I know not a tittle about any of them.

The Supporters of Eirik

As for Eirik, he was supported by Slayer-Styr Thorgrimsson, who was known not only for his skill at opening skulls but also for his word-craft; by Eyjolf of Svin Island, who owned much property; by Thorbjorn Vifilsson, whose daughter Gudrid will play a large part in this history, and by the sons of Thorbrand of Alptafjord, about whose utility I know nothing. Most likely their arms were as strong as those of any young men. – The value of this crew to Eirik was immense; his to them was dubious. Why then did they associate themselves with this desperate wolf's-head, whose enterprises had three times now come to nothing? – The answer can only be that they belonged unknowingly to the League of the Ice-Dreamers. At night they closed their eyes and drifted into a purple darkness, which presently reddened like water colored by seeping blood, and then eagerly they pulled on rich blue dream-shirts and dreamed themselves into the ice-maze that so obsessively baffled them; yet each night they thought that they were closer to finding what they wanted in the ice (although the truth was that each night they were only a night older). From a distance the floes appeared to be almost diamond-shaped, so that the fjord was a chessboard seen end-on – an effect enhanced by the fact that the dark leads were sometimes diamond-shaped – and yet they were not any shape, really, and neither was the ice; and so the mind realized that it had been tricked, and, bewildered, let the ice be as it was. – Because they ice-dreamed in spring, they walked a frozen fjord riddled with leads and channels that led them on vast detours so that they wandered over an agony of sloping ice-ridges, suntanned and dazed, with dirty water trickling to the right of them, to the left of them, and under their feet. These great ice-chips they must walk would soon be shattered and thrust against the shore like so much driftwood, there to melt, or at best live on ignominiously for a month or two. But even when the sun was hot, ice lived beneath the moss, and ice lived in Jötunheim to the north; and in time a wedge of darkness would be driven into the previously unriven day; and this darkness would let in cold and wind and ice and more ice, until winter could rush across the fjords and harden the ice to bear the weight of the most ambitious dreams; then the Ice-Dreamers could skate directly to whatever called them; and they would be laughing and their eyeballs would be rolling and swirling like the falling snow.

The Third Outlawry *ca. 981*

That spring, Thorgest and the sons of Thord the Yeller brought a case against Eirik for slaughter at the Thorsness Thing. It was a very crowded Thing. Thorgest had brought many armed men with him, and the sun was bright on their spears. Because Thing-time was truce-time, Eirik felt somewhat secure; nonetheless he avoided Thorgest as much as he could. Of his supporters, only Slayer-Styr was present. – "You must stay in your booth as much as if you were a prisoner," Slayer-Styr cautioned his friend. "Certainly Thorgest has cause for anger against you." – "That I know," said Eirik, grinning. (But when he sat in the booth by himself, he looked somewhat more cast down.) – As for Slayer-Styr, he drew away from Thorgest all the men that he could, but the balance was still against Eirik, so Styr went into the booth of Snorri the Priest, who officiated at the Thing, and talked with him privately, praying him not to set on Eirik as soon as the Thing had closed. – "We both know that he's nothing but a wolf's–head," said Snorri the Priest somewhat snappishly, and

Slayer-Styr said, "Yes, we both know that he's likely to be outlawed despite my efforts, and that is why I want you to guarantee his protection until he's left the district." – At this Snorri the Priest demurred, but Slayer-Styr promised that if Snorri did this for him then he would come to his aid were he ever to need it, and Snorri was too worldly a man not to know that eventually trouble would come to him as it came to all, so he gave his word, and Slayer-Styr shook his hand and then straightened his big shoulders and left the booth, and while Snorri sat sighing and shaking his head and rubbing his hands Slayer-Styr sought out Eirik, who had been somewhat anxious during this empty time, which must be filled by some pleasant or unpleasant result, and told him the news.

"Little enough the old fox has promised us," said Eirik.

Slayer-Styr bowed his head. "Little enough can we gain," he said. "If Thorgest has his way, there will be nowhere you can go."

"Then I'll go to Nowhere," said Eirik. "The land may be as green there as here."

Eirik was sentenced to the three-years' outlawry. As soon as the Thing ended and Weapontake began, old Thorgest, well pleased, sent his men to find Eirik and spit him on their spears, as he had loved his dead sons; but by then Eirik was gone, for his supporters had already hidden him among the islands.

The Bird-Islands of Breidafjord

Breidafjord means "Broad-Firth," and indeed it is so wide that on the south shore the sea-cliffs on the northern side, which are among the highest and sheerest in the world, appear as a low blue line interrupted by clouds. But the fjord is by no means empty. Over its grey waters rise everywhere a carnival of bird-islands, whose tenants cackle and scream and sob, offering men mirrors of meaninglessness for their feelings. So, as Thorgest's men roamed the islands for Eirik in their skiffs, choking with anger and hatred, they met themselves in the shrill troops of bird-soldiers that promenaded on the low black cliff-edges of mossy islands; as they sailed from rock to ochre-smeared rock, harshly jesting and telling each other the lying tales of their unsheathed swords, they heard the soft sobbing chuckles of birds; and sometimes when they rowed suddenly upon some hidden beach, skiff by skiff in their full warlike importance, they passed between guano-streaked cliffs from which jutted thousands of tiny pedestals, cushioned by moss, and on every one of these perches stood a grey bird, with a snowy breast and a snowy head; and because Thorgest's men were rowing quietly, in order to take Eirik by surprise, the birds did not take fright, but stood on their ledges like statues of themselves, and as Thorgest's men came closer the birds shook their heads and cried like children and spread their wing-feathers like fingers. In a cleft between cliffs, a boulder had fallen and wedged itself halfway above the sea, and upon it, too, a bird stood, ridiculously weeping and shaking its snowy head. – On other islands, which grew grey-green with grassy velvet, puffins hid in their holes. White loons laughed in the grass with upraised beaks. "Odin's chickens" (*Phalaropus hyperboreus*) cackled back at them. Clouds swooshed in the sky, and birds swooshed in the air. On every island was a flock of birds; and there were so many low rocks and low islands in that wide grey sea! – Some islands were commanded by the *skarfur*-birds – black cormorants with long narrow beaks – and the *skarfurs* paid sublime inattention when Thorgest's men rowed by, for they were busy looking up at the weather with their bright eyes, or going fishing in the sea for a moment or two, returning to stand on their white rock as they spread their wings like arms to dry themselves. Beside this white island of black birds was a black island of white birds – the *fyll* – who did not even trouble to look into the clouds; and in the sea paddled other birds, colored black and red and white . . . Puffins fluttered desperately, like fat white fish that had suddenly discovered that they were birds and had to fly, and could never stop flapping. There were eider-ducks, fulmars, shearwaters, sea-parrots. The islands were crazy and crowded with the bird-clowns, some of whom screamed until Thorgest's men were deafened. They never found Eirik. As the proverb goes, "Three things are uncountable in Iceland: mountains, lakes, and islands."

Dimunar's-Bay

Eyjolf of Svin Island had hidden Eirik in Dimunar's-Bay, which was a cold and narrow refuge set among sloping hills of crumbling lava that ended against a cold black wall of rock that sloped outward like a cave-lip; and above this wall rose two grey-green mounds like teats.* Between these hills, birds crouched screaming. Sometimes when the sea was hard and grey, mountains and clouds seemed to be mutually translucent upon the coast of Iceland.

---

* In Icelandic, *dimunar* means two hills set close together.

Eirik sat patient among the bird-cries. He scarcely thought of Thjodhild anymore. To guard against mischance and malice, she had returned to her stepfather's at Haukadale. – "I know I have caused you grief and trouble," Eirik had said to her; "I am sorry." – "So I see," she said. – On his left he saw the long blue vertebrae of Snæfellsness, which was cut lower and flatter today by a cloud-knife, and then a broken line of low black islands. Clouds hid the white dome of Snæfellsjökul, but he supposed that he would be able to find it again if he sailed out far enough so that it would rise above the bad weather like a white tower to guide him straight to his goal. The sea was flat and blue. To the west, a cloudbank met the sea at the water-horizon. Above it, the sky was the usual luminous subarctic blue, which Eirik did not care about in the least. – At midnight the sun was north, and sank down against a ridge-top, each affecting the other so that the sun took on a wide egg-shape and the ridge became notched. The sky was orange, and the sea was like a rolling plain of snow.

When Eirik's ship was ready, Thorbjorn Vifilsson and his daughter Gudrid helped him cast off. For a long time he saw the girl's slight form in the purple shadows. Thorbjorn waved him out through the rocks. – "May good luck go with you!" he called. – Eirik could see the twin dry teats of Dimunar Island for a long time. The hills were faded in the sun.

Blue-Shirt ca. 981 – ca. 985

His supporters accompanied him beyond the islands, and he told them that he was going to Greenland. The very existence of the country was debatable in those days. Eirik had heard something about it from Ulf Crow's son.* He sailed due west from Snæfells Glacier and made landfall at the base of another glacier which came to be called Blue-Shirt . . . What happened then? – That is unknown. The *Flateyjarbók* records only that he named an Eirik's Island, an Eiriksfjord and an archipelago called Eirik's Holms. – Sometimes during those winters, when the nights were separated only by feeble red wedges of daylight, and he was more alone than if he had been buried, he must have thought he heard loud voices roaring in another language, but had he rushed out into the dark black snowstorms he would have seen nothing. – Nor is it written anywhere how Thjodhild fared at home. As always in the

---

* Gunnbjorn, after whom are named Gunnbjorn's Skerries. It is said in the *Book of Settlements* that Ulf Crow had another son, Grimkel, whose son Thorarin Korni was a wizard and a shape-changer.

history of Blue-Shirt, answers are nowhere and everywhere, crowding upon
the islands of fact like a trillion separate whitecaps . . .

In the fourth summer after he had come to the new country, he sailed back
to Iceland, where he still had numerous supporters, and called for colonists.*
His shrewdness was evidently superior to his vanity, for he referred to the
place not as Eiriksland, but as Greenland, because, he said, people would
be most tempted by a pretty name.† (Most fortunate were those of limited
understanding, for whom the Idea of Greenland remained an unknown island;
for them was only a humming and rushing as something darkened the grey
air overhead; this was AMORTORTAK, the Demon with Black Arms.) No
doubt some of the colonists believed that Greenland really would be green,
perhaps a hilly misty sort of country, like Scotland, where their sheep could
graze (when in fact there were mainly rock-sheep and cloud-sheep), and their
daughters could pick berries eight months of the year. If they thought of
Blue-Shirt at all, it might have been as one of the dyed garments which they
would soon be wearing there in token of wealth. The women and children
leaned over the side, talking excitedly. Mothers put their children's hoods on;
the children looked down at the water. The sea was lavender, and the sun
wheeled round to the west, casting a shining light. In any case, twenty-five
ships set sail from Iceland in the year 985. Only fourteen of them arrived
at the icy rocks of the new coast. Of the others, some were blown back
to Snæfells, and the rest were drowned before they ever saw the cold, cold
glitter of Blue-Shirt.

Greenland at the Millennium

"The Land is wonderfull mountainous, the Mountaines all the year long full
of yce and snow: the Plaines in part bare in the Summer time. There grows
neither tree nor herbe in it, except Scurvy-Grasse and Sorrell." So wrote an
Englishman six and a half centuries later. – But accounts written before the
fatal change in climate said that Greenland's winters were not as severe as
Iceland's, and that some of the hills had trees that bore little apple-like fruits.

---

* Here it should be mentioned that when Eirik returned he had another battle with Thorgest
of Breidabolstead, which he lost, and after that, says the saga, they were "reconciled." In that
case, pears are surely partridges.

† I take this as proof that the salesman's art is unchanging, for in the *Book of Settlements*
we read that Thorolf, one of the first Norsemen to set foot upon Iceland, returned to
Norway proclaiming that "butter dropped from every blade of grass in the land which they
had discovered; therefore he was called Thorolf Butter."

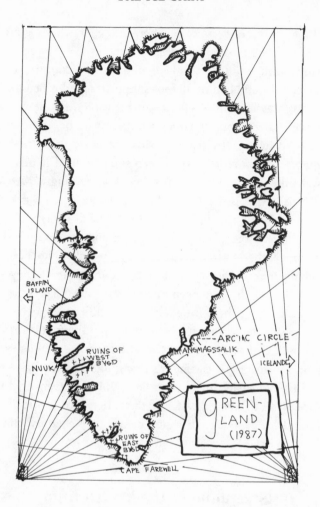

That reluctant mercenary, Nicolò Zeno, who wrote one of the last descriptions of the colony before it was lost, claimed that the monasteries were tolerably well-heated, thanks to the boiling sulphur-springs. (Not being accustomed to the cold, however, he died nonetheless.) The establishment at Eiriksfjord, near Cape Farewell, they called the Eastern Settlement (Ostrebug), and the one at Godthaab they called the Western Settlement (Vestrebug). They traded ivory, reindeer hides and walrus-skin ropes for corn, timber and iron. It was said that Greenland abounded in silver mines, in white bears with red spots on their heads, in white falcons, in whales' teeth, and in walrus' skins. It surpassed all other countries in its quantities of fish. There were many different colors of marble, and on a certain island could be found great deposits of a stone called talguestein, which was ductile enough to be worked into pots and drinking-vessels, but resisted fire. (In my arrogance I dare to hypothesize that it must have been soapstone.)

There were no Skrælings then to harry anybody, although the herdsmen sometimes found their abandoned settlements. Since the climate was mild in those days, the Skrælings had gone north, preferring the icy skerries which the polar bears preferred. They were wild people, in no way to be trusted. They returned with the southward wend of the polar ice, bestriding the huge turquoise-colored bergs. Their flat brown faces expressed nothing; their black eyes moved in a restless nomadic alertness that the Greenlanders considered ominous. They smiled only among themselves. At first they lurked among the glacier wastes of the interior, never in the same place from day to day, but it was clear that they coveted the coast. And while they awaited their hour the winters became longer and colder, stalking across more of the calendar every year. The mountains exhaled a freezing vapor. A contemporary sailing treatise seems to have been written in the chilly shadow of Blue-Shirt: "From Snæfjeldsnæs in Iceland, from which point the passage to Greenland is the shortest, the course is two days and two nights due west, and there you will find Gunnbjorn's Rocks midway between Greenland and Iceland. In old times this was the customary route, but now the ice that has been brought down from the northern recess of the ocean, has adhered so closely to the above-named rocks that no one can hold the ancient course without placing his life in danger."

The Other Greenlanders ca. 1200 – ca. 1500

In 1271, according to a Danish chronicle, a strong wind from the northwest carried to Iceland a quantity of ice laden with bears and wood. This incited the pickers and gleaners to go to Greenland. Some mariners from Friesland encountered "some miserable-looking huts hollowed out in the ground" – no doubt the traditional sod igloos or *anegiuchaks* of the Eskimos. Beside these huts were mounds of iron ore intermingled with gold. The mariners took as much as they could carry. "But when they returned to their vessels, they saw coming out of these covered holes deformed men as hideous as devils, with horns and slings and large dogs following them." One sailor, characterized as an idler, so that we need not mourn him, was caught by the Skrælings and cut to pieces with knives of unicorn-horn.

They were often to be seen after that, hunting seals and walruses in their skin-boats, which were long and narrow, so narrow that each Skræling seemed to be a part of his boat, for it was not much wider than a single ski. The boats were dark-colored. Tanned skins had been stretched tight over wooden lips to make them. They were pointed at both ends.

By the end of the century, Icelandic chronicles were reporting fearful signs and monsters in the seas around Greenland. Giant men called *halfsstrambs* rose out of the waves, with pointed heads, flippers and sad angry eyes. Sometimes the sailors saw *marguguers* – tall beings who were women from head to waist, with loose hair, great breasts slung over their shoulders, and long webbed fingers. Their appearance always presaged a fatal storm. Waves so high as to be called sea-mountains would rise around a ship, three at a time, and overwhelm it.

In their good time, the Skrælings raided and destroyed the Western Settlement. Ivar Bardsson, longtime procurator of Gardar, was, according to a narrative of 1349, among those selected by the Governor to expel them. "When they arrived there," says the manuscript in its resigned way, "they found no man either Christian or heathen, but only some cattle and sheep running wild, of which they took as many as they could carry on board the ships and returned home." The only settlement now remaining was the Ostrebygd. In 1379, according to the *Icelandic Annals*, "Skrælings attacked the Greenlanders, killing eighteen of them and carrying off two boys into captivity to be their thralls." It is hard not to be irritated by the really rather manic optimism that could have permitted Nicolò Zeno to write (*ca.* 1400) that monks and nuns held easy sway over the country. He devoted several pages to praising the luxuries of the Friars' chambers, which were heated with volcanic water. "They have also small gardens," he went on,

> covered over in the winter time, which being watered with this water, are protected against the effect of the snow and the cold, which in these parts, being situate far under the pole, is severe, and by this means they produce flowers and fruits and herbs of different kinds, just as in other temperate countries in their seasons, so that the rude and savage people of these parts, seeing these supernatural effects, take these friars for Gods and bring them many presents such as chickens, meat and other things, holding them as Lords in the greatest reverence and respect.

After Zeno's death the ice continued to tighten around the island, until landfall could only be made during the month of August. Having no access to trade, the Greenlanders were forced to live on dried fish and milk. A papal letter written in 1492 expressed the belief that no ship had sailed there for eighty years. By that time the Greenlanders had all perished.

11
Black Hands,
or,

How the Skrælings put the White-Shirt on

The Hermaphrodite
?? – *ca. 30,000* BC

GOD has made everything out of nothing. But man He made out of
everything.

PARACELSUS, ca. 1590

Elder Brother and Younger Brother lived on the ice without knowing
where they had come from. Elder Brother supposed that maybe the ice had
given birth to him through a seal-hole, because that was how Younger Brother
had been born; but whether or not that was the case, many questions lay
underfoot, like frozen tussock-beds. He had no memory of how he had
learned to be himself, striding about so utterly at home upon the black
ice; he could recollect many hunts and moons before the time of Younger
Brother, but whether his aloneness had ever had a beginning he could not
say. Sometimes he had a dream of another Brother, who had turned his
face from him and gone southward into the ice-mountains, crying out and
tearing at himself with his BLACK HANDS; and there were other nights when
he was certain that in the ice-combs far beneath him many other brothers lay
curled in frozen sleep, waiting to be born; but when he thought upon them
those fancies seemed to him fantastical, for on that entire world of ice there
were to be found but two souls: Self and Other; and between two and many
there lies a gap as wide as between one and two. Thus, Elder Brother could
never believe in a multitude of men corresponding to the seal-multitudes
he fed on; nor did it seem to him wise to make any presumptions. The ice
had taught him that: each step he took upon that surface must end with the
weight of heel and toe placed firmly upon *known* ice, never *presumed* ice that
might be no more than a film, shattering beneath him so that he fell into the
black dead sea beneath, never again to be born, perhaps . . . So he became by
degrees ever more practical, and stern and stately in his knowledge. Younger
Brother feared more than loved him. But this was a matter that Elder Brother

considered of no importance. The only important thing was getting enough for them both to eat. Being accomplished in this, he felt content that he did his duty; after all, without him Younger Brother must perish. The truths that he learned from the ice were not simple, but neither were they ambiguous. So Elder Brother strode with sureness through his ice-life.

Younger Brother was less sure who *he* was. Sometimes he thought he was a seal, and lay on his stomach barking. The wind was cold, and Younger Brother wept even as he barked, but he would not move because he wanted so much to be what he thought he must be; there were so many seals that he was sure that they were his relatives. Once when Elder Brother returned from a hunt he found Younger Brother almost buried in the snow, so long had he been there. – "You are not a seal, you know," said Elder Brother. "You are a boy." – But Younger Brother did not know what a boy was. Elder Brother was a grown man, and there were never any other people.

At other times Younger Brother was convinced that he must be a polar bear. He strutted about on his two little legs, growling and seeking to kill the seals. The seals said, "First he barks like us, and now he tries to bite us. What sort of fool is he?" They spanked him with their flippers. Younger Brother cried because he was too weak and slow to kill the seals.

One day he was sure that he must be a gull. He waited until a strong wind came; then he flapped his arms. The wind said, "What is this? A cub-animal? Good, I will pick him up and then drop him. What fun it will be to watch him fall!" – The wind seized Younger Brother and bore him high above the ice, so that Younger Brother screamed, and all the other gulls screamed back at him. They were trying to instruct him in the important skills of screaming and flying, but he did not know their language. In his fear he wet himself. The wind was disgusted at this and dropped him at once. By a fortunate accident he landed in soft snow.

After this, Elder Brother decided that it was dangerous to leave him to himself. Really he was too young to begin hunting, but there was no one to take care of him. If he continued to think that he was not human, one day he might turn into something inhuman.* So Elder Brother put him on his back and took him hunting. Younger Brother always cried.

Elder Brother was very skilled at walking on the ice. He could tell from its color how safe it was to walk on. "Never walk where the ice is black," he told his brother. "That ice is young ice; it is weak ice." And Younger

---

* In those days you had to be careful what you thought, because your thoughts would come true. Nowadays you have to be careful what you think because if you think it, it will never happen.

Brother listened because he wanted to be like his brother. – "Never walk on snow-covered ice," said Elder Brother. "You cannot see what color it is. Sometimes the snowdrifts will float on open water. That is called *mafshaak*. If you walk there you will die." – And Younger Brother listened, remembering every word.

"Sometimes you will see me walking on black ice," said Elder Brother. "Do not try to imitate me. You are ignorant and weak. I can walk on ice so thin that my foot breaks through it with every step. If you try it you will die." – Younger Brother listened without saying anything.

"See this pole with the bone point?" said Elder Brother. "This is called an *unaak*. When you mistrust the ice you walk on, use your *unaak*. Jab the point firmly into the ice. If it punctures through, the ice is not safe. If it does not go through, you may proceed." – Younger Brother listened well to these words.

The Bear-Shirt

One day Elder Brother carried Younger Brother on his back to hunt seals. For a long time they had gone hungry. They saw a breathing hole on the far side of a region of black ice. Elder Brother set Younger Brother down and told him to wait while he went to stalk the seal.

Younger Brother sat very still on the ice. The sky was seamlessly grey. The wind was blowing. He could see Elder Brother sitting beside the seal-hole,

YOUNGER BROTHER ALONE ON THE ICE

his spear resting on his knee. Elder Brother never looked away from the hole. As Younger Brother sat watching him across the black ice, he began to feel very lonely. He felt that his brother did not understand him or care about him. He began crying softly. He wished that he was something else than a boy. As he looked around he saw a polar bear crossing the black ice. The polar bear spread his legs wide and moved slowly and steadily across the dangerous ice. When the ice groaned, the bear got down on his belly and began to swim upon it. As Younger Brother watched, he became convinced once again that he was a polar bear, for his thoughts were but a succession of stars that wheeled about in his skull-sky like the moon and the sun, chasing each other through all the lovely hells. He stood up, spread his legs wide, and took his first step onto the black ice. He heard Elder Brother shouting at him, but he paid no attention. He was sure now that he was a polar bear. He felt comfortable, ferocious. His hands had become furry claws. He decided to kill Elder Brother and eat him.

Elder Brother ran toward him. There was anguish in his face. – "Stay still!" he shouted. "That ice is not safe!"

Luxuriously, Younger Brother opened his mouth and growled. Then the ice began to crack beneath his feet. At once he forgot that he was a bear. – "Help, help!" he wailed. – Then Elder Brother was there to lead him back to loyal ice, and he loved Elder Brother more than ever before; and his tear-streaked face made Elder Brother laugh. – "Now we must listen by the seal-hole," said Elder Brother. "If you have no attention for that, watch *Nanoq* and learn how he walks."

Polar bears give an impression of white snowiness, but incongruous with this is the almost triangular head, which the bear nods like a napping seal, in order to deceive other seals into thinking that he is one. Most of us want to be what we are not; but the clever ones, the predators, *pretend* to be what they are not, stalking and sneaking until their victims discover the deception too late.

Although the bear nodded like a seal, he often upraised his head for his own purposes, as if to gaze upon the evil spirits in the stars. When no seals were near he was his real self, and prowled and stalked upon the ice, uplifting his head; – and when he padded so springily upon his black-toed feet, Younger Brother understood for the first time how quickly a polar bear could move, and was frightened. The snow-bear licked his feather-arrow fur. He grinned with his black mouth. His round nostrils dilated. He rushed back and forth upon his iceberg.

"Elder Brother, can one create an ice-bear from one's thought?"

"I cannot say for certain," said Elder Brother. "So my advice to you is to not think on ice-bears." He strode on his way. – Younger Brother hopped feebly in the snow, but he could not by any means go as fast as his leader.

"Elder Brother, Elder Brother, where are you going?" cried the little one. "Please don't walk so fast or I'll be left behind."

"You must learn to keep up," said Elder Brother, turning his face away. He strode away across the mist-blown ice. Younger Brother ran after as quickly as he could, but his legs were fat and little.

The Storm, the Spirit Woman and the Island

"I feel a ringing in my ears," said Elder Brother. "A storm is coming." – That night the stars began to dance in the sky, as if they were being blown about by a strong wind. A ring formed around the moon. The next morning long clouds streaked the horizon. They came closer and closer. They were solid black; they did not reflect the white color of the pack ice. The seals lowered their heads in the water. The clouds became tinged with red in the south. A light breeze sprang up. As the hours passed, the breeze became stronger and stronger. Soon it was a stiff wind, then a gale. The sound of it was terrifying. Elder Brother could hear it coming down from the mountains before it reached him. When that far-off whistling came to his ears, he braced himself, holding Younger Brother as tightly as he could in his arms.

There was nowhere to run to, because the wind was everywhere, and the two brothers had no home. They huddled together, unable to see or hear each other but taking comfort from each other; and still the storm increased. Presently the furious chill of the sea-peaks, which could burn their flesh white, became a shelter to be desired (although they could not reach it now), because nothing else but ice-walls could break the force of that dread wind, which did not seem white to them, although it raked them with such great quantities of snow that they were almost suffocated; nor was it black, although there was such darkness in it that they could see no more with open eyes than with closed; it shattered the icebergs' bristles, splitting ice from ice so that snow gushed through the rifts like white blood foaming down cliff-sides; and the sky screamed through every crevice that it could find or make until the ocean, frozen though it was, was creaking and crashing, wrecked upon the second sea, the wind-sea. And then snow fell and snow blew and the sky's light vanished into cold opacity; the greedy storm had swallowed the sky.

At last there came a lull, although the clouds still roiled evilly about their heads. When Younger Brother looked up at his guardian, he saw that the frost had made his face into something strange and terrible. Elder Brother had great white moustaches, weeping with icicles. His eyebrows were frostbrows that went all the way up his forehead, as if Elder Brother had died and the ice had begun to grow and grow on him forever until after a million years he would be buried at the heart of some new frost-continent for a shroud, as in warmer climates dead faces quickly become overgrown with pale white mold until they are patchy and spotted like dogs' faces. To the very ruff, Elder Brother's hood had frozen into a creaking helmet of ice-hardened fur.

"I'm afraid of you!" cried the little boy.

"No, be afraid of the storm," said his brother. "Unless you are very attentive and obedient to wind-songs, you will die."

At this, Younger Brother began to cry, but his tears froze on his cheeks. The wind was rising again. Impatiently, Elder Brother cut off a strip of sealskin from his parka and tucked it around Younger Brother's face. – "Tighten the drawstring of your hood, or your face will turn to ice," he said shortly. "Now come with me. We must find a sleeping-place before the wind sings again."

After this they spoke no longer, for the storm-scream made hearing impossible. They staggered about all through that night-devouring night, but Elder Brother could find no protected spot. The little one came behind him wailing. Sometimes he could not go on; then Elder Brother had to carry him on his shoulders as he went. They were both near the end of their strength. They had eaten nothing but a little bit of frozen fish for five sleeps.

At last Elder Brother stopped in the shelter of an overhanging ice-drift. – "Here we must rest," he said.

He sat down on a rock. Snow was blowing in his face. Younger Brother fell down beside him. His mouth opened, and his eyes closed. Elder Brother pulled the boy to him and set his head in his lap. He breathed gently in his face to warm him. He himself felt already rather warm. His face glowed with frostbite. He stroked his brother's cheek. Patiently, he waited to be killed.

Then suddenly a Spirit Woman came flying down from the sky. Her eyes shone like moons. – The two brothers were astonished. They had never seen anyone other than themselves.

"Spirit Woman, Spirit Woman, who are you?" said Elder Brother.

The Spirit Woman laughed. "I am the blue snow-shadows all around you. You can always hear me; you can sometimes see me; you can never kiss me."

She bent down; she struck the ice. *An island sprang up!* It was vast and white, and there were mountains on it. The two brothers crawled feebly onto the shore, where they lay half-dead. – The Spirit Woman clapped her hands, and a snow-house sprang up around them. Then she bent over Younger Brother and did something to him, but he did not know what it was. – "Live together," she said. "I have fitted you for each other." After saying this she flung her arms up and rose through the roof of the snow-house.

Younger Brother raised his arms; he bent them upwards at the elbows; he wanted so much to be a bird! – but he could not follow the Spirit Woman. He cried.

For a long time the two brothers slept. They did not hear the voices of the birds, or the steady wind. They lay encased in sleep, which melted slowly. When he awoke, Younger Brother felt a warm wetness between his legs that had never been there before. His fresh boy-strength became as feathers whirling in the air. (But Elder Brother's arms still cut through the air like knives.) The nipples flowered on his chest, and bore fruit. Then his brother looked at him as men look at women. He pulled him to him; he kissed him.

"I won't! I won't!" cried Younger Brother.

But of course he had to.

San Francisco Transvestites 1987

Jerome had a long thin body. – "I look like an anorexic girl," he said. "Men are easily fooled. They're so stupid. Usually they just look at my hair." – He put his soft foam-rubber falsies tight up against his nipples.* He combed his long blond hair. He worked the black fishnet stockings up over his toes, his knees, his waist as if he were wading cautiously into female water. He rose; he put his high heels on. – "I should *really* get my fresh undies," he said. – His hair shone so beautifully gold and coppery on his shoulders . . . – "I like comfort," he explained. "I'm not that concerned with looking like a woman. – Oh, *where's* my black bra? That's *such* a nice outfit! Let me go look in the closet. That's where I keep my little *lingerie* bag. – Oh, good, here it is. La, la, la . . . This petticoat is really lush. I *do* have to take these undies off, though. I *have* to feel nylon against my skin." – And so he took his clothes voluptuously off to start over, kneeling thin and naked on the bed to sort through his

---

* Being a guest, I was permitted to try the dried orange peels.

flimsy things. At last he chose a fluffy black dress; lovingly he slid himself into it, but presently he bent himself on the bed and pulled the dress up to expose his buttocks ... He was famous for his paintings in nail polish. Ranks and rows of nail polish bottles of all colors stood by the window. He lay stroking his lovely clothes ... At his request he was gagged with a black scarf and a sock in his mouth. His wrists were tied to his ankles. He stared ahead of him a little desperately, it seemed, with his big blue eyes.

Despite these efforts he did not in fact become a woman until he went into the bathroom with Miss Giddings, dancing into an ecstasy of appliqué and eye-liner and rouge because the pair of them were trying for the look of weary whores. They helped each other on with their lipstick, each one the all-wise Spirit Woman to whom the other could turn for advice, for eye and lip correction. Miss Giddings made perhaps the most remarkable transformation, her lush black wig so sweet around her clown-pale face with its white makeup. But Jerome (now Miss J.) was just as much of a lady. "I *always* look good in red," she whispered to the mirror, when she thought that no one could hear. Then she made her debut. "I'm the Red and Green Girl," she announced. "I'm Miss Christmas Tree." – "*I* feel like a gift!" cried Miss Giddings. – "You *look* like a hallucination," said Miss J. – "Oh, I *love* to hallucinate! Hallucinations are my *favorite* things!" – When they had drawn on their black and gold evening costumes, they became so stately, those two, and so beautiful ... – "Oh, but our clothes simply *reek*," they said. "You see, we've been having such *excitement* ... " They told each other that they looked stunning. They clacked about in the garden in their high heels. With sublime contempt, they decried what they had evolved from: – "Boys?" they said. "They're *meat*. They're less than *objects!* They're things you *eat* and *poop out*."

Outside the Black Rose Bar (𝕿𝖍𝖊 𝕱𝖗𝖎𝖊𝖓𝖉𝖑𝖎𝖊𝖘𝖙 𝕲𝖎𝖗𝖑𝖘 𝖎𝖓 𝕿𝖔𝖜𝖓, said the pink matchbox), a woman looked at her reflection in the window as she brushed her hair before going into that place of pink lights and mirrors where women who looked like angels would take you by the hand as you walked down their row to the bathroom (the floor of which was often covered with piss to the depth of your shoe-toe), and these women would let you kiss them and put your penis in the slits where their penises used to be, provided that you paid them money – this woman, then, finished brushing her hair and suddenly yawned, and her face fragmented into a hundred lumps for a moment, becoming again a man's face, and then she licked her lips and smiled and became a woman again.

The Woman-Shirt

Before, Elder Brother and Younger Brother had been the same. Now they were different, and difference called to difference, so that they needed each other, but at best this yearning could only unite them for a space; it could not reconcile them. *She* was more capable of loving constancy than he, for, having been the younger, the inexperienced, having trembled so often in the face of his quick intolerance, she now basked in this new need of his for her. Whenever he wanted, she laid her head down for him, smelling the bitter smell of dead leaves and earth. Smiling, she chewed a tender, bitter willow-bud. He took her hand; the wind blew, and the water trickled between the stones. – To him her youngness had always been an annoyance. But now her young eyes, her taut young shoulders, and those brilliant black eyes in her pale face, hurt him so happily. It was his *need* that he enjoyed, however, not she herself, although in that first moon he thought that she was everything to him. Looking at her, thinking of her transported him, which struck him as vile because now it was hard for him not to despise the icy serenity of their earlier relations. And he knew that he should not love her, for she had been someone else whom he had been supposed to love differently. – What is loneliness? Does the lonely space between two rocks vanish when spanned by a spiderweb?

At first they did not know how to tell each other about their new feelings. They hung their heads shyly, like flowers in the wind. They thrilled sweetly to each other and kept their thrilling secret.

They decided to live on their island forever. They built a house out of earth and stones, never having seen trees to build from (even driftwood was so rare that they thought that forests, like seaweed, grew upon the bottom of the sea). From their rocky world they stood watching the sun wheel round and round in the sky, vanishing only when watery blue vapors blew over from the volcanoes of the south. Spring came, and clouds puffed their bellies just above the moss, and streams appeared everywhere, grinding and groaning and laughing and sighing, and birds sang in the rain and insects buzzed beneath the moss, which, wet, sank deep beneath Elder Brother's step when he went hunting, and the sun was a white disk in a white sky, and the weather was cold and cool and cold and warm. They tried to live quietly in that beautifully terrifying spring landscape, with its chips of blue sky whirling in the icy cloud-sea as the wind blew and the rivers roared and ground stones together (being the motors of geology), and the ice-floes seemed to form such a delicate white puzzle-set, unmoving in their matrix of black leads, more white than bleached bone, and in the fjord was an island besieged by floes and behind that rose the grand

black slab-mountains of Slab-Land, halfway up which swam cloud-spears as
the birds sang and new storm-clouds rushed in and the cold wind screamed
and grey clouds fell as low as Elder Brother's head, with more clouds behind
them, and it rained, and storms trapped the man and woman and tortured
them without meaning to or not meaning to, and as the rain began to fall
in earnest the stream-tones increased in pitch and boulders stirred in the
riverbeds and the rivers began to groan as the birds sang and the cold rain
fell, sometimes freezing as it fell, sometimes not, and Elder Brother could not
hunt, and for days they had no food, and the air was so cold, so frightening,
so beautiful. – Presently summer came. Pink and yellow flowers sprang up

ARCTIC HEATHER,
SLAB-LAND

along the sides of moss-cushioned waterfalls, and other waterfalls played in
rock-clefts, and the moss embroidered itself with spiderwebs. It was sunny on
the ice. The seals lay on their backs and folded their wet black flippers over their
bellies. The great slab-landscapes of sea-ice were stitched with white seams and
stamped with fine blue granule-lines, as if they had been yards of calico. Elder
Brother and his wife sat on the steep and rocky shore, watching the melting
of the last dirty drifts of ice, which were weak and rotten, speckled with dead
leaves, sun-wrought to treacherous pointed ridges along which it was almost
impossible to walk without mishap. Water dripped from them and gathered
in dirty puddles underneath them and ran into the clear brown water of

the fjord with its light-lines and ripples that softened the greenish-brown outlines of reflections of peaks of the blue knife-slab ridge across the fjord, and little floes drifted across the image. A gull stood on a rock in the water for a long time. A floe broke in two. On the northern horizon lay a white line of seemingly solid ice, in which was reflected a mountain made blue by the storm-cloud over it; and Elder Brother and his wife saw themselves reflected in each other's faces. The sunshine warmed them, and they were very happy. Stalks of golden grass moved in the breeze in stiff increments, their seed-crowns a precious but heavy burden. Closer to the moss, the little plants with penny-shaped leaves did not move.

Sometimes when he was away hunting, Elder Brother pictured to himself his wife's firm buttocks, which he liked to grip in his hands when he was making love to her. But then he would think to himself: My buttocks are also like that. And this thought would throw him into confusion. He could not understand the *otherness* of his wife.

The Cloud-Shirt

There were musk-oxen on their island, and many low, rolling mountains. Sometimes mornings were hot and golden, with the mosquitoes not yet born and the wind in abeyance, and from a meadow-bluff the river in all its braids seemed but a neighborhood of mild and silvery streams, and there were no clouds in the sky; and then there was one, lying on a soft snow-shoulder, and then a few more white rabbity puffs, and then the wind-sound came out of a mound of black-and-rusty boulders, so that for the first time it seemed possible that maybe the wind came from the darkness underground; and the bar of cloud upon the glacier had widened until it spanned the notch of the pass, but overhead there was still nothing but clear blue sky; so the man and his wife never knew how the weather was going to be.

When a storm first came into the sky, the grass and the moss seemed yellow in that light. The glaciers became a glassy grey, fretted with waterfall-stairs. The wind increased in tentatively stronger gusts. The noise from it seemed to emanate from the riverbeds, groaning through those long corridors of rock, and from somewhere beneath the wings of the Faceless Mountain, and the grass trembled (though the little tundra plants stood perfectly still), and the sky got darker and darker, the white sun a pale poor face now in comparison to the many snow-faces that smiled so much more brightly than the day. When the storm-weather was bad Elder Brother sometimes felt listless, doomed. He could not say why. As for *her*, she became restless. Something had begun to beat its wings inside her, something bright and shiny and hard. When the sky was overcast the mountains were exceedingly grim, and she did not like to look at them. She did not like the way that the Spirit Woman had changed her. She ought to have a new name, having become different, but though *he* was still Elder Brother, her guardian, her brother, she had lost her name. Now she was only a wife.

The Hermaphrodite-Shirt

Was a woman something she was supposed to be? But she had not started out being one, and she did not want to be one. She did not necessarily want *not* to be one, but she wanted to be several things. A woman was not all she was.

The Bear-Shirt

Some women you *penetrate*; others *milk* you: thus Elder Brother generalized to himself, for he was now a man of experience. It seemed to Elder Brother that the latter was what his wife did to him; he did not like it. It reminded him of her as she had been before her sex had changed, when she used to question him endlessly about the different kinds of animals, as if once she knew enough about the habits of seals or foxes she could become one, and then be forever free of him. So he soon lost his appetite for making love to her.

"Judge a girl by her kamiks,"* runs the Greenland proverb, "a woman by her husband's kamiks." She sewed pretty kamiks for him, but he always found fault with them. After all, what could Younger Brother know about anything that he did not know better?

The rocks on the hill beyond were white because there had been a fire there, Elder Brother said. He showed his wife things at almost every step. – Here was the kayak-leaved plant. – This heap of stones, which formed a ruined cave, had once been a trap for foxes. The bait was attached to a heavy slab exquisitely balanced so that when the fox gnawed, the slab fell and imprisoned it. – This pile of white fluff was reindeer hair. A Dane had shot it the year before, and left most of the carcass there to be wasted. Now only

---

* Skin-boots.

the hair was left. It was soft and dry, and would have filled a good pillow. – But his wife did not care in the least.

Sometimes she would get so angry at him that she felt a deep dull pain behind her heart, as if an icicle had lodged there. Then she would abuse him until he clapped his hand over her mouth, at which she would try to bite him. They had scenes that lasted all night and all the next day. Afterward she would feel somewhat satisfied, but he, exhausted and lacerated, despised her precisely when she attempted once again to be a good wife to him, for to him she seemed to be displaying a triumphant magnanimity, her attentive kindness a silky self-satisfied quality: I am content because I have made you suffer. So the more extreme her efforts became to propitiate him, the more sullen he became, until she flew into another rage and it all began again. He could not understand how she could so easily enter these states of feeling so intensely that he must always be reacting to her, as opposed to having feelings of his own; and the image of those winter nights which he preserved when he closed his eyes was of her lying motionless beside him on the skins, her body drawn as far away from his as possible, glaring at him, a single anger-tear rolling down her round cheek, as she told him endlessly of her hatred, smiling bitterly. She could have rolled back upon those buttocks that he admired so well, and done something to herself, and presently given birth to fishes, so that he and she would never be in hunger, but she would not do it because she did not want to help him.

In his resentment at this, he began to tease her. Jokingly, he said he knew that she was no woman at all, but just his Younger Brother who had carelessly lost his penis. – "You think that having your red slit is all there is to being a woman," he said. "Well, that's not so. Remember that I am your Elder Brother. I know about those things. If you want to learn how you should be, you must be more obedient to me." – He meant it only as a GAME, of course. He did not mean to hurt her feelings, for what would be the use of that? – But she took it badly. – "You don't know anything!" she cried. "You don't see anything! If something were to change in front of you, you wouldn't see it!" – After this, Elder Brother kept a watch everywhere for new things. One day he even saw a black birch twig upthrust in an iceberg.

The Ice-Shirt

His hunting often took him north, where there was still ice. What a feeling of freedom to walk along the shore-ice! Every step took him further away from her. After the agony of clambering up and down steep ridges of loose boulders with a sheep or a reindeer on his back, what a relief to walk upon that flat surface, which afforded good traction thanks to the snow that covered it, and it was white and beautiful to look at, and a refreshing coolness rose from it as he marched along it in the hot sun. From time to time he must leave it – a wide lead of emerald-hued water barred his way, or the drift itself came to an end – and then it was back to walking on stones, on the loose stones of fan-shaped streams, on the great boulders bridged by moss-tussocks which he was sometimes compelled to use as stairs, climbing cliffs of them to dodge some inlet of the sea, then descending other cliffs equally steep, clinging to the stems of dwarf willows for support, with his face in that wall of fragrant moss as he went down – but what a relief and joy it always was to be back on the ice! (For, unlike his wife, he had no striving to ascend for the sake of ascending.) – No matter that the ice might still be dangerous. It was nonetheless the child of beauty and ease. Sometimes the beached ice-drifts were covered with sand, and it almost seemed that he was walking on solid earth, except for the cold hardness which he could feel underneath at every step; and when such drifts came to an end and he must step down, he sometimes looked back at that wet white underbelly, dripping, dripping silver droplets on the stones – and then the first brown moth of summer flew out from underneath, resting on a sunny rock to dry her striped wings; and then she went off about her short life.

The Bird-Shirt

As for his wife, in his increasing absences she thought of the Spirit Woman and longed to fly away like her. She lowered one shoulder; she bent one knee; she raised her arms, as if she were a gull banking in the wind; but nothing happened. Once two little birds alighted on a boulder and sang to one another, looking into each other's unwinking eyes. She rushed upon them to frighten them, so that she could watch them fly away. She noted a certain quality of tensely sweeping flexion in their flight; she strove to bring this into her arms. When the black-and-gold flies, more beautiful than jewels, alighted upon her hands, she did not crush them, but watched their throbbing wings. – One day she found that she could leap and leap without a sound. She concealed this from her husband; *he* had never told her anything. Often, however, she stretched her arms in the night with languid, self-satisfied movements, so that he wondered what she was doing. In solitude she bird-walked backwards, stepping lightly on the balls of her feet; she raised her arms as she lowered her hands. Her arms became wings.

She built a fire in a circle of stones. When she threw a loaf of moss on it, it glowed like a tree in autumn. It was evening, and the dwarf willows cast their shadows on the rock. The flames flickered at her like wings. – Yes, yes, she told herself. She could do that. She could fly away whenever she chose.

That winter, when Elder Brother teased her until the tears came, she raised her hand; she pointed at him with her hand-edge. She whirled her hands around her like knives. She took her *ulo*-knife and she flailed at his face.

ULU

She took her bone-needle; she poked him again and again. – He drew his arms into his stomach and was silent, like a nothing, a worried little icicle. – Oh, she was contemptuous! – Then she saw that she had poked him full of holes. – Elder Brother was dead! She had killed him!

She bent his knees; she put his face against his thighs; she curled him into a ball and buried him beneath the snow. Presently the Spirit Woman came down from the sky and said, "Where is your husband?" – "Oh, he is out hunting," said the woman indifferently. She no longer cared much for the Spirit Woman; she had her own powers. – "You're certain he is out hunting?" said the Spirit Woman. – "He didn't say," the woman yawned. – The Spirit Woman paced upon the snow. She sat down. "What's this sharp bony thing I'm sitting on?" she cried. – The woman watched her and chewed a piece of dried meat. – "Look!" cried the Spirit Woman in horror. She scooped away the snow. "It's your husband! You've killed him! See how he's full of little holes!"

The woman gazed straight ahead; she whirled with outflung hands; she leaped into the air. Now she was rising, rising, among the whirling snowflakes. The snow and the sky were both white.

The Spirit Woman cried in anguish, because she could not follow Younger Brother.

A number of millennia later, Dr. W. S. Bruce, the Scot, disturbed a congregation of ivory gulls off Franz Josef Land. "The cries became louder and louder," he wrote, "and in a few minutes we were in the midst of a host of terrified yet defiant birds. Again they swooped down upon us, and it seemed quite likely that at any moment they might dash into our faces. So we passed from gullery to gullery among many thousands of birds. It was a magnificent sight: the sun was shining brightly in a blue sky, the air was clear, and these handsome birds in their pure white plumage added brilliancy to the scene."

Birds on a Roof 1987

And so we were sitting idly, backs to the wind, while the Eskimo crew re-bound my runner to the frame with tight nylon rope.

JOHN HUSSAR, *Chicago Tribune*,
"An Arctic adventure on
snowmobiles and sledges"
(*San Francisco Examiner*,
Sunday, 6 July 1986, section T)

O ne rainy day the wall-shingles of the adjoining house grew spotted and stained with the wet, but the black roof-shingles looked just the same as ever; they were so dark that rain could not darken them. A single black bird came and landed on the roof-ridge. It waggled its tail and puffed its black chest out; it strutted in the rain. The tall chimney beside the bird made it seem indescribably small and ridiculous. It took wing; it flew through the grey air; and then it returned to the roof. (Meanwhile a little fly clung to the inside of my windowpane; the fly had been trying for days to escape, because it did not know that rain was falling. If I had let the fly out, would it have died?) – Suddenly dozens of other birds came and landed on the roof, and the single black bird was lost.

Brothers and Sisters

We found a few small willows, about three inches in height, and clusters of a small white flower, name unknown.

> OLIVER L. FASSIG,
> reconnaissance diary for
> Greenland islands (*ca.* 1905)

Now that Sister had murdered her own Elder Brother, snowflakes blew from her sky-shoes to make the constellations, and the mountains thought that they heard her rushing overhead (but sometimes it was another Presence that hummed so blackly); and the dead man transformed himself steadily into ice, but the Spirit Woman who had made them one for the other was left behind. Caribou streamed down the fells, searching hopelessly for a hunter to whom they could give themselves. And the Spirit Woman gazed ever upward, envious and grieving. She desired Sister; that was why she had made her so. Now she was gone. When her grief had fully ripened, she gave birth to packs of wolves and dogs, who scoured the island and grew restless, who pulled down the musk-oxen. And the Spirit Woman blessed them. – "Go where you please and marry as you please," she told them. "But only do not take your sisters in marriage; that is forbidden after what has happened." – Hearing this, they began to fan out across the sea-ice, looking shyly back over their shoulders at her until a creamy mist boiled up over the forsaken island and their Mother was gone forever, dissolved in her own mournfulness. Then they loped voraciously toward the Sun – not that they misliked the night-shaded places below the ridges of snow, but something called them, although they could not know what it was, so they followed that excruciating beauty-circle which indeed led them round and round; they whined and lapped up puddles where the ice was bluest, cocking back their ears and listening anxiously for the sound of rock against rock, sniffing for the new lands; at long last they found them, and paired together in the crackling grass: their children were humans. – At once their shamans learned how to change themselves, singing, "*Qangattarsa! Qangattarsa! Aya!*"* Their ivory-carved ice-bears could come alive; their women's knife-severed fingers fell into the water to become the teeming seals.† Quickly they came of age and married. On their spears were carved round eyes, gaping mouths.

They wandered east, naming the islands, which then became alive, but they themselves had no name; they had not yet become *Inuit* – the People: – their nature was not fixed in them. They followed the animals, singing their songs, fleeing their old villages whose death-mists hid the hungry ghosts that thrummed like bow-strings, bending themselves on all fours like reindeer when they shot their bows. They crossed the ice without fear, brothers and sisters helping each other, never taking each other.

Now they learned to chip stones to make sharper tools. Their flint-points were pink, yellow, blue, notched into beautiful crystal-faces. They dug their houses into the ground and lined them with stones; over their doorways they placed whale-skulls to keep watch. They paddled their kayaks east, and at last they arrived in Greenland. Then they found that once again the Sun had led them in a circle, for Greenland was First Island, where the Spirit Woman had made them. – Unlike the Bear-Games in Norway, the Sister-Games were just beginning.

Where Greenland Was ca. 1390 – 1646

The Frenchman Isaac de la Peyrière in his *Relation du Groenland* (1646) reports of the island many marvels and enigmas, until in its very existence it seems to be a trembling Thing without a face, heaving its breast with many pangs to give birth, at last, to Eirik the Red's bastard daughter Freydis, whom he brought home to Thjodhild without a word, and Thjodhild said, "Where did you get this babe from? Is she yours?" and Eirik said, "Yes," and Thjodhild said, "I see that there is no help, and I must rear her," to which Eirik replied, "I thank you, wife, for you are very generous." Freydis cried for her milk, but Thjodhild had none to give her, Thorstein being already weaned, and they

* "Let us fly up, let us fly up; aya!"
† This story will be told in the Sixth Dream, *The Rifles*.

found a nurse for her, a big strapping farm-girl named Thordis, whose young son had died, but she at length refused the labor, saying that the baby hurt her very much about the breast. – "She is already proving trouble enough," said Thjodhild. "Let us wean her now, and see how she will do." – "It will be as you will," said Eirik. "I see that." – The child lived, although she cried much in hunger and wrath. And in time she began to thrive, and grew strong and stout in the Greenland air. But that strange country in which she found herself, with its ice-breath and the spectral sky-colors, was never rigged out in stout map-sails, for even her father knew not where it began or ended. – "Some say that it extends so far as to join the regions of Tartary," writes Peyrière, reciting obediently what he has been told, "but this is uncertain, as you will hereafter perceive." As to whether it joined America, his considered answer was that he really could not say. In hopes of resolving that issue, I myself have spent many hours studying the map of Nicolò Zeno the Younger (1558), made a century and a half after the narrative that it is supposed to illustrate; but the arms of its islands are featurelessly alien, like the arms of squid.* Greenland is called there ENGRONELANDA. There is a pair of gently sloping lowlands directly opposite each other on the southeast and southwest coast, but in the main the interior of Engronelanda is nothing but white mountains crowded together. The northern regions of the islands lie at the top of the map, which says evasively: TRAMATONA. The fjords at the southern lobster-tail curve of the island bear names; these may be the names of settlements or the names of monasteries; it is hard to be sure, as they are almost illegible. The map is icy-white behind its prison-grid of longitude and latitude. On the northeast side of Engronelanda is depicted a volcano spewing its black plume of fatality above a church. (This becomes less enigmatic, if more sinister, when we recall that in the year 1308, according to Danish chronicles, there were fearful claps of thunder in Greenland, and heaven-fire fell upon the church at Skalholt, reducing it to ashes with a remorselessness in keeping with the times. This event was followed by a tempest so strong that great boulders were broken from the mountain-tops. That winter was so severe that the ice remained a year without melting.) East of the church, in the ominously featureless whiteness, the map says only: MARE ET TERRE INCOGNITE. In the middle of the ocean, southeast of Iceland, is a diamond-shaped array of crosses.

---

* "Of these north parts," says our Nicolò, "I have thought good to draw a copy of the sailing chart which I find that I have still amongst our family antiquities, and, although it is rotten with age, I have succeeded with it tolerably well . . ."

Freydis Eiriksdottir

"Mother, why do you hate our sister?" said Thorstein.

Thjodhild laughed bitterly. "She is not your sister, but your half-sister. I do not hate her, Thorstein, for we strive to be Christians here; we must hate no one."

For some time after this the little boy, not knowing what a half-sister was and fearing to ask, sought to see his sister naked, for he thought that she must be missing some part of her body, but this he was never able to do, and so one day he thought to ask her himself, while they gathered driftwood together. But at this Freydis burst into tears and said, "I see that I have no friend in this house." After this she would not speak to him, and kept a great deal to herself. Nor, indeed, did this suit Thjodhild at all ill. Her father was sorry, and sought to cheer her when he could, but he had little time for her, as the farming was very rigorous in Greenland due to the severity of the climate. So Freydis was left alone.

One day she was in the eastern pasture and found a carving there, a little figure of a seal, done in ivory. This she considered very beautiful but uncanny, and she hid it, knowing that if her stepmother should find it she would throw it on the fire. Now she considered herself very secret and mysterious, and gave herself airs, so that Thjodhild found her difficult to bear, and struck her to make her more obedient, but the girl only laughed brazenly. She did her share of the work and more, for she was as strong as any of the three boys, but she no longer made any effort to please. As time passed she became increasingly ill-tempered.

The Skrælings
of Greenland 1577

T he history says that these savages are of a deceitful and ferocious disposition, and that they cannot be tamed, either by presents or by kindness. They are fat but active, and their skins are of an olive colour; it is believed that there are blacks among them like Ethiopians. They are dressed in seal-skins, sewn together with sinews. Their women wear their hair in disorder, and turn it behind their ears to show their faces, which are painted blue and yellow. They do not, like our women, wear petticoats, but several pairs of drawers made of the skins of fish, which they put on one over the other . . . The shirts of the men and the chemises of the women are made of the intestines of fish, sewn with very fine sinews . . . They are very dirty and filthy. Their tongue serves them for napkin and handkerchief, and they have no modesty about things other men are ashamed of." So says de la Peyrière.

The Moon and the Sun

Justina – Abraham Zeeb's little *kifak*.* Poor thing! She *is* simple-minded, but they tease her cruelly. And now she says she loves me – because they've told her I love her. And she's telling it about, so happily . . . She can count to ten on her fingers and to twenty by taking off her *kamiks* and counting on her toes.

> *Rockwell Kent's Greenland Journal,*
> entry for the Saturday before
> Christmas, 1931

We systematically spoilt the girls who worked in the house. Most of us were on very playful terms with them, and their company added considerably to the pleasures of the Base. We treated them exactly like children, but we brought them up in the way that no children should go.

> MARTIN LINDSAY
> (Royal Scots Fusiliers),
> *Those Greenland Days* (1932)

Once upon a time the Sun lived with her brother the Moon, and at night when the lamps were blown out somebody came to her as she lay on her deerskins and made love to her. There were many other people who lived in the house, although they were shadowy inferior souls whose best aspiration was to become planets. In the meantime, since they had not yet decided how to climb into the sky, they lay around the house year after year,

---

* Servant.

and the Sun was constantly cooking for them and the Moon had to go out hunting. – How dreary it was! Winter after winter the guests stayed, and it was always dark, and the poor Sun never learned their names, which were thin and whispery, like the puffs of breath that rose up inside the house and melted the snow-roof a little so that it dripped, dripped, throughout the dark nights and everyone must pull hides over his face to keep dry as he slept; and the guests were continually coughing and shuffling about and tinkling into the urine pot, and just when the Sun finally got to sleep her brother came in with another seal that she was required to butcher with her *ulu*-knife and flense the skin. Already the guests were chewing the fresh seal-liver that she had pulled out. When her work was done, she chewed a piece of meat and then blew out the lamp. The guests whistled and hissed in the darkness. The snow-roof dripped. She wrapped herself in her deerskins and waited with a bitterly beating heart. Presently the man came to her in the darkness; his heavy hand was on her breast; his hot breath was in her face, and she endured the inevitability of it. The other guests hissed and sighed all night. In the morning it was still dark, of course, and she lit the blubber lamp and stared sullenly into the guests' faces, her own face puffy, unhappy; but her brother did not want her to disobey the laws of hospitality, so he sent her outside to pound the frozen blubber into oil for the lamp. When she returned, she resumed her silent study of the guests' faces. But they only laughed uneasily and stuffed meat into their mouths. Who was it that kept raping her? The dark day passed; the dark night came. She blew out the lamp, and then when no one could see her she dabbled her hands in the soot. She lay waiting on her deerskins. When the man came, she embraced him tightly, rubbing the soot upon his shoulders.

"One of you has soot on his shoulders," the Sun said the next morning when she lit the lamp.

"Who? Who? Who?" sighed the guests stupidly.

She made them strip off their skin shirts, but their shoulders were not dirty. As each of them exposed his shoulders to her, he sighed and became a puff of vapor. He could never become a planet now. Finally only her brother was left. He wept; he hung his head.

"Let me see you without your shirt," the sister said.

He wept; he hung his head.

"Show me your naked shoulders or I will stab you with my *ulu*," she said.

He wept; he hung his head.

"Strip off your shirt or I will run away into the snow," she said.

He wept; he hung his head; he stripped off his shirt, and there were sooty finger-marks on his shoulders.

Now she knew that she had always known this. And he – he could think of nothing to say or do but point to her, crying, "You have black hands, sister!"

She did not clean her hands. She sharpened her *ulu*; she cut off her breast and threw it into his face. "As you seem to be so fond of me, eat me, then!" she cried. (He wept; he hung his head.) She took a stick, stuck lamp-moss on it, dipped it in seal-oil and touched it to the flame of the lamp. Then she ran away into the snow. As she ran, she began rising into the air.★ The Moon stood in the doorway of the house watching her as she rose up glowing and bleeding. He took his ice-scraper, skewered the lamp-moss and lit it. Then he ran after her. But his torch did not burn well. As he ran up into the sky, which was frozen and black, and rang under his feet, the flame went out. Nothing was around him but darkness; he could no longer see his sister's light, for she was too high above him. There was only a fading coal on his stick. Frantically he blew on it, and sparks flew out to become the stars. His clothes froze on his back; his shoes became like horns on his feet. Ever since then we have seen his glimmering night-gleam, the roundness of his naked belly which wavers and waxes and wanes (and sometimes vanishes when he must go down to earth to hunt seals), and we see that just as he was alone on this crowded earth, he remains alone in his nights of fiery unbelief, but his sister is always bright and warm, because her lamp-moss was burning when she came up into the air. – What is it about the polar heavens that fixes a transient thing for eternity? And is the Sun happy now? Can she who lights the darkness take comfort from her own light? from his snowy face? As she ascended into that bitter darkness, was she saying to herself, "Just let me reach the sky; just let me lock myself in place while my lamp-stick burns and everything will be all right?" – Oh, Sun and Moon, how can *we* be happy if you came to be yourselves in this way? My own true Sun, how long will you bleed?

★ "As our habitat is the meeting of air and earth on the world," said the mathematician C. Howard Hinton in 1906, "so we must think of the meeting place for two as affording the condition for our universe. The meeting of what two? What can that vastness be in the higher space which stretches in such a perfect level that our astronomical observations fail to detect the slightest curvature?"

A Relation, Concerning the Sun and the Moon

"As far as personality goes," said Seth Pilsk the Thin, "I think the Sun and the Moon are very much like the River. They go on about Their business, and because They go on about Their business certain things happen. I don't know if it's all intentional or not; I have no idea. But They're there, and They give you some kind of feeling. They give me a real solid, steady feeling. I imagine that They have some intentions. The Moon is very calming, usually. Even if He's menacing He's very calming. It just happens that the Arctic in the summer has no night, so you never get the Moonlight, but the Sun is what you're aware of, always. She just goes in that tight little circle. Toward the end of my stay, She would occasionally disappear behind a higher mountain peak in the gorge of the valley."

In Praise of the Sun

Now it is to be told that as the Moon made his rounds he heard a woman's voice calling, "Brother!", and consciousness warmed him because he had her again at last amidst all this emptiness whose ice-echoes would now serve to magnify and multiply her; and in desperate hope he soared higher than ever before, rocking and wobbling like a flame in a draft – but then the woman came hurrying closer on bird-wings and said, "You are not my brother! Good!" and she began to fly away into the darkness, but his heart-scream was already shattering him, so he pleaded with her, saying, "Have you seen her? She is bleeding, and has sooty hands," to which the Bird-Woman replied in her high small voice, "Well, you drove her to it, just as my brother forced me to kill him; it is all the same!", and then he was alone again. – One does not realize how much one needs the Sun's love until She is not there. For light there is only the fog-glare and the ice-blink. The horrible cold Moon grabs you by the ankles and rubs your knees and touches your belly, and everywhere He touches you you go sad and frozen; He wants to draw you down into the ground where it is always dark; here His pale shine will be dazzling, at least to Him as He sees it reflected in the balls of your frozen eyes . . .

The Air-Bridge

You who know yourself to be so stolidly solid that you do not have to worry that you might turn into anything else, ever; – how do you think it must have been in those times of frightening transformation? We cannot call them freer. The Sun and the Moon, for instance, have never again been seen on earth. They were like butterflies seized and pressed into the moving album of some Russian aristocrat; yes, they still fly, but only when he turns their page. – So at first I thought, but when I gazed up into the sky I understood that this, too, was a simplification, for the Sun she is alive! She lives mutilated; she cut off her breast for the Moon and now must live in a bright blue waste, but nobody has killed her. As for her poor pale brother, serenely menacing, he pursues her in his unstable way, waxing and waning in melancholy persistence; he too is still himself. But when you run up the air-bridge to become gods, your last mortal moment, aberrant or not, becomes the moment of butterfly-pressing. Never will she be able to forgive him. Never will he stop wanting her. Much of their light is shame-light. So in a sense the Sun and the Moon are dead.

Wearing the White-Shirt
1385 – 1987

It is reported that the waters about Greenland are infested with
monsters, though I do not believe that they have been seen very
frequently.

Speculum Regale, XVI.135

O nce upon a time Bjorn the Crusader was crusading, in hopes of
improving islands, souls and days, and it chanced that he came to Greenland.
The old stories do not say why he came; his home was in Iceland; but then
I have never understood the whims of crusaders, not being one. – It was a
sunny morning, with the sun glowing behind the snowy digits of mountains,
and a single yellow-and-white Danish fishing-boat pulled slowly across the
fjord, looking breast-heavy with its forward cabin and its tall mast, and it
turned into the harbor and vanished behind a bluff and soon its white wake
had vanished, too, and once again it was half a thousand years ago and a
wind blew so that a few white spiders of crevice-grass twitched between the
rocks, which were black and silver, and had been set by AMORTORTAK into
the moss as if they were grave-slabs, and beautiful flies crawled on them to
be sun-warmed. The rocks sloped down to the blue sea. Near the tide-line
the moss was scattered with broken mussel-shells, and then it ended, and the
rocks were slippery-green. Across the fjord were snowy cliffs, through which
sky-blue patterns showed, and in front of these was a low black tongue of
rock banded with snow. The color of the water changed from blue to grey
and back again. The rocks ran, slimy-green and pointed, a good distance
into the water, and two Skræling children, a young sister and a brother, had
gone running out on these to a skerry where there were mussels. The low

tide lulled them. They had eaten the shriveled black crowberries in the moss (which, sun-dried, taste vaguely like olives), and the sea was calm and there were no clouds, and the rocks were blue and black with mussels for them to eat, so that they did not heed the silent ascension of the tide that licked higher and higher until only a few bare points stuck out of the water; and when the children cried to each other and tried to run back to shore those vanished, too. They stood trapped on the skerry, waiting to be drowned in the sea; and then, when the tide was almost at its height, Bjorn the Crusader saw them and rescued them, although he frankly considered them to be trolls. (He was an Icelander, and so may be forgiven his ignorance of Greenland.) – "To die that way is a death not even fit for the King of Trolls," he said to Solveig, his wife. "We will take them and put them ashore." – "Ashore?" cried Solveig sharply. "You must make them understand that they are to work for us."

The children's long black hair blew in the wind. They wore trousers with the fur side out. Their coats had fur ruffs. They smiled anxiously with white teeth and peered at Solveig through their hair. They crossed their arms; they held one another's hands. There was in their eyes a liquidly honest expression, although what it expressed she could not say. It made her uncomfortable. Nonetheless, they swore an oath of fidelity to her and him; they caught food for them; they told them that they accounted themselves as dead children, but for them. – And what clever little trolls! Bjorn had but to say that his wife wanted a certain kind of meat, and they would set off for it. They had round brown faces, widening from forehead to cheekbone, with shining eyes whose whites gleamed.

Greenland "is a stark, bare, treeless land, with naked rock predominating everywhere," said Rockwell Kent (1932); but reindeer ran and leaped in the hills, and eagles swooped in the air, and everything was green and full of flowers. – Bjorn had the trolls build him a house on a soft tundra shoulder full of fuzzy-budded plants. The lichen was ankle-deep. The troll-boy was very strong, and did most of the work. When he threw himself down among the grasses and mosses to rest, his sister squatted behind him, catching the mosquitoes in her hands before they could torment him.

In Frost-Month, when the white streams froze on the faces of black cliffs, Solveig bore a baby. The troll-girl loved most of all things to carry this newborn son. When Bjorn and his wife were not there she whispered to the baby in her Skræling tongue, pretending that he was hers, for she was very imitative. But she seldom had a chance to do this, because her mistress never trusted her. – "Stop whispering into his ear, you troll-carline!" Solveig cried. "I know you!" Then the little Skræling girl had to give the baby back to her. To Solveig and her husband, the troll-speech sounded like this: – *'Im-a-ním-a-mím*. – Like so many Icelandic women, Solveig resembled an angel in appearance, with blonde-red bangs cut very short so that her face looked boyish.

Oh, how hard the Skrælings tried to wear the White-Shirt! – "Give me back my son now, you troll-carline!" cried Solveig. But they would have done anything to be Icelanders. – Often the troll-boy killed seals, and his sister skinned them so quickly with her *ulu* that Bjorn blinked, and even Solveig, who was an impatient mistress, could find nothing ill to say. – The troll-girl loved Solveig's wifely headdress, and wanted to wear it, but Solveig would not lend it to her, so she made herself one out of whale-guts. Of course she still looked like a Skræling, for that long, lush, blue-black hair fell around her oval orange face, accentuating the high cheekbones, the glossy black eyes. – "You are two queenly wives!" cried Bjorn in his good humor, and Solveig smiled, and the troll-girl smiled very very quickly.

On the short winter days, while Bjorn and Solveig lolled at their ease, the troll-boy set out across the ice, and wandered among the low snowy islands which reflected themselves as clouds in the grey sky. Soon the blackness came. Solveig sat dispiritedly by the fire, giving her baby suck, while Bjorn lay asleep, and the little troll-sister sat waiting for her brother all night, until when the cold pink sunrise glowed against the snowy mountains she went running out to meet him. He never returned without meat slung over his back. – "*Tuttu!*" she'd hear him call. "*Puisi! Sava!*" – Those were the Skræling words for animals. – "No," said his sister gravely. "You must say the Icelandic words. You must say 'reindeer'; you must say 'seal' and 'sheep.'" And her brother did his best to articulate the strange words. For he did not want to be a troll any longer. – "Yes," said Bjorn to his wife, "they are good trolls."

In the month of Winter's Wane, Bjorn said that he must be returning to Iceland, and they begged to accompany him and serve him forever. – "You are very plausible," Bjorn told them, "but the truth is that you are trolls, and I know you will never be able to change your nature. For this reason I cannot bring you back to Iceland, for I do not want to be called Troll-Bringer or Death-Bringer." – The truth was that Solveig had forbidden him to take them. She scorned and distrusted them, knowing as she did that they were the *Skrælings* with their gutskin bags, their sealskin mittens, their golden sealskin dog harnesses, their caribou skin mittens, bone needles and punches, black skull skin-scrapers to clean new furs: – they were the Skin People, the Bowl People. Every household had its tub of urine to tan skins.

The day of parting soon came. Bjørn bid the Skrælings return to their people, if they had any. His wife stood beside him. The Skrælings stood and waited. – When the ship began to sail away, Solveig came to the side and gestured contemptuously to the Skrælings to return to the hills. They thought her very beautiful. – The ship began to recede upon the sea. But the troll-children could see it for a very long time, because they stood on a high rock on the edge of Greenland; so they stood there and the wind blew their long black hair and when Solveig finally shrugged and turned her back to them forever (this is not even the first of the Seven Dreams), they killed themselves by jumping into the sea.

The Troll-Children 1987

The boy clambered down the cliff-rocks (although there were stairs), whirling stones from his slingshot. There was a tense purring in the air, and each stone vanished from sight before it hit the ground. – "Can you kill birds with that?" – "Not for birds," he smiled. "Sometime to *kill* the Danish people!" – I pointed politely from his weapon to the center of my forehead, and he nodded and was happy. – "This pouch for stone, it should be made from seal," he said. "But I have to make it from this." He pointed to the sole of his shoe. – "He is always practicing," his friend said. "But only in summer. In winter there is so much ice, we cannot find stones."*

Christian and Margethe

The name of the boy was Christian. He was my friend. He lived in one of the older sections of Nuuk, by the harbor, where little A-frame houses of vertical planks – red houses, green houses, black houses, each with its chimney, its little square windows – marked the winding margins of dirt roads, which dodged between outcroppings where nothing grew but grass and crevice-moss. These streets ended abruptly at the edge of the fjord, whose grey wave-lines served only to emphasize its flatness in distinction to the rugged sky (which was a strange bright color – maybe blue, maybe pink or grey – suggestive of an

---

* The friend had never seen his father. His father was a Dane who had known his mother for a month. The friend found out his father's name and called Denmark on the phone. "Daddy, it's your son from Greenland," he said. – The father said, "I don't want to know you. I don't want to talk to you again." – The friend knew nothing about hunting or fishing; he had no family to show him.

impending bursting-forth: perhaps of snow, or of some brilliant light behind
the clouds, a light never before seen), and in distinction to the grey snowy
precipices which soared all around, their cylindrical storage tanks for petrol,
with stairs winding around their faces; on the ground were fishing-nets. At
eight-o'-clock on a spring morning, a single motorboat could be seen in the
fjord. A yellow dog wandered behind the houses, sniffing at trucks, boats and
dirty snow-patches. A flatbed truck rushed down the street, with a dozen
Greenlanders★ sitting in the back. The men had wide nostrils, and smiling lines
around their eyes. They wore sunglasses and windbreakers. Sometimes they
carried ghetto-blaster radios, and sometimes rifles. – A fisherman clambered
down the cliff-steps in his parka and rubber boots. He had his bedroll under
his arm. Danish schoolgirls went off to their lessons, carrying their books;
and men and women walked to work. When the women's hair was cropped,
they looked very Western. – At the roadside near the dock lay fresh-dead seals,
shotgun-killed, with a hole in each stomach to display the intestines to the
sun; they lay belly-up, small seals and big seals, and their little teeth were
bloody, and blood dripped from their whiskers.† – The house where Christian
lived was green. He lived with his sweet Margethe, who was fairhaired and
fairnamed like a Dane, but who hated Danes, as he did; and mornings they
sat at the kitchen table by the sugar bowl, while Christian's little brother
stalked the walls with bow and rubber-tipped arrow, while the snot ran
down his face, and Christian got up and put some loud Greenlandic rock
and roll on the stereo.

★ That is, the real Greenlanders: – Inuit.
† Seal meat has a beefy, fishy, bloody sort of taste, which is greatly improved by the use
of mustard.

Christian was a fisherman. His motorboat had a hole in it; he had struck ice in the fjord. Now he was waiting for the money to repair it.

Christian and Margethe set out for the center of town, past the grassy cliff-ledges that were piled with beer cans and broken glass, and came to where the Bloks rose high and white. Christian sharpened or rather dulled his knife against a lamppost; Christian walked down the street twirling his knife and yelling, "I KEEL all the Danish people!", and the Danish people went about their business, ignoring him stonily, and Margethe saw an Inuit woman lying on her side in the snow, groaning, with her hands over her face. – "Maybe she think it's night," said Christian, highly pleased with his joke. Margethe bent over her. "She's drunk," she said. "We can do nothing for her." – Christian found a friend, and the two young men went into a Danish grocery and Christian whirled his knife while his friend leafed through a pornographic magazine, and then they bought packaged sausages. Margethe stood outside like a sister, spitting placidly in the street. They went down to the beach to look at Christian's boat, and the sea-waves crunched against the rocks, and the sea-birds screamed, and Christian and his friend bent over the upended boat, one in parka, one in jean-jacket, their elbows touching as they played a game with five Danish kröner, trying to move the bigger coins from the middle to the edge in five moves or less, exchanging two adjacent coins per move; and Christian's smiling face was bent low over the coins and he rubbed his moustache thoughtfully, while his friend, who had Inuit eyes but light-colored hair, watched and spat and counted his moves in Danish. Later, they tied knots with dazzling speed to show off to each other, and Christian kept embracing and teasing his Margethe, whose chestnut hair and fair skin and blue Caucasian eyes made her look so Danish, but she spoke Greenlandic best and hated the Danes because they thought the Greenlanders lived in igloos. She stood in her white parka, looking at the ocean and playing with the feather of an *appa*-bird.

My first night in Greenland, in a snowstorm in June, I did not know what the Bloks were, and they seemed very dreamy, with the snow swirling through the shine of the lights, and these vast rectangular buildings laid out in grid-rows upon the snow, everything white. The stairs stank of garbage. There was rotting garbage in bags at every landing. Most of the graffiti, being in Greenlandic, I couldn't read; however, I made out the words *I LOVE YOU* over and over, and the name *ANNEMARIE*; I saw the words *HOW ARE YOU?* – "They are at a very low level," said the Danish administrator, earnestly. "They often do not speak Danish." (And I thought, how remarkable that *he* spoke no Greenlandic!) "It is hard for them to understand us," he said.

"If they do not, we must try another method." – It was getting cold. The low sun glittered on the white exoskeletons of Bloks 1 through 5, each Blok four storeys high, each storey containing twenty-five flats, with laundry and rugs hung out on the terrace-railings, and the muddy courtyards full of puddles and Carlsberg beer cans and broken glass. There were many mothers with babies who smiled, and young loving couples who nodded, and old Greenlanders in their flats who would give you tea or beer or fish or seal-meat, and giggling girls in their ski jackets, and occasionally a young man drunkwalking unseeing, moving his fist in the air. Sometimes the older women still wore their trousers of fur, which had long colored stripes running down them.

BLOKS 1-5

Amortortak and Angangujungoaq

One night Christian's Mommy and Daddy were playing cards, laughing with friends in the kitchen and crying, "*Ehhh!*" They usually played for hours, Christian said. He loved them. In the living room, Christian and Margethe sat watching an opera on TV, but with the volume low because it was in Danish, and his Mommy and Daddy didn't like to hear the Danish language. Many old

Greenlanders were like that, he said. For his comfort and relaxation he also had the radio going, with a sports program in Greenlandic, and he leaned back on the sofa with his arm around Margethe, who was smoking a cigarette, at which Christian decided to smoke a cigarette, too, and so they sat there smoking while Christian stroked Margethe's hair and she smiled at him, and I asked Christian to tell me a story, so he poured three cups of Danish coffee for us and Margethe put sugar in it. – Once upon a time, Christian said (and Margethe smiled and yawned and put her head down on his shoulder), the Greenlanders had been at constant war with a race of giants* named the *Tunersuit*, who dwelled in the inland fjords amidst the fog and mist, surrounded by the cruel black mountains of the interior beyond which only the ice-wall rose; and Christian said that the Tunersuit were Danish people, for all bad people were Danes to him, but I was sure that the Tunersuit must have been the Icelanders, who settled up the fjords because only there could they find pasturage for their cattle, and it was very strange to be listening to this story of the fairhaired giants sitting in this living room on the ruins of the West Bygd, while outside in the sunny evening the children played ball and called to each other in a language I did not understand, and fairhaired Margethe, who hated the Tunersuit so faithfully and in whose veins the blood of the Tunersuit so surely rushed, lay fast asleep on Christian's shoulder; and I thought how sad it was that when we were in the National Museum together she loved to look at the ancient Greenlandic woman-faces with their lustrous blue-black hair and black eyes, and Margethe would exclaim at how pretty they were, and although she was just as pretty in her smiling Danish way, she could never look like that; and I was glad that she was asleep as Christian told the tale of the giant monsters who must have been her great-great-grandparents. – Now Christian said something especially disturbing. He said that the Tunersuit had BLACK HANDS. I had read old legends of the Greenlandic demon AMORTORTAK, who came in the winter darkness when the shaman summoned the people to the ceremonial house and the candles were extinguished and the shaman invoked this horror as the snow blew hard outside and the wind-scream rose and everything was black, and presently a new scream rose above the wind-scream and giant AMORTORTAK rushed among them in the darkness, yelling, "*A-mo! A-mo!*", and everyone was very still because he

---

* This odd myth of the relative sizes of the two peoples has been perpetuated on both sides. Caudius Clavus referred to the Greenland Skrælings as "small dwarves of an ell's length." In fact the Eskimos were not particularly small, but it is always easier, when dehumanizing our enemies, to convince ourselves that they are odd in size or shape. Perhaps this was the reason why the Eskimos were happy to let the Norsemen be giants.

was known to have BLACK HANDS that killed with a touch. How, then, had the fairhaired giants come to have the BLACK HANDS? – I cannot convey the sense of horror and mystery that I felt. – Once upon a time, Christian said, in the time of the wars with the Tunersuit, there lived a little boy named Angangujungoaq. Angangujungoaq was the only son of his father; he was a much-loved child. They told him to be careful, but he wouldn't listen. One day he was out gathering shrimp upon the beach, and the Tunersuit kidnapped him. They were always stealing children. Angangujungoaq's father returned from a seal-hunt and said, "Where is my only son?" – He was so angry and sad that his only son was gone that he gathered his friends together and they went rushing up into the mountains, ascending the green ridges between fjords, fording brooks without stopping to drink, and they went up another ridge, and another, a higher, steeper one, and the other men were tired but Angangujungoaq's father glared around so fiercely that they said nothing, and they climbed a mountain but they could not see the ice, so they descended into a valley whose lake reflected the rosy clouds of impending summer sunrise, and then they climbed a higher mountain, clambering up steeply sloping slabs of rock set into the hillside, and one of the men looked down and saw that the lake of the sunrise clouds was itself at the edge of a vast cliff, at the foot of which flowed the creek by their camp, and beyond their camp was a great white fjord that was white with snow-mountains and glacial silt, and he wondered if the Tunersuit might live that way but he did not dare to say anything to Angangujungoaq's father, who in fact was being guided well by his need and urgent rage, and the men climbed higher and higher, and the mountain became rockier, and every ridge-crest above them seemed as if it must be the knife-edge that stood alone beneath the red clouds, from which they would be able to see the ice, but there was always another crest above, and it got rockier and there were snowdrifts melting into little streams between banks of black rocks and white rocks; and the men ascended through the snow for a long time until at last Angangujungoaq's father pointed to a low mountain on the horizon and cried, "See, the ice!", and the men looked and at first saw only sky, but when they strained their eyes they saw a line going across the sky, and they realized that the line marked the top of the sky-colored ice-wall, that the sky was made of ice! Toward that sky-blue cliff that was banded with white they now made their way, and Angangujungoaq's father pointed and they saw a single giant footprint in the snow, and they went higher and higher up into the mountains, into the mist and the ice, until at last they came to the house where the Tunersuit lived. Quietly, so quietly, they peered through the windows, and saw the Tunersuit *touching* the boy with their *BLACK HANDS* . . . Angangujungoaq's father bit his lip for grief, and wanted to rush in to fight with the Tunersuit, but his friends restrained him and sat down in the snow with him beneath the gables of that horrible house, whispering in his ear that they had best wait until the Tunersuit were asleep, and this they did. When at last the giants lay snoring, they broke into the house and took the boy away. Presently the Tunersuit awoke, and were very angry that the boy had been stolen back. They set out in pursuit, but a fog came up to blind them, and Angangujungoaq's father ran and ran with his friends, down the snow-mountains to the knife-ridge mountain, down the knife-ridge mountain to the cloud-lake valley, over the low mountain and down the green ridges, and in his terror that the Tunersuit might capture his son again, Angangujungoaq's father ran faster and faster until he had outdistanced his friends, and he came to the end of the mist and ran down the last grassy-green slope to the beach where their home was and the orange sun-rays shot very low across the water, which was icy and mirror-clear (but past the mouth of the fjord the water went inland, toward the Tunersuit, and vanished into blue-grey icy darkness), and Angangujungoaq's father threw himself down on the sand and looked at his only son. – The boy now had the *BLACK HANDS!* The father cried and did not know what to do. At last he understood that it would never be safe to live with Angangujungoaq anymore, so, said Christian, he had to kill his son.

White Shirts and Black Hands 1987

The Bloks were eerie at one in the morning, with the luminous orange sky, and the light-globes glowing purposelessly at every doorway, and teenagers promenading in small groups, whistling in two-toned cries almost like birds. Sometimes laughter came from the distance, but its source could never be found. Three teenagers in black leather jackets strolled down the sidewalk kicking a soccer ball. An orange signal-light blinked. A car drove by slowly. – Then a door slammed, and a man came out yelling and twisted a passing girl's breast. The girl spoke quickly, placatingly, and escaped. Tears of pain rolled down her face. – A police van went down the street, and boys and girls clapped their hands. Later they made a circle and danced in the street.

Sometimes it was possible to forget that the ice was there just over the mountains, pressing down on six-sevenths of Greenland, its cold weight several kilometers thick; for the grey cloud-streaks and pink storm-streaks shrank on certain mornings when the summer sky burned through like leads in pack-ice, and drying clothes blew listlessly behind the flat barracks-like houses overlooking the harbor. A boy walked by, hands in parka-pocket. Two Danish girls tripped along laughing. A car pulled in across the street. – How could there be ice here? – By the stairs that led down the cliff to the harbor was a sign in Danish about something being strictly forbidden. An Inuit girl was coming up the steps. She was wearing sunglasses and a fashionable black wool coat. She stopped and looked out at the sign. Then she spat very thoughtfully. The white spittle tumbled in the air.*

Amortortak and Emilie

Emilie was a receptionist at the museum. When I asked her where the Inuit Institute was she looked it up for me in her directory but couldn't find it, so she said she'd help me search for it. We walked down to the ocean, Emilie wheeling her bicycle slowly, and we went up a street and down a street and could not find any Institute, so Emilie put down the kickstand of her bicycle and we sat on the beach and she took her shoes off and stood in the sea, but the water was too cold for her, so I gave her her shoes and we walked out of Nuuk and through the new tunnel that the Greenlanders had lately dynamited under the mountain, and after awhile we came to the satellite town of Nussuaq, where Emilie lived. Sometimes Emilie swung her brown leg over the bicycle seat and coasted far ahead of me, down the sea-hill, down the tunnel, down the sunny harbor-road, until she was almost out of sight, and I thought that maybe she did not like me after all or was tired of me; but then I'd presently see her, slowly walking her bike again at the next bend in the road, and when I caught up to her we'd walk together awhile until she suddenly rode ahead again. – "I live in a big flat," she said to me, "and I'm all alone; I'm so alone!" – What could that mean, I wondered? – She said that she had no friends, no friends at all. I was sorry for her. It seemed very strange that such a pretty chatty girl would know no one. Where was the brother to care for her? Sometimes when she'd ride ahead of me and I plodded down the road until she came in sight again, I'd see her talking to people for ten minutes, twenty minutes, with the sun shining from within her face, and later I'd ask her what they'd said. – "Oh, he was a taxi driver," said Emilie glumly. "He

---

* "... children like the little girl with the wedge-shaped ulu or woman's knife (opposite), soon will feast happily on fish eyes – like candy to an Arctic child." – NATIONAL GEOGRAPHIC SOCIETY, *The World of the American Indian* (Washington, D.C., 1974), p. 86.

thought I left a red purse in his taxi." – "Oh, she was somebody who used to live across the hall at the technical institute. I don't remember her name." – "Oh, he is just somebody to say hello to. There are so many people who say hello and you do not know them."

When we got to her flat, Emilie took her sweater off and bent over the table to clean it, and her breasts were bare and brown like speckled eggs. On the wall were Emilie's drawings. They were all of naked women, partly black and partly white, with their hands on their hips. In an envelope she had dozens more.

She was very restless, continually changing her clothes or getting up to do dishes or looking for things under her bed or rubbing lotion on her dark legs or going out to the store. Men kept coming by and asking for her. They did not ever seem surprised to see me. – "Are you her boyfriend?" said a blond Dane. – "Possibly," I said. – "Where is she?" he said. – "Out walking in the mountains with a friend." – "A boy or a girl?" – "A boy." – "This is very unexpected," said the Dane. "I am one of her colleagues at work. She invited three of us to dinner for this hour." – Emilie was evidently a mysterious woman.

The flat was silent. In this little Danish world I could see hardly any evidence of day-to-day life.* There was only a mattress cover on the bed. In another bedroom were Emilie's dirty clothes, crammed into a suitcase in the exact center of the hardwood floor. There was no toilet paper in the bathroom; there were no paper towels in the kitchen. But by the bathroom sink were four used toothbrushes. At six-thirty she had said that she would be back within an hour. At ten-thirty the sunlight came through the window from the rim of the other apartment buildings, and I was desperately hungry, but there was nothing in the refrigerator but milk, cartons and cartons of it, all unopened. I opened one and drank it. It tasted like coconut. Then in the back of the refrigerator I found a little jar of pickled mushrooms. I unscrewed the lid; there was a pop of escaping gas, a smell of putrefaction.

In the cabinet beneath the television were dozens of intricately scissored paper snowflakes, some in the familiar shape of a naked woman with her hands on her hips, and Emilie had colored each of those hands with black magic marker. There was also a sheaf of xeroxes of Emilie's hands, fingers

---

* How barren it was can be suggested by pointing out that even the *Islendingabók* – which rarely concerned itself with the lives of those excluded the privilege of membership in the Tunersuit – mentioned "both east and west in the country traces of habitation, fragments of tholes and stone implements, so that it may be perceived from these that that manner of people had been here who inhabited Vinland and whom the Greenlanders call Skrælings."

spread and groping against empty blackness ... At midnight a drunk rang, looking for Emilie.

The next morning she came in for fifteen minutes to change her mud-stained skirt. She took her blouse off and ironed it, standing in the kitchen leaning over the ironing board with her magnificent and indifferent breasts. Once again she put on her office clothes, and became a different person. But then she let her hair down, and for a moment I thought she looked like a Skræling, for that long, lush, blue-black hair fell around her oval orange face, accentuating the high cheekbones, the glossy black eyes. – Oh, she had sex appeal; she had *arnap angutinap!* – She was from Sisimiut, she said, where the black coast sloped steeply down to the icy sea, and long white cloud-fingers broke every cliff into a series of black ridges shimmering in mid-air, on and on into the Unknown until they came to that great blue horizon where the Ice reared, that Ice so summer-blue, so storm-grey, cloud-white like the milk in Emilie's refrigerator because it had no color but the color that the sky gave it ... And Emilie, what was she? – Was she black or white? What did her black hands mean?

III

Vinland,
or,

The cuttlefish in the current

Dressmakers' Patterns
30,000 BC – AD 1007

She makes herself coverings;
  her clothing is fine linen and purple . . .
She makes linen garments and sells them;
  she delivers girdles to the merchant.

Proverbs 31.22, 24

The question of who was going to put on which shirt had not been decided; indeed, it remained to answer the more elementary question of which shirts, once put on, could come off; and, more elementary still, of which shirts there were to make. So the dressmakers were busy drawing and cutting. Many were measured for bear-shirts; a few, like Freydis Eiriksdaughter, chose the Ice-Shirt and became coldly great. In Norway, Gunhild's successor King Olaf made many black shirts with crosses on them. As for the Skrælings, they continued to wear the shirts of beasts, fishes and stars.

Wearing the Ice-Shirt 986 – 995

As to the ice that is found in Iceland, I am inclined to believe that it is a penalty which the land suffers for lying so close to Greenland . . .

Speculum Regale, XIII.126

Now that we know as much about the Skrælings as the ancients did, I want here to tell the tale of how the dew was drunk up and how the frost came. – Venerate Bjarni, son of Herjolf Bardarsson, for he was not curious about VINLAND. He found the country by accident one autumn, being wind-blown south from Iceland in his merchant ship. It was a wooded land, with many low hills. His crew asked him whether he wanted to land and he said he did not, so they sailed north for nine days, and discovered Markland* and Slab-Land† before at last they saw Herjolfsness Promontory looming in the Greenland dusk, with Herjolf's boat hauled up on the rocks; and Bjarni stayed with his father after that and became a farmer. If he had been left to his innocuous labors and ale-stupors, all would have been well. But at the court of the Earl of Norway he was criticized for being so incurious, and the whirlpool-lives sucked and sucked. Someone was bound to come to Vinland wearing the Ice-Shirt.

"To be Great is to be Misunderstood"

ca. 1800 – ca. 1960

Only our stomachs and our pockets urged us to those high latitudes,
where under the eternally revolving sun we looked for animals frozen
to death by Polar storms . . .

WELZL

In conventional representations (lying engravings and pandering painterly panoramas), we see them with shields and byrnies and helmets like laboratory fume hoods, raising their spears at the sight of grapes, while Freydis leans against her brother's shoulder, smooths her long dress, and slits her cat-eyes. But I have never yet seen any pictures of Greenlanders in their ice-shirts; so it is now my place to provide one. Of Eirik the Red it is written, as I have said, that he had three sons by Thjodhild: Leif, Thorstein and Thorvald. Freydis was his bastard daughter. She was married to a rich man at Gardar. Of all these it is necessary to write, and of Thorstein's wife, Gudrid Thorbjornsdaughter.

---

* Possibly Newfoundland or Nova Scotia, but, more plausibly, Labrador.
† Baffin Island.

IV

Freydis Eiriksdottir, or,

How the frost came to Vinland the Good

Gudrid the Fair

But at midnight the north wind goes forth to meet the coursing sun and
leads him through rocky deserts toward the sparse-built shores.

Speculum Regale, V. 89

Of Gudrid it is to be told that she was a beauty; and men compared her
to Gudrun of Lunde, who was called the Lunde-Sun for her fairness of feature;
but her father Thorbjorn Vifilsson was the son of a freed slave. In *Eirik's Saga*
we read that it was Aud the Deep-Minded, the daughter of Ketil Flat-Nose,
who brought Vifil to Iceland from the British Isles. She gave him land when
he asked it of her; and men did not speak ill of him, for he had learned not
to claim his descent from other than thrallish race. At last he brought a wife
home to Vifilsdale and got two sons on her, their names being Thorbjorn
and Thorgeir. They went courting to Einar of Laugarbrekka's together, and
each paid fifteen *örers* of silver for one of his daughters, Thorbjorn taking
Hallveig, and Thorgeir, Arnora. In other respects the brothers were not such
mirror-likenesses, for Thorgeir was not cursed with ambition, and thereby
escaped mention in the strife-pages of the *Flateyjarbók*; as for Thorbjorn, to
be Vifil's son galled him. He meddled much in affairs of honor. When Eirik
the Red was outlawed from Haukadale, Thorbjorn gave him good welcome,
and helped him on his way to the bird-islands with good gear and provisions.
When Eirik rode against Thorgest the Yeller to regain his bench-boards,
Thorbjorn rode with him. He accompanied Eirik out past Snæfellsness and
wished him luck in Greenland; he brought Thjodhild and her sons back to her
foster-father's house. – Thorbjorn of Haukadale stood in the doorway. "Well,
namesake," said he, "think me not ungrateful for your help and care. But now
be on your way, for you are poor company for Thjodhild, being but a freed
slave's son. Take this silver for your trouble." – "Never," shouted Thorbjorn
Vifilsson. "Never!" He spurned the coins, and left them lying in the grass.

Thorbjorn Proves Himself to be a Person
of Quality *ca. 988*

For a time Gudrid lived as foster-daughter of Thorbjorn's friend Orm and
Orm's wife Halldis. Gudrid wore her long yellow hair wrapped around her
belt. Next to her body she wore a chemise of silk, so that her breasts were
partly uncovered. There were many gold rings on her hands. – I have often
noticed that when cut roses in a vase begin to droop there remains one to
stand awhile; looking away from those bowing crimson bells that once com-
panioned it, it drinks the light as long as it can, although its narrow-tongued
underleaves have already lost their strength. Why that one flower survives
the others I cannot say. It did not bloom any later. It had not seemed any
healthier. But now it stands alone, and becomes the more beautiful for that.
Fair Gudrid rose alone long after those who loved her had fallen into the
mass of decay. – At this point in time, when we first look upon her, she was
surrounded and protectively nourished by other roses, for although Thorbjorn
Vifilsson was descended from a slave, he had done very well on his farmstead
at Hellisvellir, and so possessed cows and sheep and rings of gold. However,
he had accomplished his success more through a combination of anxiety
and luck than through shrewd management. For one thing, the land in the
Laugarbrekka district was slightly superior to that in Vifilsdale, and had it not
been for his marriage he would not have had access to it. For another, Gudrid
was a beautiful child from the moment of her birth, and men often rendered
Thorbjorn little assistances of one sort or another solely to be in sight of her.
Fearing at last that something harmful might come of this, Thorbjorn asked
his friend Orm to foster her. – Gudrid soon made herself well-liked, not
only for her beauty, but also because she saw her duty and was industrious.
Her foster-mother Halldis taught her the spells called *Warlock Songs*, for in
those days Iceland was not yet a Christian country, and so neither Gudrid
nor Halldis thought this ill knowledge. – By now, though he did not see it
immediately, Thorbjorn's luck was beginning to turn. In the summer after
King Harald Greyskin's fall, he obtained a chieftainship at last, but this prize,
though it brought him honor, made him liable to many expenses. So he slept
poorly, his honor and his life-fear watching over each other as in the old days
of Herlaug and Rollaug. He dreamed that a thrall-collar was being fastened
upon him, albeit one of gold; this collar was choking him, and he screamed
very dreadfully in his sleep. – "Is it so dire, then," said his father, "that I was
once a slave? For you know that I came of high race in Ireland; and I was a

slave for but three years. Surely the Icelanders have forgotten these things."
– "You are old," said Thorbjorn, "and rarely go out. If you did, you would
see that they have never forgotten." – "Perhaps you are right," replied Vifil,
stroking his grey beard. "I know little of what goes on around me. In my
dreams I often find myself in Ireland." – It was important to Thorbjorn that
his farm be among the largest in Laugarbrekka, and this, too, bore its cost.
With his wife dead, he was compelled to take on new thralls to do her duties.
They cost more to feed than she had done; it was a by-word that thralls were
gruel-greedy and careless, for after all the property did not belong to them.
Presently it began to be common knowledge that Thorbjorn's money was
dwindling, but he refused to alter his habits, and he instructed Orm that
Gudrid not be informed. She, therefore, continued in her happiness, and
being so, she was beautiful, so that other roses never bowed away from her
(or so it seemed to her, at least, in her sundrenched blindness of growing
and rising and standing and waiting for she knew not what). – "I am not
quite sure," the young men said, "whether it is her mouth or blue eyes that
I like most." And many of their summers were spent debating this point. It
must be reported, however, that out of all of them only one was prepared
to make her an offer, and that was the odious Einar Thorgeirsson, a fellow
with "a taste for the ornate," says the saga. – Oddly enough, his father, too,
was a freed slave. He wore a purple cloak, and on his head a bearskin cap.
Gudrid thought him ridiculous. However, some thought him dashing, and
his father's wealth encouraged friendship towards him. It was with precisely
that argument that Einar persuaded Orm, whom he knew in connection
with some sea-trading, to approach Thorbjorn as his go-between, and to
ask Gudrid's hand in marriage.

"As I am sure you can imagine," said Orm carefully, "my foster-daughter
is particular about husbands. Her hand is not to be had for the asking." –
"But surely it can be had for *my* asking!" cried young Einar, smoothing an
imaginary crease in his purple sleeve with such great concentration that he
seemed almost to have forgotten about Orm and Gudrid. "I mean, after *all*,"
said Einar brightly, "I have money, and Gudrid's father will soon have none!"
He had only once seen her, passing through a doorway, but her shape had
intrigued him. Knowing her descent, she seemed to him a perfect match.
How adorable it would be to take her trading with him in Norway, to present
her before the court of King Olaf Trygvesson! – and if, as seemed likely, she
was high-spirited, well, his gold could tell her beguiling tales, or, if need be,
read her lectures to which she would be obliged to listen.

"I certainly consider myself your friend," said Orm, "but I would rather

not be the one to take your proposal to Thorbjorn. He is a proud man –
not that I wish to offend you, for you are fine in every way. I hope you
understand me." – "Proud?" said Einar. He meditated. "What is pride? Pride
is the quality of heart that comes when a man can give gold rings to all who
are loyal to him. Can Thorbjorn do this? Today he can, but tomorrow, I fear,
he will not be proud anymore." – "I see that you too are proud," said Orm,
"so there is nothing left for me to do but let you have your way." And he
promised to raise the matter with Thorbjorn at one of those lavish feasts that
the latter was always having, for he liked to be considered a man of generosity.
(As for Orm, both he and his wife Halldis were like ghost ships, that blew
rudderless across the sea in accordance with others' wills.) While the other
guests were occupying themselves with ale and meat, Orm sat swallowing
miserably, and Halldis said to him, "Shame, husband! You promised Einar,
rightly or wrongly; now you must uphold your honor!" – "That is all true,"
said Orm, "but I wish that I had not promised." – Having said this, he got
to his feet, and walked the length of the long-fire to the high-seat, where
Thorbjorn Vifilsson sat ordering his thralls about. – "May I speak to you
alone?" said Orm. – "What!" cried Thorbjorn. "Is the ale gone already?" And
he laughed at his own words. But he arose, and ushered his friend outside.
Now there was nothing for it; Orm had to take up Einar's proposal. No
sooner had the words left his mouth than Thorbjorn picked up an axe and
threw it down, cleaving the turf between them. "I never expected such a
thing from you," he cried. "Imagine! My daughter married to the son of a
slave!" And he refused to let Gudrid live at Orm's house any longer. When
his money was gone, he set sail for Greenland to get land from Eirik the Red.
Orm and Halldis accompanied him, and they both died of a plague, along
with half the people on the ship. Gudrid and her father, however, survived
very nicely. All the Vifilssons had that knack.

A Mournful Banquet in Greenland

Wishing to avoid the bitterness consequent upon dreaming too much, Gudrid
kept herself busy in Greenland. Because the ship was blown about on the sea by
evil winds until the autumn, by which time the ice was already clashing against
the shore, they were compelled to winter in Herjolfsness. The chief farmer
there now was named Thorkel (for poor Bjarni Herjolfsson, the incurious
discoverer of Greenland, had by now vanished forever from the pages of the
Flateyjarbók). He gave them hospitality, and Gudrid immediately set herself

to work weaving and spinning like a spider, so that all thought her a most industrious girl; and her father became puffed up with hearing her praises.

"What lies over that mountain?" said Gudrid.

"That way?" laughed Thorkel. "Nothing but mist, ice, rocks and trolls."

That winter came a famine to Greenland. From behind her loom Gudrid saw the house-men go out hunting and return empty-handed. Thorkel's heavy footfalls told her that he no longer expected any luck; and she heard him in speech with his wife Helga, who was saying, "Never before have you come back with nothing from the Reindeer Isles," and Gudrid span her woolen threads, and Helga said, "You saw no seals?" and that night as the moon shone on the ice like copper Gudrid refused to join the others at table, saying that she was not hungry, so that later her father came with a candle into her chamber to ask her privily if she were ill and she said, "I cannot bear to eat their meat any longer," to which he said, "I had not thought that you were capable of such rigor!" at which she flung her bedskins down indignantly and sat up, crying, "I cannot bear it, I tell you!" and Thorbjorn smiled and said, "Indeed, my Gudrid, you are proud but I know you!" and he went out and returned with a bit of seal-meat and left it there. Tears coursed down the girl's face, and she sat up in bed and prayed, watching the steam of her breath ascending to Heaven from that cold room; later she devoured the meat. The moon sank below the ridges, and her father's candle went out, and the night was black and ugly. The next day Thorkel set forth once again for the Reindeer Isles with his neighbor, an older man named Gunnar, who brought both his house-carles for the chase. The sky was an ugly purple-grey, like a wound, and sleet came sizzling down. Two days after this Thorkel returned alone, half-dead with cold, and said that the others had been lost. He slept all that day and part of the next, while the others went about their business in a hush, and mist thickened around the stead. When Thorkel awoke he called his wife to him and they spoke in whispers; he rose, drank down hot broth, put on his cloak and went out again. This time Thorbjorn went with him, even though he was a poor hunter; and perhaps it was that famous Vifilsson luck or perhaps it was something else, but they returned with a young seal. Gudrid sprang up and embraced her father; she thought that she had never loved him so much. When he descended to the fjord to gather driftwood, she threw on her cloak and followed after him. It was very windy there. Ice glared on the wind-blown rocks; and the horizon was livid. – "I had not thought that Thorkel spoke truth when he said that there were trolls here," said Thorbjorn, shearing a branch with a stout axe-blow; and Gudrid said, "Father, what do you mean?", and Thorbjorn said, "Just after we killed the seal, we spied two devils on a hill – or at least they were dark and devilish-looking little men, with round cheeks like babies. When they understood that we saw them, they ran away. Thorkel and I agreed not to tell the others, but I wanted you to know." – Gudrid had turned pale. "Do you think they mean us evil?" she asked in a low voice. – Thorbjörn shrugged. "I think we will never see them again. But now I wish that I had not lived beyond my means, and been forced to leave Iceland." – With this, he began to chop at another log, and the conversation was at an end.

The famine continued, and the cows began to die of cold in the byre. Gudrid always ate what was set before her. One day she took out a length of golden thread which her father had given her to use when she was married, and began to embroider pretty rune-patterns as her foster-mother Halldis had taught her, and Helga came over to watch for a moment and said, "You take great pains to please us, Gudrid; do not think that you are a burden to us!", and Gudrid smiled so brilliantly and said, "No doubt some do say it," and Helga said, "What do you mean?", and Gudrid said, "It is kind of you to compliment me; I too think that this pattern will be very pretty when I have finished it."

The next day Thorkel went out again for reindeer, and again returned empty-handed.

Now murmurs began to go up from neighbor to neighbor that it was time to inquire of Thorbjorg, the Prophetess of that settlement, how long the famine would last. (For Greenland was not yet a Christian country at this time.) Every stead seemed to be in straits. Hearing this, Thorkel said, "It does not seem that we are to be allowed much ease. I think that we must make a feast for the Prophetess."

Thorbjörn Vifilsson spoke out against these pagan practices, and Gudrid also, but she only a little, wanting always to endear herself to others. So in the end it was only Thorbjörn who swore to leave the house when the old witch came.

Helga and Thorkel stood together in the doorway when the Prophetess came, and greeted her as respectfully as they could. She hobbled past them with scarcely a word; that was her way. – "May I help you take off your skin cloak?" pleaded Helga. – The Prophetess said: "There are so many beautiful clothes here!" and Helga hastened to present her with a fine wool serk that she and Gudrid had woven together, meaning to give it to Thorkel. Then Thorkel led her to a high-seat that had been specially prepared for her and Helga brought the cushion stuffed with hen's feathers, which the Prophetess took without saying anything, seating herself in the high-seat as the others lined up to greet her. And again Helga said, "Welcome to our house!" and the Prophetess grimaced; and second in line was Thorkel, who said, "Thank you for the honor you show us!", to which the Prophetess answered, "Yes, Thorkel, honor is a thing you have need of," to which no one dared to reply. Next came the cringing house-carles and carlines one after another; and last in line was Gudrid Thorbjornsdottir, who bowed her head and said, "My name is Gudrid, and I also greet you and thank you," and unexpectedly the Prophetess smiled and said, "A lovely girl! And such beautiful eyes!" (Then Gudrid thought to herself: Now will Helga gouge my eyes out and offer them to her?) Thorkel, who had managed to put the Prophetess's insult out of mind, said, "Will you come with me to look upon house and herd?", and the Prophetess got up sighing and leaning on her staff and went through the stead without a word of blessing, so that the host's face was wrathfully tinged. Then she sat down in her high-seat again. Helga and Gudrid rushed to bring her the goat's milk gruel that she always required, and the dish of seals' hearts, the dish of reindeer-hearts, the dish of snow-rabbit hearts . . . They sat down to their own meager meal as the Prophetess sighed and grunted, cutting her food with a knife whose point was broken, and refreshing herself avidly with the gruel, shoveling it into her mouth with a strange brass spoon whose like Gudrid had never seen before. Even so, the others finished before she did; there was little enough for them to eat. – "Oh, the Ynglings knew!" said the Prophetess in great satisfaction, licking the last drops of heart-blood from her knife. "But *that* game is not finished yet; we still have the wild grapes." And she looked at Gudrid very shrewdly.

"How do you like my stead?" said Thorkel at last.

"I will answer your questions tomorrow," she replied. "Make up a bed for me and leave me in peace."

But now Thorkel was on his feet. He put on his cloak and left the house.

"What is it he seeks to do?" said the old woman querulously. "Never mind. Where is the bed that you have prepared for me?"

"I will take you to your place," said Gudrid. "Here, let me help you." She extended her hand.

"Oh, but she is a *sweet* little maid!" said the Prophetess to the others. "Her name is Gudrid, you say? If only she had been my daughter. I am the youngest of seven sisters and they were all Prophetesses; now the others are dead. Soon there will be no more of us – *aiee!*"

That night Gudrid was frightened, and wondered if she had done wrong to permit herself any friendship with this heathen woman. And yet she could not help it. Just as ladies poured out the feast-ale, so Gudrid longed always to pour herself out for others to taste of her and be refreshed. It would be far better now, she knew, if she were to join her father at Gunnarstead. But Helga needed her; she owed Helga so much. As always, Gudrid knelt upon the cold floor and prayed to CHRIST. And she made a resolution that she would do nothing to bring her into dishonor.

In the morning there was a stir among the waiting folk when the Prophetess rose at last. – "Oh, what gifts can I give her today?" wailed Helga, but Gudrid comforted her and said that there was no need. The sky was a moldy patchy green, like badly cured leather, and the wind rattled the house. Truly it was a very ugly morning. Gudrid longed to be home in Iceland. – "Now we must have women who can help me sing the *Warlock-Songs*," the Prophetess said, and Thorkel (who had returned very late) inquired of all his thralls, but no one knew the songs. But the Prophetess sat in her high-seat with her eyes half closed, saying, "There is someone here who knows – the Spirits tell me so!"; and at last Gudrid said with folded hands, "I am no sorceress, but in Iceland my foster-mother Halldis taught me songs she called *Warlock-Songs*," to which the Prophetess said, "Well, child, it seems your knowledge is timely!", and there was a silence and then Gudrid said, "That is the sort of knowledge I want no part of, for I am Christian, having hearkened to the words of King Olaf's priest," but the old Prophetess frowned and said, "It may well be that you could help us and not be a worse woman for it!"

Gudrid hung her head.

"Come," said Thorkel sharply, "it cannot possibly be CHRIST's command that a young girl refuse to help the folk who sheltered her!"

"I know that my father and I have been a tax upon you," said Gudrid. "I promise you that we will leave on the first day of spring!" Her lip was trembling.

"But it is not that that we ask of you," said Thorkel. "You need not believe the words you sing; but you must sing them, unless you want us all to die of hunger. How well do you think your CHRIST would like you then?"

Gudrid caught her breath. Her face was very white.

Thorkel stood up. "Is it right that I should be insulted by every guest who comes?" he shouted.

"Hush, hush," said Helga. "Pay him no mind, Gudrid."

The Prophetess wore a blue mantle, which was as heavy with stones as all the seas with islands. Her necklace was made of glass beads, and they tinkled one against the other when she moved. Her hood and gloves were lined with white catskin. – Gudrid hated her. Smiling, she sang the *Warlock-Songs*.

"My daughter," said the Prophetess, "I have never heard lovelier singing.

The Spirits shunned us before, but they could not resist you. – Truly I cannot imagine anyone who'd resist you! – The Spirits came down from the ice-mountains; they danced around your head, my Gudrid; they promised to lift the famine before spring comes. (Oh, they have BLACK HANDS, you know! I heard that from the Skrælings.) And I can see that you will make a distinguished marriage here in Greenland."

Eirik's daughter, Freydis, who valued praise the more because she so seldom got it, would have loved the Prophetess had she said those things to her. As for Gudrid, she hated the Prophetess just as much as before. – Kneeling, she thanked her for her words and kissed her.

So Gudrid bore the winter at Herjolfsness as patiently as she could, and spring came at last.

Spring on Baffin Island 1987

Even as I watched I could see the streams increase. The noise of the wind became mingled with the sound of waterfalls. The smell of the sea came into the valley, and gulls flew crying. I ran across the mudflats to watch the advancing water. I saw the reflection of Ulu Peak in a puddle. The sand became ribbed mud, imprinted with the three-toed feet of birds. Every little channel reflected some snowy mountain. I stood on a little spit of mud and watched the water come in all around me. Although it moved in starting and stopping pulses, it approached very quickly, for the tide was also coming in; the ocean came and met the streams of melted ice. It was very cool and wild, and the birds sang. I could see no one else in the whole world . . .

Two Grateful Guests ca. 990

When the spring was well advanced, Thorbjorn and Gudrid sailed with their thralls to Brattahlid, and Red Eirik welcomed them. The seasons passed. Gudrid could not understand why her father was in no hurry to ask Eirik for land. She fretted and drooped, like a rose whose stem has finally lost its resistance to death, so that the scarlet bell of beauty becomes an insupportable weight; thus Gudrid wove and span at Brattahlid with her hair bedraggled. They wintered with Eirik and played at chess and draughts. Eirik's son Thorstein was very enamored of Gudrid. He stayed at home with his father, for which reason men considered him a more promising youth than his brother

Leif. Eirik said that he would be quite satisfied if Gudrid was pleased with his son. But Gudrid did not care much for Thorstein. Often Thorstein would come to the door and say to Thorbjorn, "Where's Gudrid?", and Gudrid would cower back and pray that her father would not tell him that she was there, but Thorbjorn would smile a big comfortable smile and rest his hand on Thorstein's shoulder and say, "Why, Gudrid's right here. Gudrid! *Gudrid!*" and Gudrid would have to play at draughts with Thorstein. – Now the lovely rose began to droop somewhat more. "Why must you say that I am there?" she demanded. – Thorbjorn paced up and down the room, smiling sadly. "Eirik has been good to us," he said at last. – "He only pays the debt he owes you!" cried Gudrid. "You guested him when he was outlawed from Haukadale; you helped him hide from Thorgest . . ." – "Yes, I helped him," said Thorbjorn. "I helped him when I had the means to do so. Now I have almost nothing. The more he pays me back, the greater my new obligation. Greater still, because I cannot meet it. Thorstein is fond of you. You should be grateful for the chance to please. Do you understand me, Gudrid?" – Gudrid sat down slowly, biting her lip. It was very sweet to see the way her hair swept down above her eyes. A single blonde strand of it curled lovingly around her neck. Her little white hands rested in her lap, clenching and unclenching. She turned her head away, but Thorbjorn saw a single tear running down the straight sweep of her cheek. – "Oh, well," she said. "It seems that prostitution happens in the best of families." – When Thorstein came that day, Gudrid smiled and rose and smoothed her sleeves. Her shirt had a blue tint.

In the month of Sowing-Tide, Eirik gave the Vifilssons land at Stokkanes, where his bench-boards had first washed ashore, so that it was considered a lucky place. – "Can you carry up my loom for me, Thorstein?" asked Gudrid. "Oh, you are as strong as a bear!" – They had a little bay for their harbor, and above the beach the land rose at an angle of forty-five degrees, rich with moss and lichen, and, after flattening just enough to provide space for a commanding house, it became a steep and mossy shoulder of the sky, behind which were snow-peaks. The lichen was green and grey; Gudrid walked ankle-deep in its foamy blooms. In the sky were always eagles. Dwarf poplars grew thick and green in the streams that rushed into the fjord; from every rise Gudrid and her father could see another stream. Sometimes the streams were full of waterfalls and foamy rapids, so that throughout their length they were the color of the snow they came from.

For the first few days Thorbjorn and his thralls were busy consecrating their ownership of the new land. They traveled all over it, and lit a fire at the mouth of every river. Thorbjorn's house-carles wanted to build a temple to THOR, but Thorbjorn and Gudrid would not allow it. – "This is good land," Thorbjorn said. Wherever a man lives and farms, he considers the land to be good land, and sees abundance and fertility. Just as the Skræling word for crowberry means "earth-apple," as if it were the harvest of some great hot garden of richness, although to those who live south of Brattahlid the crowberry appears to be a wretched little fruit, so Thorbjorn saw the beauty in his land and made up his mind to be contented with it. His farm was hardly as big as the one he had had in Iceland, but he did not complain. He farmed there at Stokkanes until his death.

The weather was sunny and mild.

Thorstein without Gudrid

Afterwards, on those midnight summer nights, Thorstein closed his eyes and saw blonde Icelandic women leaning in doorways. It was a great grief to him that the Vifilssons were gone. Gudrid had made him feel that he was about to do or be someone infinitely more wonderful than he could ever have imagined, as if his desires were white reindeer running over tundra plains beneath a keen bright sky and he was there, too, running among them, galloping toward the inland ice; but now that Gudrid was gone he had shrunk back into himself, and his longings hung upon him loosely, like the wrinkled belly of a fat man who has starved; – Gudrid would not help him play the Changing-Game! His brother Leif, who was well-traveled in his sharp-keeled ship, told him not to despair, for when the Queen was taken, often some pawn could be found. In fact, Leif had just come away from a delightful affair in the Hebrides. He had sailed to Norway to winter at King Olaf's because he and his father were always quarreling, and Olaf was known as a generous man; as for Olaf, he was well-pleased that Leif had placed himself under obligation to him, because he would not at all mind becoming King of Greenland as well as King of Norway, and when that time came Leif would have open to him the choice of Herlaug or the choice of Rollaug.

Love and Honor

Of Olaf it is related that he was a devout Christian. He slaughtered many pagans, and burned the sorcerers in their houses. For a time it was his dearest dream to get Queen Gunhild, Eric Bloody-Axe's widow, into his hands; for not only had she killed his father and harried his mother into foreign lands, but she was also known for her poisonous witchcraft; it would be a deed to bring a smile to GOD's face if he could punish her as she deserved. But Gunhild, now bereft of all her sons save King Gudrod, lurked on the outer islands beyond the knowledge of him who had supplanted her, so that he could but twist his beard in his hands and curse, at which his serving-man Blue-Shirt said, meaning to console him, "Take her escape not so hardly, Lord, for after all she was baptized, and her son Harald Greycloak pulled down all the idols." But at this King Olaf flew into a rage and shouted, "You consider her a Christian, do you?" and Blue-Shirt fled from his presence. Now King Olaf shot the absent Gunhild with insult-arrows day and night, pronouncing her the most villainous of all Norway's Queens, but this led him to think upon the GOOD and BEAUTIFUL Queens, the better to make a contrast with her wickedness, and before he knew it he had fallen in love with the idea of taking one for himself. The men of his court were relieved at the change of subject, and encouraged him, saying, "Yes, Lord, indeed it is your duty to give us the gift of an heir!" at which King Olaf began to smile, saying, "I will not say no to that," and his men swore to support him with all their power. In due time, therefore, he became engaged to Queen Sigrid of Sweden, who was surnamed *the Haughty* because of her habit of burning her suitors alive. – "I will make those small Kings tired of coming to court me!" she said. – With her Olaf, however, she was justly content. He was a surpassingly handsome man (whispered her serving-maids), and very skilled in arms – and, of course, he ruled all Norway. – The King now razed a pagan temple near Drontheim, and took from it a great golden ring which had hung in the door. His carles cut down the idols with their axes and worms came out; the axes split THOR's skull; then the men stripped that place of everything rich and goodly, and burned it. But King Olaf joyed in the ring that he held. So large it was that it would easily slip over his pretty Sigrid's head ... Then she would come into his arms, so cool and slender and soft; and only he, he at his pleasure, would be the one to lift that treasure-collar from her shoulders; and then she would fill his mead-cup. This vision came to have the strongest hold over his inclinations. In the end he sent the ring to her, for it was considered a most distinguished ornament. But the Swedish goldsmiths sneered to see it. Then Queen Sigrid's eyes flashed and she said very quietly, "What do you mean by these grimaces?", and the goldsmiths turned to one another like fingers curling inward to make a fist, each waiting for the next to speak. And Queen Sigrid smiled and said even more quietly, "Well?" and the pikemen waited for her command and the goldsmiths said, "Let us weigh this ring," and the

Queen said, "Do so," and the goldsmiths set up their scales and put the ring in place and puzzled over it and then said joyously, "Queen, this ring is false!" and Queen Sigrid turned very pale and directed that it be broken into pieces, and inside it was only copper. Then Sigrid flew into a rage. – Strange it was that that ring, which first had been meant to be a token of worship, became next a token of love, then of deceit; and yet its inner self never changed. – In the spring, she met her sweetheart in Konghelle to complete the discussion of their marriage, and Olaf said that she must be baptized. – "I am satisfied with my own faith, which is the faith of my fathers," said Sigrid. "But I will not object to your believing in whatever god pleases you best." – He slapped her in the face with his glove and called her a faded heathen bitch. – Queen Sigrid the Haughty stepped back. A welt was rising very slowly on her cheek. "That may well be your death," she said.

Waiting for Favorable Winds

In the spring, Leif, not wanting to rush too far down the road he had taken with Olaf, elected to return to Greenland and court his father somewhat, because he did not want to let Thorstein supplant him in the enjoyment of his rights; so he set sail, but unfortunately the winds were against him, and he was blown straight to the Hebrides. He spent the summer there waiting for favorable winds. Of course he was not about to stand on the docks wetting his finger every second to see if the breeze had changed, not when there were friends to make, such as noble-born Thorgunna, who went to such lengths to welcome him! – She was a tall, strong woman, says the *Erbyggja Saga*, and somewhat plump. She had a pale long face, with big eyes, green eyes as big as marbles, within which the dark pupils seemed glittery and freckled, like watermelon seeds. Her teeth were very white, and when she smiled they glittered with a purity made eerie by the dark red fall of hair around her shoulders, so dark and red that light seemed to vanish into it. When she smiled, little lights moved in her eyes. She took Leif to the Callanish Stones and made runes, for she was a woman of much knowledge; and for his delight she called hedge-riders down from the blue-black clouds to bewitch the town, raising her pale shoulders, outstretching her arms to pick ghosts from the wind; and he sat beside her in the grass-grown mound of a forgotten god, feasting upon milk, cream and blæberries, and thinking to himself, "Never has there been such a woman!" Thorgunna had a way of leaning her head back on his shoulder and pursing her lower lip, which he considered charming. – How lucky he was to be here! – The sea was so still that summer, and the grass so green, that Leif's pleasure had safe residence. (There were no trees anymore, of course; the Vikings had set fire to those when they routed out traitors.) In the fjords, beams of cloud-light moved across the water, and Leif exalted himself in cool tranquility and felt the breeze upon his face. He let his idleness travel up the long blue inlets; he watched the crows aswarm around the Vikings' stone forts ... Because the mountains were so dark, their reflections in the sea resembled shadows. – "Look!" said Thorgunna. "Do you see those great stones on the hilltops, like gateways? Those mark the road for the SHINING ONE. He walks only from hill to hill; I have seen Him in the wind. – And do you hear the cuckoo singing? He must have two full meals of cherries before he can change his tune." – She wore a blue kirtle. Leif liked to watch her breasts heave under it. For her part, when it was all over, she never forgot how he used to bury his dark-tanned face in her white neck, worrying and worrying it like an animal, with his many-ringed hand about her neck, pulling it against his face, and then when he pulled away she looked straight ahead, breathing fast, but he kept his head turned toward her and presently pulled her face toward him again, kissing and kissing her mouth with such force that she could not breathe. It seemed that he could not get enough of her. – So the summertime passed agreeably enough for Leif, as Thorgunna took him to gather brown crabs and cockles. Oh, so often he took her chin in his hand; he pillowed his head on her creamy white thighs . . . – But presently, as was often the case in Leif's life, the wind changed, and he went in to see Thorgunna and tell her that he must be going – for, says the *Grænlendinga Saga*, he was always moderate in his behavior. Although Leif was not yet nicknamed *the Lucky*, in those days he did have an idiot luck, for it never dawned on him that Thorgunna was not only a determined woman, but also a formidable witch, and that although he might take his leave of her now, she might not choose to take hers of him. She lived with clenched teeth, schooling her bastard son Thorgils in hate-craft, raising him on adders' hearts; and never did she put Leif out of her mind. When the boy was old enough, she sent him to Greenland to work witch-woe on his father Leif as best he might; then, when she had gathered venomous nectars to rub in whatever wounds he might have made, she bought passage to Greenland on a trading ship, happy now only to inflame her heart still further by tasting herself already burying her teeth in Leif's side; and she had taken a private berth, so that she might lie the more contented in the dark with her fixed smile; and the ship bit the waves and sped toward Greenland, but then a fog began to infuse the sea and the fog became more and more luminous the closer they drew, so that the

Captain became leery of shoals unseen; but in her berth Thorgunna used her
arts so that the ship broke through into sunlight and began its crawl upon the
surface of an immense blue-grey plain of fog, beneath an omelette sky of blue
and white, in which there loomed far off the great shoulder of Blue-Shirt, and
Thorgunna smiled as before and the ship sailed on; but closer to Greenland
the clouds drew together and started looking like sandbars upon which the
ship was doomed indeed to run aground, since Leif's luck-wind had sprung
up (Leif all unknowing of the fact, for he lay whistling and passing the time
with a concubine from the Orkneys), and though Thorgunna lay calling upon
her familiars until the veins stood out in her neck, she could not have her
desire despite her possession even now of sufficient Power to see how it
would have been if only her Wave-Riders had been able to thrust the ship
north on their ice-wet shoulders while she gave birth to her wolf-bitch self
of vengeance whose red mane of hair stood straight up on her back like
long-fire as she howled with the joy of the Changing-Game; now, outstripping
the Wave-Riders in lust, she would have leaped into the sea, darting from
wave-peak to wave-peak until she saw that first low ice-cliff of Greenland
– for a moment she even believed that she did see it, having lost hold of the
difference between the certainties and conditionals which she used to gather
like pebbles in the shell-beaches below the Callanish Stones, sorting them one
from the other, each for its own use; but now she could not do that because
Leif's luck-wind had blown her back down inside herself where she lay chilled
by sweat-drench and tear-drench; and very slowly her eyeballs rolled up like
the bellies of dying fishes and when a sea-lurch banged her head against the
wall she did not feel it, and the wind blew all her clammy Wave-Riders away
and caught the sail in its whirly palms and nudged it eastward as the traders
began to swear and pull at their beards; and over the ocean the clouds were
like flat white tundra polygons, with blue sky-cracks in between. At last they
swept, all unwilling, into Snæfellsness Reef. Through the clouds punched the
white-capped pyramid of Snæfellsjökul. The snow was like a spider on top
of it. Spider-legs of snow crawled down its sides. The whole blue peninsula
swam in cloud like a crocodile. There the ship lay, rocking and rocking all
summer in the bad wind. Many Icelanders went to chaffer with the ship for
her trade-goods, which the merchants let go for low prices, being desperate
not to lose all profits to the west-wind; seeing how matters stood, the Icelanders
saw yet more, and in time it got about that a certain tall woman with dark red
hair had many fine clothes, although she would not sell them. There was a
woman in Frodis-Water named Thurid, who, being vain and covetous (the
one implies the other, for vanity is a form of insecurity, which must enshroud

itself in costly cerements) decided to have her people row her out to the ship, in order to see Thorgunna's clothes, and, being a woman of means, she was sure that a sufficiency of red gold would make Thorgunna strip herself half-naked, if need be, like a butterfly becoming a caterpillar again for the sake of a leaf, so that Thurid could have whatever of her finery she desired. Off she went one day to the listless ship, on which the traders paced to and fro, cursing the wind; and Thorgunna sat by the prow, gazing dully into the water. She had aged; Thurid thought her a very hale woman of fifty. There were now little ridges on either side of her eyes, which had sunken into deep black pits, although they still gleamed green like stagnant well-pools. – "I've come to look at your clothes," said Thurid, perhaps a bit too briskly, for, having taken note of Thorgunna's sad and desperate face, she gloated in the likely success of her purpose; but Thorgunna looked up at her very slowly and then looked down at the deck again and said, "Well, I'm wearing them, so look at them if you like, but please don't trouble me;" and Thurid's anger was inflamed, but the truth was that Thorgunna wore a *very* becoming purple wind-cloak, so Thurid said mildly, "If I may, I'd like to see *all* your clothes," so Thorgunna rose rather heavily and led her down to her berth. In a wooden ark, which she now unlocked for her guest, Thorgunna kept blue serks and kirtles that Thurid snatched into the light and held before her in a critical ecstasy, sniffing at them to see if they were perfumed and caressing the weave of them more lovingly than she had ever caressed her husband, for she thought that she would become a finer person if she wore them (*again* that game of Changing!); and in the ark were also belts of silver and gold, and many festive *slædur*-dresses of different colors that made Thurid's breath come quickly, and cloaks lined with velvety *pell* that Thurid placed in her lap and stroked like cats, so that Thorgunna had nothing to do but listen to Thurid exclaiming over how lovely the clothes were. And Thurid set many of them aside and put the rest away with due reverence and wanted to know how much it would cost to buy what she had chosen, but Thorgunna smiled coolly and said that her clothes were not for sale, that she was not some rag-merchant, and Thurid did not believe her and offered to pay a great price for them. But Thorgunna chopped the air with her hands and said again that her clothes were not for sale; and as she said this she remembered Leif sliding his hand into her kirtle, caressing her strong white shoulders and ripping off her fine clothes until they lay in a heap at his feet, and she stood before him, the wonder of it being she had let him do it; – and now here was this Icelandic woman inspecting her clothes as though Thorgunna had no feelings. So Thorgunna took her clothes from Thurid's lap and replaced

them in her ark and closed and locked it while Thurid sat in the stillness
of disappointed envy, and Thorgunna smiled pleasantly, and Thurid rocked
herself, her eyes hard and shiny, and presently invited Thorgunna to dwell
with her at Frodis-Water until the wind changed, for it was in her mind that
she could make Thorgunna part with her pride and all her fine things, if only
she had leisure enough to do it. – "Thank you," said Thorgunna, smiling
wearily. She knew now that she was not fated to get to Greenland. – They
left the ship together on Thurid's skiff. All the way, that covetous woman
kept fingering the stuff of Thorgunna's mantle, but Thorgunna merely bit
her lip and turned her dull gaze to the bird-islands of Breidafjord, which
were still much the same as when Leif's father Eirik had hidden in them;
and the black *skarfur*-birds curved their necks to gaze down disdainfully at
each other's toes, and they stood on their white-dunged rocks and shook
themselves, while the sea foamed grey and green over low rocks, and kelp
swam in the waves. – "Nothing good will come of this," said Thorgunna,
but Thurid pretended not to hear. She gave her guest a bed in the hall, which
Thorgunna covered with English sheets and a silken quilt. Thurid came and
watched her arranging the bed-hangings, and presently said she wanted to
buy them, but Thorgunna's little nostrils flared, and she said quietly that she
wasn't about to lie in straw for *her*, no matter how fair-spoken she was; she
preferred to pay for her keep with labor, she said; and she also wished it
known that she would do no wet work. – Although she went to church
every day, people thought her reserved and ill-tempered. For example, she
never got along with Thorgrima Witch-Face. When she worked at the loom,
she often wove figures of women whose heads were howling dogs, so that
Thurid wondered whether she might be mocking her, but nothing was ever
said about it; in the matter of the hay-drying, Thorgunna was equally peculiar,
for she would not do it until they made her a special hay-rake that no one but
she was permitted to touch. – One day it was very good hay-drying weather,
and Thorgunna was working in the fields with Thurid's husband Thorolf and
the others when a black cloud appeared on the horizon, and this black cloud
came closer and closer until Thorolf directed that the hay be raked up, but
Thorgunna ignored him and went on spreading the hay with her special rake
until the cloud was directly overhead, and then it rained blood. – Thorolf
asked Thorgunna what she thought this meant. – "I imagine," said Thorgunna
lazily, "that it will mean the death of someone here. It's hardly a good omen,
now, is it?" – Most of the hay soon dried, but Thorgunna's pile never did, and
neither did the rake that she had used. – When her thralls told her of these
events, Thurid strode triumphantly into the field, saying, "Now, Thorgunna,

you will have to pay for the hay that you wasted with your carelessness!" and Thorgunna said, "I can guess what you want me to pay for it!", but the color had fled from her face and she leaned upon her bleeding rake for support, as if her strength were leaving her. It was now hot and sunny again, and Thurid walked away and Thorolf gave the order to spread the hay back out again, but Thorgunna raked very slowly, and her tines left glistening red furrows of blood in the hay. After awhile, though the day was still far from over, she went into the stead. She took off her bloody clothes and climbed into her bed. That evening she did not come to dinner, and they heard her sighing in her fine English-hung bed, so they knew that she was ill, and in subsequent days her condition worsened, until it was clear that she would never rake hay anymore. She called Thorolf in, and he came uneasily. – "Well," she told him, "I'm going to die tomorrow. Thurid may have my scarlet cloak, so that she can feel she's gotten something out of me. But my bed-hangings have to be burnt. I don't really expect you people to have the intelligence or good faith to do it, but at least I've warned you. And I want to be buried in Skalholt." – Thorolf promised to obey her requests. – Thorgunna died, and they laid her out in church while Thorolf made her corpse-chest, with four iron bands around it, and a great bolt which he nailed shut. Then he kindled a fire for the bed-hangings. Perhaps it was in these that her Wave-Riders had dwelled, for while she was alive they often flickered and rustled like the surface of the sea, even when there was no breeze, and the odor of the sea had come from them. But now, at any rate, they hung as listlessly as becalmed sails; they did not tremble in terror at the glowing fate that Thorolf now prepared for them, hoping meanwhile that he could do it decently, without his wife making a scene; but no, of course here she came rushing into the death-chamber, almost sick with greed; she threw herself down at his feet and embraced his knees and begged that he might spare the bed-hangings, because, she said, Thorgunna only wanted them burnt for spite, so that she should not have them, and Thorolf felt sorry for her but he said, "It is an ill thing to disregard the wishes of the dead," and Thurid shouted, "Why do you think I wanted her here but because I could see that she was *fey**?" Then Thorolf said, "Surely she was a witch," but Thurid cried, "I do not fear her! You *must* not burn her goods! You *must* not!" and her aspect was so wild that he began to fear she might do herself an injury, so at last, deeming this evident peril to be of more consequence than mere forebodings that would probably come to nothing, he agreed to let her have her way. – The result of this was that Thorgunna's

---

* Doomed.

corpse began to haunt them. At first she helped rather than hindered their doings, for they were obeying her will by bearing her to Skalholt for burial. – Sometimes the stones formed a pavement at the base of the green, green hills, but Thorolf knew that in a certain other direction they formed black lava-bridges over which only the bravest fool might walk, crossing high above the flat brown plains strewn with stones, wandering among the mountains until at length one must cross great rivers bursting down from snow-ridges, rivers so wide that no one could see across them, rivers roaring down lava-steps, and then at length the country became grey and orange with volcanoes, and sulphur springs trickled through the yellow grass, and far off might be seen the steam-clouds rising up from Kraela, the Pool of the Damned – and to Thorolf's mind this was where Thorgunna ought to go. – But no sooner had he opened his mouth to say so when he heard a knocking and a bony rattling inside that corpse-chest! – "This is very strange," his men said, growing pale, and Thorolf said, "By HEIMDALL, I would that I had burned those bed-hangings!" – and the tears came to his eyes. – On the first night of the funeral journey, Thorolf and his people had crossed the North River, which ran narrow and silver between the mountains, and it was night, so they knocked on a bonder's door and asked him to give them something to eat out of hospitality, but he refused them. They lay themselves down cheerlessly in a shed. Late that night there came a clatter in the buttery. A tall naked woman, with dark red hair, was standing there, putting meat on platters. She brought it out to Thorolf's party, and served them. When the bonder saw this he feared greatly, and no longer withheld anything from them. – They buried Thorgunna at Skalholt, and returned home. But now the haunting assumed a more murderous character. A half-moon went backward and widdershins around the farm, and many people about there began to die, so many that the events came to be known as the Frodis-Water Marvels, and the be-molded dead molested the living, as the saga says. Finally they even came to the Yule-feast. Then the people burned Thorgunna's bed-clothes, and held a special Thing at Frodis-Water to banish the dead back to their graves, at which the hauntings ceased. – Leif never knew any of this. Nor could he have believed it, for Thorgunna LOVED him.

When he told her of his resolution, they were sitting together on a bluff, watching the birds fly above the sea-foamed rocks. Leif had just lifted his head from her lap, because he had gotten tired of the crawling clouds in the sky, and he judged that it would be better not to be touching her in any way when he told her.

"I want to go with you," said Thorgunna. – Leif had expected this. (Her

lower lip was very red and full, he remarked to himself, but her upper lip
was as thin as a pink ribbon. She had ears as pale and pink as translucent
shells. – What a beauty she was!)

"You are such a nobly-born woman," said Leif, "that it would be cruel of
me to make you endure the hardships of the voyage. I am afraid the wind
might change again."

"I am stronger than you think," said Thorgunna.

"And will your kinsmen approve?" Leif wanted to know.

"I don't care about that."

"So they would probably not approve, I take it," said Leif very lightly,
bouncing on the balls of his feet. He did not want to be outlawed as a woman-
robber.

"I'm perfectly confident of your ability to defend me," said Thorgunna,
shrugging her white shoulders, and he did not at all like the way that she
said it.

"Well, now," said Leif. "Well."

"You *are* willing to have me accompany you?" said Thorgunna.

"Of course I want you with me," said Leif, "but I'm not certain it's wise
to abduct such a well-born woman as you, being in a foreign country as I
am, and even when all my men are together there are so few of us. I'm
glad you're confident of my abilities; I think you may be more confident
than I am. But it's your beautiful confidence that I love and admire in you"
(and later, when he was relating the tale to his younger brother Thorstein
– who sat wide-eyed and open-mouthed, which Leif found gratifying – he
explained to Thorstein that it always helped to say kind things to a woman
during these scenes; it was a *prudent* thing to do, like greasing the axles of
an ox-plough).

"For the last time I ask to come with you," Thorgunna said. "I don't think
you'll like the alternative."

"I'll take that risk," said Leif, annoyed now.

"Then let me inform you," said Thorgunna, looking at him steadily from
beneath her narrow red eyebrows, "that I'm carrying your bastard in my
belly. I think it will be a son. I'm going to send him to Greenland as soon
as he's old enough to travel, and I don't think he'll bring you any joy. And
I'm going to come to Greenland myself in the end." She folded her strong
fair arms across her chest; she looked him full in the face, and Leif saw that
she was weeping silently, weeping for grief and wrath. Her hands gripped
each other. The rings on her fingers dug into her flesh.

So Leif had to give her a gold ring, a mantle of cloth from Greenland, and a belt of walrus ivory. All in all, however, he considered himself well out of it. His son Thorgils did indeed come to Greenland, and Leif acknowledged him, though he was pale and high-shouldered, and men always said of this Thorgils that there was something uncanny about him.

Fathers and Crows

Leif sailed back to Norway in the fall. King Olaf heaped him with honors and made him feel accomplished. The feast-hall was richly adorned; the tables groaned under the weight of all the meat and drink.

"Are you intending to go back to Greenland in the summer?" said the King.

"If you approve," said Leif winningly.

"I think it would be an excellent idea," said King Olaf. "I'm sure you're anxious to see your father again." (At this they both smiled.) – "Now," said the King, smiling at Leif, with his face very close to Leif's, so that Leif could see nothing in the whole world but the King's face, and the King's eyes were looking into Leif's eyes with such intensity that Leif slowly lost sight of the King's other features, and although he felt the King's breath on his face it seemed to him that in the universe was nothing but the two blue worlds of the King's eyes, "now," said the King, "you're going to go to Greenland on a mission from me. You're going to preach the True Faith in Greenland."

"That's for you to command," said Leif in a panic, "but I think it will be difficult."

"Of course it will be difficult," said the King. "But I have great confidence in you. That's why I bestowed so many honors on you. And I know that I'm not the only one who has confidence in you. People who know you feel the same, all the way to the Hebrides." And the King slapped Leif on the shoulder, and with his own hands he poured Leif another cup of ale.

Thus it was Leif who began in Greenland the age of crabbed and ascetic bishops, whose black eyes and black robes would later sweep across Vinland like the wings of crows. True, they had white beards, white hands. But their narrow faces expressed only equivocal love (with bishops everything is equivocal). His mother Thjodhild was converted at once, and so was Thorstein, but his father refused to have anything to do with the new faith. After Thjodhild became a Christian, she refused to live with Eirik anymore. She could do as she wished, for by law one-third of the household wealth was in her power. Then Eirik hated her, and he hated Leif. Thjodhild built a church just over a little rise from the main farmstead at Brattahlid, so that Eirik would not have to look at it. She laid a polar bear skin in front of the altar, for the health of the perpetually kneeling priest.

Gudrid and Thorstein Eiriksson

In Thjodhild's church they sang and were silent and prayed and were silent. The women sat with folded arms (partly because it was cold). Bleak white light came in through the windows. Gudrid sat very still with bowed head. Thorstein trembled every time she shifted in her seat. He so much wanted to kiss her white throat. Her hair was the color of sunny wheatstraw. From behind, Thorstein watched her blonde hair fall down her shoulders like a waterfall, its ringlets making love to each other in complicated ways like the wooden ringlets of his father's bench-boards. But even then Gudrid had the round white cheeks, the smooth forehead of a prospective nun. – So they sat there in church for hours, while the grey light failed.

On the Lord's Day, Gudrid walked around on the hillside eating Arctic violets. She threw herself down on the sweet tundra. Sometimes the rocks were grown with white lichen-spots like clumps of daisies. There were many grassy spaces to lie on, and walls of rock, black and white, in the crevices of which grew egg-shaped cushions of moss. Later she and Thorstein sat together on one of those private seats. A tiny stream trickled down the rock beside them. Spiders span just above the moist places, and mosquitoes came to see if the water might be blood.

"And your father prefers you to Leif?" said Gudrid, smiling lazily. "You're sure?"

"Yes," said Thorstein, flushing.

So they were married. Gudrid slept with her cheek on her knuckles.

The Land of the Counterfeiters

By its delineation of Greenland, casting a solitary shaft of light through the darkness of five centuries, the map makes its strongest claim on our curiosity; and it is this feature, perhaps even more than the delineation of Vinland, which most clearly seems to lift the map out of its period, and might even suggest – were the converging evidence to the contrary less strong – the work of a counterfeiter.

> R. A. Skelton, Thomas E.
> Marston and George D. Painter,
> *The Vinland Map and the Tartar
> Relation* (1965)

Here it must be inserted into the tale that as Leif was sailing from Norway to preach King Olaf Trygvesson's new faith, he once again encountered difficult winds; and his ship was swept far south – all the way to Wineland the Good, in fact. There were great fields of wild wheat; there were grape-vines and maple-trees. Although King Olaf's priest waxed dangerously anxious, like a mosquito, Leif persuaded him that they would best fulfill their mission to the King by first exploring the new land to see if heathens or Christians lived there. – The weather was very fine. They saw a pretty island, dressed in gold and green. Leif led his men ashore, and they all rushed to drink the sweet dew. Then they sailed around the headland, and up a river to a place where there was a lake, and here they anchored. Between the lake and the sea was a rise, and on the far side of the rise they built turf houses, because it seemed luxuriously easeful to winter there. Wineland was a place without frost. – "This seems to me a very kind country," Leif said. "I'd have to say it's superior to the land my father discovered." Then he ate more salmon and grapes.

They filled the ship with timber and grapes on the vine. In the spring they set sail, with a favorable southern wind all the way. In three days they came to Markland; in two more they passed Slab-Land with its glaciers; they crossed the great abyss, Ginnunga Gap, in which fire and ice first mixed to create the nine Norse worlds; and then, just as the ice-peaks of Greenland came into their sight, Leif with his nervously keen eyes spied a shipwreck on a reef. He rescued fifteen people from the wreck, laying claim to their cargo of timber, and so returned home enhanced in wealth and reputation. People called him Leif the Lucky.

"But I say his luck and his ill-luck balance each other," Eirik said sourly. "He may have saved a wreck in the ocean, but he also brought that troll-carle of a priest here."

"People always say that I've inherited your luck," said Leif when he heard this. "If I have inherited bad luck as well as good, that must be due to you. And it seems to me your prestige was better when you led the settlers from Iceland than it is now."

"I see that you mock me now that I am old," Eirik said. "Ten years ago you would not have dared to say what you say now. You think yourself a bold enough whelp now. Time will tell whether or not you are humbled."

A Monkish Error

Here the *Flateyjarbók* says an odd thing: – namely, that the leader of the shipwrecked crew was named Thorir, and that he was married to Gudrid. But other sources insist that Gudrid was in Greenland during these years. In any event, the career of that much-married woman would not at all have been affected had she been espoused to Thorir, for the *Flateyarbók* now brings her home with Leif, whereupon Thorir conveniently dies during the winter and Gudrid marries Thorstein. – Certainly Gudrid and her marriages did not matter much to Eirik anymore, for he, old and defeated, died that same winter.* Greenland was now a Christian country, as was Iceland, where King Olaf had sent another mission while keeping some important Icelanders hostage. He did have a very zealous soul.†

---

* The *Hauksbók* keeps Eirik alive until Gudrid's subsequent marriage, so we will do the same.

† This almost-saintly Olaf is credited in some accounts for bringing six countries to the True Faith: Norway, Iceland, Greenland, the Orkneys, the Shetlands and the Faroes. May ODIN the High One have mercy on him.

The Death of Thorvald Eiriksson ca. 1003

Leif being surnamed the Lucky and Thorstein being married to Gudrid, the third son, Thorvald, decided to win his own fortune in Vinland. – Oh, he was rushing, rushing . . . – In the following year he borrowed Leif's ship and manned it with a crew of thirty. The autumn winds sped him to Vinland, and he settled in Leif's houses for the winter. There was an abundance of fish, and they never saw any frost. In the spring they sailed west, in the summer east, exploring at their ease among the fair forests that came almost to the shore. One day they came to a thickly wooded headland between two fjords, and Thorvald and his men wandered ashore, Thorvald exclaiming over how beautiful it was, and how much he wanted to make his home there, and then as they strolled back to the ship they saw three humps on the sandy beach. The humps were skin-boats, and under each one three Skrælings were sleeping. – "These must be outlaws," said Thorvald. "Kill them." – They divided into groups and seized all but one, who managed to escape in his skin-boat. Quickly slaying the other eight, they scanned the country more closely and saw other humps at some distance up the fjord, which they reckoned to be settlements. From these soon came a great army of Skrælings in their skin-boats, and Thorvald ordered his men to set up a defensive breastworks on the gunwales of his ship and ride out the attack there, conserving themselves and their weapons as best as they could. The Skrælings swarmed closer and closer and then began to shoot great clouds of arrows, which hummed across the water like insects and stuck in the side of the ship until it bristled. – "See the string-birds!" cried Thorvald, laughing. "See the glad-flyers!" – After a time the Skrælings gave up and paddled back up the fjord as quickly as they could. When they were out of sight Thorvald said, "Is anyone hurt?" – "No," said his men. – "Well," he said, "an arrow flew past my shield, and here it is." He pulled it out from under his armpit, and blood gushed forth. "I guess I will settle here for awhile after all. It's rich country; look at all this fat around my guts." Then Thorvald died, and they buried him there. They raised no rune-stone to him, but put a cross at his head and feet, and the place has been called Cross-Ness ever since. Then they filled the ship with grapes and grape-vines, and the following spring returned to Greenland.

The Voyage of Thorstein and Gudrid

Thorstein mourned for his brother, and said that Wineland must be a dangerous place, but Gudrid said that the grapes there were certainly very fine, at which

Thorstein said that the ship was full of them, so they hardly needed to bring back any more, at which Gudrid said that she wished she had married Leif. Gudrid sat at her loom, which was over two ells high, with its cross-post that always made Freydis think of a gallows, and strings of wool fell from the half-completed garment like rain, almost down to the ballast-stones; and she refused to speak to her husband until he agreed to go to Vinland. Then Gudrid kissed him.

Gudrid's father had a ship, and they manned it with a crew of twenty-five and set out that spring. But they encountered unfavorable winds, and were blown around all summer, sometimes to Iceland, sometimes to Ireland. A week before the onset of winter they made landfall in Lysufjord in the West Bygd.

In the West Bygd 1987

The white grass blew in the wind. The place seemed to be merely a tussock-bog at first, so long had the grass been growing. Then I saw the ancient stone-lined ditches, hidden under the hair-grass, and the huge rooms, now roofless and carpeted only with green grass; and I walked through the foot-wide passage-ways between, waist-deep in the ground. A black tree was growing in one of the old rooms. – There was a little rise, lined with straight stones, on which we all sat for a moment, enjoying the sun. In the hollow beyond, great slabs had been set in the ground. Then came a grassy dyke, and another chamber floored with moist moss. By the far wall of that pit were two slabs set upright, with just enough space in between them for me to stand in the grass, as in the old generations horse after horse had done: this was the one surviving stall of a stable. – I clambered up the little wall and saw another rise that bore a stone building whose floor was a single slab. (From a distance it looked like a square array of fire-stones.) Then came low ridges, and then the milky-blue fjord, whose face was traversed by thick lines of cloud-shadow.

The Greenlanders wandered through the ruins laughing. Their trousers were stained with sheep blood. The woman with the wide golden face threw herself down in the soft grass and began to sharpen her knife on a foundation-stone. The men wandered surely along the wall-tops; the boy found a feather and played with it before he gave it to the wind.

But why was the vegetation so lush here? I found the answer underneath the overhanging grass, which could be parted with the same degree of difficulty as a mop of human hair. There was a long rectangular cavity above the wall of stones which was full of something black and wet and moldy. It was what remained of charred wood after seven hundred years. It seemed most probable that some time after Ivar Bardarsson had made his journey to the West Bygd and found it as deserted as Roanoke, the Skrælings had come to this farm and set it ablaze.

The Talking Corpse

... so long, so darksome, and so bitter a winter ...

PELLHAM

That winter Thorstein and Gudrid were guests of Thorstein the Black. "You will be well provided for with food and lodging," said Thorstein the Black, "but you will find it dull here, because there are only my wife and myself, and I am quite unsociable. I am also of a different faith than yours." A disease soon came among them. The first to catch the sickness was Thorstein the Black's wife, Grimhild. She was a big woman, with almost as much strength as an ice-bear, but there was nothing for her to fight, unless she were to tear herself open with her hands, and so she declined, day by day. Then Thorstein Eiriksson fell ill. They lay down, and soon Grimhild died. Thorstein the Black went outside for a board to lay her corpse on. – "Don't be too long, dear friend," said Gudrid. (She was already calling him dear friend, just in case.) – Then Thorstein Eiriksson said weakly from his bed, "Look at Grimhild. I see her raising herself on her elbows." – Gudrid looked, and saw dead Grimhild slowly pushing her feet out of the bed and wriggling her grey toes like worms and feeling blindly on the floor for her shoes. She screamed, and Thorstein the Black came rushing in, and Grimhild's corpse fell back on the bed again, so heavily that the whole house creaked. The husband stood still for a moment, then said: "You will have to be content with your lot, Grimhild. It is too late for you to change yourself. But I will make a fine coffin for you." – No one else said anything. – At dusk Thorstein the Black went down to the landing-place to help his men put away the fish they had caught that day, and suddenly a house-carle came running down from the farm to tell him that Grimhild's corpse was trying to clamber into bed with Thorstein Eiriksson. When Thorstein the Black came into the house, that huge grey woman was at the edge of his namesake's bed. Thorstein the Black threw her down on the floor and drove an axe into her breast.

At nightfall, Gudrid's husband died. In the window was what in those times was called a Weird Moon, whose silver-yellow face foretold a death; and it seemed to Thorstein Eiriksson as he died that the moon was coming closer and closer to the window until he could see nothing but a coldly shining ball looming over him; what he actually saw was the grieving face of Gudrid bending down to take his death-kiss; and he felt her breath on his lips and suddenly remembered her on their wedding-day when she took a silver hairpin, whose head was a golden dome crowned with gold, and smiled at her husband and put up her loose maiden-hair; she covered her head like a married woman, and Thorstein, seeing the change in her, was grieved because he loved her hair and felt that it was his fault she must put it away, for she looked more than ever like a nun in her head-cloth; so now this passionless nun-head approached him like the moon, refreshing his eyes with light; and Thorstein could not tell whether he was falling into the moon or whether the moon was falling down upon him but he felt lost and lonely in the white light and jerked his body trying to swim out of it, so that Gudrid thought that he was pushing her away and stepped back, cut to the heart, and all at once the white light became silvery, and then black, and he was dead. Thorstein the Black took her on his lap and rocked her in his arms and tried to comfort her and promised her that in the spring he would take her to Eiriksfjord with her husband's body. Gudrid thanked him warmly.

Then the corpse of Thorstein Eiriksson sat up very slowly, and said, "Where is Gudrid?"

Gudrid prayed to GOD and asked Thorstein the Black if she should answer, and he said that she should not.

"Where is Gudrid?" said the corpse again.

Once again Gudrid said nothing.

"Where is Gudrid?" said the corpse, and Thorstein the Black walked over to the death-bench and sat down with Gudrid on his knee and asked his namesake what he wanted.

"I want to tell Gudrid her destiny," said the corpse. "Gudrid, you must not marry any Greenlander, because an Icelander will be your husband. Your descendants will be bright and excellent; the sacred dew will sweeten their blood. After your husband's death you will be ordained as a nun." Then the corpse fell back and was still forever. To keep his spirit from wandering again, they laid heavy stones on his grave. (I hope he is in it still, slumbering upon some sweet snow-breast.)

After this, Gudrid stopped calling Thorstein the Black her dear friend and began waiting for the Icelander who would increase her fortunes. In the spring Thorstein the Black sailed her to Eiriksfjord, and there he lived for the rest of his life. He was considered a man of great spirit. Gudrid went to stay at Brattahlid with her brother-in-law Leif. Soon afterward her father died, and she inherited everything.

Gudrid and Thorfinn Karlsefni

A trader named Thorfinn Karlsefni sailed from Norway. He was an Icelander: the son of Thord Horse-head, the son of Snorri, the son of Thord of Hofdi, whose wife Fridgerd was the granddaughter of King Kjarval of Ireland. It was known that he was a wealthy man; his sword-hilt was made of gold. He quickly fell in love with Gudrid and she married him. Until he died in Iceland many years later, they ate from the same bag and drank from the same cup. Between them was the silence of a stilled need. As is written in the *Flateyjarbók*, "Gudrid was a woman of striking appearance; she was very intelligent and knew well how to conduct herself among strangers."

These things came about as follows: – When he hove into Eiriksfjord, Karlsefni was welcomed, as he had much news of Norway and of the change of Kings there (for Olaf Trygvesson had been waylaid by the kin-friends of his former fiancée, Queen Sigrid the Haughty, whom he had slapped in the face so long ago, and her men cut his men down one by one and strove to overcome him as he stood on the prow of his Long Serpent, hurling spears, until at last matters were such that he was beneath the sea and they were above it and Queen Sigrid clapped her hands for joy); to which relation Eirik the Red listened several times over, glorying in the fall of any Norwegian King – for he hated them all; and Karlsefni bore a cargo of fine goods as well as fine tidings: silks, and woolens, and gilt-inlaid axes, and many similar things, which he invited Eirik to choose from as he desired; in consequence, Eirik's reputation obliged *him* to ask these Icelanders to stay with him through the winter and receive his best hospitality; and so self-esteem entertained self-esteem until Frost-Month, when Eirik began to get low in spirits; for though he was chieftain of all Greenland he did not have the resources to celebrate the Yule-days properly, it being impossible to grow any grain in Greenland, by reason of certain boreal winds that chilled the seed in the ground. Karlsefni, however, was delighted to continue playing the game of giving, and so he told Eirik to take as much malt and meal and corn from his ship as the feast required. It is not improbable that Karlsefni had already decided by then to ask Eirik for Gudrid's hand; certainly Eirik was content, for by giving Gudrid he repaid

Karlsefni for the ale-malt, and simultaneously assured Gudrid a successful future. So his honor-banners continued to brightly wave.

At Christmas the men sat in their brownish-blackish robes, laughing and shouting and staring into the fire while the women filled their cups. Karlsefni stroked his sleeve-buttons, which marched in a close-set army up to his elbows. – The women's robes tightened a little at the waist, whereas the men's fell straight. I know the robes better than the people, for I have seen photographs of the clothing excavated from the frozen graves at Herjolfsness.

So they made the red ale, in which bubbles rose to become bitter, cream-white foam, and they drank it and it tasted sweet, and soon they were happy by the hearth-fire and Leif walked up and down telling of blue-eyed Ingebjorg, King Olaf's sister, whom he had been quite unable to get out of his mind since he had returned to Greenland (and Karlsefni nodded blandly, not caring to tell Leif that Ingebjorg was now married to Sigrid the Haughty's nephew, Earl Rognvald); and Leif's sister Freydis was there with Thorvard, her husband; Freydis hoping that everyone would admire her new scarlet feast-cloak which was ornamented with lace (she had bought it privily from Karlsefni), but because the Christmas feast had become Gudrid's wedding-feast people did not pay as much attention to Freydis as she considered that she deserved, so she became drunk and abused Thorvard and even pelted him with bones, which all thought great sport to see, and Thorvard pulled his skin-hood over his face, which had colored, and took her hand as if to lead her home, but she did not want to go away from this warmth and noise and brightness back to Gardar, which was nothing but a black island in a black sweep of fjords, grinning with the white glare of snow-trails on blackness, grinning with long narrow fjords whose blackness vanished into blackness, and she wrenched her hand out of her husband's and said, "Many things will come to pass differently than you imagine." – "She holds his honor of little worth, it seems," said Karlsefni to Gudrid, but in reply, she only grimaced. Old Eirik the Red, who became drunk on a single draught now, stood by Leif telling over all the wrongs that he had suffered in his feuds, while his wife Thjodhild filled men's cups as Freydis scolded Thorvard more shrilly, and Eirik raised his voice, saying, "King Harald Fairhair's race has decayed, and I am glad of it, but when will the blight strike all those proud fools in Iceland?"; and when Leif strove to put in a good word for King Olaf Trygvesson, whom he liked better and better now that he was dead, the father leaped up to strike with his fists at the guests' bright shields that hung above the benches, so that there was a great din and clashing (at which Karlsefni's men grinned and whispered, "How the old dog barks!"); but soon the hearth-fire softened Eirik's anger, and he let his head fall on his breast and slept, his breath catching sometimes as if he were sobbing. So it was a very merry Yule. – Karlsefni and Gudrid played at chess. Both were expert players. ("The Icelanders," says Olaus Wormius, "are accustomed, during the long nights of winter, to cut out various articles from walrus teeth. This is more particularly the case in regard to chess-men.") In my mind's eye I can see Gudrid and Karlsefni at the game, like two facing visages of the temples of Angkor, whose stone noses are higher than ten men (now their faces are long since covered with jungle creepers); and in the background I see a herd of dark caribou running along the narrow white strip of an Esquimau carving. For all of this happened so long ago! – The ale was sweet in their heads; their skulls were honey-hives, like the lion's head undone by Samson, and so Karlsefni, his cup empty, drank Gudrid's face in his long low glances from the chessboard, and thought to himself: What a sweet brave girl! – for his head was muddled. Finally Gudrid saw that his soapstone cup was empty save for the foam-rings, and, smiling at him so gently, she filled it.

All that winter Gudrid kept talking to her husband about Vinland. Finally he agreed to sail there with her in the following spring. He purchased several ships, and took on a crew of sixty men, with five women accompanying them to serve their needs. These arrangements suited Gudrid very well – as they did her former sister-in-law, Freydis Eiriksdaughter, who saw in Gudrid's plans a chance to enrich herself.

Freydis Eiriksdaughter

Shee cast her greedy eyes upon us, and within full hopes of devouring
us shee made the more haste onto us, but with our hearty lances we
gave her such a welcome that shee fell down, and biting the very snow
for anger.

EDWARD PELLHAM, describing
a white bear in Greenland (1631)

Freydis was an excellent-looking woman, but her disposition was evil. We
already know the tale from the *Heimskringla* of King Onund's son, Ingjald,
who was fed a roasted wolf's heart to make him stronger and braver, and
after that he became wicked. So, too, Freydis's selfish cruelties were not
originally hers by nature, but came about simply because her stepmother
Thjodhild would not own her in her heart – or so it is incumbent upon
a historian to believe in this age of compassionate first causes, for how
could we hope, if people could be born wicked? – As a green stalk may
bend in two without breaking, so Freydis suffered many things when young
which would have killed her later. Once she was playing with Thjodhild's
coarse-wool comb, with its tine-spaces each as wide as a finger, and she
lost it and Thjodhild whipped her, saying, "I don't know who your mother
was, but she must have been a thief if she was your mother," and Freydis
turned pale, but said nothing. Later Eirik gave her a silver penny to smooth
her grief. In the evenings, when the farming work was done and they were
sitting by the long-fire, he taught her the names of Kings by letting her
play with coins from his store: – here were silver pennies from the mint
of Eric Bloody-Axe, of Canute, King Olaf, King Svein Forkbeard . . . and
Freydis loved the pennies and craved them. In her dreams she saw a hoard
of silver: silver spiral arm-rings, and finger-rings with dragons' heads, and
Byzantine reliquaries engraved with the faces of saints, and silver filigree
brooches, whose raised patterns wandered like gleaming berry-embroideries

in moonlight; and silver pendants for her to wear, and silver beakers that no one but she would be allowed to drink from; because, as with her father, her quickness longed for assurance. The mazy designs of these imagined treasures were for her as the bench-boards had been for Eirik, as the uncanny fjords had been for the Ice-Dreamers: the future was in them. So her love of gain was hard-bound to her, overpressing on her love of others until that was all gone. If Eirik had known what she dreamed about, he would have pitied her even through his anger at her greed; for never could she hope to have such riches in Greenland, where even iron was scarce, and ships were held together with tree-nails and baleen lashings. (Once, we read, some hunters burned a stranded vessel just to carefully pick the nails from the ashes.) – But Eirik did *not* know his daughter's dreams, because she concealed what was on her mind. From a great height, the roiling ocean seems as fine as a girl's skin; and Freydis's mood-twists were similarly imperceptible even to those who knew her well. When she dreamed, she was happy, because her foster-mother's insults passed entirely out of her mind. – Of course, the next day, and every day, she had to live beside her doing her wool-work. – When it rained, those two women sat by the long-fire weaving and carding wool and hating each other, and the rain ran down the translucent bladder-skin windows.

Thjodhild's Dream

This aged, lonely person went to bed early, cold and aching in her joints. She dreamed that CHRIST was in her. In those days the building of churches went on apace. In Iceland, the priests promised men as many places in heaven for their people as there were sitting-places in the churches that they built, so a great number of churches were erected. Through the loving kindness of the WHITE CHRIST she had been herself permitted to build a place of worship, in despite of her husband, and whenever she could she knelt down on the cold stones. Now in her dream she found herself glowing with the light of CHRIST; she was a lantern for His light because she had given herself to Him; she dreamed that this light penetrated through even to her stepdaughter Freydis until the girl was heart-scored with it and knelt at Thjodhild's knees begging for forgiveness; then Thjodhild blessed her and forgave her freely; but when she awoke, her heart and other hearts were as they had been before. So in the end Thjodhild had of that dream nothing but bitterness.

Queen, Castle, Rock

Sometimes when Freydis was little her father took her down to the mossy river where it was so bright at night, and daily it was bright; or he bought her a dress from Herjolfsness; or he let her sail with him all the way to the West Bygd in the spring, when little blue icebergs rested like clouds in the sky-blue calm of the fjords, and the farmers all gave her milk to drink and her father took her hunting in that vast stretch of low brown ridges threaded with snow and green water (puddles, lakes, rivers), and he pointed and she saw birds rising from the mountains to go to the inland ice; and once her father sailed west to kill whales and Greenland shrank and shrank until it was only a long blue ridge, white-topped, and Freydis was afraid that everything would go away but Eirik laughed shortly and said that everything was a big nothingness anyway, and she clung to him amidst the rocking of the boat, the soaring birds, the waves, as in a wind a fly clings to a tree-trunk, and everything was so joyous but presently he put her off from him, for weariness at Thjodhild's scenes. – "I never should have married that cow," he said often to himself. "Her horns are too sharp." – So Freydis tormented herself with her various griefs; and in time everything that she and Thjodhild did to each other was mutually checked and countered, as if their actions had been the ivory chessmen, then white, now glowing yellow and translucent brown, some carved like stacks of coins, others with serene blank faces, some like salt-shakers and the rest like whales'-teeth, army and army of them confronting each other now and forever in the National Museum in Reykjavík, and never a move to be made. Freydis grew up to be a pretty but rather sullen girl. People said she would not turn out to be very even-tempered.

The Hall and the Little Milkmaid

In those years of her father's middle age, Brattahlid stood proudly above its green plain, with the sheep grazing all around, and mountains rising across the water by Gardar and Hvalsey – for the hall was on a hill, fronting the water, so that all the Eirikssons had timely warning of anyone's approach. Behind it stood the home-mead, the barns, sheds and trading-booths. It too was wrapped round with turf. The floor was made of stamped earth and flagstones. A spring burst out between the pebbles of the floor, and Eirik had made a stone-edged gutter to lead the water into a well-basin in the middle of the long hall, where the water gathered and bubbled. The overflow ran through another narrow channel of stone and went out under the opposite wall. – "Here not even haughty Queen Sigrid can burn us out," Eirik liked to say. – Brattahlid was worshipfully attended by its hay-barns and cow-byres, which were thickly turfed around the walls, and their doorways curved as they went outward so that no snowy winds could harm the shivering cattle. Twice a day in winter Freydis had to go into the byres and squeeze between the dumbly suffering animals to dole out hay from the barn. In bad winters she had to feed them on fish and birch leaves. They became so weak and thin that in the spring they had to be carried out of the byres. Then they stood looking around them stupidly. After a long time they began to nuzzle the green shoots of the plant whose wood was called by the Skrælings qajaasat.* The sun shone upon their bony shoulders, and the wind blew, and the mountains stood behind great green tundra-bluffs spangled with ice, and the shore of the river below was still lined with it. It was very summery in the fjord, which was guarded by snow-peaks. – Freydis milked her cows, and dreamed of riches as she stood working among the butter-tubs. In the summers she took the sheep to pasture, and drove them home again across the wide and shallow streams.

Sometimes it was very windy, and the grey sea was covered with straight black wave-lines that made the fjord into a plain of rocky slabs. The dwarf poplars shook their heads violently against the wind, but because they were so low Freydis could look out across the land and retain an impression of stillness. The rocks did not move; the narrow white spill of Troll Falls did not change, but fell steadily in its silent stream (which from a distance seemed frozen), down a green cliff-top, down a white cliff-face veined with black, then down a steep green slope into the fjord. Birds still sang; the snow on the cliffs did not move; the clouds presented no new bellies, and only the wind itself expressed the storm that was coming. Even the sun still shone. But no matter how hungry they were, the poor thin cows would raise their heads and moan in low snuffling bellows at the weather, for they were afraid. Always they were afraid that it was winter again. When Freydis saw them failing to eat, she flew into a passion and lashed them with rope. But suddenly she would cease, and fall to comforting the creatures, because she could tell to a nicety (so she believed) when she was being watched from Brattahlid, by the prickling of her head. In fact, everyone in her family was

---

* "Little kayak." The leaves of this shrub are shaped like kayaks. Native Greenlanders say that a tea brewed from them will give strength to a hunter.

well aware of the cruelties that this little milkmaid inflicted, but Eirik chose
to say nothing, and the others, who came increasingly to dread her rages,
also held their peace.

Demons and Stones

When Freydis was a little girl her father took her on his knee and told her
the stories of the old times, and once he told her how good King Swegde
had gone looking for ODIN all through the world with twelve men, and he
came to Turkland, but ODIN was not there, and he wandered through the
Great Swithiod★ and into Vanaheim,† where he got a wife named Vana, and
he brought her home to Sweden and they had a son named Vanlande and
everybody said that King Swegde should stay home and be a happy King
for the rest of his life, but King Swegde had sworn a vow to find ODIN,
so after a time he returned to the Great Swithiod and went eastward, and
ODIN was not there, and King Swegde got drunk and despairing and it was
evening and the sun fell behind the forest, and then he saw a stone as big
as a rich man's house, and there was a door in the stone, beneath which a
dwarf was sitting. King Swegde was very drunk. He ran toward the stone
shouting. The dwarf leaped up and stood in the doorway, through which
King Swegde saw a glimmer, and the dwarf called, "Swegde! Swegde! Come
in, and I will bring you to ODIN!", and Swegde ran into the stone, which
closed behind him so that there was no door anymore; there had never been;
and King Swegde never came home. His son Vanlande succeeded him, but
Vanlande was destroyed by a Finnish witch. – Freydis believed this story,
because Greenland was inhabited by those artful and treacherous dwarves,
the Skrælings, who were known to be sorcerers, although the appellation
of "dwarf" rings now with an irony that Freydis could not have appreciated
because in M. Vahl's work of 1928 a researcher who dug up the frozen bodies
of fourteenth-century Norse women gives us "the picture of a race, greatly
deteriorated and degenerated through intermarriage and undernourishment,
a community of almost dwarf-like people crushed down by all the bodily
infirmities resulting from lack of proper nourishment . . ." – nonetheless, it
was true that when a Skræling wanted to become an *angágkoq*, or shaman, he
went into solitude and sat in silence beside a large stone, and when the time
was right he took a small stone in his hand and rubbed it against the

★ Russia.
† The Don River region.

boulder until his ecstasy came. Then he was given his assistant spirit; then when the people blew out the lamps in the snow-houses he could summon spirits, crying, "GOI! GOI! GOI!"; he could even call upon the dreaded AMORTORTAK, the giant black-armed monster, who yelled, "*A-mo! A-mo!*" and could murder with a touch (his victims, as I have said, turned black and died). Freydis, who was wise and intelligent, remembered this and resolved to call upon Him. She was very ill satisfied at having been born a bastard.

Amortortak 1987

"This is the medicine man's friend." The Inuk showed me a white carving, with wide eyes and big teeth, a carving that could leap. "And this one. All these. They hear the medicine man. He has an enemy and he sings; they come alive, kill his enemy."

"Are there medicine men in Greenland now?" I asked.

"No. The last one is dead."

"Will there be again?"

"Now we all believe in the GOD," he said contemptuously, "so it can never be again."

Her Soulscape *The Bay of Fundy, 1987*

The grass, brown as if pickled, is all smoothed down by the tide's enormous hand. A flat plain of it goes on and on. Half of the time it is covered by the sea, and the water is as the weather is, and one cannot see Freydis's underlying nature, but as the tide is out now we may walk farther and farther inside Freydis, our feet sinking deep into the welcome of that rubbery grass, on top of which, here and there, rest patch-flakes of mud; and there is mud in the little channels that are filled with the vinegar-colored sea. In those channels the water is very still, reflecting the overhanging grasses, except where loose algae-clots, seemingly dissolved, smear themselves across the picture. The channels drain into larger brown lagoons. The sea is so calm that it is hard to see any waves. Rich green grass grows on the mudbanks; grey gulls fly over the grass. In the mud are thin pointed slate-bits. – At the edge of the brown grass lie furry lumps of mud, which at first impression seem to be the scattered limbs of some dead animal. Then there is a little mud-cliff, waist-high, which affords a view of a sodden grey mudflat pricked by green stubble, stained by green algae and red clay, littered with rocks and oozing from furry puddles. A rock cast down into it sinks almost completely, with a wet squishy sound. The mud has the consistency of diarrhea. – Along the sides of the lagoons are places where the grass has been rubbed raw, exposing sand beneath; here can be seen tiny white shells. – It is possible to leap the wet mottled banks of some narrow channel and stand upon the mud hoping to see the fled ocean, but then the grass will give way with a ripping sound and the mud will give way and you slide helplessly, long brown hairs of grass sticking to your shoes, into the filthy stream, up which a long green string of half-dissolved algae swims, giving you your first hint that the tide is coming in. Presently things will be hidden again. – A good way inland, you can stand on a firm meadow of grass and dandelions and think that you have put that muddy vileness behind you, but then you will find inexplicable piles of rock-flakes, each flake as thin as a gingersnap, and you know that you are still not and never will be away from it.

Wearing the Dream-Shirt

I shall make his blue cloak red.

AASMUND GRANKELSSON, just before spearing
Asbiorn Selsbane (1024)

We all dream one dream. But Freydis dreamed seven. On the first night she dreamed of her silver hoard; on the second, of ice-bears; on the third, of black faces in the mountains; on the fourth, of rows of shining axes; on the fifth, of the death of her father. Then she dreamed the sixth dream. As a bleached white tree-bone, startling in its beautiful gruesomeness, may hang suspended against a wall of dark trees, so this sixth dream stood out in her thoughts. She saw her father holding a dream-shirt in his hands, shaking his head and hesitating as lately he so often did, having grown old. – It was a shirt with ribbed darkness inside, the ribs sprung and whorled into almost floral patterns, like some initial letter of the Codex Frisianus's *Heimskringla*. Carved black channels rushed between the white whorled bones. But it was immense; a mountain could wear it on its chest. Eirik wanted to put it on, but he knew that it would be too big for him. Shrunken and white-bearded, he stood holding the shirt and blinking. Suddenly he seemed to see Freydis. He beckoned her over to him and put the dream-shirt in her hands, and she saw that by no means was it too big for her . . .

In a happier family she might have called everyone to her to hear her dream. But when Freydis awoke, she told only her father.

"So it's you who will inherit my Blue-Shirt," said Eirik.

"But is Blue-Shirt a shirt that you put on, father, or is it inside you? – For you wear no blue today." Freydis asked questions such as these because she was a very practical woman.

"Blue-Shirt is a shirt you put on, as you would any shirt." After saying this, Eirik would say no more. But for a moment he put his arm around his daughter's shoulders.

The Whirlpool-Dream

What fiend is that   who guards the threshold,
and prowls round the perilous flames?

DAY-SPRING, on a visit to the Frost Giants

On the next night she dreamed the seventh dream. It seemed to Freydis in her dream that she had approached the table of some great King, who sat among his house-carles. She noted well which ones he smiled upon, and which he turned to with displeasure, chastising some, dismissing others; and when she felt sure that she had identified the men to whom the King most often turned his sunny face, she smiled at them and cultivated their friendship, until she could ask them to bring her before the King, so that she could go into his service. At length the King arose and swept open the casements, through which she saw a great white mountain on a sea-coast, surrounded by lakes of water that were of a dead nature although they boiled furiously all the time. Branches falling into these bodies of water became stone. In the sea were many whirlpools, and in them she saw the whirling faces of the King's courtiers, smiling or frowning as the King had smiled or frowned upon them. They whirled and whirled until the sea had stripped their flesh from them, and they became skulls. The mountain rose high above the revolutions of those lost souls. After a time the sun came out beside it, and turned it blue.

"That mountain is Blauserk," Eirik said when she told him her dream. "That was the great blue glacier I first saw so many years ago when I sailed west from Snæfellsness."

"But why have I dreamed that dream?" cried Freydis.

"Because you must go there," her father said. "Go alone, and tell no one."

The Evil Traveler

Freydis set out in her finest clothes. She combed her hair; she put on her bronze brooches (which are now green in her grave). She was wearing a mantle dyed with black and scarlet. It was high summer when Freydis set out upon her way. – The wind sounded like women laughing together riding down a waterfall.

Down the fjord she sailed, with two thralls who were to wait for her. The sun went round and round in the sky, but the clouds were arrows pointing behind one black snow-cliff. The other cliffs were black and white and green. Sometimes there were lines on their faces like rivers. At night the sea was blue; the mountains were blue and gold. – She wondered when she would return. "What will I become by then?" she thought. "What have I become?" (Perhaps the only time when the meaning of life becomes an issue is when you are waiting for something to happen.) – Shortly after midnight the sun went behind a ridge, and thereafter, as Freydis continued on her way, the snow and the sky seemed paler, though no less luminous. The green fjords, where her father's settlers had built, became olive-brown as she passed them, and then they receded like memories. The ridges merged with the mountains behind them, so that it seemed that the peaks were but ridge-caps. – At last she came to the open sea, and then her craft sped down past Herjolfsness, where Bjarni Herjolfsson had returned from that accidental Vinland voyage, where Gudrid and her father had first wintered in Greenland; and then Herjolfsness was gone and a mist came and went, and Freydis had rounded Cape Farewell. Leif's luck-wind was working neither for nor against her; so it was with Leif. – She followed the coastline north and east. Here for the first time she began to encounter ice. At last she could go no further. Mount Blauserk loomed high above her with chill shining from its horrible blue shoulders. So her father had seen it, when he first fled Iceland and sailed due west from Snæfellsness. So the Skrælings would see it a thousand years later, although by then the ice had bleached a little. – "Wait for me here as long as necessary," she commanded her scared thralls. She fastened the *skóbrodar*-spikes to the soles of her shoes. Then she slung her traveling-bag over her shoulder, grasped her staff, and stepped onto the ice.

The Edge of the Frozen Sea

At low tide the ice was muddy and made a constant trickling sound. Rocks and ice-boulders rested in the middle of it. Every few moments came the smash of ice breaking. Sometimes there was a little rustling noise, but it was only sand spilling from crumbling sandhills. The wind made a steady sound above the walls of the valley, each of which was a series of slabs seamed by ice-rivers. As ice fell down the cliffs, the noise of its smashing echoed like cannon-shot. It was a daunting place, but just as a stream may travel slowly down its way-course, deflected by stones but unhindered, so Freydis held to her direction – although whereas a stream is remorselessly patient, she herself would not wait a thousand years, and it was that failing which enslaved her to Blue-Shirt.

The water in the leads was blue and green. Sometimes the edge sheared off the floe that Freydis was walking on, or the floe tilted and began to sink, or her foot broke through a rotten spot in the ice. Every step was a gamble; if she fell, she would die. The leads made long rivers which she must sometimes jump across. Although the middle of the fjord was frozen smooth, getting there involved clambering over rough drifts of shore-ice which were often unstable, so that she fell into jagged ice-troughs in which the sea-water had pooled. It was an immense labor to drag herself across this waste, although she was a strong woman. At ebb-tide the channels became dripping canyons, with stones and darkness at the bottom of them. After she had achieved the smoother ice, the heartbreaking flatness and endlessness of the ice impressed upon her the tedium of her way ahead, and later, after many days upon the floes, the long ridges of stone which she must traverse one after the other made her want to cry. It was too early for the purple flowers, and even had it not been she would not have cared.

FROZEN FJORD IN SLAB-LAND

The Vestibule

The western wall of Blue-Shirt's valley was formed of slabs, each slab being a tall narrow pentagon, so that the ridge-top was a series of sharp black points. In the evening the sun came just over the wall, and the little rivers gleamed unbearably, as did every speck of mica in the granite boulders. The sun was hot on her cheek.

Skulls and Loneliness

She saw a grey rabbit skull frozen half in the ice. There was snow in its eyes, and there was ice on its teeth. It was waiting for the midsummer thaw so that it could be ground into the mud and buried. Here as in Slab-Land the boulders waited out the good weather, half-sunk in the mud like crocodiles. Some had faces. The little streams waited to become terrifying columns of water that fell from mountains to roll boulders as if they were marbles. The ice waited to fall in lethal slides (not that it meant to do harm, for after it fell and killed reindeer it was still waiting for something). Considering full well the fact that red hair lightens upon a putrefying human head, but blonde hair darkens, I conclude that Freydis must have walked a tightrope of decay; so now as she went higher and higher along the knife-ridge of death (though she came proudly dressed, because she did not want Blue-Shirt to believe that her hand could be had for the asking), she maintained a fixity of purpose to steady her; oh, yes, she was one of the Ice-Dreamers. – In the moss was a perfect lemming skull. A flower grew through its eye. – Freydis's skull, not yet freed, grinned inside its bloody flesh.

The Dead Land

As she walked across the sand, the wind blew in increasingly fierce gusts. The valley was very sunny and empty. Sometimes there were little rivers to jump over or wade through, rushing through the sand, their beds black or cobbled with colored pebbles; near these streams she often sank in wet sand up to her ankles. Hour after hour she walked. There was no place to rest from the wind, for here the valley was a bowl, its sides dull with sand-fans from slides. At length she saw a solitary boulder far to the east, and made for it thankfully. Sitting down in the sand, she rested her back against it and ate. The wind knocked down her walking-stick and swept over her face. Shivering, she fastened her hood. Despite the wind, sounds remained as inhumanly perfect as crystals. Sometimes she could not tell whether what she heard was the sound of a distant ice-fall or of her own thongs striking the boulder she leaned against.

Farther north, the valley was packed hard with tiny stones, a flat, ringing pavement broken up by blue streams. As Freydis looked down, she saw a spider crawling along in the flatness, with a great leaf on its back. The insect stopped for a moment and studied her as she studied it; then it continued on its way. Two black geese quacked and quacked at her. When she came near to kill them, they took flight, showing their feather-skirts in a rush of black and white.

Presently her way began to narrow. There was a gap in the mountains, through which the wind howled, and on the other side the V-gaps between the black pentagonal slabs were filled by hanging glaciers. At this spot was a stony rise, down which flowed many milky streams which Freydis must

now cross. Thrusting her staff into the water for balance, she strode from
stone to stone, grunting like a bear as she shifted her weight.

She slept in a wretched spot, a sandy hollow surrounded by dark tombstone-
like boulders, behind which was an icefall. There were bear-prints in the sand.
At night the sand hissed in the wind, blowing in her face, and the sun glared
at her from atop a row of black mountains. As the skin-tent fluttered, so her
heart beat in the wind. – In the morning it was very cold. Mica sparkled
in the sand. The sky was clear, but a white cloud hung over every icefall
that she could see. As she prepared to go on her way she heard a rumbling
noise, and then the steady deliberate rhythm of something heavy walking
down the mountainside on boulders. Her heart pounded. But she could see
nothing. She searched behind the boulders and found a cave formed by a
pile of grim black rocks. In front of this lay the vertebrae and ribs of some
small animal, dislocated from the carcass and left immaculate.

Whiteness and Wind-Voices

As the valley continued to slope upward, the greenish-white streams between
the gravel-bars became wider and wider. Little white points of foam danced
in them where they struck rock, but this whiteness was not of the same
character as the whiteness of the icefalls and tumble-block glaciers on the
cliffs around her, for while the stream-foam had about it the lightness of
motion and seemed less chilly than it was, the ice was dirty, blue-white,
massive and very still. At some time it, too, might well move, but that Freydis
did not want to see. – Mount Blauserk reared ahead, an ominous blue tower
of ice. – Now she must traverse steep sand dunes overlooking the river, and
sometimes the sand was beset with funnel-holes down to the melting ice
beneath, and the wind ruffled the water on the big green river and chilled
her as she walked. It often seemed to her that she heard voices in the wind:
– sometimes the laughing talk of two women, other times a man's whistled
tune, but the melody proved always to be the cries of birds, and where the
women's voices came from she could never tell. The crumpled icefalls were
motionless and blue.

Next she had to ford waist-deep rivers, which task she did not love at all,
but even though her likeness was uncarved in her father's bench-boards she
was well aware that she could not change her fate. The water refreshed her
feet at first, but by degrees those went numb, and so also her legs, until
she could no longer feel the bottom beneath her save as a ship's mast in

Gore-Month knows the ice that girdles it. Therefore she grabbed with her pole for hidden pits of stumbling; she hen-stepped along with locked knees; but her pole bent and trembled and the current forced her knees apart and turned her downstream. She knew that if she were pulled down she would likely be killed, so at last she had to back out and stand on the bank shivering, rest a moment, and then go upriver or downriver, to a wider place or a place where there were whitecaps, which meant boulders that she might be able to step on. When she forded one braid, there was always a rise of loose boulders, and then many more braids all green and silver in the sun. All around her she heard the loud and steady buzzing of the rivers, the rocks grinding together into sand, the humming starting and stopping abruptly, changing pitch inexplicably. (In the clear creeks she often saw, caught between colored stones, the crescent of a leaf, which gleamed silver like a Skræling's *ulu* blade, or blue like a mussel shell.) – Sometimes the rivers were green and sunny, and then she liked them, particularly when she was thirsty. They seemed calm, like grief smoothed away with gold. But in the evenings, when the runoff increased, the rivers whined and she could hear the boulders sing with the voices of drowned people, in a dim gravelly underwater chorus. Then poor Freydis was as scared as a child.

Again she slept, crowded by black dreams. The next morning was so cold that she dreaded to put on her damp shoes, which had become half-frozen overnight. The river gleamed golden in the sun, the mudflats orange. The great scarps, bastioned by piles of their own jagged debris, were softened by the snow upon them which rounded their peaks into shapes almost within the calculus of mercy. But ahead were other towers too steep for even ice to cling to. The landscape became one blue and orange jaggedness, scarcely relieved by the few stretches of grass, moss, even flowers which Blue-Shirt contemptuously permitted to grow. And every meadow was blasted by grey lichen-frost.

Once again the pass narrowed, and its walls steepened until she was forced to descend into the wilderness of rocks just above the river-cliff, and the river breathed its chilly spray-breath and fog-breath on her until she was soaked to the skin. The boulder-edges she clung to cut her hands. The roar of the river was maddeningly loud. It pressed upon her like the weight of that cold grey water, which would sweep her away with it if she were to fall. But she must go where her dreams led her. Her hand-holds were icy-wet from waterfalls. A cataract drenched her, and the cold made her ache to the bone. Meanwhile, though the sky was mild, a thin white mist of cloud covered it. The white roofs of the mountains now gleamed all the more splendidly. In the sand, little mica-grains shone more brightly now that they need not compete with the sun. White falls of water spilled down the cliff-rims from overhanging glaciers, to be lost in shadowy crevices from which no rainbow came, and then presently to reappear lower down, much stronger and wider as they rushed into the river that coursed so ruthlessly down toward the far-off Ice Sea, sliding around the sharp grey polygons of rocks, falling and leaping and making its sinister whitecaps; freezing, drowning and crushing all but the strongest who sought to cross it, killing even with its mist, chilling those who remained too long beside it; and yet it had no malice. – But Freydis thought that it did, because she saw others as she saw herself. – In fact the river's only desire was to release itself from everything, rushing away and away and away, growing stronger and more fulfilled in itself the farther it went, until at last it was satiated in the loving coldness of the sea.

Presently a cruel rock rose in front of her, wet and icy. Freydis could not climb over it. Heartbreaking as it was, she must turn back through the jumble of frozen boulders, clinging to them with bleeding hands with the river grinding in her ears, until at last she found a way to climb a hill of dangerously unstable scree, and then, trembling a little (but only a little, because Freydis remained an exceedingly single-minded woman), to traverse a steep wall of sand which crumbled beneath her feet, with the river a good distance below, and always the crack of falling rock and ice about her; and the higher she got the more voices she could hear in the wind; and after clambering up a jumble of boulders she found herself upon a plateau at the foot of a single mountain that rose in many mad black columns, with the sun very white behind it, and the grey lichen now looked soft and welcoming to her, because it was the only thing that grew. Black boulders burst out of the earth with fractures like downturned mouths. There was music in the wind. Hard cruel women were singing, women much harder and crueler than she. Their lyre was made of mountain-teeth. In their song she could hear only a few words – something about white witches over the sea. Beyond rose Blue-Shirt's peak, and it was shining hurtfully with the Ice-Lights.★

★ "Some hold," says the *Speculum Regale*, "that fire circles about the ocean and all the bodies of water that stream about on the outer sides of the globe; and since Greenland lies on the outermost edge of the earth to the north, they think it possible that these lights shine forth from the fires that encircle the outer ocean. Others have suggested that during the hours of night, when the sun's course is beneath the earth, an occasional gleam of its light may shoot up into the sky; for they insist that Greenland lies so far out on the earth's edge that the curved surface which shuts out the sunlight must be less prominent there. But there are still others who believe (and it seems to me not unlikely) that the frost and the glaciers have become so powerful there that they are able to radiate forth these flames" (XIX.150–1).

In the evening a wild hare, snow-colored, saw her from across a stream and was not afraid. Blue-Shirt Glacier was a pillar to mark her way. The sun wheeled round and round the mountains, making each snow-tip orange in turn, while the rocks fell and the ice shattered, instantaneously swelling the roar of waterfalls, and the creeks trickled and the tundra meadows moved scarcely a muscle in the wind. It was all unspeakably grand and beautiful. The world was still being created here.

Love-Song for Amortortak

Picking her way up a moraine of white boulders, through which a creek flowed, Freydis Eiriksdaughter clambered from stone to stone as if ascending stairs, and they endured her weight, though giving forth grating sounds. The sun was hot on her knees; the wind blew her hair in her face. Ahead of her the hillside steepened, and the glacier trough was littered with huge slabs resting on the river of smaller boulders, ready sometime to continue their tumble to the valley floor, as other rocks and ice-rocks did every few moments; and Freydis was a little daunted; but greed was her bravery, so she clambered along upon the slabs, and so continued. Mount Blauserk dancingly vanished and reappeared before her shining eyes. There were little hummocks of green grass and ankle-high trees on either side of her. Presently she came to the end of the slabs, at which the mountain steepened still further, and she had her choice of a smooth inclined wall of stone streaked with black tracks of rockslides, or the scree of those slides, and after some thought she chose the scree because on it her feet were less likely to slip. The peak rose sharply ahead of her. It was in the shape of an *ulu*, and was called Ulu Peak by the Skrælings, although Freydis knew neither of these things. To the south of it was a sort of saddle joining it to another mountain; this saddle formed a steep hollow that glittered with stone and ice. Another stream was born here, and made its cold and silvery way to the icebound river below.

At this spot Freydis took a stone in her hand and struck it against a boulder three times, calling on AMORTORTAK as she had seen the Skrælings do, for she knew that AMORTORTAK and Blue-Shirt were one and the same. – Nothing happened. – Crying loudly, "*AMORTORTAK!*", she struck the boulder again, this time with all her strength so that the stone cut into her hand and a white flake chipped off the boulder and there was the smell of sulfur and ice fell from the rim of the western cliff and smashed upon a boulder with a terrifying sound, and then a drumming began from behind the hills which did not stop, day or night, until she found Him.

At the Foot of the Ice-Mountain

Now there was nothing but Blue-Shirt, Blue-Shirt, drumming in her blood; every beat of her heart was for Him because she had not possessed Him yet and coveted Him so badly that she was sick; and she rushed upward among the mountains faster than prudence would have advised, but was certain that she climbed charmed stairs of rocks that would not fall because *He* had called her in the Dream of Ice as He had called her father; so Freydis had faith. Now Mount Blauserk rose so high and close that it was like the sky. Boulders were heaped up against its ice-walls, and it was among these that she now wound her way. – Sometimes the rockslides were so old it seemed the very rocks were moldy, being covered with mounds of white lichen; occasionally even the lichen was overgrown with moss and crowberries. – The drumming sounded fiercely in her ears. Whenever she stopped for a moment to lean gasping on her polestaff, the drumming grew louder still and then a boulder would roll past her down the mountainside. This made her uneasy. For awhile, therefore, she turned from the stream and walked upon the meadow, stepping from mound to mound of moss. Halfway up she came to a stone like a canted pyramid. It had an up-grinning mouth, so she knew that she was going in the right direction. – Here and there the turf was ripped up from rockslides. Huge boulders were sunken into the moss, and the earth around them was raw and wet. Ahead was the great blue Ice-Mountain, which became more vertical the closer she got to it. Little white chips of stone lay upon the moss. The Mountain was a busy place, and none of its business was for Freydis's good.

The sun lurked behind the western ridge, so that the valley was in shadow. The water had advanced considerably across the mud in the last day. Little chunks of ice floated in it. Soon the bottom of the valley would be one vast riverbed. To the south she could still see the ice-sheet, but it was cracked and contracted now. Freydis felt so lonely that even that creaking waste of frozen ocean would have been as home to her now. – Ahead of her, the Mountain glowed in the sun that was too high to reach her. It was golden and magnificent and terrifying. (Most frightening would be if AMORTORTAK were not there; if No One were there.)

Skulls and Clouds

Now Freydis could see the way she must take if she would go on to her master. Above her, sky-high over Ulu Peak, the glaciers were cloud-roads,

hanging over the edges of mountains just far enough to tempt her, but to
walk such a road (which she knew she would have to do) she must first climb
a mountain of dirt and gravel, slipping as she went, the dirt crumbling away
beneath her every step and hissing down to the river far below; and sometimes
the rocks she stepped on slid away as well, making landslides as they rolled
down to the river; and after this ordeal came the brittle glacier-edge that
projected into space, wet beneath with icy stream-heads, and if Freydis were
to go under it a piece might break off and fall on her, but if she went onto
it it might break off beneath her weight and then she would fall down the
cliff, down to the sunny green river to be shattered and drowned; so she must
walk among the loose boulders alongside the glacier until she judged it solid
to walk on; and even after that she must watch for soft spots and crevasses. But
she had to do it. Blue-Shirt was all around her. – Freydis combed her hair; she
fastened on her fur-lined woman's cloak, which had a hood of costly felt. She
secured the cloak-ends at her right shoulder, with a fibula of gold. Then she
bent her knee (to Whom you well can guess). – "At all events," thought she,
"I have done what I can to succeed in my ends." – Sucking on this conclusion
with satisfaction, she strode along until she saw a likely glacier that would take
her past the grey slab-mountains rising above gravel-shoulders, and then, her
resolution squared by a breath, she began to ascend. A shy half-moon was
in the southern sky. The sun was in the west. Cloud-wisps supplicated the
moon behind ridges. Because the sun was riding the top of the slab-wall,
that cliff was in shadow, while the river was still sunny and green.

The glacier was a wide blue road that became the entire world as she went
forth upon it. It was slippery, slit with crevasses and black with dirt. It seemed
to fall away from her at every step, curving down into the clouds. Here again
she must fasten the *skóbrodar*-spikes to the soles of her shoes. – Moistening
her lips, Freydis squinted ahead at the glazed sunny snow. The valleys and
mountains below had become very distant. Above her was a slanting wall of
icy boulders; below her was the same, all the way down to the river below.
She was so high that she could hear the sun launching spear-beams against
the ice; she could hear the wind blowing far below her. – Vertigo, vertigo! –
The palms sweat, the face sweats, the knees grow weak, and she must look to
neither right nor left. – Finally there were only sunny rocks, tightly compacted,
each one as brittle as ceramic. They clinked and slipped melodiously as she
trod upon them. She was in the middle of a frozen stream of boulders. They
were poised above her with their sharp edges. As she followed the glacier's
ascending spiral, stones brushed her right elbow and her right cheek, so steep
was the mountain here. Presently the way was broken by a steep tongue of

JOLLNIR PEAK, SLAB-LAND

ice a dozen ells in breadth. It was smooth, glassy and treacherous. Below
were clouds and Nothing. Here she longed piteously to return, but her will
sent her forward to cut footholds in the ice. She crossed it, she clung to it;
it brushed her elbow, her cheek. (Thus Blue-Shirt first caressed her.) There
was a rock in the middle of it, and on the rock was a bluish-white spider.

Round and round went her road, and as Freydis struggled up that great
blue wall she had the sense not of being watched but of being *known*, known
so well that AMORTORTAK and His creatures took no trouble to spy on her.
When her way seemed especially dangerous, this comforted her; at other
times it irked her, but her eager need never abated. – Then the weather
began to change. It had nothing to do with her, she was sure; Blue-Shirt
could not be bothered to put on his weather for *her*. – First she felt His wind
on the backs of her hands. The cold took her breath away. That wind blew
so cruelly! It blew and blew, continually changing its direction. It numbed
her face. It wrenched the golden fibula from her cloak and flung it into a
crevasse. Then her cloak-ends began beating her in the face, no matter how
tightly she crossed her arms, and though at first she relished the stinging in her
numb cheeks, the beating went on until the blood came. The wind-scream
was so loud in her ears that she could not hear His drumming anymore and

became confused, and staggered on the ice. At the same time the difficulty of going forward increased, so that at times she must clamber straight up from ledge to ledge of that night-wall that imprisoned her no less because she clung to it of her own free will (the wind would gladly have taken her); and how much farther Blauserk might rise into space she could not tell. – But she knew that she towered over the shattered ice-plain of the frozen sea! She could see a dark outline of her reflection gliding with perfect ease just beneath the surface of the shiny ice; by some freak or witchcraft she could also see her own face retreating as she advanced, so that it seemed that her double was walking unwillingly backwards, giving up the low ground that *she* seized to take the higher, and her hair was matted and her face was wild; now suddenly she perceived a third, a fourth reflection; there was an image of her in every facet of the great ice-crystal that she climbed; and her face was writ small in every stray snowflake that swirled in the wind; there were so many of her that she could not be counted! – "I'm an army!" Freydis said aloud. "I'm bringing my army to you, Blue-Shirt, and I'm going to conquer you and take what I want! They'll call you Bare-Back when I'm done with you, do you hear?" – For the height, the cold and the dizziness had crazed her a little. – Now the wind died down, and she heard a ringing of bells in her ears; it sounded like the ringing of a bell called Joy which her stepmother Thjodhild had presented to the church; but the drumming of AMORTORTAK was louder. The bell tolled; she thought she saw it swing; she thought she saw the ice-peaks rocking in the wind. The weather grew worse. Freydis felt as cold as if she were naked. She shivered; she leaped recklessly upward from ledge to ledge to warm herself; she whirled her polestaff around her head, yet still she could not keep warm. Then the wind began to whistle again; she could hear it coming from far away, from somewhere on the other side of the mountain where the inland ice began (it went on forever). There was a great clamor of rocks falling in that wind. In a panic she ran along her ledge to find some refuge, for she knew how easily the wind could pluck her away when she was hemmed between cliff and abyss. But of course she could find nothing. At that moment she hated Leif for inheriting the family luck. (She did not hate Blue-Shirt because she was already His.) – Again for a space the wind subsided, and she used her grace to spring higher while she could, hoping that the ice-cliff might be somewhere riddled with caves, in one of which she might huddle (it seemed to her conception that Blauserk must be an anthill of ice, extending under the entire world with its rotten passageways and swarming trolls – but this notion was entirely due to her faith; for she had not seen a single sign of Him: not a single skull, or iron

arrow; still she *must* believe her dreams). She fled up ledge to ledge, and in
due time she reached another wide glacier-shelf, which wound round and
round the mountain as before; once again that was her road. Now there
were places of a hundred ells' width where the glacier was punctured by
great sharp boulders, between two of which she spied a hollow lined with
rocks, lichen and snow, which might afford a little shelter. The stones in
it were round and blackish-green. Many of them were set into mud and
moss, so that Freydis had no difficulty in prying them loose. But as soon as
she began to erect her skin-tent, the wind screamed and knocked it down
and tore at it and snatched it into the air, beating it and shaking it even as
it buffeted her, and almost tearing it from her grasp. With all her strength
Freydis held to one corner and slowly, slowly drew it down to her, pulling
during the weaker wind-breaths, and at other times merely waiting, for she
could do no more. Her hands were muddy and bloody. Moment by moment
she struggled to reclaim what was hers, dragging her tent out of the
wind's fists and clutching it to her heart, ell by ell, as if it were her most
darling treasure – as indeed it was, for without it she might well not live. So
at last she was ready to begin again. – By now it had begun to rain. It was a
cold, heavy, stinging rain. The raindrops struck her face like nails. When the
wind-gusts momentarily abated, Freydis weighted down each corner of the
skin-tent with a stone so heavy that she could barely roll it into place, but in
doing so she stripped the moss away and left wounds in the raw mud, which
the rain soon washed away until the smooth ice showed beneath like bone,
and then the roaring wind rolled the stones away on the ice and bent its
wooden poles until they snapped. – Freydis was soaked and filthy. The rain
had turned to sleet, and presently became snow, pelting her crumpled tent
until it was a white drift. Then the wind lashed it, and it twisted and writhed,
but the snow clung to it as the snow clung to her; for she was now so weary
that she could scarcely brush it off. – Freydis understood at last that she could
not hope to raise her tent. There was nothing to do, tired though she was, but
continue on her miserable way. It took her half an hour to roll the tent around
the poles again, such was the wind. There was no chance of rest. She tightened
the drawstring of her hood as much as she could; then she must raise her face
to the storm once again, and at once her cloak-ends began beating her face,
and she staggered upward through the fog and wind, with snow piling up
on her elbows and head and shoulders.* The mist had thickened to such a

* What straits she was in cannot be imagined by those who have not been alone and
at the mercy of an Arctic storm. The edge of the sharpest and most cunning word is dull
in comparison to a knife of wind.

degree that she could barely see her own feet. Although she did not know it, this saved her from many vertiginous dangers, for there were now several places where the way was but a hand's breadth wide, on either side of which waited destruction from crevasses, but because the Nothing was filled with fog she could not see it, so it could not draw her down. Freydis clambered up the stony ice, gasping for breath, and her breath-clouds mingled with the fog. Often she thought that she must have to abandon the attempt, but had she done so there would have been no hope for her, and that was the only reason that she staggered on, pulling herself up by means of icy slabs she could barely see, sobbing words of praise to Blue-Shirt for His road that guided her up His great ice-wall; and whenever she was compelled again to embrace the ice while working her way up from a narrow ledge she rested her ear against it and listened for the drumming sound she craved, as one might put ear to a mother's belly to hear the movements of the fetus in her womb; though Freydis could not be sure that she heard anything, yet somehow doing this comforted her; and blindly, faithfully, with her head sunk almost upon her breast, she followed Blue-Shirt's road – first, as a baby follows its mother's face with its eyes; then, as she continued on in that hellish white darkness, the drumming came into her heart again, and she followed that crag-way with mature and steady purpose, as was her duty; but then hailstones rattled down on her and broke open the skin of her frostbitten face in many fresh wounds and the wind slowed her steps and aged her; and finally, as she pulled herself from ledge to ledge, her own dear drumming faded as her last strength left her, and when she came to another shoulder on the ice she hobbled as slowly as a crone, praying to Blue-Shirt: "Please let me die!" – So she called on Him a second time. (Never before or after in her life did she say these words.) Then it seemed that He was satisfied, for all at once she reached a sort of cave formed by two great slabs of stone leaning against each other on the hillside. She crawled inside that cold dead womb and fell down upon the stone. There she fainted, and slept out the storm, her strength returning by degrees as she slept (and the drumming once again grew loud and confident in her ears), so that at last, when after many hours the sky became sunny and icy-blue, she awakened, and her intention was frozen harder than ever in her. – Freydis was one of the bravest women in the world. She had to be, because she had only herself. Or so it seemed to her. – Thus she clambered up the Ice-Mountain, which was sheer, and every foothold was slippery with ice. She climbed seven thousand ells. At last she could see the summit rising in a snowy wall that was sometimes silver, sometimes blue or gold, depending on the mood of the Sun, and up this wall Freydis went, cutting steps with

her double-bladed axe, ascending through light and clouds and light and
clouds with not a shadow on that metallic snow whose colour could never
be defined: – it was not blue, not really.

The Palace of Amortortak

For the wonders of Iceland and Greenland consist in great frost and
boundless ice, or in unusual display of flame and fire, or in large fishes
and other sea monsters.

Speculum Regale, X.105

Atop this mountain was a castle made of ice, like a skull on the mountain's
blue shoulders. The walls were fortified with frozen stones and beams of ice
seven ells thick. Upon the battlements walked demons and little misshapen
Skrælings armed with horn-bows. A ramp ascended to the main gate; down
its middle was a set of rails, at the top of which was a wagon loaded with
hailstones and boulders. Demons stood on either side of this cart, holding
fast to ropes made of walrus-hide. In the event of any attack, the wagon
could be let down upon the rails so that it would rush toward the besiegers
faster and faster until finally the demons pulled upon the ropes to check it
suddenly, and the missiles came flying out upon the men below to crush
them. Forty ells below the parapets of Blue-Shirt's castle, guards strutted upon
wooden brattices, walking round and round the walls like flies, so that they
could see movement from any direction. Atop the ramparts were cauldrons
of ice-stones so cold as to burn, feeding upon their own chill; this molten
frost could be poured down upon anyone who approached the castle walls, so
that he would freeze and fall down tinkling into a thousand shattered pieces.
Demons leaned upon great poles of sea-horn shod with points of iron-hard
ice; these could be cast like spears. In addition, the ice all about the base of
the wall was mined and covered with snow carefully raked, so that no one
unfamiliar to Blue-Shirt would know where he could safely step, if he were
to go off the main path. These mines were deep and narrow pits filled with
silently burning flames of cold-fire. Above the castle-roof was constructed
a second roof of ice and snow, set upon thick ice-posts, so that an armed
host hurling stones over the battlements could do no harm.

Boldly Freydis approached. In truth Blue-Shirt's fort was a grim place,
but she felt such joy and relief to have reached her goal that it held no

terror for her. – "Certainly they know how to defend themselves here," she said to herself, "but it may be something worries them, or they would not take so much trouble over it." – As for the sentries, they scrutinized her in silence, marching round and round on their brattices with their hands on the hilts of their swords. But when she reached the base of their ramp, the demons all shouted and grinned at her, and the troll-guards urinated down on her. So well did they know her. – Biting her lip as she suffered this treatment, Freydis ascended the ramp, at the top of which loomed that great hailstone-cart, and the demons made as if to loose the ropes that held it in such steady suspense over her. Once again Freydis affected not to notice. But it was certainly very disagreeable to her to be treated as she treated her own thralls. The demons sniggered. Their repulsive features, which were neither yellow nor black in hue, twitched in their merriment, and their naked bodies shook so hard that their arrows rattled in the quivers. When they blocked her path, Freydis shouldered them aside. – "LOKI's bastards!" she yelled, and they laughed like oafs. – A great troll of a Doorkeeper threw open the gate without even challenging her, and stood aside to let her enter. – Now Freydis was very cautious, recalling the words of ODIN the High One:

> At every threshold,
> ere you enter,
>> you should spy around,
>> you should pry around,
> always hesitating
> lest some foeman should be waiting.

So, as Freydis stood almost within that barred gate, she determined to guard her words somewhat. She could never be sure that she was not among foes. Thinking that she hesitated, the Doorkeeper grinned and winked and tittered impatiently. Truly he was the ugliest troll she had ever seen or heard tell of. Once Eirik had told her of a far place called THE GREAT BLUELAND,* where the people were burned almost black by the sun, but they were said not to be ill-favored, whereas *he* . . . He wore a cloak of ice-blue livery, but his shoes were iron. The balls rolled continually in his narrow little eyes. He licked his lips with his pointed tongue, and scratched at himself with great yellow claws. When he opened his mouth to yawn, she saw rows and rows of spiked teeth grinning in its darkness, as if he had been some sea-reptile such as her father had often told of finding in his nets when he fished in Iceland. – Seeing her stare, the troll spoke to her for the first time, saying

---

* Africa.

angrily, "Think not to steal the treasures from my belly, for the gold that I swallow would kill you with its venom." And he shook his knife at her. – Freydis snatched her own knife from her belt and waved it in his face, crying hotly, "It was never my intention, *thrall*, to scoop your stinking shit from your guts!" – "No need," said the troll sourly, "since you already stink of piss." – But he put his knife away, and after glaring at him Freydis did the same. She was beginning to learn how to deal with the folk here. – Once again the troll scuttled aside on his hairy spider-legs as Freydis came forward undaunted, and so she strode into that dark and icy castle. The troll slammed the gate behind her. – Without a word, Freydis gave him her mantle to hold. She took off her gloves, knowing that one must appear before great lords with ungloved hands. She looked at her image in a little ivory-backed mirror that she always carried (for Freydis was vain) and made certain that her hair was brushed smooth. – The troll laughed and presented her to a pair of demon-hags more ugly even than he. They sniffed at her and wrinkled their noses. – "Oh, my!" they said fastidiously. "You must wash, sister!" they said. – "I'm no sister of yours!" cried Freydis. "My tits don't hang to my knees, and I don't stink *after* I wash!" – "Oh my, oh my," the demon-hags grumbled. "It seems we have a Queen to wait on." Then they led her through the channels and bowels of the castle, whose corridors were shored up everywhere with beams of iron and other ignoble metals. – "Don't breathe so hard," said the hags peevishly. "You'll melt the ceiling." – They hobbled groaning down a winding flight of slippery blue ice-stairs, and so brought Freydis presently to a cellar that smelled of saltpeter. In a corner were many diverse ice-casks, which the hags now proceeded to prise open one after the other, looking for the right kind of snow for Freydis to wash herself with, and arguing all the while in such disagreeably screeching voices that she wished she could have killed them. At last they found what they sought, and shoveled a bushel of it into a pail. Then they made her strip herself and scrub with it. It seemed to Freydis no different from any other snow she had seen, but she said nothing, because she considered any words she might utter to these monsters to be words wasted. – "Very well," they said to her when she had finished. "Now we'll take you to people of rank, and we hope they kick you back downstairs, stinking whore that you are!"

Now at last Freydis was introduced to folk more after her liking, for, while goblins they were, they inhabited the loftier ice-rooms of the upper storeys, and wore grand blue robes. Though it was quite dark in the heart of the castle where they lived, the Ice-Lights illuminated them tolerably well, especially when they nodded slowly and earnestly at something that she had said and she could see the smooth white moon of a cheek or a chin rising in the darkness; and their eyes glowed with ice-fire, and there was a greater darkness in their mouths. Sometimes the ceiling creaked when their King paced heavily in the room above, and then their faces rose slowly toward the sound, like a dozen rising planets (for I like to think that they were the guests of the Sun and the Moon, who, once their hosts had abandoned them for the skies, became in time hungry and anxious, and so fell into Blue-Shirt's orbit). – They did not abuse her as the thralls had done, but greeted her civilly, for her father's sake; they asked her for news about the lower parts of Greenland where men lived, and hospitably refreshed her with sugar-ices. – These were Blue-Shirt's house-carles. Freydis in her turn cultivated their friendship, and, as her dream had told her to do, she asked them for advice.

"You must avoid the indulgence of your spiteful desires which once satisfied the purpose of your life," they replied, "for now, my girl, you have more important things to live for. You must keep a watch over your tongue, and say only what will please others, for that way you will better be able to please yourself. You must also keep a watch over your behavior. If our King exalts you, then many people will turn their eyes upon you, and if your deportment is petty or dishonorable then they will become weary of you, and that will make them difficult to manage. Even a milkmaid speaks lovingly to her cows, and soothes them, though not out of love, as perhaps they imagine, but simply because cows believing themselves loved are more easily milked."

(But at this, Freydis smiled, remembering how she had always whipped her cows when there was no one to watch her.)

"Be sure only of this," said the trolls, "that you show proper conduct to Him, as befitting a King."

"I thank you for your counsel," said Freydis gravely, "and will do as you suggest."

She walked forward with her head erect; the demons whose friendship she had sought walked before her. So they led her into their Master's presence.

Amortortak

They tell me here that human flesh tastes quite as nice as bear-meat;
but that you can always read in a person's face if he has eaten it, and
that those who have been compelled to do so shrink from speaking
about it.

LINDSAY (1932)

AMORTORTAK sat atop a slanting wall of ice. He had cold and cloudy temples.
His beard was frost. He wore a helmet of bluish-white ice. His hands were
quite black. – When Freydis came into the demon's presence she was well
received. She declared her errand, explaining her disposition to Him frankly
and asking for His help and friendship in attaining her ends.

"I am sure you know," said Blue-Shirt, "that I already appropriated to Myself
all rights in Greenland ages ago. The Screechers* hold the country only as a
fief. The same goes for you Icelanders. You are all bonded to Me by virtue
of your blue eyes. When your father first wintered here alone, I made him
acknowledge Me and become My man. Now I will give you this condition,
Freydis: if you also swear and declare your vassalship – for a willing servant
is more valuable to Me than a dozen of the other kind – then I will enrich
you here and in Wineland, and we will see what can be done in the two
kingdoms to increase your power. But I tell you frankly that you will never
be greatly loved if you follow Me."

Freydis considered carefully. Although she was well aware that there was
much to be said both for and against the demon's offer, in the end she chose to
deliver herself into His power. Then Blue-Shirt was well pleased, and claimed
her body and many rich presents besides, and she became His vassal under
oath. As she was preparing to return homeward out of the rock, He saw that
she was somewhat downcast, as indeed it was only natural that she should be
after the bargain that she had made, so Blue-Shirt smiled and touched her
with His BLACK HANDS and said, "I at least will always love you, as long as
you continue to fulfill My demands," but this answer pleased Freydis even
less than before.

---

* One possible meaning of "Skræling" was "Screecher" or "Flincher."

Ships and Coffins

Even a potato in a dark cellar has a certain low cunning about him
which serves him in excellent stead. He knows perfectly well what he
wants and how to get it. He sees the light coming from the cellar
window and sends his shoots crawling straight thereto: they will crawl
along the floor and up the wall and out the cellar window; if there be a
little earth anywhere on the journey he will find it and use it for his
own ends.

BUTLER, *Erewhon* (1872)

Polar men don't wait until the last minute to think of what they are
going to do when winter is over.

WELZL

She married a pliable man, who was easily enticed by her ways, just
as King Harald Fairhair had been enticed by the Laplander Svase to meet
his daughter Snæfrid, a lovely longhaired girl who stood before him in the
hut and looked into his eyes until he thought he could see inside her all
the sons that she was going to give him – to wit, Sigurth Bastard, Halfdan
Longshanks, Guthroth the Radiant and Rognvald the Straightlimbed – and
now Snæfrid filled his mead cup and he saw her naked arm and the sound
of the mead-foam in the cup drove him wild and her lips glistened and
Harald knew now that he loved her so passionately that he must make her
his wife, at which the Laplander Svase looked him up and down with the
utmost insolence. Seeing this, Harald threshed for a moment in the nets of
Snæfrid's witchcraft, but he could not help himself. When she died he sat beside
her for three years expecting her to come to life again, and he bestowed costly
coverlets upon her and she seemed to him unchanged, until at last Torleiv the

Wise cured the King of his sad delusion by bidding him to honor her further by raising her and changing her dress, and when this was done all sorts of foul smells came from her body and it turned blue and worms and toads and newts and reptiles crawled out of it and it crumbled into ashes. – Like Snæfrid, Freydis was longhaired and slender. Freydis's husband, Thorvard, was a rich man from Gardar,* where the promontory was narrow between the sea-arms and fog hung over the mountains. Freydis seemed to him an unknown flower which had never existed before. – "I don't suppose you'll have much trouble with him," her father told her. "You'll live in comfort; you'll have whatever you need."

On their wedding day, Thorvard gave her a pale blue dress which came from foreign parts. It was the most beautiful dress that she had ever owned. Freydis put it on and looked at her reflection in a slow-flowing stream. She laughed and laughed all alone. Then she rushed into the hills to masturbate.

If Freydis had been as handsome a woman to look upon as Gudrid, she might have enforced her ways on people more quietly, gently snubbing the men who were enamored of her, for instance; and turning a radiantly intense countenance upon the others until their friendship was also excited, then siding with their wives. As it was, she was somewhat strident at times, and people dreaded her. – To Thorvard, however, his wife was always beautiful. When he lay rutting in her, she smiled coolly and endured it, and when Thorvard asked her if he did not please her, she replied, "I prefer to keep the advantages on my side." – Often Thorvard pondered this answer, but it admitted of many interpretations – none necessarily of great favor to him.

But now Freydis, seeing from her successful marriage that she was held in high regard by AMORTORTAK, became more grasping and open in her greed. Even on the Lord's Day she set her thralls to gathering driftwood (for in those days the coasts of Greenland were still congested with salty tree-trunks that had floated from Siberia). She made great stores of cod and seal-meat and birds' eggs, far more than she needed (though here her husband agreed with her, for he too was a hoarder). On the farm she superintended everything. A thrall who spilled a few drops of milk would be whipped. She wore seven gold rings, and hoarded many more. Perhaps AMORTORTAK knew her nature and was not surprised by this. In any event, He said nothing to her which would have prevented her bringing herself down, and neither did her brother Leif, though people spoke to him about her arrogance and ostentation. – "I do

---

* Now known to the triumphant Greenland Skrælings as Igaliko, "the deserted cooking place."

not have the heart to reprove my sister in anything," he said. – In fact he was afraid of her.

Just as grey mountains and green mountains become blue when seen from a distance, but white ice-mountains never do, so Freydis's schemes kept their

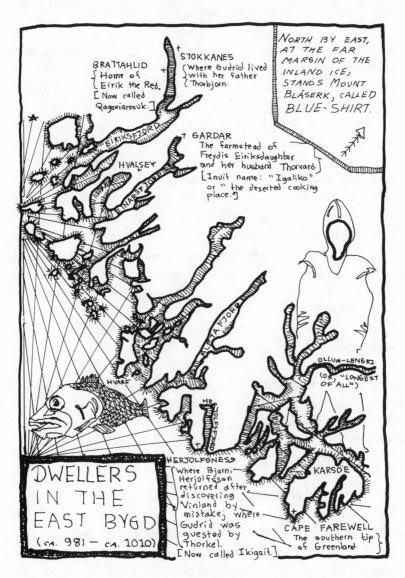

BRATTAHLID
{ Home of
{ Eirik the Red.
[Now called
Qagssiarssuk.]

STOKKANES
{where Gudrid lived
{with her father
{Thorbjorn.

NORTH BY EAST,
AT THE FAR
MARGIN OF THE
INLAND ICE,
STANDS MOUNT
BLÁSERK, CALLED
BLUE-SHIRT.

EIRIKSFJORD

HVALSEY

NARSEFJORD

GARDAR
The farmstead of
Freydis Eiriksdaughter
and her husband Thorvard.
[Invit name: "Igaliko"
or "the deserted cooking
place."]

ALT-AFJORD

HVARF

OLLUM-LENGRI
(OR, "LONGEST
OF ALL")

HERJOLFSFJORD

DWELLERS
IN THE
EAST BYGD
(CA. 981 – CA. 1010)

HERJOLFSNESS
{Where Bjarni
Herjolfsson
returned after
discovering
Vinland by
mistake; where
Gudrid was
guested by
Thorkel.
[Now called Ikigait.]

KARSOE

CAPE FAREWELL
The southern tip }
of Greenland.

color through the years. She remembered the name "Wineland," and one night Blue-Shirt visited her in a dream and told her that He had been watching her, at which Freydis said that she had not expected anything different, and Blue-Shirt said, "Neither ice-crags nor the Frozen Sea will hide you from

My sight. Now, as I once told you, there is a place called Wineland where you may go, if you wish to be rid of Me, but I tell you this because I expect you will prefer to bring the ice there, and extend My kingdom. Then, even though you are but a woman, I will let you sit in one of My earl-seats, and you will have great influence and all the power that is needful to carry out your wicked designs."

Hearing this, Freydis conceived a great desire to go to Wineland, and asked how she might manage it.

"I leave that to you," said Blue-Shirt. "You have enough cunning to do whatever you are determined to do."

And Freydis saw that He mocked her somewhat, but she said nothing, because one must humble oneself when craving boons of one's betters.

Freydis's next task was to convince her husband that the two of them must go to Vinland. Here perhaps she took less trouble than she might have, because Freydis was a proud and impatient woman. He, therefore, feeling himself not so much convinced as bullied, said that he was quite content where he was. Here in Greenland, he said, at least he had solid ice under his feet. Who knew how firm the ground was in those fabulous countries? Freydis railed at him horribly, but he became more and more silent and at last she sat beside him in a silence of her own, expressing hatred for him in every part of her, from her bitter eyes to her sharp elbows.

"I regret that we didn't understand each other," her husband said the next day, but Freydis was stiff and silent.

"Well?" he said.

"I regret that we still don't understand each other," said Freydis coldly.

Just as white lichen resists the Arctic winds without even stirring, but crumbles under a touch, so Thorvard too had his vulnerabilities. The long and the short of it was that he agreed to go to Vinland.

The Seduction of the Brothers

Freydis, who was a plausible woman, immediately made people feel friendly towards her. She rode over to the stead of the brothers Helgi and Finnbogi and asked them to go to Wineland with her. Whereas the brothers considered every aspect of the matter at length, and took their time before entering into the agreement, Freydis immediately accepted any condition which they asked of her, for when Freydis could not defy she supplicated. Natures more suspicious than theirs might have wondered whether instead of being accommodating she simply cared nothing for her own promises, but they were strangers in Greenland, and knew little of people there; so once again the long and short of it was that Helgi and Finnbogi agreed to go to Vinland with her; for when she spoke the distant call of Wineland's sun-birds was already deep inside her, and those birds were what Helgi and Finnbogi heard. (At that time she was still considered an excellent girl.)

Freydis and the brothers made a compact to take no more than thirty able-bodied men apiece, with as many women as each party desired. That way, if there were some treachery they would be equally matched. Freydis broke the compact at once by making arrangements to conceal five extra men on her ship. She saw no reason to take any chances.

Gladness

Of course she herself did not want to go. But whom could she cry to? Vinland terrified her the more she insisted on going there. In her imagination the Skrælings were already waiting for her in Vinland, their skin-boats swarming through the tall-treed fjords in search of her; and there were cruel smiles on their painted faces. – "But after all," she said to herself, "I am Blue-Shirt's thrall, with thrall's rights. If any harm is done to me, Blue-Shirt will take compensation." Then in her mind she saw hundreds of Skræling corpses floating in the warm, bloody water; their eyes were open, and their chests were pierced with spears of ice. So she was reassured.

The Axe

That winter her father Eirik died at last on a bed of sickness, and a magnificent coffin was made for him. In the spring they laid him in a mound away from Thjodhild's church, since he had never accepted the True Faith, saying that he was content to let matters stand where they were. For this reason he and his wife had had very little to do with each other in the last years. As soon as the howe was sealed, Thjodhild took up Eirik's bench-boards from the high-seat and threw them into the fire, although Leif argued with her, saying, "Mother, I myself am pictured there, plucking the grapes of Vinland!", to which she replied, "The worse for you!", so Leif let her have her way, as she was freshly widowed. It is said that when the bench-boards began to burn, a scream came from them, and the carved figures were seen to writhe, as if they sought to save themselves, but Leif's priest said a prayer and then the wood shattered and began to burn briskly, with much smoke and stench. – "Now we must look to new ways," said Thjodhild, "and change ourselves cleanly, with the help of CHRIST." – And they all knelt and praised Him. – Freydis bought a fine ship with her inheritance and announced to Gudrid that she would join her convoy to Vinland, and so would the brothers Helgi and Finnbogi. Gudrid and Karlsefni were not greatly pleased to have her, but they could not refuse her without incurring the consequences of her ill will,

and anyhow, as Gudrid said to her husband, Freydis was a staunch woman whose courage might be useful if they met the Skrælings. And so the ships gathered at the landing in Eiriksfjord – "those sea-beasts with heads bent low," as Snorri called them – and the Greenlanders loaded them with cattle, provisions and weapons – especially weapons. Freydis took hewing-spears and string-spears with gold-inlaid sockets. She took arrows and shields and bows. And she did not neglect to bring her axe.

Preparations for Trade

Now it is to be told that in those last days of winter Gudrid's husband Karlsefni had not been at ease in his mind, and spoke often, too often, to Leif concerning the way to Vinland, and the Isle of Dew, and the path to Leif's houses, which questions Leif answered with a will, for Gudrid was his brother's widow; but he began to wonder at last whether Karlsefni might be a nidderer; as for Gudrid, she was occupied with the provisioning of their ships (for if Vinland was as good as was said, she expected to live out her life there), so that she had no time at first to find Karlsefni's disquiet out; but presently it seemed to her that he watched sideways when the black snow-winds came; and he was sleeping poorly, so that she stroked his hair and requested him to tell her whether he were still resolved to carry matters through, and he looked out the bladder-window into the darkness where Eirik lay frozen in his coffin and Karlsefni's ship endured in its berth, piled high with snowdrifts; and he said, "It is no matter, Gudrid; I am one of those men who is a coward before the battle, but not when it happens. I think that that is the way with us traders." – They were in their bed. The night was very cold, even though the mattress was piled high with reindeer-skins. Gudrid perched herself on her elbows above her husband, gazing down upon him as she had done with the dying Thorstein; coolly she asked, "Do you think it will be a battle, then?" – *so* coolly, so gently like Sigrid the Haughty rising with the imprint of King Olaf's slap freshly red on her cheek as she whispered, "This may well be your death," but Karlsefni thrust that comparison aside and replied, "I am sure there will be little enough fighting, except perhaps with Skrælings, and they are scarcely men at all, as I have been told, but ignorant trolls who may easily be killed." – Then Gudrid smiled at him and laid her head down on his breast, at which he was enveloped in her warm cloud of sureness, as if she had let down her hair like a maiden again to refresh him; and he was content; but later that night, when he still could not sleep, the story of Queen Sigrid came back to his mind like water dripping from an icicle, and he knew it well, having been in Norway when Sigrid won her triumph at last. – But why should this plague him? It was not at all that he mistrusted his wife, and thought her kin to Sigrid in her behavior, for he knew that her heart was true to him; no, it was *Vinland* that menaced him. He could arm and provision himself for Vinland, but it was still an unknown country. Once when Eirik the Red was still alive, the conversation had come around to Greenland in the first days and Karlsefni had asked what it was like to discover that country, to which Eirik replied, "This is a beautiful country, and I am very satisfied to have taken it." – Karlsefni said, "Indeed you made a success, which seems to me more marvelous still when I reflect that there was no one to help you on your first voyage, when you were outlawed." – He said these things only to please his host. But the shafts of flattery seemed to have hit a different mark from the one intended, for Eirik was displeased. "If there was help, it was help that I well earned," he said, and would say no more, but screwed up his features most sourly. Karlsefni saw that he had troubled him, and turned the subject; but ever since that day he was convinced that Greenland must not be so fair a country as it appeared. (Nor did it appear so fair now, to tell the truth, in that sunless space between Harvest-Month and Sowing-Tide.) As for Vinland, what might it be? That promontory, or isle, seemed to glower across the sea at him like Queen Sigrid; nobody knew her; no one could guard against her. Olaf Trygvesson had been brave indeed to slap her in the face with his glove and call her a heathen bitch, for he must have been told her reputation. But then, never had he been afraid of anything – not when he struck down the pagan images with his axe (as he first ascended the throne he proclaimed: "All Norway shall become Christian, or *die!*"); not when he baptized in Viken and Agder and Hordaland, mutilating and torturing whoever would not submit. – No, he would not have feared Vinland; after all, what was there in that country for anyone to fear?

Karlsefni had a friend from Iceland named Snorri Thorbrandsson, whom he knew to be shrewd and reliable, for he had often bested these Greenlanders at trade. Snorri and another captain, Bjarni Grimolfsson by name, had both agreed to accompany him to Vinland. So it came into Karlsefni's mind to share his forebodings with them and listen well to whatever they might reply. When the opportunity arose, he sailed to Herjolfsness, where they were being guested with all their men at Thorkelsstead, and called them aside.

When he put the case to them, Bjarni stood frowning (he was a melancholy fellow), but Snorri chuckled and said, "That was ever your way, Thorfinn, to act like a new bride who knows not which will come first, her churching or her childbed. What danger can Vinland hold for Norsemen such as ourselves?"

"Mark you, I have no notion of withdrawing from this voyage," said Karlsefni, feeling somewhat foolish.

"Of course not," said Snorri. "Your wife has a mind of her own, so people say."

"What do you mean?" said Karlsefni.

"Thorkel guested her, you know. He and Helga remember her well. They ask after her father Thorbjorn."

"Thorbjorn Vifilsson is dead."

"Well, well," said Snorri. "At all events, Gudrid is a very accomplished woman. I wish you much success."

Then Bjarni Grimolfsson said, "Is it the Skrælings you fear after all?"

Karlsefni was quiet for awhile. "No," he said. "And yet, I suppose . . ."

"If it is the Skrælings," said Bjarni, "you need only tell your men to guard their weapons. For the Dwarf-Folk never came to Vinland, as it seems, since the Skrælings know not the use of iron. With our axes and swords we shall always bring the matter to a good ending."

Snorri interposed, "Remember that we are all traders. There may well be profit to be gained from these Skrælings. Of course there is little enough room on our ships for trading-goods, if we mean to bring all our cattle and other possessions with us. But perhaps something bright and gaudy, of little value, might help our luck."

"You know that Freydis Eiriksdottir and her husband Thorvard are coming with us?" said Karlsefni. "It seems he too is quite the trader."

"He has a sharp mind for money, they say, and little else," said Bjarni. "He is no man. But I believe that he is bringing a few bales of trade-cloth with him."

"Well, and I shall do the same," said Karlsefni.

After this talk he felt much easier, and thought that his fears and fancies had been childish. Yet his mind, being a trader's mind, often translated among currencies, so that the equation between Vinland and Queen Sigrid was not such a strange one for him to make. Karlsefni decided to be vigilant in the strange country, just as King Olaf should have been.

The Seduction of Leif

In Ram's Month, when she was certain of finding him in, Freydis sailed up the straight and narrow fjord to Brattahlid, and paid a call to her half-brother. Although he preferred Gudrid to her, Freydis had insisted that *she* be the one to ask him for the loan of his houses in Vinland, for so she hoped to make the others indebted to her. – Gudrid was beside herself with rage at this presumption, but Karlsefni (who underestimated Freydis almost to the end) said merely that he supposed Freydis craved her importance, and he did not begrudge it to her; for he was not a smallhearted man. – With this, Gudrid's party yielded to Freydis.

Leif was sitting by the long-fire, which burned blue and green with the salt from driftwood logs, and he stared out the window at the snow-swirls, and the wind keened songs of beautiful cruelty from the Ice-Mountain and Leif drummed his fingers on the arm of dead Eirik's high-seat – his now, for all that that mattered to him. Matters had not gone badly for Leif of late, but neither had they gone especially well. Certainly it was pleasant to be the master of Brattahlid; certainly it was pleasant to have money and reputation, but now that he had attained those things he was not certain what to do next. He should probably marry, for he did not much care for this pale creature of a Thorgils who had lately come to Greenland – his son by Thorgunna Witch. He did not propose to let Thorgils inherit Brattahlid. Nor, to tell the truth, did he desire Freydis to do so. – So there sat Leif the Lucky, at the peak of his prestige, and the peak was not as high as it had once seemed, and ahead of him waited the Valley of Death, as it waited for all; and Leif did not much like this.

"Leif," said Freydis, "it is our wish to use your houses in Vinland. Will you let us have them?"

The brother looked up. He was the last of Red Eirik's sons, and this is the last time that we will see him. – "You're only a hanger-on in this," he said. "Why are you asking for my houses? Go bring Gudrid to me and let her ask me."

Freydis smiled bitterly, but said nothing.

Leif threw another log on the fire. – "Still here, are you?" he said contemptuously. "By the slit of your slut-mother, you're a stubborn one! Very well. You can borrow my houses, then."

The Disappointments of Thorvard

Thorvard had expected to feel an exhilarated sense of suspense before sailing to Vinland, and at first he did, but certain events instilled in him a melancholy fear and a sense of being dirtied, these involving the unexpected disapproval of others concerning actions of his which had seemed to him either well-handled or else so trivial as not to be worth any judgement. In particular was his use of Leif's houses there, which he thought his wife had gotten cheaply (i.e., for nothing), until one of his friends told him almost angrily that he had paid too much – for now he had incurred a great obligation. – He's jealous, Thorvard said to himself. But this thought distressed him even more, that one of his friends could be so jealous of him as to hate him. – Of course no one was jealous of him at all. Everyone pitied and despised him somewhat, because he was Freydis's husband.

A Ship among Ships

Freydis's ship had a sail with blue and red stripes. It was painted on the bows. Her husband had commented somewhat on the expense, but Freydis said, "The money is mine, not yours. Anyhow, don't you want to show Gudrid and the others that we are people of quality just as they are?" – Thorvard said that he had not thought of it that way, and after that he kept his peace. – Freydis's heart bounded up like a rushing sun when she heard men comparing her ship to Gudrid's and judging it the better of the two. It was now Gudrid's turn to be silent, which she was. So Freydis, unopposed by any word, thought that she had begun to come into her desires at last; for most of all she wanted her name on men's lips; she wanted to be remembered. Her gold necklace was sometimes a heavy, choking weight upon her throat, but she had to wear what suited her.

The Norse Ship-Berths 1987

On that happiest summer of my life we walked along the cobbled beach, the real Greenlanders and I; and there were three rectangular berths for Viking ships, grass-grown now, each with its rolling lip of silt and sand; but the

Greenlanders said you could still bring a ship in at high tide in the spring. Nearby was a stone trap for foxes, made by Greenlanders. On a bushy rise stood the remains of a many-roomed stone house where Tunersuit had lived. – "There are more houses over there, where the grass is green," said Jónar. But we did not look at them, because at that season the bushes were full of black spiders whose gluey webs stuck to your mouth.

The Greenlanders ran up a rounded tundra ridge, exclaiming in delight whenever they saw a reindeer. The ridge was soft and wide. There were bright green shrubs; there was white lichen to cushion our steps. Ahead, beyond a grey pass, was a Mountain of ice.

We found a stand of the kayak plant. A hundred years ago, reindeer hunters ate them to be strong. We chewed them; they tasted a little more astringent than wintergreen. – "Look!" cried the beautiful girls, picking yellow flowers. "It smell like licorice!" – We ran through a dwarf poplar jungle, and the girls leaped across a rushing stream, carrying the flowers in their mouths . . .

The Voyage to Vinland
ca. 1007

No man becomes master while he stays at home, nor finds a teacher
behind the stove.

PARACELSUS, *ca.* 1590

We were fain to grabble in the darke (as it were), like a blind man for
his way.

EDWARD PELLHAM, 1631

The Greenlanders, then, having decided to explore new countries, put
out to sea from Eiriksfjord. For weeks they watched the waves rise and fall
and rise again unexhausted. Sometimes the wave-crests were spotted with
the foam, so that they resembled marble. The ocean curled and foamed
and drenched them with its cold scum. Few icebergs pursued them south,
for the colony was in its sunny early days, but even so the sea resembled
curled ice, and the froth of it blew in their bearded faces as powdered snow
will fly when driven by the wind. Sometimes the ships were lifted on the
waves taller than mountains, so that the timbers creaked, and the voyagers
could see a black hint of coastline far off, or a dullish green wall of ice.
They sailed through the stormy and excessive cold of the spring. After a
squall the sea became insidiously smooth. They sometimes saw birds flying
around their ship at these times. Some landed in the rigging to rest, and
were killed by Freydis's crew. Others circled round and round in the mist
until they were spent. Then they fell into the sea and were drowned. Their
white bodies bobbed for awhile on the waves, which were sometimes green
and sometimes as black as smoked glass.

The Map of Sigurdur Stefansson *ca. 1590*

To Freydis and her crew it must have seemed that they were enclosed by land, for they believed that Greenland joined Jötunheim, land of the Frost Giants, to the north and east, and Jötunheim eventually joined Norway, and Norway was a part of Europe which ran south to Africa; and meanwhile on the west Greenland was connected to Flintland, which was connected to Woodland, which was connected to Skrælingland, which was connected to Wineland.

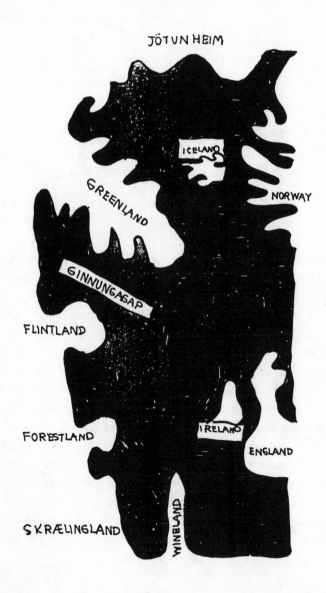

Waves and Loneliness

They continued to sail southward and west on the grey foggy sea, which presently subsided somewhat in its wave-peaks and became a dreary plain of chill, with the white mist parting beneath their keel like fat under a knife. At times the sky was mist, and the sea was mist, so that it seemed that they were suspended in a cloud, and Freydis wondered if Blue-Shirt had deceived her, and there were no Vinland; being of a solitary, mistrustful nature, she even suspected her brothers Leif and Thorvald of having plotted to send her to Jötunheim. She felt as her father had felt when he was outlawed. – But just as sadness itself has its borders, which may be discovered by blundering through its white fog, across its grey sea, until suddenly the sky becomes visible, though slatey, and then after another long weary time come the first blue intimations of heaven, so the northern waters, too, had their margin, decorated with kelp-runes in imitation of the *Flateyjarbók*. – Freydis saw them first, for her ship was the best wave-biter. – So the wave-hills rolled more smoothly: although it might have been that by countenancing this the ocean merely gained clarity to express its unhappy urgency, which beaded every face with cold and salty drops, and thrust up whitecaps more jaggedly shortlived than starfire, to illuminate its cold and salty sickness.

Ginnunga Gap*

South of the white line of pack-ice, the sea was specked with swirls of ice-powder like a pebble beach. The ice formed dazzling white polygons bunched together so that in appearance the form they made was similar to that of a Nevada desert salt-wash, except that one could see the white jigsaw pieces undulating in the waves, and the ocean could sometimes be seen between the cracks. The distinction between sea, sky and ice was confused. Everything was blue and white, blue and white; there were so many broken patterns. This was Ginnunga Gap, the abyss where the nine worlds had been created from fire and ice, for to the south was Muspelheim, the Kingdom of Fire, whose sparks rose up to make the stars; and to the north was Niflheim, the Kingdom of Cold; and rime-breath met heat-breath in Ginnunga Gap and melted into drops, from which the first being, evil Ymir the Frost Giant, was born. His offspring killed him. The sky was made from his skull; and in Helluland I

* Probably Davis Strait, between Greenland and Baffin Island.

have seen the mountains created from his bones. – Ginnunga Gap endured. It was now the channel to the sea called MARE OCEANUM that enclosed the entire world in its ring; and at the bottom of the Mare Oceanum lay LOKI's hateful offspring, the Serpent of Midgaard, that stretched around the world with its tail in its mouth, waiting for the bad day when Fenrir the wicked Wolf was going to swallow the moon and the Troll-Child would destroy the sun so that the sunshine became black; and the Serpent of Midgaard lashed the waves with its hideous tail that was longer than all the continents and the black waves rose and eagles screamed in the wind-scream and the world-tree Yggdrasil creaked and groaned, and then the men from Muspel came sailing across the sea with LOKI as their steersman and LOKI was laughing and laughing very awfully with tears of poison crawling down the sear-tracks in His cheeks and His eye-sockets were black and blind because the Gods had tied Him to a rock beneath another serpent that spat acid in His eyes, for He had murdered BALDUR the Good, so that no punishment could be terrible enough for Him; but now the Murderer was free and He was going to murder the world! So He steered the Muspel-men blindly, laughing in the wind because everything was going to be destroyed; and now Fenrir gaped his jaws, and his mouth was ODIN's grave; and then Valhalla was destroyed with all its gods and the earth died; and that was the doom that had to be, but that did not mean that we could not face our death with hate and brave defiance, as when THOR went fishing and drew the Serpent of Midgaard up from the deeps with His fish-hook, and the lividly spotted Serpent squirmed and stared with hatred at its mortal enemy whom it could not yet harm, and it spat venom at THOR and THOR beat the Serpent with great blows and finally threw it back to the bottom of the Mare Oceanum.

Harder by Helluland,* a plain of ice stole to the horizon, impregnated with great adjoining ovals surrounded by leads, the effect being one of a microscope slide of crystalline cytoplasm; and then there came the sharp lines of the shattered ice-mirror, some still showing from above the lines of their original joining, but there were missing shards, too, their place held by water. The closer the Greenlanders came to Helluland, the more solid the ice became. When there were dark blue sea-places, they were frosted over. Presently Finnbogi called out that he saw the headland, which was hardly anything but knife-ridges outthrust into the ice, presenting fingers that were cliffs on either side, with snow above and snow below; and then came more islands full of snow, and pale blue frozen lakes, and channels of the rich blue

---

* "Slab-Land" or "Flint-Land" (Baffin Island).

sea, so rich a blue (almost indigo) as cannot be described, each glittering with
its translucent crystals of ice. At last came the slabs from which Slab-Land
got its name, great slabs that were really mountains sunken into the snow
and topped with snow. These blue cliffs gave way to black cliffs arranged in
a circle like stadium seats, all around a blank flat circle of snow (here, Freydis
thought to herself, there must be some secret), and then over a frozen river
were more black hills, and so on to the horizon.

Helluland

That first land they sighted, then, they called Slab-Land, for it seemed to
be nothing but a slab of rock crowned by glaciers. The shore was without
grass. When they landed on it, they found the beach littered with slabs as
long as two men lying end-to-end. Considering the country worthless, they
returned to their ships and set sail. – Not a great deal has been written about
Slab-Land, so I will print here the Narrative of Seth Pilsk, as told to me
in 1987. How hard it is in Wineland to believe in this Country of Flints! –
because here today it is so sunny and warm and the afternoon is blue and
the houses are yellow and gold and happy.

The Voyage of Seth Pilsk the Thin 1984

"Well, when I got to Baffin Island, I was feeling really good, 'cause it was
sunny all the way up, and it was just so exciting to look down and know
where I was, and what it looked like. It was funny, too, 'cause we went
into Frobisher Bay on a 727 and they served us a drink and that kind of
stuff, 'cause it was mainly businessmen: – oilmen and natural gas men going
up to Frobisher Bay. It looked like I was the only camper. Also there were
some Eskimos going up, that had been just visiting down south. When we
got to Frobisher Bay, I got my pack and just started walking. I had a layover
for a day before I could go up to Baffin Island. And so I just walked up from
the airport, out towards the fjord where I was going to camp. It was great,
'cause as soon as I got away from the airport and that strange-looking town,
all the sudden I got off the gravel road, and I was on the tundra and I felt
really good, 'cause I was familiar with it from the summer before. I really felt
like I was at home and I knew what I was doing, and I felt really confident;
I felt *great*. And all the little flowers were out. And I got to camp on this nice

high spot overlooking this river, and everything was pretty idyllic. It was pretty
warm, too. And so the next day I got on this nice big propeller plane which
took me up to Pangnirtung. That was also really nice, too. It was cloudy, but
nice. But the thing about the whole trip was that I was feeling *so* confident, so
utterly unrealistic about my abilities. I thought I knew everything, because I'd
been to Anaktuvuk Pass, and I'd hitchhiked some, and I just felt invincible and
superhuman. I felt like I knew what I was doing, and in reality I knew *nothing*
about the way nature works, and I *still* don't. You know, I could learn all
the names of every single species of plant in the world, and it won't mean a
thing. – At that time I didn't even know any of the plants. I didn't hardly
know how to recognize one plant from another, or where I was, or why

the rocks were there. *Anything.* And I guess I had a false feeling, because the Arctic really made me feel good. And so I got into Pangnirtung. I just signed what I had to sign, and started walking. I got to the end of the road, past the garbage dump, and there you are.

"It was a really wonderful walk, just going through this tundra. To the right were some mountains that keep getting bigger as you go along, and to the left was a fjord. That first day I just walked until I got acclimated, kind of getting used to walking on the tundra. I had a real heavy pack. It must have been about a hundred and forty pounds at the beginning of the trip. I was able to stash some food and some of the gear with some friends in Montreal, so it was probably around a hundred and fifteen or so – you know, a heavy pack. So every step I'd take, I'd just sink into the tundra. You know the feeling. So I just got used to that, and I walked a good ways, and I was able to camp in between where the valley would rise up into the real high hills and a little rise or point between me and the fjord. It was on a nice swale, so it was really dry, and you know what that tundra is like to sleep on. It's just better than any mattress you could ever buy. And so everything was just so *perfect*: I had plenty of clean water, it was a perfect place, and there wasn't a cloud in the sky, and everything was Absolutely Ideal, and I just felt so high, so superhuman . . .

"The next day I went out, and I did a whole day of hiking. A lot of it was quite careless hiking. I would go right on the shore between the land and the fjord, where there was a lot of ice, which was so much easier to walk on; a kind of snow-covered ice, with plenty of traction, but I was utterly careless. I had this huge pack on, and I would just have a bounce in my step, and think nothing of jumping over crevasses or going over real iffy footholds that were just absolutely stupid; I could very easily have broken a leg or something. I saw a lot of beautiful waterfowl along the way. I had an encounter with a mother goose and her little ones, which I took for amusing, but looking back on it I'm kind of ashamed that I even got so close and threatened her goslings like that. But I *did*. I kept going, and I'd been going all day with a heavy pack, and I was really tired. And I got to this really major stream which braided out to – I don't know, oh, a dozen braids, maybe, big and small braids, out to the fjord.

"And so I just crossed these little braids with no problem, and I got to this one really major braid. It was a really tough current. It was really deep, and there was a lot of slippery rock underneath. So I wasn't sure exactly what to do. I was really tired, and I had my camp spot picked out on the other side. It was very similar to the one the night before. I just let my laziness and

TIROKWA PEAK, BAFFIN ISLAND

confidence get the better of me. I *knew* that if I would just wait an hour, the tide in the fjord would go down, and I'd be able to make a perfectly safe crossing, but I just figured that nothing could possibly happen to me, that I was just being *cautious*, as I had accused you of being the summer before. So I dutifully (although I thought it was silly, but out of some weird feeling of obligation I did it) undid the belt of my pack and put all the hundred plus pounds over one shoulder and stepped right in. The water went well above my knees. Maybe halfway between my knees and my waist. It was cold as hell. My legs just immediately went numb. So naturally, halfway through I just got swept away."

The Voyage of Seth Pilsk the Thin Continued

"I don't know how I got to the other side. I was lying among the rocks, with my legs in the water, and my pack had slipped from my grasp. I was pretty beat up. I didn't care whether I lived or died. After awhile I got more conscious and thought, well, maybe I should do something and let myself live. So I kind of crawled over to where my pack was. It took all my energy. I could hardly even stand up and drag it to some high ground, so I just did that. Everything in my pack was just drenched. A lot of my food was ruined. But just through sheer stupid luck my sleeping bag was dry. It was the only thing that was dry. So I took off my clothes and just got into the sleeping bag. It got to the point where I was shaking, and I knew I was on the mend. I started shaking pretty uncontrollably, both out of the cold and the fear. The sun was still out, which really helped. There was kind of a breeze coming from the fjord. But I dried out, and after awhile I quit shaking. – It took a long time to get everything ready because I was kind of weak and really bewildered, and pretty vulnerable, but the first thing I did was set up my tent. Then I just went through my pack and laid everything out. It dried pretty fast in the sun, 'cause it was on the rocks, which were pretty warm at that point from the sun, too. And a nice wind helped them dry out fast. Then I just camped out and started thinking about what had happened and my whole attitude. – It seems like there's nothing like a close brush to bring you down to earth, and make your priorities in your mind very clear (for a good while, anyway). I started considering what the fuck I was doing here and realized that while I think it was a step in the right direction, doing that kind of thing, my priorities were all fucked up, that I just had to quit doing things so much for show, just start doing things just 'cause I wanted to. Real honest things that I wanted to do. I was so ashamed of myself. After that I had kind of a miserable night. Thought entirely too much. And in the morning I packed up and headed out."

"Was it in that same river that you saw that drowned girl?"

"Yeah."

The Voyage of Seth Pilsk the Thin Concluded

"I came back down that way. I was kind of weak, 'cause I'd poorly planned my diet, poorly planned it with a lot of food I didn't like. So I didn't eat enough to catch up to the amount of work I was doing. So I wasn't having a good time. And I didn't know much about where I was. I couldn't get very far between the two big walls of mountain. It was tough going, and I just couldn't do it. So I gave up. I was at Overlord, the first path-camp. The park actually had a few picnic tables and emergency shelters. I spent the night there, and early that morning I heard these frantic footsteps by my tent and somebody yelling for me. Just kind of loud sounds. I couldn't make out any words. And there was a very panicky Swedish guy outside the tent, and he wanted me to help. So I told him I would, and I got up.

Turns out this fellow was part of a team of Swedish climbers. They were trying to climb a certain face of Mount Thor, one of the mountains that had never been climbed before. They'd tried it the year before, but they lost a man trying, and they eventually had to give up. They couldn't make it. We'd heard that they'd successfully climbed it this time. After a strange mixture of sign language, drawing, a little French, and Swedish, I finally ascertained that one of the members of their group had been swept away trying to cross that same stream.

"Apparently they'd been really giddy and high about having successfully completed the climb. And on their way up to Canada, in New York, they'd met another Swedish woman, who befriended them, and they took her along, and she didn't participate in the climb, just tended to the base camp, and for whatever reasons – we thought that maybe she'd felt a little left out, had something left to prove since she didn't go on the climb – they'd tried to cross the stream before it braided out at all, and it was really just a torrent, and it was utterly impossible for a human being to get in and make it across. It was just crazy. They didn't rope up, and they didn't use sticks. Even I, who had stupidly crossed those heavy braids, find it inconceivable that you would even set foot in such a place, but she did. She walked right in, and was immediately swept away. She probably died in the first half-minute. It was probably painless. She probably went totally numb as soon as she got in the water, 'cause it was pretty *cold*. – So I spent that day with this fellow, going at just a breakneck pace, through this tundra and ice and stuff, trying to get back to this spot. It was amazing, 'cause this guy didn't have any gear. He must have been in such a panic, and been so frightened at seeing this woman die, that he had run all the way to where I was with nothing but tennis shoes. That's just a hell of a distance, and a hell of a terrain to run over with tennis shoes. He was just so pumped up. I had him calmed down a little, got some warm food into him. We weren't thinking too much. We just wanted to get to that spot as soon as possible, just on the outside chance she might still be alive. Every time we took a break, we just got going, 'cause we thought that the minute we took for a break might be the minute she was still alive. So we got there and we looked around. There were some Eskimos there from the village. And the helicopter did come. But nobody'd found her. And it turned out when we got near the river that the fellow who'd run all the way up to get us had a severely sprained ankle, and didn't know it, 'cause he was so pumped up. So for about the last half-mile we had to carry him.

"The next day we spent in the river, looking for the woman, whom we unfortunately found. We weren't the first to find her, but some other people did, and we got a glimpse of her. It was really horrible. She was really beat up, and had an absolutely anguished expression on her face, and her hands were all clenched up like claws. It was pretty dreadful. Her eyes were open. – I wouldn't say that we were depressed about it, but we were – well, I'm not sure. We were all very quiet. So that night we got set up, and there was a lot of driftwood up from the town, so we built a little fire, and relaxed, or tried to, and one of the Eskimo guys came up, and he was a guy from Ellesmere Island who was just telling us how much he loved the country and loved being there; and he had the most beautiful eyes that were wide open all the time, and just seemed *at ease*, very happy. He said that it was too bad, and he said that this woman had probably died at about six-thirty in the morning, about the same time as his wife gave birth to a little girl. That was – very comforting. And that night we were sitting by that same river, and it was just moaning all night. A very eerie feeling, and a very nice feeling, too."

"Do you think the river has a spirit?" I said.

"I really do," Seth said. "But I don't think a river wants anything, except to be itself. Just like anybody and anything. I don't think it claimed a soul. I don't think it's at all vindictive or vicious, just itself. It just seemed very honest. If you hear a river moan, you know it has life."

The End of the Light AD 1007

As the Greenlanders sailed southward, the sea began to shine more vehemently. It glowed even through the fog, so that they could not shut it out even by closing their eyes. The frosts lessened, and finally ceased altogether. The hazy sky became pink and dim with orange clouds, and they went farther south and it got warmer. They stared at each other in that pale, exciting light – but it was not far enough south because it was still light at night. A round ringed cloud hung in the sky like Saturn. Then the sea was warm and misty and lavender, and they thought they saw a tree-coast. There were big silvery rivers in that greenness. Ahead, finally, was an orange bar of sunset, and then the promised darkness. Presently the sea grew grey, but it was not storm-grey but *dark*-grey beneath a sky which was dark, and they passed an island which was light like a last white cloud, and then the sky was banded blue and black and the black got bigger and bigger and they sailed into that hot delicious darkness . . .

How strange it was not to be able to see things! The moon pretended to help, and sometimes it did, but they sailed without a care through its long bright tendrils that rested so easily upon the water.

DWARF WILLOW,
SLAB·LAND

Markland*

They sailed for two days before a good northerly wind, until they sighted a second land, which was flat and wooded, with white sandy beaches that sloped gently down to sea. They called that Forest-Land, as Leif and Bjarni had done before them. From Woodland to Wineland it is not far, Leif had said. They could already smell the honey of their land, borne to them on the sea-breezes. Freydis smiled through her teeth and said that Wineland was certainly due by now. As for Helgi and Finnbogi, they merely ran their eyes over the waves, whose crests were as numerous, distracting and unfathomable in their arrangement as the black lines on birch bark. – Presently the weather changed, and they found that they were not quit of Markland after all. In

---

* "Forest-Land" or "Woodland" (probably Labrador).

the dark grey sea, a dark cape arose, against which the whitecaps crashed. A petrel flew in the rain. The forest was greenish-grey. Hugging the coast because of the storm, the Greenlanders sailed past dark grey rocks, grey lakes and rugged, tree-shagged hills. Atop the low, rocky cliffs, wiry little trees grew out of the yellow grass. They sailed along the edge of a yellow plain, with grey rocks beside them and grey mountains too high to be mountains ahead of them. They rose up into the sky, those mountains, and Freydis thought that they must be wrapped in cloud until her ship came closer to them and she saw that before they vanished into the real clouds they flaunted snow on their greenish teats. Those mountains, seen indistinctly through the rain, reminded her in a ghastly way of Blue-Shirt, and once again her heart sank, for here were the trees and grass which he had promised her, but how horrible it all was! Still she wondered if he had tricked her, and she had become his for nothing. (Freydis never really understood how lofty Blue-Shirt was.) – No one else shared her feelings. She heard Helgi and Finnbogi talking about how rich in timber the country was. They would be quite content to stop here. – "If you stop here," said Freydis dryly, "it will be without us." – *That* kept them quiet. – The mountains were vast grey trapezoids in the mist, inset with ovals and diamonds of snow. Low spruce forests rolled south under the storm clouds, run through with wide grey streams that cherished little sand-islands at every bend. Hills of green and yellow trees folded in on themselves in the rain. Sometimes the ridge-tops were high and flat, forming horizons that ended abruptly with the land. The land opened out before them, but the trees were packed so tightly together that in places it would be difficult for a man's body to force a passage between them. At the edge of the coast, their roots twisted and stampeded around each other to burrow into the solid earth; the weaker trees leaned slowly into the ocean, their roots exposed by the wind. Freydis, who had never seen so many trees before, was almost revolted by their lushness. The struggle of the roots reminded her of worms in a corpse.

The plains of Markland went on, interrupted by dark cliffs with snow on them. The hills were greenish-black in the fog. The ships sailed slowly past dark bays whose cliff-walls were patched with snow, then along a plain of windblown fog through which little could be seen but orange-brown grass and silver ponds that were mirrors of the sky and scraggly, wind-twisted trees ("tuckamores," the Newfoundlanders call them now); and the sea merged so closely with the fog that they might have been sailing through the sky, were it not for the black rocks to starboard, with their whitecap shallows, which were thick with gulls at low tide.

After a time the blue sky burst from the suddenly mild clouds and enriched the colors of the trees. Ahead was a long narrow rectangle of blue between a flat tree-ridge and a flat cloudbank. Here they stopped for water, and Gudrid found many fossil shells. Thin white weed-stalks ascended from the grass like smoke. – They returned to their ships, and sailed past many low blue ridges dairy-dappled with snow, white clouds and blue sky. Though low, these cliffs were sheer, and their faces were lined with ancient strata. A single bird hung in the sky.

The ocean was very black and clear. In the shallows, where it met the white sand, it was green as the land was green with scrubby spruces all the way to the horizon . . .

"Let's find the *big* trees!" cried Freydis. And they sailed south for two days and two nights.

Wineland the Good

When [the sun] first comes to visit the east with warmth and bright
beams, the day begins to lift up silvery brows and a pleasant face to the
east wind. Soon the east wind is crowned with golden glory and robed
in all his raiments of joy. He eases griefs and regretful sighs and turns a
bright countenance toward his neighbors on either side, bidding them
rejoice with him in his delight and cast away their winterlike sorrows.

Speculum Regale, V.87–8

The sun arose upon the sea and made it gold. A little later, when the
water was pale blue and translucent, the sky was still gold, flaming like another
world beyond the highest pitch of the Greenlanders' yearning. Still they sailed
south, upon the wrinkled blue plain of the sea, so that their vessels scarcely
trembled. Their long wake-road vanished into the sun's golden spangles,
while a low white cloud lined the horizon. When the sun was fully up,
the sea was a dark, dark blue, foaming and hissing beneath their keels. The
white foam lay upon the water like ice.

At midmorning the sea became as smooth and insidious as smoked glass,
and they saw a low land lined with trees. It was a peninsula, from which
other peninsulas extended, none of them more than the height of two men
above the waves. Low skerries barely broke the ocean-skin. The land's skin
was grass of a rich brown-green color. Rocks reflected in the water their
cleavages, subdivided by the ripples. Beyond, the ocean went on again. In
the bays, the sea was shadowed brownish-green from grass.

The land curled around the ships. Dark green trees grew on its fingers. They
entered a low lagoon, whose ripples were like a thousand smiles. Warm and
blue, the sunny water streamed peacefully. Across the firth was a meadow of
golden green, rolling over a rounded hill to where the evergreens started. The

warblings of the alder-birds made the only music. Black hawks flip-flapped slowly in the air, and the sunlight was like liquid about them so that they seemed like clots of blood-jelly in water. The grass blew in the wind, and all around was the smell of the sea. Wide-leaved little ferns had risen through the dead grass, and they danced in the sun, Wineland being Sunland, Summerland where there had never been Bear-Kings; and the Greenlanders rushed ashore to drink the sweet dew out of flower-cups and they thought that they had never tasted *anything* so sweet, and they were happy. – "The trees that stood with dripping branches and frozen roots," says the *Speculum Regale*, "put forth green leaves, thus showing their joy that the sorrow and distress of winter are past." – Oh, they came before the frost *ever* did! – When Freydis came ashore her husband tried to help her across the sea-mud, but he slipped when she leaned her weight upon him, and she stood upbraiding him in her muddy shoes. "Now I know what a poor husband you are," she cried, "since you cannot even help me across a muddy spot." – Everyone laughed at Thorvard, and he stood smiling and blinking and leaning on his fancy spear. – As for Gudrid, she felt gay, and went running among the rolling hollows of low evergreen trees, and all around her were little lakes full of forested islands. On the beach she found a black mussel shell as blue and white inside as china. The sand was unbroken save by the three-toed imprints of birds. The pale blue waves came gently to the beach, which sloped slowly up, a smooth white shelf, to the unruly grasses, where fast black birds skittered low in the air. Where the sand was wet, Gudrid's feet sank in as if she were walking on butter. A gull-feather lay upon the sand. There were dandelions around the little lagoons. Ahead, there was a blue-green city on the horizon, but all the towers were trees.

Pinpointing their Landfall

From the astronomical observations that they took, we know that they must have landed near New Jersey. But other scholars, some of even greater repute than I, say that the Greenlanders stayed at Cape Cod, in Maine, in Newfoundland, in North Carolina.

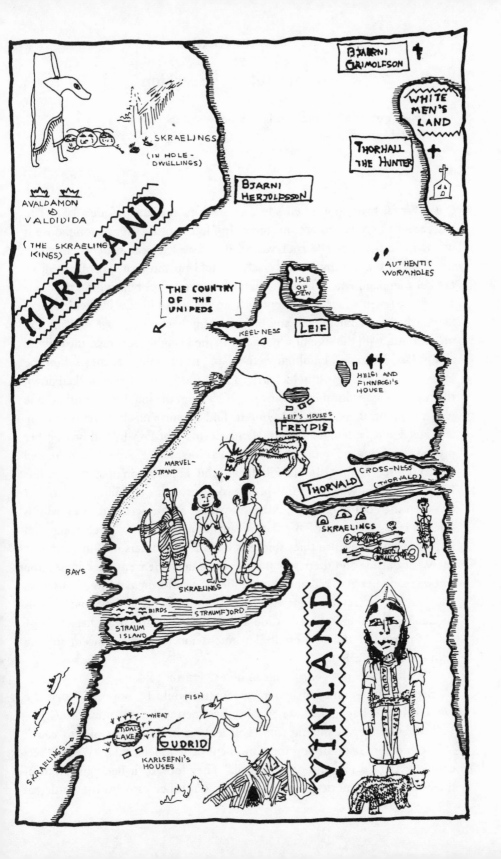

Freydis Takes Possession

Every woman is the freyja of her property, and she who has a
household is a hús-freya.

Yngling Saga, XIII

It was Freydis who found Leif's houses, in a fine meadow beside a lake. The
tall grass had grown up around them. Inside the peat-shagged longhouse it
was dark and moist. The roof was made of peeled beams, between which
smaller sticks were fitted transversely to hold up the peat. Freydis went to
get her men, and when she came back there were fires burning on the floor
and warm green water was dripping from the peat-block walls, which were
like stacked soil strata, green and brown, going back to the Age of King On
on the floor, with the Age of Queen Sigrid the Haughty very near the ceiling;
and in fact, Helgi and Finnbogi were talking of old things as they sat on the
long-benches, for their ship had arrived first; and Freydis's men walked down
the timbered corridor to see if anyone else was in the longhouse, and no one
was for the brothers' men had gone to find Freydis and show her the path;
and Helgi and Finnbogi stopped talking, seeing that Freydis had broken her
promise to bring no more than thirty warriors, and Freydis's men looked
to her to see if they should kill Helgi and Finnbogi in that windowless
longhouse, from which the fire-smoke rose through the ceiling trap so that
not even the cool blue sky could see anything, and it occurred to Freydis as
she leaned against one of the dark beams that she did not need Helgi and
Finnbogi anymore since their ship was harbored with hers in Wineland, and
she went outside and there was no one there, and she went back in and the
smoke made her eyes red and she blundered against the cold wet soil-bricks
and her men were standing with their thumbs on their axes; and Freydis
suddenly yawned and went outside and the grass on the peat-shagged roof
was blowing like the hair of dead women, and then she came in smiling
with her mind made up.

"Why have you put your things in here?" Freydis said.

"Because we assumed that our agreement would be honored," said the
two brothers. They looked at her thirty-five men without expression.

"But," said Freydis smiling still, "Leif lent his houses to me, not to you."

The brothers said nothing for a moment. Then Helgi said, "We brothers
could never be a match for you in evil." They took their belongings out of
the houses and went deep into the woods, until they came to the border of

a lake. Here they built themselves a house; here they labored to glut the hold of their cargo ship with timber, making axe-music among the white blossoms of the cherry trees, the white daisies on the grass-sea like wave-stars reflecting the blossoms above. The brothers shared whatever they had with each other and did not hoard it, for they knew the saying: "Oftentimes, what was meant for a friend is saved for a foe."* Their thralls also worked seriously and well: they were all Icelanders. Helgi and Finnbogi instructed them to hold themselves apart until it became clear where the Greenlanders stood – "for," said Helgi, "their Queen Bitch has already once played us false." – "Oh, she is not the Queen, though she thinks she is," said Finnbogi complacently. "It is that Gudrid who will put her in her place." – "Gudrid?" cried Helgi. "But she does not carry herself like that!" – "Wait and see," said his brother. – As for Freydis, she too commenced immediately to set her people at felling timber for a cargo to Greenland. She was severe and cruel with them, but very clever, and so she soon had filled her ship with maple-wood.

Gudrid and Karlsefni

For Gudrid the new country offered so much of freshness and greenness that for a time her requirement of being first in all things was forgotten, and she kept gazing out at the Isle of Dew where Leif had landed and shaking her head in wonder at the richness all around. – "Even the breezes here are so sweet I could almost make a meal of them!" she exclaimed to her husband. – "There is no question of that," he laughed. "Here in Vinland are more substantial feasts." – Truth to tell, they were both somewhat intoxicated at all that they saw. – They killed a big rorqual† in the shallows on the first day, even as they were bringing their hammocks ashore to Leif's houses, and the meat was good. Almost every week some fine whale would be stranded on the beach; so they had everything they could want. Deer abounded in the forests and meadows around them, and the lake was so plentiful in fish that Gudrid could catch as many as she liked with her hands. – "Oh, there is wealth here!" she cried. – When Freydis heard this, she waded in the lake up to her armpits and swept up all the fish she could into her net. The net was so heavy with fish that she could barely drag it home. – "I see you are

---

* "Let no man stint him and suffer need of the wealth he has won in life," said ODIN the High One. "Oft is saved for a foe what is meant for a friend, and much goes worse than one weens."

† Species of whale with a dorsal fin and wrinkled skin about the throat.

hungry today," said Thorvard mockingly. – For once Freydis did not lose her temper with him. – "Don't you see," she said patiently, "that it is summer now, but when winter comes it may well be as it was in Greenland? Then you will thank me for this." – "No doubt I will," said Thorvard, "but you had better smoke them quickly or they will rot." – "Thralls!" cried Freydis, snapping her fingers. "Build a fire of green twigs and dry these fish for me. And don't eat a single one, because I've counted them!"

As for Gudrid, she sometimes set an especially fine fish aside to be smoked, for she knew that such could be sold for a higher price in Iceland or Greenland should she return there, but the little trout and perch she kept for her own table; so her ships filled up more slowly than Freydis's single ship, although her cargoes were better in every respect. – Nor did Karlsefni immediately load his ship with timber, but left what his thralls had felled on a rock to season. – "There may well be maggots in these unknown trees," he said to his wife, "and this way we will kill them. As for your sister-in-law, if she has a cargo of maggots then her ship will go to the bottom on the way home." – "I pray to CHRIST that it may be so," said Gudrid.

By this time, she was sure that she wanted to live in Vinland forever. She told Karlsefni that if he acted decisively he could easily become chieftain of the new land, as Eirik the Red had done in Greenland. – "We can protect ourselves from the Skrælings," she said. "They must be frightened of us, for we have not seen a single one as long as we have been here." – "These things are in my mind also," said Karlsefni, playing with the buttons of his sleeve. "We have men and ships enough to carry on trade with the home countries. As for the Skrælings, we will see about them when we meet them. It may be that we can burn them all out, and take their lands for ourselves. But remember, Gudrid, that the country we see around us already belongs to Leif. When we have good cargo in all our ships, then we can explore the fjords to the south."

Helgi and Finnbogi

As for Helgi and Finnbogi, nobody knew them except Freydis, and she had quarreled with them several times, so they were seldom visited. They worked their fields with plough and sickle; their men-at-arms and their five women kept to themselves. Karlsefni had gone to their house once and invited them to move closer to the others, for reasons of safety should the Skrælings attack, but they said they would rather take their chances with the Skrælings than with Freydis. Karlsefni could not but find this sensible, especially since they had seen no Skrælings at all.

The Swimming Games

Karlsefni's men did much to support themselves and enrich him. As yet there was no ill-feeling between them and Freydis's men, for Freydis had not so far overstepped herself as to refuse to share Leif's houses with them as she had done with Helgi and Finnbogi. Often they played games in the summer evenings (all marveling at how quickly darkness came on), and the women yelled what they thought would best incite them to good sport. Sometimes the men went swimming in the lake, and made contests between them to see who could stay underwater the longest, for this had come into fashion at the court of King Olaf Trygvesson in Norway. It was said that King Olaf surpassed all other men at this; and indeed I can well believe it, for in the Year of Grace 1000, when pressed in a sea-battle by his enemies King Swend, Earl Eric and King Olaf of the Swedes, he stood on the gangways of his ship, the Long Serpent, and exhorted his men so that they defended him until their swords were dull, "and the fight went on with battle-axe and sword," and the King stood from morning till night shooting with his bow and throwing two spears at once, and finally he went into the forehold and opened a chest that he kept beneath his throne, from which he took many sharp swords, which he passed to his men one by one; but as they received them from his right hand they saw blood gushing down into his steel glove, but he would not say where he was wounded and they did not ask him, so the battle went on and the King's men began to fall, at which his enemy, Queen Sigrid, standing on the bank with her thralls, so far forgot her dignity as to clap her hands; while Eric's men swarmed round the Long Serpent and boarded her, and King Olaf Trygvesson stood fighting on the quarter-deck, protected by his last men, but they, too, fell one by one, and when King Olaf stood almost alone he sprang overboard; and Earl Eric's men tried to grapple with him in their boats, but he raised his golden shield above his head and sank into the sea; and such was his skill at that game that he has never come up since. – So Gudrid's men wrestled laughing with Freydis's men in that clear blue lake that gazed up at the Sun like an eye, and they dunked each other in the water and pulled each other down and shouted to their rivals, "Come, your kingdom is below the waves!" – Karlsefni did not like this mocking of a King, but Gudrid said gently into his ear, "Let them play. They serve us better for it." – As for Freydis, she lay on the shore laughing at the play, while Thorvard sat twirling his spear in his fingers . . .*

Freydis bore herself well in those days. She called Gudrid "sister-in-law," and held several feasts for the people at Leif's houses, as if she were the hostess there. Although some found her overbearing, she was at the peak of her prestige.

Freydis Eiriksdottir

But high summer passed.

---

* Of Olaf's disappearance beneath the waves Halfred Vandrædaskald made a verse that is a constellation of questions and speculations. Did the King doff his mail-shirt under the sea and make his escape by swimming beneath Earl Eric's long-ships? Halfred's conclusion is not definitive:

> "I scarcely know what I should say,
> For many tell the tale each way.
> This I can say, nor fear to lie,
> That he was wounded grievously, –
> But more than this is hard to tell,
> For no news comes, nor good nor ill."

Wearing the Ice-Shirt

It began to blow and raine and to be very darke . . . The nights and the
frosts began to grow upon us.

PELLHAM (1631)

Well, no rune is good or bad, but if you want like to make things
PERMANENT it's best not to use the Rune of Destruction.

Alcoholic on the Bus (1987)

T he pasturage was very fine in Vinland, and the livestock soon became
frisky and difficult to manage. Gudrid had roses in her cheeks; she was pregnant.
She and her husband sometimes sailed along Keel-Ness and Marvel-Strands to
look for stranded whales. Not far away was a cove whose beach was made of
smooth round rocks, and the sea was so clear there that the orange rocks and
white rocks in its bed were as distinct as eggs. Orange cliffs, not much more
than a man's height, ringed the cove around. In their fissures grew manes of
wet salt sea-grass. Above them was a wall of evergreens. Here Gudrid and
Karlsefni sometimes came to talk of private matters. Now that Gudrid had
finally achieved a marriage which was satisfactory to her, she came to love her
husband dearly, for that was her clear duty. As for him, he sometimes thought
that they had achieved a perfect understanding. Gudrid knew this, and took
pleasure in it. But she could not let it stand in the way of her plans.

Two Lessons on Beauty

One day when the sun was sweetly mild and they were in their cove gathering
mussels, Karlsefni gazed at her admiringly, for Gudrid remained pleasing in
men's sight no matter how often they looked at her. – "I can hardly believe

we've been married half a year," he said, "for I never tire of your face."
– Gudrid flushed and smiled, but said nothing. – But Karlsefni could not
stop praising her. – "Beauty is a strange thing," Gudrid replied at last, in
a rather low tone. "Men have been telling me all my life that I have it, but
what is it? Look at that bird in the sky," and Karlsefni, gazing where she
pointed, saw a pretty black bird with white wings, and then Gudrid said,
"Now how much would that bird be to your mind if someone cut off its
wings with an axe?" – "That would be an ill deed," said her husband. –
"Yes, an ill deed," said Gudrid calmly, "and ill-looking that bird would be
without wings. How black and ugly and beaked and clawed, like a troll!", and
Karlsefni said nothing; and Gudrid went on, "Sometimes I'm afraid my luck
is too good. Husband, would you like my face as much if Freydis strangled
me in my sleep? How much would you care for me then?" – "Beautiful you
may be," said Karlsefni, "but those are ugly words to utter. Let us hope they
never come to pass. You know that I dislike Freydis as much as you do, but
it would be better for both of us if you refrained from saying such things
without cause." – "Oh, now you find me heavy to bear," laughed Gudrid,
"but it was you whom I thought so interested in the subject of beauty! And
to think that was only my first lesson to you! – My second lesson is that
people often think something beautiful because they do not understand it.
Do you like that sweet bird-song?", and Karlsefni listened and smiled at the
bird-music that came from somewhere near them, and Gudrid said again,
"Do you like it?", and Karlsefni said, "Well enough." Then Gudrid shook
her head sadly (but, her husband thought, somewhat falsely) and pointed
to a little brown bird almost like a mouse that was cheeping behind her
in the grass, and Karlsefni saw that a green snake with a white stripe along
its back had put its head in the nest-hole to eat the bird's eggs; and now,
having finished that operation, it was eating the bird; Karlsefni saw that the
bird-music was a bird-scream; and at last the snake had crushed the bird into
a ball of twitching blood-furred flesh that it could swallow, so it gaped its
jaws and entombed the bird in itself; and then the snake whipped itself away
from that empty place, and hid beneath the waxy orange cups of flowers.
– "There we have Freydis," Gudrid said, and Karlsefni, meditating like a
monk in the recesses of reason, wondered now what snake or bird his own
wife might be. – "You're certainly determined to make your opinion of her
clear," he said at last. "But I well remember that in Eiriksfjord you were the
one who praised her courage to me." –"If you don't care to do something
about her, then I've had enough of the subject," said Gudrid. "But I will
be happy when we go south to find our own land."

The truth was that Gudrid was very weary of Freydis. It was impossible to avoid witnessing her ordering her men about with shouts and blows. She seemed so unrestrained in Wineland now that people wondered at it; she seemed almost wild. Certainly Thorvard was wretched on account of her. Once Gudrid and Freydis were preparing the day-meal together, and Gudrid said to Thorvard, "What's your favorite dish?", and Thorvard looked a little shy but said finally that his favorite dish was whale-meat, and Freydis said, "No, whale-meat is not your favorite dish, Thorvard. You prefer seal-meat, don't you, because it's easier for you to hit a seal over the head!", and Thorvard went red in the face. For no reason that anyone could see, Freydis's anger had come out like a knife, clean and sharp and shining. – Gudrid, who had always been able to rule (so she fancied) through a beautifully calculated sweetness, intensely disliked Freydis's way of managing her affairs, for she had no understanding of the difficulties that Freydis suffered under. Gudrid also had little fondness for Freydis's men, who were sullenly taciturn, but raped her with their eyes. She considered them outlaws, wolf's-heads and home-takers. In the evenings, when the work was done, they stood in the doorway of their dark house.

The Search for the Skrælings

As for Freydis, she was restless. Although she was enriching herself beyond her greediest dreams, she had not fulfilled Blue-Shirt's commission, and did not know how to go about it. She had no familiar in whom she could confide her wickedness, for her men, since she had picked them to suit her, were tools, not counsellors. Each day was beautiful; Freydis wished, however, to improve the day. At length it occurred to her to search for the Skrælings. Despite the others' complacency, she knew that there must be some. Had they not killed her brother Thorvald? Freydis had always associated the Skrælings with magic and evil; surely they worshipped some relative of AMORTORTAK whom she could go to for assistance and instruction. (She hated the Skrælings for being little and dark, like thralls.) So she often wandered, with an axe in her belt, among the birch-trees, beyond which a grey-blue light played over the lakes. Freydis followed those lakes and found spruces, hemlocks, and rivers like brown mirrors which were disturbed only occasionally by rapids whose tassels of white water did not in the least prevent the surrounding water from reflecting the fractured planes of the rocks, in which grasses and mosses grew, and sometimes deer came to drink, and saw themselves in the

water without being frightened, and ferns and maple saplings grew all around
in the moss. (Sometimes Helgi and Finnbogi also went roving through that
forest and threw themselves down into beds of moss. The moss was so thick
that they could have hewn blocks of it for seats.) But she found no sign of
the Skrælings. – There was a wide blue lake. Freydis waded in. She stepped
on speckled granite pebbles (black spots on white), which glowed richly in
the clear water. She waded toward the low, forested islands. But the Skrælings
were not there.

The Leaf-Sun

There are some people who give warnings of their darker moods. Such was
Killer-Glum of Iceland, who (so says his saga) turned pale and wept tears
the size of hailstones whenever his slaying-fit was on him. But Freydis gave
no sign of her most horrible thoughts, so the sagas seem to indicate; – and
yet I think that everyone reveals himself somehow.

In the forest beside Leif's houses was a tall tree whose leaves were spiked like
suns. In the summer Freydis plucked one and folded it upon itself, tormenting
it into glossy leaf-jaws full of teeth, then letting it open upon her palm until
once again it was a leaf-sun transfixed upon the sun's own thorns. – It was
a holly tree. – Freydis closed the leaf again, so that the Sun was tormented
upon her own thorns, those thorns twisted and ingrown all the way to the
Sun's heart; then she let the leaf go, and it sprang open again; and she folded
it so that it was a glossy green leaf-mouth with teeth . . .

The Dream of the Ice-Cliffs

At night it was very dark, and there were noises that Freydis had never heard
before, teeming noises of joyous indifference. The flickering of the fire cast
shadows on the trees, so that it was the trees that seemed to flicker, not the
stars. Now the logs in the fire blackened and looked very very old before they
crumbled to embers. Searching the sky a little desperately, Freydis thought
she saw a grey light in it to the far north where her home was, but the light
was interrupted by a smudge of cloud. The trees stood out with illusory
distinctness against that light, every branch and needle of them, and for a
moment Freydis felt radiant and fine. But presently the light died and all
she could see were the last embers, almost blood-red against the darkness.

Whereas the dreams of the other Greenlanders moved south night by night until they dreamed joyously of moonlit flowers, rilling dew-cups, and Gudrid dreamed that pink and white flowers from heaven kissed her lips, Freydis must wear an ice-shirt for her night-shirt, and so at best she could but dream of Slab-Land with its low blue ridges spattered with snow. She wandered across an endless flat brown landscape, streaked with ice-puddles and snow. Her bare feet were shoed in ice as she went her aimless and dreary way, and the wind smote her with frost. Sometimes the snowdrifts were shaped like animals, but they were always distorted, deformed beasts which would have been able to live only as monsters, like Gudrid's wingless bird. Northward the land was traversed by many gullies where the snow was thick. Presently the white and the brown appeared in equal proportions, and then the white ruled. The land seemed less dreary when it was that color. But it did not seem any better a place to be. Rock-ridges underlined the snow, and there were blue-white mountains almost like lumps of shattered frozen glass; they had almost as many faces as crystals. Milky-blue fjords insinuated their wide arms between the peaks, and dark-blue traceries informed their ice. Ahead were big blue cliffs. They grinned like teeth. They swung apart as Freydis neared them, and she could see a dark fjord winding deep into mountains and snow and more mountains, and then the cliff-teeth began to chew and the fjord salivated icy rivers because the cliffs saw her coming and were hungry, and Freydis woke up sobbing in the longhouse and Thorvard was rocking her and stroking the sleeves of her night-shirt and for a moment she actually loved him as she would have loved anyone who'd rock her after such dreams.
– Poor Freydis!

Later in the summer they often slept outside, until the Skrælings came. – Who knows why the starry sky is full of brightness? – It was all so joyous, because Wineland was a place of joy.

Freydis in the Forest

Up in the northern headlands Vinland was a little more like Greenland, with steep hills of loose rock shining in the sun, and secret Skræling paths along the cliff-sides, beside white waterfalls; but the gorges were clothed by birches which grew taller than any Greenland trees, and in such great numbers as to almost exhaust her cupidity.

Here by the ocean were spruces which the wind had bent at right angles to their trunks, so that they grew horizontally, dead grey in color like witches'

brooms. The low hills were ranked with these trees, whose grey trunks and
white trunks stood like rib-bones planted upright in the darkness. Ravens
winged through the fog. Freydis could sometimes see the air between their
pinions. The grey breasts of the unknown trees were covered with ivy, as if
they were knights dressed in ring-armor. She pushed her way between these,
and entered a forest eaten by bugworms. Here and there a tree-corpse had
fallen, wrenching up roots, dirt and turf with it like a toppled pedestal. The
farther she went, the closer together grew the spruce trees. Their grey twigs,
which seemed white in the shadow, formed wiry shelves on which Freydis
hung gold rings as an offering to AMORTORTAK, for the place was cursed in
her imagination. When she had finished with her work, there would be dirty
patches of snow here even at the end of Sun-Month, hiding between the
trees on the steep hillsides. But as yet there was still no winter in Wineland.
– A plump grey rabbit sat beneath a tree, its forelegs resting against its folded
hindlegs, its ears raised. When it saw her, it shifted its legs, but it did not
otherwise move, not knowing what she was, so she speared it easily and
hung it from a tree as a sacrifice. Then she turned away from the forest,
its cold and shady branches raking her on every side. Although the sky was
clear, a grey cloud-stone was poised in the north, ready to fall down over
everything and blot it out.

The Grove of Uppsala ca. 800 – ca. 1000

In Sweden, dead horses, dogs and men hung from the trees. During the
nine-day assembly in honor of the gods, men were impaled on spears and
raised into the trees, where they hung and rotted so that flesh-gobbets dangled
from the black claw-branches and ODIN's ravens picked at their faces and
hooded them beneath their black wings. Skeletons creaked in the breeze like
lanterns. In the summer the horse-fat sizzled in the sun and dripped from the
free-spinning hoofs that clanked and clanked so restlessly. Flies lived beneath
the tree-leaves, happy in sun and shade. Ravens lived in ribcages, feasting
on livers and then nesting there like the half-hidden faces that had been
carved in Eirik's bench-boards, so that when the new victims were raised
up the ravens flew into their safe bone-houses and peered cawing between
the rib-bars until the groans and struggles had stopped; and then they flapped
cautiously through the leaf-sky like shadows, ready at any time to read menace
with their sharp eyes and hide in their nests, which were lined with beak-torn
scraps of the dead men's clothes, so that for the first time the men wore their

robes inside them instead of outside, and the plump black mother-ravens hatched their eggs there and fed their young on the maggots that writhed as white as living bones. – When the people killed their victims, they sang beautiful songs. Sometimes they drowned them in the springs that watered the grove, and if the gods were delighted the dim white bodies vanished in the water, transubstantiated into heaven like the lucky inhabitants of Hiroshima. – The holiest assemblies lasted for nine days, and at them sacrifices were required every day, for the wooden god-images were watching and waiting in their dark wooden house, which was red and white with gold ornaments that gleamed and sent their sun-rays upwards through the trees to pass between the rib-bones and so ascend to Valhalla, where the gods were pleased, FREYJA especially, for gold was Her tears; and because gold belonged to FREYJA it also belonged to Freydis, who had been named for Her and dedicated to Her just as her dead brothers Thorstein and Thorvald had been dedicated to THOR for their good, their strength. At the name-fastening their father had given each of the boys a hammer-token with which to bless himself and protect himself from evil, but all that was laid aside when Greenland was Christianized. – Beyond the god-house rose a great sacred tree that was green in summer and winter. That tree, of course, was the World-Ash, Yggdrasil. Many died when Yggdrasil died.

A Depiction of Yggdrasil in a Seventeenth-century Icelandic Manuscript of the Prose Edda*

Yggdrasil grows high, with a crown like an artichoke, and green and yellow banana-leaves. An eagle peacock crows in crest-heaven. Below are the four mischievous squirrels, Dain, Dvalin, Duney and Durathror, scaling the green trunk in their hunger and agile malice, the first pair of them almost at the crown, the others ascending from the tree's great and wild blossoms, no two of which are alike, some being star-shaped, some fruited or flowered; and then the trunk of Yggdrasil speeds down, down, down, through infinite space, coarsening as it goes until it has become a chain of oval orange vertebrae branching into world-roots, beneath which waits the horrid Midgaard Serpent.

*AM 73846 'Okunnur listamathur.

The Trees of Vinland

In Markland and Wineland the trees rose high and green. Markland of course was Tree-Land, and trees of great magnificence could be found there, but Wineland was WINELAND THE GOOD; and it was here, if anywhere, that Freydis might find Yggdrasil since she was not in Sweden. Here, so the sagas read, the grapes on the vine made men drunk. Somewhere in Wineland, then, must be a great Tree of Splendor whose leaves were moist, whose fruits were sweet, whose blossoms were of every color. She had thought upon her mission to Blue-Shirt even upon leaving Gardar with its foggy mountains, Gardar with its low green ridge-wrapped bay; for as she stepped aboard her ship (Thorvard trailing behind on the dock, with many backward looks at their fine stone house) she knew that her duty to Blue-Shirt lay undone; and Freydis was a great respecter of her duties to others when they were more powerful than she. They sailed down the straight sea-arm that they had often sailed the other way to Brattahlid; they went south to Herjolfsness, for Thorvard had a little trading to do there on the way, and then they left that last fjord, leaving behind the shelter of its black slab-walls; and they sailed deeper and deeper into the Greenland Sea until they could barely sight the rocky tip of Herjolfsness twisting like the tail of a seahorse, and the black blocky headland above it vanished in the clouds; and then they were alone in the sea, and all the time Freydis did not know what she must do in Vinland to plant her frost-seed; and now she was alone in the forest amidst a delicate airiness of trees and still she did not know what she must do; and white light slid up and down the taut spider-threads stretched between the forks of shaggy trees, upon which shadows shimmered (while on the surface of a shallow creek, the light trembled as if only it, not the water, were moving); and under the trees many extended raspberry-arms rose and fell quietly, while the ferns rocked themselves in sunlight as in darkness: until Freydis was lost and confused, and peered up a steep slope of yellow-green and evergreen at the peaceful darkness in which more deeply losing herself would have been a luxury because then she might have lost the imperative which Blue-Shirt had strapped to her shoulders. When she craned her head she could see, at almost the extremest angle toward the vertical, a few blue chinks of sky, like tiles set into a stained-glass window; and the sun pressed lovingly down and struck a single golden tree, while everything behind was filled with shady wonder; and still Freydis did not take the hint, although the tree-boughs rode the sea of wind so silently and tirelessly that they seemed uncanny to her, for she had led a treeless life; and suddenly she recalled the fear she had felt upon walking late one evening down a forest path, soon after she had come to Vinland, and perceiving that in the absence of any breeze *one* tree's branches were waving; she could not understand how this could be, unless there were spirits; and now the sun came lower and set all the trees on fire, and she saw one tree streaming with golden glory and wholly believed in YGGDRASIL the Summer-Tree so that her faith was beating in her breast with great heart-strokes, and Freydis decided that for Blue-Shirt's sake (which was her sake) she would find Yggdrasil and cut it down. It did not matter so much to her. She was, after all, a Christian woman.

The Dream of the Seven Birds

Meanwhile, Gudrid also dreamed a dream. It seemed to her that there were seven wood-brown birds flying through the forest, and then suddenly one of them turned white and fell down dead.

Skins for Milk

The man who is to be a trader will have to brave many perils,
sometimes at sea and sometimes in heathen lands, but nearly always
among alien peoples; and it must be his constant purpose to act
discreetly wherever he happens to be.

Speculum Regale, III.79

I n the following summer, Karlsefni and Gudrid sailed south, with most
of the other ships in their expedition. Their foam-trails marbled the sea. –
Freydis, however, remained in Leif's houses. After all, she reminded everyone
again, he had loaned them to *her*. She considered this time, when the others
were away, an excellent opportunity to find the great tree Yggdrasil. Her
men, having been idle for some time, had begun to chafe at her leadership,
and might soon have seized their liberty, had Freydis not taken them into
her confidence. – "There is a certain tree I am looking for," she said. "Its
wood will bring a high price at home. I will give a good reward to whichever
of you finds it. And if you meet the Skrælings, I give you license to rape
and to rob as you desire, provided you bring me back one prisoner alive."
– Thus incited, her men set off into the trees, singly and in small groups,
as they would. – As for Helgi and Finnbogi, no one consulted them any
longer. They stayed in their house with their thirty men, their five women,
and no one knew what they did.

The other ships sailed south for many days, until they found a tidal
lake around which wild wheat grew in abundance, waving and shining like
Gudrid's hair. On the higher ground were more grapes than they had ever
seen, even those among them who had been to Germany. Their purple
juice was very sweet. A cupful of it made a man drunk. In the streams of
the fjord were so many fish that the Greenlanders had but to dig trenches
at high tide to trap all the halibut they wanted. The forests were full of

far more game than they could eat. Gudrid and her husband formally took possession of this country; burning no THOR-fire, however, as they too were Christians.

They had been there a fortnight when early one morning they saw nine skin-boats coming up the river. As the Skrælings approached them, they began to wave long rattle-sticks in a sunwise motion, and the Greenlanders were confounded.

"Have your weapons ready, but not obvious," ordered Karlsefni. He stood there watching the Skrælings. "I wonder what this whirling of sticks means?" he said.

"Perhaps it is a sign of peace," said Snorri Thorbrandsson. "I suggest that we go to meet them with a white shield."

"That seems wise," said Karlsefni, and that is what was done.

Wading ashore, the Skrælings stared at them astonished. They had never seen anyone like the Greenlanders before. To the Skrælings they seemed great big people, with wide legs like bears. The women, though smaller, seemed very stiff and straight to the Skrælings; their hair was a golden wonder. The Skrælings could not understand where these tall people had come from. For a long time they looked at them, and then they got back into their skin-boats and paddled away.

Snorri Karlsefnisson

Gudrid wanted to winter where they were, and as usual she got her way. The Greenlanders built houses on a slope by the lake, some close to the water, some far, and upon Karlsefni's orders they erected a palisade around the settlement. The livestock were let out to graze as they would. There was no snow at all. Shortly after Christmas, Gudrid gave birth to a son, whom she named Snorri. He was the first white to be born in Vinland. Laughing, Gudrid took him in her hot arms.

Two Dear Friends

"Mistress, you must hurry south!" cried Freydis's men when they found out what had happened. "Gudrid has had a brat and taken possession of the best land in the south, and there are Skrælings!" – "Very good," said Freydis coolly. She threw them a golden ring. But she was shaking with excitement.

– She set sail the same day. Her husband, too, was anxious to make the voyage: he smelled trade. – When Karlsefni saw that pair of vulture-birds, he became flushed with rage, for Gudrid had incited him unwearyingly against Freydis, but now it was Gudrid herself who said, "Well, husband, we have seen Skrælings after all, so now she may prove useful." – Then Karlsefni shook his head and let the matter rest. – As for Gudrid, she greeted her guests heartily, and gave their men quarters in one of her longhouses. She played the hostess with Freydis as Freydis had done with her, and none of this was lost on anyone. – So only Helgi and Finnbogi remained with their men by Leif's houses. Everyone else was now living in Gudrid's country.

Freydis's Milk

In the spring (it would be the last spring) the Skrælings returned, a vast horde of them, swarming up the river in their skin-boats and waving their sun-sticks sunwise. There were so many of them that their numbers blackened the river. – "Raise your white shields," said Karlsefni. The others did so, and the Skrælings landed and approached them. They made it clear by signs that they wanted to trade. – Oh, but they were evil-looking little people! Their cheekbones were broad; their hair was coarse; their skins were a swarthy darkness! They dressed themselves in skins, like shape-changers. The Greenlanders despised them. But trade was trade.

Now, what did the Skrælings have to offer? The women brought their reed-woven bags stuffed full of moose-meat; the men offered arrow-points of stone. But the Greenlanders had no use for such trifles. Then the Skræling men threw down their packs, and took out pelts and sables and furs of all kinds, pointing to the Greenlanders' spears as if they craved them. – "We will not let them have weapons, no matter what they offer us," said Karlsefni. "Remember, they are friends today, but they might be enemies tomorrow." And all the Greenlanders deemed this a wise principle.

"Let us trade them red cloth," said Freydis's husband Thorvard. He had never seen furs so fine. There would be a tremendous market for them at Herjolfsness. – Freydis smiled at him; and he looked up at her, rubbing the sleeve-buttons of his robe. Freydis knew that his purse hung at the belt of his undercoat, dangling and wobbling like his bloated testicles.

Thorvard approached the Skrælings with his bundle, smiling and twinkling his eyes. Here at last he was in his element. The Skrælings watched him cautiously. When he threw down his bundle they leaped back, but then they saw him open it; then, when he took from it span after span of red cloth, they shouted with excitement. So they traded red cloth for grey pelt, and the Skrælings tied the cloth around their heads as soon as they got it and danced for happiness, for red was sacred to them.* Now the other Greenlanders ran to get all the red cloth they had, and the trading went on until the red cloth ran short, and Freydis cried, "Cut it smaller, you fools!" – Thorvard was the first to try this trick. He took a span of cloth, and solemnly sliced it into pieces no more than a finger's width. The poor Skrælings, having never before seen public dishonesty calmly and graciously performed, thought that the smaller cloth-lengths must be more special and sacred than the others, and so they paid even more pelts for them, and all the Greenlanders liked Freydis that day and Freydis laughed until she was almost sick. – But at last the red cloth was exhausted, no matter how small the Greenlanders cut it, and the Skrælings were still standing there with skins in their packs. – "Let's pay them with milk!" said Freydis, intoxicated with her own shrewdness. – "Bring them milk, all you women," said Karlsefni. – The women went inside their houses and came out with pails of milk, Freydis going first because the others were afraid. When the Skrælings saw the white liquid they sniffed it and wrinkled up their faces in puzzlement, as if they did not know what it was, for there were no cows in Vinland. –"Don't you even know what *milk* is, you animals?" Freydis screamed at them, quite carried away with herself. "Don't your women have *milk* in their tits?" – And she pointed to the milk-pails and squeezed her own breasts through her robe, to make the Skrælings understand. – But at this gesture they cowered back, and Freydis saw that they feared her when she did that. – "Oh, you don't like my tits?" Freydis mocked them. She stopped playing with herself and put her hands on her hips. "Well, the milk isn't from me. Go ahead and taste it, you ugly thralls! Drink it up and give us all your skins!" – She seized a dark Skræling boy by the hand and forced his head into a milk-pail. He drank, and when she let him go he was grinning and dancing. The others touched his milky face with their fingers and licked them. They they rushed up to drink the

* In those days there was Power everywhere. You did not have to be wise to find it. Power lived in pretty feathers; Power was in stars and owls' beaks; Power was in the patterns that the women painted on everyone's shirts so that they could find the animals they hunted and kill them; they could bring back meat to eat and clothe everyone in their skins and they could all dream of the Star People who dwelled on the black roof above the trees and sparkled at their images in brooks and lakes; they dreamed also of the Plant People who came on green legs bringing corn-gifts and tobacco-gifts; and all the gifts had Power; but the most Powerful color was *red*, and the women made paint from red earth and birds' eggs and painted special things on everyone's shirts, so the red cloth of the Jenuaq was highly prized.

milk. – "Well done, Freydis!" cried Karlsefni. – And so the Greenlanders got all the Skrælings' pelts, and the Skrælings got some milk and some scraps of red cloth. (Who is to say who traded most advantageously? For they are all dead now.)

The Seduction of Kluskap

The Skrælings came often to trade after that, to the pleasure of both sides, for Karlsefni's cows produced plenty of milk, and his storehouses had plenty of room for skins. In time the Greenlanders and the Skrælings could understand a few of each others' words. It was Freydis, too clever in many things, who talked to the Skrælings, and found out that their god was called GLOOSKAP. – In fact He was not a god at all, but a shape-changing Person with Power; Freydis, however, not having known any such, assumed that He must be a god, that He must take worshippers, that He must be in league with AMORTORTAK. Just as, seeing in the face of a stranger features similar to those of someone you've always known you let yourself be lulled into trusting the external resemblance, so Freydis, knowing that both were gods, trusted that both were cruel. She called upon GLOOSKAP, and asked Him to make her richer, and promised that soon she would bring the frost from Greenland. She was so fertile in her dreaming; in her lust for a master she was so sunnily adulterous . . .

The Skull in the Sea

Just over a rise from the settlement was deep grass, and then the ocean, as if the Greenlanders' houses had never been. Young hard spruce-buds kissed dandelion-caps and lovely purple irises in this bee-meadow whose buzzing ascended pleasingly to the sun. In the tidal lagoon beneath was a grassy bluff scattered with bleached driftwood logs, and then a wide tongue of pebbly beach on which Freydis stood by herself, irresolute. It was the month of Egg-Tide. A cold wind was blowing in from the ocean. Freydis walked north to a low and lonely point, where the white surf crashed against the fractured rocks, upon which were only breeze-stirred salt-puddles. East and north of her she could see nothing but ocean. She knelt with her face in the north and prayed to AMORTORTAK, her noble and most excellent Chieftain: "I wish to thank You for giving me Your peace and forbearance for so long when I have not yet fulfilled my promise to You. Do not be impatient with me. I will do my part. I am like a gold ring which You have sent out among your people; I know You desire my safe return, so that You may add me once again to Your hoard." – So she spoke at length, praising herself to Him so that

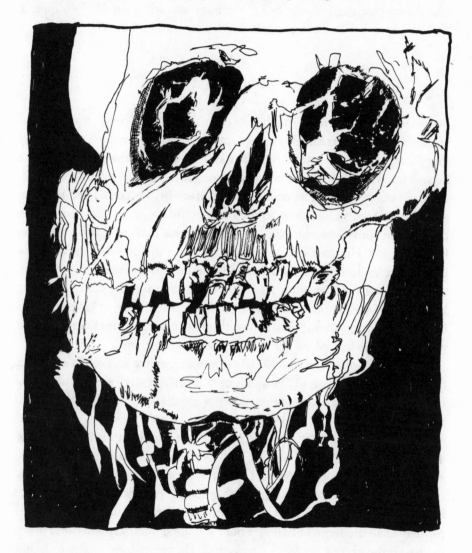

HUMAN SKULL

He would be reminded of her value, and swearing anew to do His will. Then, walking south across the point, she came to a beach where boulders formed themselves into double arches, like the eye-sockets of a skull, through which the milk-grey sea gazed mildly, while the forehead was flat and green-grown,

and though the skull had no mouth the teeth were scattered thickly about: –
smooth pebbles, black, orange, red and white. Because this was a prodigy,
Freydis considered that Blue-Shirt had heard her prayer. She bowed again,
and a cloud-shadow came to the edge of the ocean. (In those days, as I have
said, the shape-changers were dying out, but it was still possible to do quite a
bit with prayer.) – The place is still there today; it is called "The Arches."

The Luck of Skofte Carrion-Crow

Meanwhile Freydis's men had not been idle. In small bands, they ranged
among the low green islands that decorated the lakes, slaughtering whatever
they found. There was one among them called Skofte Carrion-Crow, because
he was known to follow in the footsteps of others, and to swoop away with
whatever booty of theirs he could. For this habit he was considered less than
a man, but Freydis found him all the more useful the more despised he was,
because she could make him do unpleasant chores for her, in order to retain
her protection. He acted as a pimp for her in many things. – The deer were so
plentiful in Vinland that Freydis's men killed them whenever they saw them,
taking only whatever portion was convenient to carry; so Skofte, following
behind, was never hungry. – "Ha, ha!" the men would laugh. "Leave the guts
for Skofte Carrion-Crow!" Of course they left him far more than that, as it
was less trouble in Vinland for them to be compassionate.

It was Skofte who first discovered an encouragement to Freydis's designs,
for as he was grubbing in the belly of a fawn that the others had left he
came across a mass of browse in which a great leaf lay undigested. It was
gold and red and green; it glowed like radium, and it was from an ash tree.
– Skofte capered with joy. He clutched the leaf tightly in his bloody hands.
This was the first lucky thing that had ever happened to him. (Those who
are genuinely ill-favored by luck, I have found, are often thrown a crumb of
undeniable richness, so that they can no longer pretend that richness does
not exist anywhere, and then, when their usual run resumes, they will be
tormented all the more.) Skofte set out for Gudrid's country at a run. He was
in the northeast, not far from Cross-Ness. He swam from island to island,
with the leaf in his mouth. He ran through the trees and swamps until the
sea-smell came into his nostrils, and he swung north to avoid Helgi and
Finnbogi's uncanny house, and thence poled his skiff down the coast to
Freydis.

"Well, well," said she dryly, seeing him. "What now?"

In answer, the little man held out the leaf to her, which blazed and shone with a wonderful fire, so that for a moment Freydis was timid and perplexed, but seeing that it had not harmed Skofte, she took it boldly into her hand.

Freydis, Gudrid and the Great Tree

After this, Freydis went looking everywhere for Yggdrasil, but she could never find it because her purpose was selfish and so she was blinded by the goldness of her own self-light; great spikes of gold light pierced her eyes like spears so that she wandered seeing sunny meadows and sunny trees; and everything sent up a shout of golden rejoicing to her god JEHOVAH, whose Son on earth we call the WHITE CHRIST (although to Red Eirik He was BALDUR, the son of ODIN the High One); but Freydis cried in this joyous light because she could not find what she wanted to find; yes, the tears rushed from her eyes in round drops that caught the sunlight and seemed gold to her (for, as all men know, the kenning for gold is "FREYJA's tears"); but her selfishness maddened her with pleasure at the same time that its consequences hurt her; so the gold light she saw in everything was the light of herself, the gold-perfect self that she had been born with and lost to Blue-Shirt, so she rushed through the trees calling her own name and wanting to make love to herself; she laughed when she glimpsed her face in the pools of slow wide rivers, and tried to drink herself up; she kissed her own lips in the water; she drank and drank the sweet water but she could not become any more herself than she already was; she made love to tree-trunks that might have her shape; so she staggered through the forest, forgetting her scattered clothes, ignorant of the blood that streamed from the cuts in her feet; but of course it was because she loved herself so much that she had given herself away. She had never been able to give herself to anyone who wanted to have her except Blue-Shirt, and in Him she had made such a terrible bargain that she did not want to think about it. So she blundered through golden spiderwebs, and golden beetles tumbled from the trees and crawled in her hair ... At last it was night, and the sun-madness left her, so that, sour, naked and footsore, she could stride the long ells home to Gudrid's houses.

At last it became clear to her that she could not discover Yggdrasil by herself, so she prayed to Blue-Shirt and asked His advice, and in a dream He told her to send Gudrid to seek it, for while Gudrid was by no means a superior person (said Blue-Shirt with a sneer), she was nonetheless unblinded, since,

though she had prostituted herself before, she had at last married someone
for whom she could feel love. Freydis did not care to understand this. It was
very bitter for her to be forced to ask Gudrid's help in anything. Nor, of
course, did she care to tell Gudrid that what she searched for was Yggdrasil
– for all the Greenlanders remembered how in Herjolfsness Gudrid had
refused to sing the *Warlock-Songs* for the Prophetess even though the need
pressed, and her mind was changed only by force of the farmer Thorkel's
rebuke. – So Freydis must hatch a plot to deceive Gudrid. (Happily, Freydis
could hatch plots as well as ever a hen hatched eggs.) At length, therefore,
she called Skofte Carrion-Crow to her and gave him back the leaf he had
given her, directing him to present it secretly to Gudrid, and to make her
swear to reveal its secret to no one else – for that way Freydis would be
called on only to watch Gudrid, and no other. As for her own men, they
were gold-greedy enough to be silent about the matter. – "But I tell you,
Carrion-Crow," cried Freydis, "if you're slipshod in this, oh, how I'll beat
you and beat you!" – "Fear not," said Skofte. "I love to deceive highborn
ladies." – Freydis laughed.

... "That is a pretty leaf," said Gudrid, turning it over and over in her
hand.

"Yes," replied Skofte. "As you see, mistress, it is gold, and it comes from
a great Tree that I have been searching for."

"It is not like Freydis to give you leisure for such errands as wooing trees,"
Gudrid said a little sharply.

Now Skofte had been warned that Gudrid would raise this point. So craftily
he hung his head and said, "Mistress, I am not happy to be her thrall, though
I would not have this widely known. When I find this Tree, I will strip the
wood-gold from it and buy my freedom. If you wish to help me, I will gladly
share with you equally. But you must swear to tell no one about this, not
even your husband, for since he is the leader of this expedition there are
those who listen behind him, and I would not have someone deprive me
of my gold-right."

Gudrid was suspicious, and did not like this proposal. Nor did she approve
of this thrall's stealing away from Freydis his labor, which – however much
Gudrid disliked her – certainly belonged to her by right. But, as Skofte well
knew, Gudrid was also an ambitious woman. He made her see how thrilling
it would be if she could enrich herself and her husband with this fabulous
tree-gold. So at last she agreed to go looking for it when she could. And,
in her pride, and her hope of surprising her husband, she swore not to tell
Karlsefni.

"Very good, mistress," said Skofte when he saw that she was resolved. "Now surely since I have helped you, you should give me some gift."

Gudrid flushed with anger. "Here," she said, throwing him a bolt of cloth. "Take it with my curses, thrall."

"A curse does not decrease the value of cloth as fine as this," laughed Skofte as he went his way. And when he told Freydis of it, she thought it a very fine saying.

Freydis and Thorvard

"What do you think everybody's talking about in the longhouse at night, when you're snoring and burping?" This friendly question was addressed to Thorvard by his slender longhaired wife. (What if women became more and not less lovely as time passed? Seeing true beauty one can only despair. – At least she was getting uglier, Thorvard consoled himself; at least she was losing her power over him.)

"How should I know?" said Thorvard. "Timber and women, I guess."

"Mainly they're talking about what a laughingstock you are," Freydis said. "They know you don't defend me. Last night I heard Gudrid say you probably couldn't even satisfy me as a husband."

"And what did you say to that?" said Thorvard wearily. He was all too used to this.

"I said nothing," said Freydis calmly. "It's your place, not mine, to reply to such accusations."

Thorvard said nothing. His marriage had long been a chimera, like King Halfdan's Yule-feast.

"Everyone can see you don't defend me," repeated Freydis. "Everyone wonders how bold Gudrid's men can be before you'll doing anything. Yesterday they waylaid me in the woods and abused me."

"If they touched you," said Thorvard, "I imagine their fingers got frostbitten."

Freydis and Gudrid

Gudrid loved to bathe herself and little Snorri in a pool screened round with oak trees; there she knelt on one knee on a soft ring of moss that ran round the pond, and dangled her white ankle in the water; she undid her hair and let the baby play with it; she gave him suck; she sat in the water and sang to him, while Freydis watched her white body from behind a tree: – oh, how beautiful Gudrid was! – Freydis wanted to chop her guts out.

Wearing the Gold-Shirt

Never did Gudrid suspect that the beautiful leaf which she fingered day and night was BÖLVERKR's.* Oh, just as the Bear-Shirt made men see red-leaf forests through a hot rainy haze of blood; just as the Blue-Shirt made the wearer's world glitter cold and grand and beautiful in a thousand twinkling mirrors, so the Gold-Shirt glared and shone like the sun's eye, so hot and bright that only an unseeing rose like Gudrid could open herself to it trustingly and lovingly and feed upon it and grow from it; she was warm and happy; she was thrilled with the gold she longed to feed on: – how her husband would value her then! Though she knew she gave of herself simply by being herself, because she was so beautiful and gentle, Gudrid longed to present Karlsefni with gold. She did not crave it for its own sake, as did Thorvard; she did not want it for what it could buy, as did Karlsefni; she wanted only to give him material proof of her love, for she had now entered that time of her life when she longed to give something back – not exactly to appease the giving spirits of her father and Thorir and Thorstein Eiriksson and Thorstein the Black, but more to reestablish an equality with the world which had given her so much; then, too, when her son Snorri had reached the age of reason, it would be deeply satisfying to her to give him gold to help him start out in life; what a fortunate woman she would be who did this! – So she drew on the Gold-Shirt; she smiled and kissed her baby; she lashed him to her back and set out in the forest whenever she could evade her husband's loving vigilance (and she did not know that Skofte Carrion-Crow always followed her); and her hair was golden, so she hooded herself in gold . . .

Thorvard and the Skrælings

As for Thorvard, although Gudrid pitied and despised him and he for his part rarely thought of her, he wore the same shirt that she did. Every night he counted the pelts in his long low sea-chest, rubbing those ermine-beards and beaver-beards luxuriously against his own, wishing he could keep them all for himself because they were *valuable*, but knowing that he would sell

* Name for ODIN meaning "the Evil-Doer."

them all for precisely that reason when he got back to Greenland. Every dawn, every noon he went down to the river to look for skin-boats. When he saw Skrælings he rushed to cut his red cloth narrower and narrower. If he saw them wearing the cloth that he had sold them, an ache went through his heart because it was *valuable*: if he could have it back again he would be able to sell it to them for more skins! – If only he had thought to bring other red things from Gardar! If only he could put on one of his many skin-shirts forever: – then he would love himself; then he would be *valuable* . . .

New Clothes

To the boy Snorri, who was now two years old, the world smelled of pine-logs and peat; and he laughed without understanding at the red eyes of the long-fire winking so merrily at him; his mother, who adored him, often smothered him in her arms, for she was not nearly so hard-pressed by her tasks here as in Greenland; the country was kinder and so was she. Once he was playing with a twig just outside the doorway when he heard a marvelous noise that made him clap his hands; it was the sound of a sentry's horn, for the Skrælings were coming to trade. But his mother, instead of being overjoyed by the noise as he was, snatched him quickly into the house and bolted the door. For the first time, something sad and heavy stirred inside the boy's bowels like a snake. But he soon forgot it, because the fire flickered at him so brightly. Now he heard the strange Skræling voices (for the People of KLUSKAP, as they always did, pointed at the chests of these Jenuaq crying: "*Muskunamu'kwesik!*" – in truth the white people's hearts *were* so icy-blue!), and he listened because his mother was listening; he watched her draw back her lips in disgust saying, "Skrælings!" and the boy jumped up and down in delight at the odd word and said: "Skrælings! Skrælings!"

How the Skrælings Whitened Themselves

Oh, how astonished were the People★ at these white giants! They called them *Jenuaq* to each other; in discussing them they used the word *Wŏbálŭse* – to

---

★ "The name Micmac comes from their word *nikmaq*, which means 'my kin-friends'," as a Canadian schoolbook explains (1983). "The Micmac used this word as a greeting, when speaking to the newcomers from Europe. Later the French adopted the term and began addressing these Indian friends and allies as *nikmaqs*. Over the years, the word came to be written as 'Micmac.' The Micmac . . . referred to themselves as 'The People' . . ." – In this, of course, they were not unique.

whiten oneself; for they could not conceive that the strangers had been born with such white skins; they must have rubbed them with the white earth of their country; or perhaps with this strange white liquid of theirs that they sold to the People for pelts; for it tasted so rich and sweet that it must be very potent in its properties. Some of the People wanted to be white, too. They loved to paint themselves, and white was one of their four Power-Colors. (Every woman painted her robe; every man's skin-shirt was painted by the woman who lived beside him.) – But now the white-wishers were warned, for from among the Plant People and Animal People came the Person called KLUSKAP; He appeared to them in a dream they all shared and told them to be cautious, reminding them that Jenuaq were demons. They knew the tales of the Jenuaq who had come in grandfather-days from the north to eat them, KLUSKAP said; they could kill the People with strange loud sounds. – Or perhaps they were not demons; perhaps they were only men who had gone crazy because they had not had enough moose-fat to drink, for Vinland, too, had its share of haphazard shape-changers; in any event their inimical character was known, as they longed to crunch mangled man-bones in their jaws: yes, they were demons; yes! – Once, it is true, a Jenu came hungry and roaring through the trees and a woman of the People saved herself and her family by calling him Dear Grandfather and smiling upon him and serving him all the food he wanted until slowly, slowly, he ceased to glare at her; slowly he began to return the family's greetings; slowly he chose to smile at them, to help them, until at last when his brothers came south he defended the People against them. – There were some in the tribe who cited this story and said, "Let us be friends to these demons, and not kill them. Their cloth is very red and holy, and it may be that they will protect us against others." So they brought Thorvard many skins, and although the red cloth strips he gave them in return were thinner than ever they said nothing; like the woman who had saved herself they were determined to bear the Jenuaq optimistically. – There were others still who said, "Brothers, let us put on this new white shirt! We will be cloud-white; we will gain new powers; we will defeat the Jenuaq with their hearts of ice!" For they had never heard tell of the brother and sister in Greenland who had drowned themselves. So, each for his own reasons, the People came often to the camp of the white, white Jenuaq; smiling or impassive, they fingered the stuff of their clothing; they clutched the wonderful red cloth to themselves – "It is more brilliant than blood!" they laughed – they listened well to their language, which was to the People as the cawing of ravens, the creaking of wood, the falling of stone on stone. Most of all they admired the weapons of the Jenuaq: the spears whose tips shone as brightly as the sun, the long bright swords that glittered like ice-teeth (but of course in those days the People knew of ice only from those regions to the north of Markland; sometimes in the spring they saw lovely icebergs come drifting by in the blue, blue water; sometimes they paddled their canoes out into the strait and moored them to a floe with a spear-cast; then they patted the belly and flanks of that white animal with their hands, laughing at how cold it was); they practically split their cheeks in joy to see the *sax*-knives that curved like a dolphin's jaw; but of highest excellence they rated the blue axes, those pretty bone-biters, those gleaming wound-gashers . . . However, the Jenuaq guarded them jealously.

The Axe

There was a chief among the People named Carrying the War-Club; he was tall and straight, and bore himself well, so that he enjoyed the respect of all.★ Carrying the War-Club said: "It is clear to me that Powers live in those axes. You men, watch and wait. If you can steal an axe from the Jenuaq, do so. I myself will go in search of KLUSKAP and bring it to Him. He will tell us how to enjoy the axe-Power for ourselves." – Another chief named Dreaming of Bad Days shook his head and said: "This is cloudy counsel. You know that the tribes across the water call us the Porcupine People, because we are prickly and irascible. Let us live in peace with the Jenuaq. We give them skins; they give us the blood-red cloth; they give us the sweet white syrup." – Then Carrying the War-Club stamped his foot and said, "These are the words of an old man. Look how the Jenuaq cheat us with their cloth! They are not honest men, but demons. And they have established another nest in the north, by the old demon-houses. They have brought their demon-women; they are making demon-children to plague us. Have you not seen the little white demon-babe whose hair is white like sea-foam? Do you want him to have brothers? Do you want his brothers to eat our hearts? We must get the axe-Power of the Jenuaq; we must not wait until their numbers are too great for us. Let others call us the Porcupine People! Let them call us the Panther-People! Ha, ha!" – So saying, he incited them all to pull on the Bear-Shirt. – Dreaming of Bad Days was not happy, and prophesied evil.

★ "It is a historical fact that the Beothuk men were tall and well-formed," wrote Farley Mowat. "The last chieftain of the race, who was murdered by white hunters on Red Indian Lake in 1819, was stretched out on the ice by his killers and measured. They reported that he was more than six feet tall."

But the matter of the red cloth so incensed the People now that they paid no attention to him. So they agreed to steal an axe at their first opportunity, and in the meantime to dissemble their purpose.

Names and Gifts

Freydis was often among the People, for she wished to learn more of their god GLOOSKAP. At first she bribed them with milk, but presently, noticing that they grew less shy of her, she discontinued these unnecessary payments (though she accepted their skin-presents just the same). – What ugly dark thralls they were! They wore weasel-skins; bear claws and wildcat-teeth clicked around their necks, so that they sounded like skeletons when they moved. They gaped at the sun; they played with stones as if they were children. – When they saw her in the forest (for she did not choose to meet them in plain view of the other Greenlanders), they croaked at her like raven-people; and she could easily imagine them creeping about on battlefields like ravens, pecking and pecking at the slain, stealing armor and gold rings, cawing in good men's blood; – "*Kwe!*" they always said. This

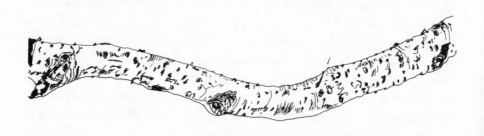

BIRCH TWIG   (NEW HAMPSHIRE, 1987)

was their uncouth greeting. – "*Kwe!*" Freydis replied sourly. She hunkered down on her hams among them; scowling, she suffered them to stroke her red-gold hair. – Oh, how she hated them! But she must learn more of their speech. The first thing to do was learn their names; then she could deal with them. – "Freydis," she said, pointing to herself. – But all the Skræling women – ugh! how withered and little they were! – promptly pointed to themselves and called themselves freydises. – "No, no, no, you dolts!" screamed Freydis, and they cowered back and whispered. – She touched her heart. "Freydis," she said. She beckoned to a scared Skræling girl and said, "You! What's your name?" – But the Skræling girl hid herself behind her blue-black hair. They never would give her their names. But she learned that a Skræling woman was called an *e'pit*. Every Greenlandic woman they called *puoin*, and she was with them many times before she understood that that meant *witch*. At first her face darkened with rage, but then slowly she began to smile. – "So I'm a witch, am I, you Skrælings? A witch among trolls? So be it. We'll see whose sorceries win out in the end." – And the Skrælings laughed and gave her roast moose-nose, because they could not understand her.

By pointing at the sea and sky she learned at last the word she so longed to hear: *MUSKUNAMU'KSUTI* – blueness. She never forgot it, because it was the attribute of her LORD. (She was hawk-keen; she was eagle-keen.) Finding her so eager and grasping in the way she whispered this word over and over among the trees, the Skrælings taught her *Muskunamu'k* (blue), *Muskunamu'kwesik* (bluish), *Muskunik* (blue cloth). But the word she prized was *MUSKUNAMU'KSUTI*. – "Yes," she said to herself; "now I can worship Him here; now I can put on the Blue Shirt in Wineland as my father did in Greenland; now I can invoke Him in the presence of GLOOSKAP Himself!"

Maktāwāākwā

To the People KLUSKAP★ was one Person among many. They admired His Powers, and sometimes sought to visit Him. But equally they admired the Powers of colored stones in streams, of knurled bones: these things they kept in skin-pouches with their rattles and used to guard against sickness, to summon the moose and caribou. But Freydis was a Christian, and must only believe in one God. The games of Power that the Skrælings played with their pebbles were as slow and useless to her as chess, which she had never had the patience to learn from her father (and Thjodhild never much enjoyed it, either, although she played with Eirik before Leif was grown and later again when Leif and Eirik had a falling out over religion because it was better for her that she do that than leave Eirik to fall into a sullen rage of boredom and horror as he squatted on his heels, pulling at his beard and cursing into the fire, and the wind shrieked outside and the days were as dark as the nights and when the wind-gusts desisted for a moment Thjodhild could

★ For KLUSKAP/GLOOSKAP, see Note on Micmac Orthography, p. 354.

hear the cows in the byre, lowing thinly, with a quavering shivering sound, so Thjodhild moved the ivory pieces around on the board as patiently as she could, until her husband began to curse her and her Christian ways and then she rose up wearily, silently, to go back to her loom); so Freydis must play by the rules of the black Crow-Fathers, who did not know that in Wineland pale sad Sister SUN was a Grandfather Whose hair was softly streaming light, Who was tranquilly unassailable, Who had created the People in pairs, Who had divided the world into lakes and lands; – nor did Freydis know about COOLPUJOT the Person of Seasons, nor yet about Chief EARTHQUAKE . . . but when she heard the old man, Dreaming of Bad Days, call gently upon GLOOSKAP (and his voice was like the sighing and shimmering of leaves), then she became determined that GLOOSKAP would be the Only One to help her speed her designs in Wineland – and because she thought so, so it would be. She could put on whatever shirt she chose. – The People marked out for Freydis a map on the ground. – "Go this way," they said politely. "Here He lives: He is NIKSKAM, our Grandfather; He is KISU'LKW, our Maker." (They said that about everyone with Power; they were indeed a courteous People.)

Thus it seemed to Freydis as if she had acquired Blueness in Wineland just as in east Greenland she had struck upon the rock and called the name of AMORTORTAK. She needed the Skrælings precisely because she despised them: being trolls, they knew what she must know. Just as each country's sky is its own shade of blue (and just as what you see depends on who shows it to you), so one must put on the same shirt over and over in different climates: – that was how it seemed to her; therefore that is how it was. So she collected His Names as she had once hoarded the silver coins of King Eric Bloody-Axe, and the word *MUSKUNAMU'KSUTI* enriched her, and she laughed and hugged herself while the Skrælings looked on (they never painted themselves blue); she had gained something else of theirs without paying for it. – As for them, they could see something flickering, something crawling behind her eyes. So when they spoke of her they did not use the word *MUSKUNAMU'KSUTI*; instead they said *Maktāwāākwā* (blackness); they said *Maktokōkŭnŭmăse* (to paint something of one's own black).

Gudrid and Gudrid

Then cherish pity, lest you drive an angel from your door.

BLAKE, "Holy Thursday" (*ca.* 1790)

One day in Haymaking-Month they were trading with the Skrælings, and Gudrid was sitting in the doorway of the longhouse giving her little boy suck when she felt a shadow on the back of her neck, and looking up she saw a woman dressed in black, who was very pale, and had eyes too big for human eyes. "What is your name?" the woman said.

"My name is Gudrid," said Gudrid. "And what's your name?"

"My name is Gudrid," said the woman in a very strange voice, so that Gudrid could not tell whether she were mocking her or repeating what she had said without understanding it or whether her name really *was* Gudrid, which was possible since she did not seem to be a Skræling. She had chestnut-colored hair, round which she wore a headband. Leif had once had bad dreams about Thorgunna; he woke up crying out every night for seven nights, and Gudrid remembered how he said that Thorgunna's eyes seemed to be getting bigger and bigger the closer she came to him and her face got paler and paler; but for Leif the most horrible thing had been the iron-cold malice in Thorgunna's face, which he might melt away no more than he could any other glacier in Greenland; this other Gudrid, however, seemed to be not so much a person with intentions as a presentiment (for such things still happened in those days, although not so much to Christians). The woman walked closer and closer to Gudrid, gliding as if without volition, and her shadow stretched all the way to the door; and she plucked aimlessly at her tight black kirtle, as if it were hurting her and she could not pull it off; it was tight about her wrists and neck, which were livid, but the rest of her was so pale, so pale; and her eyes were like polished beach pebbles. – What shirt had Gudrid Thorbjornsdaughter put on? The *Flateyjarbók* presents it as a matter surpassing conjecture; and yet I think we ought to suppose that Gudrid's double meant to tell her something that Gudrid (whose soul was as fragrant as asphodels) did not want to understand for the same reason that she did not want to remember her foster-mother Halldis's *Warlock-Songs*; she was content now to act, agile and naked, within Karlsefni's husband-shirt. – The other Gudrid stared and stared, until Gudrid thought that she was going to scream because she did not want to be fey. Her own wool shirt now seemed to be shrinking and tightening and hardening on her like drying leather; her collar swallowed more and more of itself, like the Midgaard Serpent; it was choking her; and little Snorri was weeping and she sank to a bench with her eyes almost popping out of her head like the other Gudrid's eyes, until in her extremity she remembered the Power – not of CHRIST but rather of her own smile; so quickly she put on the rosy shirt of smiles as if she were not at all asphyxiated and smiled and smiled, wider and wider; it was Gudrid's most beautiful smile ever. – "Sit down with me," said Gudrid, and the other Gudrid smoothed her black kirtle with both hands and stepped slowly over to her, when suddenly there was a crash, and the woman vanished. A Skræling had just been killed by Karlsefni's men for attempting to steal a sword. Shouting and crying, the Skrælings fled, leaving their packs of skins behind.

"Now I think we will have some trouble," said Karlsefni, but Freydis laughed when she heard this and said, "After all, we got their skins for nothing this time. Have a drink of milk, Karlsefni!" – Karlsefni turned upon her. "I will take no notice of you this time," he said, "but someday my patience may run out." – At this, Freydis abused him until he turned and went into his house. She called after him, "Go and pick crowberries with the Skrælings!"

As for Gudrid, the instant that her double had vanished she could breathe again, and not a mark on her neck could she find. – "What is it about my life that strangles me?" she wondered. "There is nothing so ill about my babe and my good husband, though certainly I will always be restless; I would enjoy going linen-bound to a wedding again . . ." – "Why so pale?" said Karlsefni, coming in. "Are you unwell?" – "Yes," said Gudrid weeping.

The Quiet Days

Now the men of Karlsefni and Gudrid put on their battle-helms; they raised their axes and polished them; they strode frowning upon the meadows, with their arms folded across their breasts; they talked seldom, and traveled always together. (But Freydis's men despised them for cowards, and continued to roam the forests. Freydis had no worry that they might talk too much about her yearned-for Tree because they had less and less to do with the others.) As for Karlsefni, he often spoke with his wife alone, shaking his head, stroking and stroking the buttons on his sleeves. – "Now you have got us all into the raven's beak!" he said to her; "you enticed us all here, and who knows when the Skrælings will attack?", but Gudrid smiled ever so gently and stroked his beard . . . The baby cried; Karlsefni paced and paced and began to shaft his arrows . . . Again, for no reason that he could see, he found himself thinking upon King Olaf, who had truly been a splendid fellow. Once Karlsefni had made him the gift of some finely made falconer's gloves (for that year he had had a whole cargo of such goods); and in return the King gave him a gold ring; he had it still. No, for all his manliness, King Olaf never forgot to be courteous, as when he rode the fish-road to Salten Fjord with the Bishop and a tempest blew against him for days and days until at last he called upon the Bishop to pray, which the Bishop did at ship's-bow, with tapers and incense; then a sea-way was parted beneath the wave-peaks for them by the hands of GOD, and the Bishop said his AMEN and King Olaf struck sail and directed his Christianizers to their oar-work; after rowing fully a day and a night, with the green-flecked ocean-shoulders rising so high on either side that they obscured the mountains (but the Bishop's path was as smooth as oil), they reached Godö Isle, where there dwelled a most benighted and stubborn pagan named Raud the Strong, as Trygvesson well knew, for he had come to convert him; and the sky was black and the mountains were black and slick with rain as the King's dragon-ship slid into harbor, so that Raud did not see; then the King raised his hand and the men seized that place, killing, beating and imprisoning Raud's house-thralls as they liked, but even now (so fine were his manners) King Olaf spoke to Raud in all good humor, saying, "Let me offer you baptism, Raud. I will not take your property from you, but would rather be your friend, if you might only make yourself worthy to be so!" and he looked at Raud so longingly, as if *Raud* were the King and he himself but the humblest thrall in the land; when Raud refused, however, Olaf changed his face, and had Raud bound, and forced an adder into Raud's mouth with a red-hot iron; so that the snake crept down Raud's throat, and came out below the armpit, giving Raud his death; then King Olaf seized all his silver and gold. Doubtless, then, he thought that he could likewise prevail against Queen Sigrid if need was. And yet she was *very* cunning and had foreknowledge from her father Skogul Toste, who was a Swede, and therefore, as all Norwegians knew, a warlock. – Sigrid had many great estates in Sweden, so that she was often wooed. Now of the wooers that she burned, perhaps the most remarkable was her foster-brother King Harald Grænske, who one summer went a-Viking to the Baltic, "to gather property," says the saga blandly; and keen-eyed Sigrid sent her men to invite him to a feast, because she knew that he was destined to father King Olaf the Saint; and Sigrid longed for the distinction of being the mother of so holy a King; therefore she lured King Harald to her with all his followers, and feasted him grandly, sitting beside him in her high-seat and smiling upon him so that he thought: "This Queen has the greatest understanding!", and later he thought: "What blue eyes she turns upon me!", and later still she had her carles put up a bed whose linen hangings were much finer than Thorgunna's had been – if only Thurid of Frodis-Water, who had so badly coveted those, could have been here in Sweden to see them! – But then it is likely that she would have burnt her fingers. The world-circle was embroidered on it, from Jötunheim to Wineland the Good, so that upon going into his bed King Harald felt as if he were clothing himself in the whole world (for he did not think that that was also what dead men did, when they were covered in earth). For a time he sat there upon the bed yawning and rubbing his beard, for he regretted most keenly his night-parting with the Queen, and was loath to lay himself down, but ale enthralled him, so at last he threw back the coverlet. There were few men in the lodging-house that night, says the tale; and Queen Sigrid's breast was heaving in excitement as she thought to fulfill her designs. Now King Harald took off his serks and lay naked in that pretty bed, at which Sigrid parted the hangings softly and sat down beside him, and her eyes were glittering in the darkness as she filled a bowl for him to drink with her own hands, and they drank together until they were drunk. – But what did she truly desire in all this? Perhaps she never intended to bear Saint Olaf under her heart at all – for she worshipped FREYJA – perhaps (unlike Freydis Eiriksdottir, who always acted according to a purpose) Sigrid was nothing but a bored and vicious woman-cat playing with mice whom she whirled about by their tails until she tired of them and bit off their heads; for in the morning she got up not from King Harald's bed, but from her own, where she had laid herself down at the last; and the sun was bright upon the water as she crowned herself and the entertainment went on as brightly as ever and Queen Sigrid was so lively as to uplift the hearts of all, teasing her foster-brother the King, making sport of other countries behind her hand, even of his dominions (at which he frowned a little), opening her mouth wide in a laugh to say that she valued her estates in Sweden much more highly than his kingdom in Norway! at which he lost all his pleasure in the day, in the year, in himself. The following summer he steered again for Sweden, this time beseeching Sigrid to marry him, at which she said, "How now, Harald? For you are already well-married to Queen Aasta Gudbrandsdottir!" – "Aasta is a good woman," said he, "but in beauty and importance she is nothing to you, my Sigrid." – "Oh, I'm beautiful now, am I?" she said. "Am I your little dove? For so you named me that night when I came to your bed." – And here King Harald could say nothing, for in truth he had been so drunk that he could not remember whether he had fondled Sigrid, or whether he had striven to, or indeed denied her; as for Sigrid, such was her genius that no one ever found out. She fanned the midges away from her neck as they walked on the strand together; she said to him, "Aasta may be lower born than you; but still it is true that she is pregnant with both your fortunes; for Saint Olaf now lies in her womb, not mine." – King Harald then became very heavy-hearted, as the tale says; but still he followed her up the country to her house, where she burned him as he slept, and the Russian King Visavald also. What she wanted from Harald in the end, then, remained as mysterious as Wineland; indeed it must be said that she behaved in a very contradictory way. – King Olaf might very properly have learned from this tale (so considered Karlsefni, tossing in his bed in Vinland, with Gudrid beside him – she always slept perfectly) to watch every quarter of the sky, having scorned so dangerous a woman – but of all men that King had been the bravest; for he never turned aside from anything: *he* would have gone to Vinland – why, he had fixed his shield on the very peak of Smalsar Horn, which no man before him ever reached! and it was told that in descending he came across one of his strongest followers, who for loyalty had sought to follow him, bristling with furs against the chill, but was now piteously trapped on a narrow ledge so that he dared to go neither up nor down; so King Olaf slung him over his shoulder and carried him down the Horn, setting him gently at last upon the plain and chuckling, "Return to your fellow palace-carles, man, and think not to go mountain-climbing again!" – So King Olaf went about his life. (But Sigrid, hearing this news, said, "He is not so sure-footed as he thinks himself." And her heart clanged with anger against him like an iron bell.) In Viken he killed King Gudrod, the last son left in life of Bloody-Axe's widow Gunhild, and was joyous, saying, "Now at last I have paid back that witch!"; in Drontheim he slew a highborn pagan called Iron-Beard, who sought to make him render sacrifice to ODIN; and when that carcass had fallen (at the very doorway of THOR's temple, as is told in the *Flateyjarbók*), then King Olaf took hostages and baptized all the Drontheim people, so that the deed became a famous success. Now the thin corn would languish, for none could pour out the sacrificial blood any longer, as had been done from the days of the Ynglings; now the Cross took root. To compensate the kinsmen of Iron-Beard, Olaf took Gudrun Ironbeardsdottir to bed with him to be his wife; and the hangings closed behind them like rippling black water, and he said, "Do not be angry with me, maid, because I slew your father," and she said, "How could I be angry with my Lord?" at which King Olaf was much content, and in that darkness they sank deeper and deeper into each other, but as soon as she thought him asleep a silvery fish swam in her hand. Snatching the blade (for like King Gudrod's brother, Harald Greyskin, he was rarely so careless as he seemed), the King arose and went to his men to tell them what had happened. Gudrun pulled her clothes on in a frenzy, biting her lip, and went away with all her serving-men, to grieve upon her father's mound; she never again entered Olaf's bed. Surely (thought Karlsefni) the King should have taken alarm at *this* happening; for if a mere girl could try such a thing against him, how much more dangerous must be that subtle Sigrid, whom he had no less outraged! But Olaf was well used to juggling three knives in the air, after all, catching them in his hand as they flew point downwards. – Sigrid married King Swend Forkbeard of Denmark. The Danes had always been the enemies of the Norwegians, but even yet King Olaf did not take caution. His sister Ingigerd, the one whose eyes made Leif forget Thorgunna Witch so easily, was now due to be married; and Olaf gave her to Earl Rognvald, even though Rognvald's father was Sigrid's brother! Truly matters had gone beyond slapping Sigrid's face; he was slapping the face of Fate itself, which duly sent him Thyre, King Swend's sister, who was Christian and had fled the Russian marriage to which she had been assigned, praying to Olaf to protect her from lapping at the sacrificial bowl with those pagans. –"Well, you are a fine-spoken woman, and also good to look upon," said Olaf. "I will gladly protect you, if you are minded to become a Queen." – Now at last Sigrid the Haughty had him in her power; for every morning as she woke beside King Swend she would say, "That Norwegian King, Olaf Trygvesson, has taken your sister without your leave! By all the snow in Sweden, it is a wonder to me how you suffer it!" So at last, King Swend sent word to his kinsmen-in-law (that is to say, Earl Eric and Olaf of Sweden, who was Sigrid's son); these hounds set out upon the hunt, and soon brought Trygvesson down. – But why should Karlsefni think upon this? Why?

Amortortak and Kluskap

. . . spontaneity is only a term for man's ignorance of the gods.

BUTLER, *Erewhon* (1872)

On the way to the place where GLOOSKAP lived, the Skrælings said, you first clambered down a little cliff onto a long shelf of rock, riddled with fissures in which barnacles and snails clung by the thousands, and there was a constant trickling at low tide as the water drained from tide pools through channels no wider than a finger, down to the sea, which was calm when Freydis came to it, the waves slapping almost inaudibly against the wet kelp-green rocks that served as a token barrier. The kelp drooped, wet and rubbery with yellow bulbs. Snails crawled on it. Clams and mussels rested in the peace of the tide pools, their shells ajar. The sand was whorled with designs of algae, mussels and agates.

You turned inward, the Skrælings said, through the forest, where the low sun shot its rays between the dark trees in a way that seemed sinister to Freydis. The trees were very thin but densely crowded. She could see no sky between them. For her, whose mind held always a gloomy cast, it seemed already much darker than it was. Each new winding among the trees led her into another funnel of darkness. Everything was grey and vague. The color had gone out of the world. The tree-boles rounded upon her like the heads of reptiles. Crooked sticks beset her way like snakes. She walked along a deer trail, through muck and mucky meadows, across stone outcroppings the same dark grey as the cliffs and the tidal shelf below; and presently the trail ascended into the low SUN, Whose satellite constellations were lily-of-the-valley, crow's-foot, starflower, clubmoss. Some pines had bare branches, like rungs of ladders leading into the evening. As she rounded the first bend in the cape she saw the ocean through the bushes; she heard the gulls. – Presently she came into a high place of ferns and mossy maples,

between the trunks of which the sky and the sea could be seen, both of them
very near the ground; the SUN seemed so close to her head that Freydis could
almost have jumped up and seized Her, as would Fenrir the Wolf of Doom.
Everything was lonely and blue and green as the light began to fail.

It was her intention to kill GLOOSKAP. She had prayed to Him, but He
had not helped her. Now the Skrælings were hostile, and she and her men
must therefore expect difficulties – difficulties which Blue-Shirt might not
necessarily excuse. – So GLOOSKAP didn't want the frost, did He? Well, she'd
stuff frost down His throat! She could see trees and sky reflected in the silver
mirror of her knife-blade. And yet she kept thinking to herself, "Perhaps this
is an unwise course to follow." (For GLOOSKAP was a god.) But she had to
do her duty to Blue-Shirt. – Well, perhaps GLOOSKAP *would* help her! She
would see. – She hesitated; she slid her knife back into her belt-scabbard;
but then she pulled it out again, screaming silently behind her teeth.

Amortortak 1987

I know now what Freydis was, because one evening in Greenland,
as darkskinned Christian sat waiting for money to come so that he could
fix his fishing boat, and Christian's Mommy and Daddy were playing cards
with friends in the kitchen again, laughing and crying, "*Ehhh!*", and sweet
Margethe laid her head down in Christian's lap to sleep because tomorrow
she had to work early at the hospital, Christian lit up a cigarette and told me
about Qivittóqs. A *Qivittóq* was a man who was desperately unhappy because
his family didn't like him or because the girl he loved wouldn't have him;
and he sweated in the bright nights of the hot Greenland summers and the
ocean creaked in his ears and the mud stank and the mosquitoes swarmed
on his face and he was so weary, so alone that the unhappiness screamed
and screamed inside him and suddenly he could take off his shirt! He could
go inhumanly naked, like a stone; he could put on the Bear-Shirt, the Blue
Shirt, the Ice-Shirt, or any other; then he could take it off again! – oh, it
was glorious; that was what Greenlanders had *always* done, Christian said
proudly, until the Danish people had come and taught them to jump into the
sea, to hang themselves, to shoot themselves like black-handed Tunersuits. –
But a few still remembered how to be Qivittóqs. A Qivittóq went rushing
into the mountains; he lived alone there for the rest of his life, howling on
the steep green ridges between fjords where the water shone silver and gold
in the sun; or sometimes milky-blue as it was in Ameralik Fjord, just beyond

which, about a century ago, the great explorer Nansen began his crossing of the Greenland icecap; and the Qivittóq was pierced by all these colors (in Slab-Land the lichens were black, white and orange, the island brown, the sea blue and the sky grey; but in Greenland there was so much screaming greenness and silver and gold . . . ; he ran up cliffs whose hair was green grass; he crossed the fjords by leaping from sandbar to sandbar and rushed toward that blue ice, rushed faster and faster toward that inland ice that called him; then as the wildness beat in his heart he began to acquire great powers. He could change himself into any animal; he could fly anywhere. When other men came near, the Qivittóq would turn his back to them and be silent if his disposition was good, for otherwise he could not help killing them with his eyes, his terrible voice. – Ten years ago, Christian said, there was a very powerful Qivittóq in Kapasillit. He hunted two brothers and killed them in the long yellow grass. At first it was thought that one brother killed the other and then himself, but the younger brother's son would not believe that. He went into the mountains and saw the Qivittóq running faster than a man should run, up and down the ridges. The man went back to Kapasillit and told the police. The police had a helicopter in Kapasillit at that time because they were shooting reindeer. They flew over the mountains in their helicopter and found the Qivittóq still running, so they hovered as close to him as they could and shot one of his legs out from under him. Then they took him to the hospital. He screamed like the wind (it is wind that makes wildness). – He had had a wife in north Greenland, but she wouldn't stay with him because his face was hairy like the face of an animal. He was crazy. They took him to a mental institution.

The Way to the Sea

Pieces of birch bark were scattered on the trail ahead like mysterious signs. It was twilight, and the blue had now washed out of the sky. The bark was rubbed to ribbons on the trees, as if something large had recently been here. A bare tree loomed, painted in circles of red and yellow. Then suddenly Freydis heard a sound like a dog, like creaking wood, like someone in pain. It was a gull's cry. The gull rose in front of her and beat its wings warningly. The ferns were upcupped like supplicating hands. Louder and louder was the sound of the sea. – She came to a dark grey cliff. There was a rocky beach far below. The water was very calm. – Then the path burst out of the trees and onto a grassy shoulder, with nothing around her except sea and blue peninsulas. The SUN cast Her golden wake on the water as She departed. Half a hundred steps beyond the edge of the precipice stood a rugged column of cliff, grass-grown, and on its top, which was only a few paces wide, the gulls lived. At her approach they rose and cried their hoarse alarms in two syllables, the second rising; they swooped and glided. In the air they were black against the westering SUN; later, resting once again on the grass, when they saw that she could not hurt them, they were white, with greyish-black wings. They groaned contentedly, like suckling babies. – Freydis looked down over the edge. – "Ha!" she said scornfully to the cliff. "I've seen worse than you!" – She let herself down with a walrus-skin rope; she stood upon the shore in that fatal sunset. Not too far away, she saw the silhouette of Someone walking on the beach.

A Person among Persons

KLUSKAP, the Living Power, walked slowly by the edge of the sea. The coast consisted of great grey slabs, worried through with thousands of ledges wide and narrow. Pebbles and mussel shells tinkled under His step. He strode past tide pools in which the rocks were round and green like turtles. The kelp-flowers and sea-moss made of each pool a garden suffused with green algae-light. Here lived snails and hermit crabs. The kelps were trees with ripe green-golden berries, which the snails relished. Here, if anywhere, might Freydis have found Yggdrasil.

At KLUSKAP's left shoulder was the ocean, beyond which lay Markland with its blue cliffs and grey lakes. On His right stretched the forest, where dew lay in the hollows of strawberry leaves. Indian tobacco grew everywhere, with its white and yellow flowers. Oaks and junipers cooled the day; their shadows were full of dew.

He was very tall (for People with Power must stand higher than people without) and He was handsome of feature. He held His head high. His black eyes shone; His black hair fell to His shoulders. He wore a blanket-robe of white moosehide that fell loosely to His knees, for He was a shape-changer and would not be constricted. On his breast were painted all the birds and animals known in His country, from foxes to whales, worked in the Power-colors: red, yellow, black and white. All these creatures were alive. The hems of His sleeves were painted with every tendril, root and bud; – with the heart-shaped leaf of the groundnut, the fragrant sweetflag plant, the Indian tobacco with its flowers like bells, the straight stalks and firm heads of cattails, whose pollen and roots fed His People; the great, irregularly serrated leaf-lobe of a bloodroot; and each of these, too, was alive; each was a Plant Person who brought food to KLUSKAP's People or gave them fragrant medicines. KLUSKAP knew them; He knew the Animal People and the Star People; the Stone People; He was one of those People with Power. He wore mooseskin leggings fringed with colored porcupine quills; His moccasins were ornamented with wampum beads. A tobacco pouch was slung over His shoulder.

As He strode there waiting for Freydis, He smiled slightly. People had come to importune Him before. If she chose to be meek with Him and her aims were pure, He would help her. In any case He would treat her as she deserved.

The twilight was very calm. – "*Āoobŭlogeâk'*," said KLUSKAP, nodding His head. "The wind goes down with the sun."

The Frost-Seed

In Vinland there is a plant called twinflower (*Linnaea borealis*), so known because from its sweetly creeping stalk rises a shoot with two pink flower-heads looking down at their own round leaves. KLUSKAP and Freydis made such a picture presently, for they stood very close together on the beach, she sheltering herself from the sea-winds beneath His arm (and always she thought, too, that since Gudrid could have *her* way by smiling – oh, how easy it looked to Freydis when Gudrid did it; she did not know the labor of a smile – so now she thought to win GLOOSKAP's favour by casting her smile towards Him, although her smile was no more attractive than a splitting seam); and both their heads bowed down in the last orange bars of sunset, looking at something that GLOOSKAP held in His palm. – "Well, granddaughter, this is your frost-seed," He said. "I hear you want to bring winter here. If you plant this little blue seed at night in the shade of the woods, then winter will come, and we will also have creeping snowberries." – "Yes, yes!" cried Freydis in delight. "That's what I want!" Her second heart, her wolf's heart, almost came alive. – "Then take it," said GLOOSKAP, sighing. "Take it from My hand." – Eagerly Freydis snatched the ice-crystal from Him, but at once she shrieked in pain and dropped it in the sand, for it was so cold that it burned her. Where it had fallen it became merely a grain of sand among the sands; it was dark, and she could not find it, and if she did she would not be able to take it . . .

KLUSKAP puffed at His pipe. He never laughed at anyone. "Granddaughter,"

He said, "what do you really want?"

"I want to be rich," Freydis said.

"Well, here you are in My country. Everyone who comes here is rich. Some of My People say you Jenuaq are rich already. They don't mind it, but they know what you're doing here. Your ship is full of timber and grape-vines. Your men must have all the game they want, because they leave good buck-deer rotting for Skofte Carrion-Crow. I've seen that. We don't do that here. Your husband is happy trading milk for skins – that was a good idea of yours, Freydis Eiriksdaughter! – and Gudrid and Karlsefni have found a place to live, where the berries are as many as stars, and the fish are as many as hairs on your head. Of course my People are angry about the man you killed, but I can smooth that out with them if you pay compensation. What more do you want?"

Sullenly, Freydis dug her heel into the sand. "I want *everything*," she said.

"At least you're honest, granddaughter," said KLUSKAP. "Well, what you've asked is hard, but I'll see what I can do for you."

The Four Wishes

At that time men and women wore loincloths of soft skin. Because the frost had not yet come to Wineland, they went otherwise almost naked, and needed to wear no perpetual shirts. Occasionally it did get chilly in the winter months, and then they wore blanket-robes of leather or beaver-fur. But even these were tied rather than sewn; for at night the People took them off and used them to cover their beds. – So shape-changing was possible for them as it had been for the Jenuaq in the days before King Harald Fairhair, but it was never easy: just as a rime-stiff Ice-Shirt can be donned or doffed only with effort, nakedness is its own stern honesty which resists the shimmering falseness of fabrics. – It is true, however, that the People had as many teachers of fashion in Vinland as they would have elsewhere; for the trees put on green leaf-shirts in the summer that turned ever so many colors in the end before the black trunk-chests stood bare again throughout the foggy winters when dead leaf-swirls lapped and eddied around the trees' knobby knees; the People knew how the midsummer mountain gulleys put on brook-shirts in the spring, how the blue sky put on the Cloud-Shirt; and once an iceberg had run aground near Cross-Ness and on it, trembling, crouched a white hare; they took the hare alive and presented it to their shamans and wise men, who kept it through the spring and marveled to see how its white coat

turned brown so that it was no longer any different from the hares that ran
in their own forests; in short, the People knew about the various
shirts, but not everyone could put them on. The best shape-changers had
Power; they were Power Persons. (KLUSKAP was one; there were as many
Others as fish in a river.) They helped the shamans fly to the Land of the
Caribou, giving ointments in Their kindness so that the shamans could pull
on the wing-shirt and swoop between the sunny mountains and speed above
the tree-plains and ride the wind high over clam-beaches and agate-beaches,
listening to the brightness of the ocean; then they could enter the kingdom
of tussocks and brooks and snowbanks; now they rushed lower in the air,
calling upon the Power Persons and trembling their hands just as sparrows
seem to tremble in the air while never in fact deviating from their flight;
and the shamans whizzed a thousand miles with meadows on every horizon,
searching and searching until at last they saw the great caribou herds browsing
where the grass was sweetest; and politely the shamans asked the Power
Persons to shout and the Power Persons shouted and the caribou pricked
their ears up and started running, running, running south toward summer,
toward the trees, toward the People who wanted to eat them, so many
running caribou as could not be conceived; then the Shamans were so
happy and proud that they flew where the sky was bluest and looked
directly into the face of Grandfather SUN until their own faces burned with
light and they came hurtling home between the trees and the great stone
cliffs, crying out: "*I have seen them!*", and they could tell the hunters where
to wait for the caribou – but before and after, the shamans must praise the
Power Persons Who had helped them. The Power Persons healed the sick
if proper gifts were made to Them, if proper songs were sung; the Power
Persons had many fine shirts to give. When red people were unhappy with
the way they were, therefore, they called upon Them: they called upon
Grandfather SUN, or COOLPUJOT THE BONELESS, or many Others of Whom
Freydis had no knowledge; they called upon KLUSKAP. – Thus it happened
once that four men set out among the trees to go to Him. The men saw
Labrador tea; they saw Indian hemp. – "*Kwe!*" they greeted those Plant
People. The forest was carpeted with ferns that shook their rows of green
blades. – "*Kwe!*" they said to the ferns. – Behind almost every little rise was
a fair lake. They sought Him from one springtime to the next, and then on
to midsummer, wading through blue-grey water, toward blue mountains,
threading their way among little green islands; and they did not know where
they were or where they were going, which was how it had to be because
KLUSKAP could be found only by seeking, seeking: it did not matter where.

It was a long journey; sometimes their spirits wavered like grass on a windy cliff. They picked blueberries and wild grapes as they went; they hunted, and roasted the meat. They were never far from the sound of the sea. (The grain of the sea-waves was like the creases in an old man's neck.) – In another version of the story, the travelers had to cross seven mountains; they made their way past two dragons with flickering tongues; they sprinted under a wall of solid cloud that sometimes slammed against the ground like a hammer; in any event, their patience was finally rewarded by a blazed path; then they came to a wide river whose sunny ripples were as mysterious as wood-grain, and they walked along the river and came to a lake, and the path led them out onto a narrow tongue of land that was green with high trees; and cattails clothed them on either side; and they climbed a hill and saw smoke ahead of them, rising slow and bluish-grey through the trees, curling like entrails. Moose and caribou roamed in great herds; they were as tame as cattle. – "Could KLUSKAP live down there?" said the first man, shaking the arrows in his quiver. "Oh, He has led us a long way! I am so angry with Him that I want to shoot Him!" – for he had a bad temper; that was what he wanted KLUSKAP to cure him of. – "Perhaps it is one of the Yellow Birch People," said the second man. "This smoke smells of birchwood. But I hope not, for they would have little to offer us but wood and sap-juice. If it is not KLUSKAP, then may it be a rich chief who will reward us well with gifts!" – for he was somewhat like Freydis; riches was what *he* wanted of KLUSKAP. – "I cannot guess who lives there," said the third man timidly. "But I hope they are not hostile people who will hate us and kill us!" – for it had always been his lot to be despised, so he was fearful. He wanted KLUSKAP to make the People respect him. – "Whether or not they kill us scarcely matters," replied the fourth man despondently. "We will die anyway." He prayed night and day that KLUSKAP would grant him long life.

Unlike the Jenuaq Bear-Kings, they never thought to have Power inside them. If they wanted to Change, they had to ask Someone most worshipfully.

They saw a wigwam in the trees, and the closer they came to it the taller it grew, until it was as high as a hill. It was perfect. Trees bowed themselves toward it, save only the white birch, from whose bark it was made, and the blue spruce, whose boughs were permitted to line it; and birds circled above it. So tall and white it was that the men rubbed their eyes and wondered that they had not seen it before. The whiteness of it was the whiteness of the Jenuaq milk-soap with which the People longed to lave themselves; it was the whiteness of icebergs and clouds blended, but birchbark-grain ran through it so that they knew that it was the same as their wigwam-skins at home, except perhaps more Powerful. It was painted mainly with red designs of Power (red was the highest color), but yellow and black patterns were also to be seen. Fish-spears and war-spears leaned against it. In the grass was a canoe upended (a long time later, when KLUSKAP left the People, He turned it into a long shore-stone, upon which trees grow now), and His many dogs crouched silently by, lolling out their tongues and gazing upon the visitors with a gaze like shining stars (they too were to become sea-rocks), and a pretty butterfly displayed itself against the whiteness of the wigwam and changed into a bird, a seed-pod, a feather of milkweed-down, and floated away. Seeing this, the men became shy and cautious. The closer they came, the more their shadows lengthened. – In the doorway, a blanket trembled in the breeze, like the twitching of an upper lip. – What lay beyond must be some naked perfect greatness superior to the four men's naked need, but whether it was good or evil depended on the uncoverer, and the four men understood that very well, so for a moment they stood watching the blanket flap and flap in the shadows, with meaning in the flapping that they could not read because they were not Wind People and had no Power: they knew nothing; they had nothing; they were nothing. Someone was watching them through the blanket; they knew that, too. Someone was watching them and waiting for them to declare themselves. The timid man and the death-fearing man found themselves wishing that their journey had a bit yet to run; that way they would still be safe (oh, there are always new things to wish!); as for the poor man and the angry man, they were so eager to put on whatever shirt might be provided for them that they wanted nothing but the end. Soon it would all be decided one way or the other. Soon GRANDFATHER SUN would look upon four new men.

How strange that the wigwam did not change moment by moment! Only the blanket flapped at the door. Everything else was the same.

"*Kwe!*" called the angry man at last. – "Who are you?" said a deep voice from inside. – "We are strangers, seeking KLUSKAP," said the death-fearing man. – The voice that the men had heard was a pale green shoot that grew inside them and spread its leaf-hands above their heads and blossomed with a single flower that was the face of their expectation. So the angry man saw a demon; the poor man, a chief who smiled; the timid man, a shaman; but the man who was afraid to die shivered, for it seemed to him that he looked into a skull-flower whose white petals gnashed like teeth, and in the flower crawled a fly. – "Come on in and rest yourselves," said the voice; and the four men went behind the blanket.

It was very dark inside. An old woman sat by the fire-embers. Beside her, a young man squatted, carving moose-figures out of wood. His name was Marten. He was very faithful. Behind the fire sat KLUSKAP. A smoke-wisp from the fire whirled round and round His shoulders. He was very tall and powerful and silent. He looked steadily at His guests, and His eyes hurt them, so brightly did they glitter; the four men shaded their eyes as He looked at them; one by one they looked away. They were impure in the light of His purity. – KLUSKAP was a thorn-bush to make them bleed; KLUSKAP was a maple tree full of sap for them to drink; KLUSKAP was a wide spruce-tree with many springy fragrant boughs, between which were soft dark spaces. In the storms of Power that few feel, KLUSKAP stood letting the rain beat down upon Him, sheltering those who humbly asked it of Him; later, in the hot dry times, Power-rain came down from His branches in little gushes, and sometimes it reached the little ones who stood beneath with hands upcupped like funnel-leaves. (As for doubters, traitors and strangers, He quenched their thirst with poison.)

"Come up to the back where it is comfortable," said KLUSKAP. – There were beds there, of soft fir-boughs. KLUSKAP lit His pipe and passed it around, and the four men smiled to inhale the smoke of His good tobacco; they sat cross-legged in the manner of seemly men, and leaned their backs against the wigwam-posts, each one of which had its own name. Just as the word *lmu'ji'jmanaqsi* sounds like what it is, a willow tree rising high and flowering and sending down so many green rainbows that rustle in the wind and tangle sweetly in each other, so the speech of KLUSKAP the Great Chief breathed like many green leaves as He now spoke words of benignity to His kin-friends. His manservant, dapper little Marten, made up the fire and filled the kettle. Red sparks danced in the air; they spun themselves around KLUSKAP's shoulders like threads. The angry man watched the sparks and they reminded him of his anger; he felt very red and fiery inside; he was furious with KLUSKAP for making him come so far; but KLUSKAP glittered His eyes at him, and the man looked down at the floor, ashamed. – Old Grandmother hung the kettle up and began scraping bits of an old beaver bone into it; it was soon filled with fat and succulent flesh, for this was Vinland, where even hoofs and skeletons merely needed to be thrown into a creek to grow new bodies. (But just as KLUSKAP's canoe was fated to be a stone and His dogs would be stones, so in time this kettle, too, would become a stone; KLUSKAP would overturn it disgustedly and fling it into the water as He departed: it is now Spencer Island.) – Raising her hand, Grandmother bade the guests help themselves. No matter how much they ate, the kettle never became empty. They ate; they slept; they ate again. –

But the man who was afraid of death tried always to sleep with his eyes open, so that he could keep watch in case anyone came to kill him. This he could not do, so sometimes he simply pretended to sleep, looking round him through almost-closed eyes. He saw Grandmother sitting upon the floor, dragging herself slowly to and fro; she pulled the leaves off strange herbs and mixed their juices with moose-fat; she was always busy making ointments. He saw KLUSKAP going in and out; he saw Marten setting forth on KLUSKAP's errands. One morning he saw KLUSKAP washing Grandmother's face; her wrinkles vanished, and she became young and beautiful. Then for the first time in many years the death-fearing man was gladdened in his heart, for he could see that he had come to the end of his quest. But later a nightmare woke him, and he saw Grandmother lying asleep in the sun, seemingly dead but for her steadily heaving breast, and the pulsing in her throat; her face was very pale in the strong light. Then the death-fearing man was afraid again. He said nothing of this to his companions. And they dwelled there for many days.

"Now, what can I do for you?" said KLUSKAP at last. He said this very gently, like a hunter making soft low sounds to lure birds.

"I am angry, and want to become mild and tranquil in my temper," said the first man.

"That's easy enough," said KLUSKAP. And He smiled at the man.

"I am poor, and crave riches," said the second.

"As many as you like," said KLUSKAP pleasantly.

"No one respects me," said the third. "I wish to be listened to as a man of authority and wisdom."

"I can oblige you there," said KLUSKAP.

"I don't ever want to die," the fourth man wept. His tears fell into the kettle; he was still eating and eating desperately, because he could not exhaust KLUSKAP's measure. "Please, Great Chief, grant me eternal life; or if You can't do that at least let me live as long as possible."

KLUSKAP raised His eyebrows; He puffed at His pipe. "Well, grandson, you've asked a tricky thing," He said. "I'll see what I can do for you."

The next day He gave each of the first three men a little box from His medicine bag; He gave them beautiful new skin-shirts that Grandmother had painted for them; He guided them home and left them. (Perhaps they had never been away, for the People believed in acting out their dreams. It might well have been that they walked their year-journeys in a single day among the wigwams of their kin, that they had made the medicine-boxes themselves. But they believed their dreams; their dreams changed them.)

Each box contained a holy ointment, and the three men anointed themselves. The angry man became sweet and devout; the poor man became a leading hunter; the despised man became fragrant in body and spirit.

As for the fourth man, KLUSKAP led him into the high, dry hills. He raised him up; He twisted him into the ground; He conjured above the man's head and he became an ugly old cedar tree. – "Nobody will bother you here," said KLUSKAP, glitter-eyed. "I think you will live a very long time." – The tree twisted its branches in supplication; it lashed its branches in horror, but KLUSKAP was already gone.

A man's robe hung in tatters on that tree for many long years, eaten by vermin, pecked at by birds, until at last a great storm blew it away and then the tree stood truly naked, creaking and shivering and growing older and older and older . . .

Freydis and Kluskap

Just as low trees may join their branches together to form a sort of cave, in which the green plants swim like phosphorescent fishes against the deep black earth, so Freydis thought to screen her glowing hopes and hatred by peeking at GLOOSKAP from between clasped fingers; He, of course, knew her every thought. The birds screeched scornfully at her from His shirt; on His shoulders the panthers rolled their eyes.

"Well," GLOOSKAP was saying, "you've asked a hard thing, granddaughter, but I'll see what I can do for you."

"I know I am deserving, for my race ranks with the highest," said Freydis proudly. "My father Eirik was Lord in Greenland; his father Thorvald was Lord in Norway, and his father Thorstein was King of Jæderen in the days before King Harald Fairhair. And when my father first saw me he said, 'This child will be named Freydis, and I expect her to be rich in costly things on account of that name.'"

At this, KLUSKAP merely smiled, but she read His smile truly. Then she

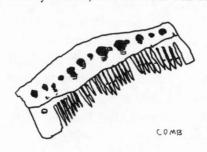

COMB

esteemed Him highly, for she believed that anyone who was not envious of her must deserve her envy.

"But first tell me," KLUSKAP suddenly challenged her, "why do you want to cause such misery by bringing the frost here?"

Freydis shook her head heavily. "I don't know," she said. "I don't know." She felt that she must say something further to establish her rights over Him, but a blue mist was in her head; suddenly she could not understand anything (for this was one of the things that AMORTORTAK did to His thralls; He fed upon them from inside, like a wasp upon a caterpillar, and slowly desiccated them and left them hollow until their consciousness was a dead King sitting on a chair within his dark grave-howe, everything dark and musty and evil-smelling, and all his royal treasure taken by robbers, except, perhaps, for a missed gold coin or two, over which the snails crawled and crawled, leaving black trails). – But Freydis knew that she must recover herself. "I want to bring the frost here," she insisted, angelica-sweet, "I want – I want . . ." But then once again she could think of nothing to say. In truth there was no *reason* for the sad deed that she was called upon to do.

GLOOSKAP looked at her with His quick eyes. His long black hair fluttered in the wind. He worked His wide shoulders, never looking away from her. His powerful silence made her uneasy. "I'm not sure you're asking such a thing for yourself," He said at last. "I think Someone Else is asking through you; I think I see Him in your eyes."

Wearing the Master-Shirt

KLUSKAP had an evil Twin, for to every man has it been commanded by ODIN the All-High: *Over and over must you fight your brother.* (If you are Younger Brother, he will tyrannize you until you rebel; if you are Elder Brother, then to defend himself against your Firstness he must learn the dark knowledge of Blue-Shirt; and *you* must tread him underfoot to crush his vileness.) As They lay in Their dark womb-home, which They named *Mooskōbe*, the two Brothers opened Their glittering black eyes and conferred together as to how They should be born. – "I will be born as all men are born," said KLUSKAP. "That way I will cause the least harm to Our Mother. You too should choose that way." – "Ha, ha!" laughed the Twin. "I can see that You think Yourself superior to nobody. As for Me, I know Myself; I elect to burst out through Mother's side! Ha, ha, ha!" – KLUSKAP was born first. Then the Twin emerged in that hideous way that He had promised, killing

Their Mother. – The Two grew up together, and often They quarreled, in scenes no more loud than unmanly (for Their blood-ties prohibited Them from striking one another).

"Tell me, KLUSKAP, said the Twin. "How can You be killed?"

"With a sharp blow to My head with a cattail flag," said KLUSKAP. But He lied. – Then He said, "And You, brother, how can *You* be killed?"

"With a handful of bird's down," said the Twin. "I wish You long life, brother!" Then He laughed, and disappeared into the forest. KLUSKAP saw that He was walking in the direction of the marshes, where the Cattail People lived; so He prepared Himself. Presently the Twin crept behind Him and smote Him with a cattail flag so hard that He was stunned. – "Ha, ha!" laughed the Twin. "Now I am the eldest!" He left His brother for dead, and went capering along the seashore. – But KLUSKAP soon came to His senses again, and rose and gathered down from the Duck People and the Swan People. He squeezed the down tightly in His hand to make a ball, and then He stalked His Twin in the shadows; He found Him, he threw that hard-packed ball at His head, and the Twin fell down dead. – "Now I am the eldest again, it seems," said KLUSKAP.

The Invitation

Freydis shook her head stupidly; she slapped her cheeks and pinched herself, and at last she remembered the Word that the Skrælings had taught her and shouted it out in GLOOSKAP's face: "*MOOSKOONAMOOKSOODE!*" – He grimaced and stepped back from her. A wind began to blow from the north. It blew all night; it blew so hard that the stars seemed to be carried along in it like daisy-heads in a stream. At dawn, as KLUSKAP stood waiting on the headland, a mist sprang up on the sea and He saw the silhouette of an immense iceberg coming closer and closer to Him through the fog and Someone was breathing cold-breath on Him and the iceberg ground slowly against the beach with a crunching sound and Someone strode ashore. – KLUSKAP knew exactly what would happen as soon as Freydis uttered the Name. – How He wanted to blot her out! But she fell under a different jurisdiction. He must wait. So He did not become a grove of flowering stars to blind her with His sparkling light; He did not seize her and kill her. – For her part, no longer did she desire to love Him, for He did not seem powerful to her. Then she remembered that anyhow she had never loved Him, nor desired to love Him; she desired to *kill* Him . . . but when she looked for her knife it was gone.

"Well, granddaughter, you will hear from Me or from Him in a dream," said GLOOSKAP graciously. "Have a safe journey back, and know that My People have been commanded to follow you unseen and protect you from panthers."

How the Brothers Greeted Each Other

Chuckling, Blue-Shirt strode into KLUSKAP's country. He wore a studded mailcoat. The ocean froze behind Him; the grass went rime-white under His boots. "My whore called upon Me in Your presence," He said with a sneer (and His familiars followed behind Him in a sleet-cloud). "Now at last I can throw You down and tread You underfoot. With a curse I greet You!"

"Well, brother," said KLUSKAP quietly, "welcome back from the land of the dead. I would greet You as You greeted me, but there is no need, because You will curse Yourself no matter what You do."

Now Blue-Shirt grinned like a great crack in the ice and ripped up four great pine trees by the roots. He paced off a square a hundred ells on a side and marked each corner by thrusting one of his tree-poles deep into the earth. (Black crows flocked to the branches from all over the world; there they sat silently, waiting for blood to drink.) – "Let this be Our playing-field," He said, and KLUSKAP replied that it would be as He wished.

To KLUSKAP, Blue-Shirt seemed like the man who had feared death, who had been afraid to take off his shirt and become anything different; that was why KLUSKAP was determined to make Blue-Shirt's chest naked. – "*Kwe! Ya! Kwe! Ya! Kwe! Ya!*" sang KLUSKAP fiercely. – Old Grandmother whispered her luck-wish in His ear; she painted red and yellow stripes of Power on His face; she brought Him a basket of smoked moose intestines stuffed with fat, meat and berries; and little Marten brought Him a kettle of the fattest stew to give Him strength; but AMORTORTAK watched Him eat with ill grace, for no one offered any to that foul King of Trolls. Sullenly He strode to the sea and caught a dozen seals; He ate their meat and crunched their bones in His teeth and rubbed Himself with their fat to make Himself more supple and slippery in His armor if KLUSKAP should chance to wrestle with Him. (And the clams, KLUSKAP's enemies, sang Him songs of their hatred for KLUSKAP, but because Blue-Shirt wore only His own shirt He did not understand.) Now He somewhat repented of the contest between Them, for He remembered that KLUSKAP had bested Him once before. But He was lustful and greedy of extending His dominions; the frost seethed inside Him in swirling storms, and He longed to impregnate the world with it, to raise great snow-mounds for His treasures, to send the glaciers creeping, rending, grinding down the fells and hills to blot out the green grape-vines that He hated so. For rage had long ago enlarged His heart. So He stepped onto the trial-field, and KLUSKAP did likewise.

The Mountain and the Hill

How different They had become from each other, those two Who once were twins, can scarcely be imagined, for the God-Shirt is a prison with heavier bars than any shirt *we* in our little inconsistencies could ever don. – Blue-Shirt stood tall and black, like a crag. His limbs were hairy and icy. His beard was frost, and there was snow on His shoulders. He was His own ice-mountain. His mail-shirt bristled with ice-spears. He seemed to embody everything heavy and hard and fixed, that even wind and sand must weary in wearing away. His eyes burned horribly in His blackish face, and He gnashed and gnashed His teeth. And no steam came from His breath, but only mist. – KLUSKAP was somewhat more slender, and shorter by a head, but He was lighter and faster on His feet, and His black eyes were living and alert. On His shirt the catamounts hissed and arched their backs, the eagles darted their beaks fiercely at Blue-Shirt, the bears raised their great killing paws, the weasels and wolverines chattered their teeth angrily.

The First Bout

Now the two Powers circled round each other and took each other's measure. And KLUSKAP swore in His heart that He would not let His brother set His wicked mark upon the land. They swung Their fists at each other: and AMORTORTAK creaked and splintered like spring ice: KLUSKAP groaned like an axe-bitten tree. AMORTORTAK bided His time, and when His enemy seemed least prepared He rushed upon Him like a wolf; He lifted Him off the ground and hurled Him down. – Then old Grandmother wailed, for she thought that KLUSKAP was dead. For a space He lay there, very pale, with blood trickling from His head, and the colored stripes that Grandmother had painted on His face were smeared with sweat and blood and dirt; and Blue-Shirt strode round and round Him, debating with Himself how best to end His life. At length He leaned down toward Him to strangle Him, but from that wondrous shirt of many creatures a marmot bared its little teeth and chattered, and a falcon fluttered its wings in Blue-Shirt's face so that He grimaced in startlement and drew back, and KLUSKAP sprang to His feet. Then Grandmother clapped her hands, and Marten laughed aloud. – KLUSKAP pulled up one of the tree-poles, and hurled it into AMORTORTAK's chest. AMORTORTAK staggered back growling; He wrenched the tree out of Himself and snapped it in two and threw both halves at KLUSKAP, but He stepped aside, and they flew harmlessly into the forest.

The Armies

Now KLUSKAP looked over His shoulder and saw Blue-Shirt's trolls swarming out of the sea. They were ice-caked; they were salt-caked. They shook themselves like rats; they bared their yellow teeth at Him; they came scurrying up to the field of battle. And Blue-Shirt laughed to see them come. – So KLUSKAP called to Marten, saying, "Go quickly! Bring my THUNDERS and ECHOES! Bring KEWKW here; bring COOLPUJOT!" – And Marten rushed off on his way. He was back in a twinkling, and he did not come alone. So KLUSKAP and AMORTORTAK marshaled Their spirit-armies just as the boy-Kings Ingjald and Alf had done in Upsal so long before; – but these were real Spirits; their eyes shone like the MOON's eyes. – Here came Blue-Shirt's demons, with their wings and claws and webbed toes; here came His trolls; here came His greatest house-carles, FELL, FROST and GLACIER. – But here too came KLUSKAP's familiars, His THUNDERS and ECHOES who lived in the storm-mountains and the rocky valleys; here came KEWKW, Whose other name was EARTHQUAKE, and here came faithful Marten rolling COOLPUJOT THE BONELESS along with a spear! Now the THUNDERS were puffy and stout and bluish-black in Their faces, but the ECHOES had no faces, being invisible spirits. As for EARTHQUAKE, He was a great giant, who could pull the earth apart with His hands. He traveled as well under the ground as on it. – COOLPUJOT was but a sallow fellow; He could not sit up, or raise His head, or even twiddle His fingers. Medicine-roots grew underneath Him in His shade. Marten nibbled at these as he rolled Him, and COOLPUJOT laughed and wheezed. – "Look at that carle!" laughed Blue-Shirt to His army. "He's nothing but a lump of whale-puke!" – "Ha, ha, ha!" laughed the trolls. – But KLUSKAP puffed at His pipe and said nothing.

So they stood facing each other in two lines, those Spirits, while AMORTORTAK and KLUSKAP clapped Their hands.

At first it almost seemed that those Two watched Their own contest like Gudrid's men and Freydis's men gathered in separate factions to see the swimming-bouts of their champions, sometimes cheering, sometimes merely waiting unsmiling with folded arms to see who might win the competition. In the same fashion stood the Brothers side by side. – COOLPUJOT lay gangling Himself in the grass; bloated and sickly-white He looked, for Blue-Shirt was nigh and it was winter, but COOLPUJOT was a Power of power nonetheless, as shall be seen. As for the trolls, their eyes goggled just above their long thin necks, and they rolled their rubbery tongues in their mouths.

The Second Bout

Now, when EARTHQUAKE came the earthquake came, and AMORTORTAK screeched and fell down a great shaft into the maw of black rock, and the air hissed behind Him as if a tower had fallen; and EARTHQUAKE stamped His foot and the earth closed; and EARTHQUAKE walked upon the earth, and it trembled, and still KLUSKAP was silent, but He smiled and His eyes glittered. – Now the yellow trolls came swarming from between tree branches and dug into the earth with long fingernails to rescue their LORD. And He lay almost upright in the black earth, like a ruin, smiling horribly, and when His trolls had freed Him and ministered to Him He jumped up out of His grave-pit and the air whistled again and He breathed a breath of ice; and although EARTHQUAKE now stamped with all His might to make a great pit into which AMORTORTAK *must* fall, AMORTORTAK grinned and spat, and His spittle flew into the crack and froze so that the lips of that earth-wound could not pull any farther apart; and though EARTHQUAKE stamped and stamped He could not shatter that ice, and so He retired from the battle, swearing oaths as heavy as unburst stormclouds.

The Third Bout

Now KLUSKAP stirred and took Marten's spear and rolled COOLPUJOT a little east, so that it was spring again – for COOLPUJOT was the Power of the seasons (and to the Greenlanders in Gudrid's country it seemed that the good weather would never end and they almost drowned in good greenness and the green grapes and red grapes burst with sweet juices that dribbled down their chins so that Gudrid's baby laughed for the first time, and the peat flowers sprang up higher than ever before); and all the trolls shielded their bulging froglike eyes and cried tears at the terribly sunny warmth of that spring; and the SUN brushed back Her golden hair and smiled down at KLUSKAP, happy to see Him so soon again; and Her brother the MOON chased after Her in the darkness over Greenland and the Jötuns trod the glorious mountains but they could not seduce Him from His sister. – Feeling the warm sun-rays upon His brow, AMORTORTAK became somewhat wan, and drops of whitish sweat rolled down His face.

Now KLUSKAP threw a handclap around a circle of THUNDERS and ECHOES; when it reached AMORTORTAK's hands it scorched Him and ice fell from His face. But He held it and grinned and hurled it back among His black trolls, and every troll added something to it as it went so that it got louder and more awful like rockslides and glacier-slides among His lonely mountains with the MOON circling round and round above as that great handclap rushed from hand to hand, until the last of those evil trolls clapped it full into KLUSKAP's face and He grimaced for a moment and became very old and the wrinkles in His face were as the strands in the spider's web; but then He gently took the handclap in His palm and breathed on it and wiped away the foulnesses of it and returned it to His shirt where it became a lightning-bird singing among the other birds. (But the trolls threw spiteful hail-balls at KLUSKAP, and AMORTORTAK laughed.)

The Fourth Bout

Now the play began to get somewhat rougher. The faces of both were bloody and flushed. KLUSKAP was dismayed at how much His brother had grown in strength and cunning; as for AMORTORTAK, He felt nothing but fear and rage. AMORTORTAK would have liked nothing better than to be able to strip off KLUSKAP's shirt; because just as the wearer needs the garment, so the other way around; and if He could pull KLUSKAP's shirt off then the Plant People and Animal People would fade and die and Vinland would become a dull grey rock of lifeless neutrality, which He could then clothe in the Ice-Shirt. For this reason He stalked close to KLUSKAP and seized the shirt by the hem, grasping and pulling with all His power, but He could not rend it; He cursed and let go when the chattering squirrels bit His hand. Now KLUSKAP flung Him down upon the rocks; but He stood up and battered KLUSKAP about the face; so KLUSKAP leaped into the air and became a hot blue rain-cloud that showered itself down on AMORTORTAK, seeking to melt Him, but AMORTORTAK merely grinned and clapped His hands, and His servant, ugly wizened little FROST, climbed upon His back, and the rain became sleet and hail as it neared His face and shoulders; so it fortified His armor with another layer of rime, and KLUSKAP gave over the attempt.

The Fifth Bout

Now AMORTORTAK clapped His hands again, and His servant FELL, a big sullen fellow with rocky grey brows, ran across the trampled grass to KLUSKAP and embraced Him around His waist and became a great high cliff-well in which KLUSKAP was trapped. – He stood for a moment running His hand through His long black locks; He puffed His pipe and thought inside the dark mountain whose sides rose sky-sheer about Him, so sheer that even Blue-Shirt's trolls found it hard work to scrabble up the outer walls to get at Him; they were going to drop boulders down upon Him and crush Him. But KLUSKAP became a seagull and flew up, up, high above the mountain, and FELL retired to His master discomfited. – The next essay was made by great GLACIER, Who threw heavy slabs of ice at KLUSKAP and also crept behind His back like a snake of cold to ensnare Him. But KLUSKAP rolled COOLPUJOT a little farther east, so that GLACIER began to sweat and groan and grow faint, and the day grew brisk and warm, until at last poor GLACIER sank to the grass in a faint, and bled and sweated and melted Himself into a merry little stream. – Blue-Shirt heaved a rock into it in disgust. – He now turned Himself into a gruesome ice-bear and sprang upon KLUSKAP, but a grizzly bear charged out of KLUSKAP's shirt and hugged the ice-bear and worried Him with his fangs while KLUSKAP sat catching His breath, and then AMORTORTAK became Himself again and KLUSKAP threw boulders at Him and smashed the ice of His face so that He was even more trollish to look upon, and AMORTORTAK bellowed and His face was black with pain and rage and He seized KLUSKAP by the hair and raised His axe and chopped off KLUSKAP's arm so that He sank down fainting to the grass and Grandmother and Marten cried out and then AMORTORTAK stood gloating over Him, but KLUSKAP took back His arm to Himself and held it against Himself and it grew back whole in its place, and He leaped up, racing round and round like a greenish tornado, shouting: "*Kŭskimtŭlnàkŭnuhkwŏde!* I have a hundred feet; I am a centipede!"

The Sixth Bout

Now KLUSKAP called upon the SUN and cast a spear of burning goldness into the heart of His brother. Blood ran down AMORTORTAK's chest and froze upon it, forming ice of a rich dark color like the red algae of Greenland (which makes what the explorer Ross called "crimson cliffs"); red ice glistened on His mail-shirt. He staggered; He glared at KLUSKAP with eyes of darkness; rocks and ice thundered down from His heaving shoulders. He called upon the Moon and pierced KLUSKAP through His shirt with a spear of white ice-light, and KLUSKAP became pale again and trembled. Seeing how terribly this had molested Him, AMORTORTAK laughed and prepared to cast another Moon-spear against Him, and as many more as it would take to destroy Him. But the Plant People on KLUSKAP's shirt took root wherever He bled and sent up green shoots that kissed Him with leaf-curls round His neck, and tobacco-leaves cooled His forehead and sweetflag leaves brushed against His lips so that He smiled at these His kin-friends and opened His mouth to chew their green medicine-leaves, so that a little more Power beat in His heart. His color returned somewhat; the red and yellow stripes glowed upon His face; He rallied Himself, and His breathing came fast. Yet it was still certain that Blue-Shirt would destroy Him, for He was shattered in His powers. He fought against Blue-Shirt with hands and feet, like a spider; He failed; He fell, and AMORTORTAK rushed to trample on His face with shoes of creaking ice ... but as the wicked one crushed that bleeding body, smearing blood and paint upon the ground, KLUSKAP came sauntering out of the woods, with His pipe in His mouth, and He was fresh and full of strength, for He had not been there at all before; He had only sent a seeming of His shape: the Name "KLUSKAP" means "Liar."

The Seventh Bout

From His pipe KLUSKAP sucked in the smoky goodness of the Tobacco People. He thrust His shoulders wide, He seized AMORTORTAK, He shook Him and He struck Him. The rising moment came, the moment when

everything must cover its face. KLUSKAP raised both His arms; He clenched
His fists –

... *and the trolls scuttled away sidewise like a centipede's legs without the body;*
He clapped –

... *and black trees fell to the ground.*

AMORTORTAK crashed down like a great rock, and a hollow sound rang
from His stony, icy chest.

Freydis's Dream

In a dream KLUSKAP came to Freydis and said, "I have killed
MUSKUNAMU'KSUTI again; that is how I have fulfilled your wish to
be rich in everything. Now you need not be bound by your word to
Him. Load your ships with My maple-wood; trade cloth with the People
for My skins, and cheat them as much as you like; gather My grape-vines,
and everything else besides. Your Ice-Shirt is melted, and you may put on
any other shirt you choose." – But when Freydis heard these words she
turned pale; she wept; she sickened like a fir-tree stripped of its boughs.

Black Hands

You will remark, sir, that nothing rots or becomes corrupt in this land; corpses, which have been buried for thirty years, are as fine and sound as when they were alive . . . To say the truth of these northern countries, dead bodies keep well, but the living always fare ill.

ISAAC DE LA PEYRIERE,
Relation du Groenland (1646)

"Ho, ho!" laughed Blue-Shirt, clapping and clapping underground. He had wanted to die.

Giants and Trees

I remember of yore   were born the Jötuns,
they who aforetime   fostered me:
nine worlds I remember,   nine in the Tree,
the glorious Fate-Tree   that springs 'neath the Earth.

'Twas the earliest of times   when Ymir lived;
then was sand nor sea   nor cooling wave,
nor was Earth found ever,   nor Heaven on high,
there was Yawning of Deeps   and nowhere grass:

ere the sons of the god   had uplifted the world-plain,
and fashioned Midgarth,   the glorious Earth.
Sun shone from the south,   on the world's bare stones –
then was Earth o'ergrown   with herb of green.

Sun, Moon's companion,   out of the south
her right hand flung   round the rim of heaven.
Sun knew not yet   where she had her hall;
nor knew the stars   where they had their place;
nor ever the Moon   what might he owned.

The prophetess VALA

I f I have passed over the tale of Leif's foster-father, Tyrkir the Hun, who discovered the grapes and became drunk on them; if I have omitted the account of Thorhall the Hunter, who invoked a whale from THOR that made all the Christians sick, it is not because I wished not to tell them, but because no one can land on every story-island in Breidafjord in one lifetime, not even Thorgest of Breidabolstead, as we saw when he sought for Red Eirik to slay him; and Gudrid found the same when she sought to devour every fresh lake-island in her country, searching for the Tree she refused to call Yggdrasil. – "Why do you wander so much in the forest?" said her husband. "You will end by becoming fey, like crazy Freydis." – "Have no fear of that," smiled Gudrid, "for I am already that." – "But what of the Skrælings?" he cried in despair. "You know they lurk about.

You know they killed your dead husband's brother. Surely they will kill you, too, if they can, for we have done them an injury." – Gudrid could say nothing to that, for she knew that it was true. But Freydis had thrown the Gold-Shirt over her, and she could not escape its dazzlement.

Carrying the War-Club and Dreaming of Bad Days

Although she knew it not, Gudrid was perfectly safe in her travels for the present. – "There she is!" cried Carrying the War-Club's men. "Look – the white she-devil with young! Shall we take revenge for the death of His Spear Is Straight?" – "Shame on you!" said old Dreaming of Bad Days. "What honor will you gain by killing her?" – "We have heard your views before," said Carrying the War-Club scornfully. "Yes, you are a man of peace; perhaps you weep when your sons bring you beaver-meat to eat. Yet this once I say that you are right, for this Jenu woman carries no axe, and that is what we want to transform ourselves. Let us wait and watch; if once she brings an axe among the trees I will shoot her in the throat. Meanwhile, warriors, send runners to the other villages, and we will prepare to attack the demons in their houses."

Karlsefni's Preparations

Karlsefni gathered his men together. (But Freydis's men were absent. They traveled in the forest in packs, and though they carried axes and spears the Skrælings feared to ambush them.) – "Now we must make a good plan," said Karlsefni. "The Skrælings have visited us before. I expect that they will visit us one last time, and their trading then will be blood for blood. I want ten men of good spirit to set up camp on the headland north of the river. The Skrælings will see you first, and attack you first. The rest of us will move into a clearing in the forest. We will build a palisade around it, higher than the one we have here. We will keep our cattle inside with us. I have noticed that the Skrælings fear the roaring of our bull. When you men on the headland send word of their coming, I will come out with the other armsmen and we will set the bull on them."

Everyone listened closely, and agreed that it was a good plan. Gudrid mourned somewhat about abandoning the houses they had built, but when she raised the subject she saw a gleam of ill-temper in her husband's eye for

the first time, and wisely said nothing more. The next day, while he and his
men sharpened their axes, she put her baby on her back and slipped away
once again to the forest . . .

How Gudrid Found Yggdrasil

Although Vinland seemed but a promontory to the Greenlanders, the truth
was that it went south and south and south, widening as it traveled into the
places of hot and steamy darkness. Gudrid's country was by no means at
the end of it; it seemed not impossible that Vinland might stretch all the
way to the MARE OCEANUM that was so black and cold and misty, where
the Midgaard Serpent waited with its tail in its mouth . . . I am maddened
by the impossibility of describing Vinland, how it *was* in the Sun's light with
golden trees rising higher and higher the farther Gudrid went into the forest –
golden trees that Freydis could never have found, for the landscape around us is
but a shadow of the landscape within us, so that Freydis found mainly crooked
black trees; or when she walked into the golden light she was tormented by
it, as I have described; and from leagues away sardonic KLUSKAP could see
her pale head swimming disembodied in its own inky darkness, bereft at last
even of desperation and despair so that she strode calmly; but for Gudrid the
trees rose harmonious and golden, their leaves more velvety than *pell*, which
was why the Skrælings sometimes clothed themselves in those green skins.
– As she went on her way, with her baby on her back, Gudrid hummed a
tune to make him sleep, and she never thought what the tune was, but it
was one of the songs that her dead foster-mother Halldis had taught her,
and the words were:

> An ash I know   called Yggdrasil,
> the mighty Tree   moist with white dews;
> thence come the floods   that fall adown;
> ever green overtops   Fate's well this tree.

and Freydis knew the same song, but she sang it thus:

> I know an ash   called Terror's Horse,★
> the sky-cliff Tree   slimed with snow-dews;
> thence roar the floods   that death-foam down;
> ever green this tree   over Well of Weird.

★ The real meaning of Yggdrasil. One name for ODIN was "Ygg," meaning "Terror."
Yggdrasil was ODIN's horse because He once rode it as men ride the gallows, hanging Himself
as a sacrifice to Himself so that from His suffering He might learn the sacred runes.

for there are two kinds of everything; and Freydis's forest-dreams were haunted always by Yggdrasil's clammy green shadow rippling on that Well of Weird at the bottom of which lay ODIN's eye, ripped from His head as payment for one drink of that water; but Gudrid's song was happy, the happier still for her because she did not remember what it was; and she came almost at once to a Tree that was gold and green in the sun (although much of it was dead) and birds of many colors nested in the crooks of its branch-arms and they sang for her; and a spring bubbled out of the moss between two roots; and the Tree's leaves made music in the sun for her, and all its dead leaves were real gold. – Gudrid laughed and clapped her hands. – "It is beautiful, by CHRIST!" she said. – But at that Name, of course, there came a terrible screeching noise from inside the Tree and the birds flew away and the leaves withered and the Tree became black and dead.

Then Gudrid understood at last that she must have been involved in some plot of Freydis's to do a thing unholy; so she cursed both Freydis and her thrall Skofte, and resolved, insofar as the teachings of CHRIST permitted, to revenge herself upon them both. But for the time being she said nothing. – Skofte, who had followed her lurking among the trees (but he had seen nothing that she had seen) soon reported to his mistress that Gudrid seemed disinclined to go out anymore. – "Should I question her?" he asked. – "No, fool," said Freydis sharply, "for then she'll know for certain that you have been spying on her. Do you think she'll like that?" She thought for a moment. "Take me to that spot where you say she exclaimed to her CHRIST. Maybe I can see something there."

They set out the following day. Freydis took her axe and a great candle of deer-tallow.

How Freydis Found Yggdrasil

There was a narrow lagoon over which leaning oaks made a roof, and the black silhouettes of their branch-arms and leaves were reflected in the water, which was almost perfectly black with those reflections, and when the breeze blew, the real branches shook but their reflections moved very differently because the water streamed and rippled with them, so that it appeared to Freydis that they had bones no more than did an octopus. Here she made her way with Skofte, and the trees grew thicker and thicker around her. Yet because she was not trapped in that black world upon the water, she was not stifled; she did not feel as if she moved in darkness; and indeed, all through the forest that morning spiderwebs and tree-hairs were white in the sun. Spiderwebs brushed against her lip. A lightning-struck tree-wreck, long since hollowed after burning, remained like a fencepost set into the forest floor. Caterpillars had eaten archways in it. – "This is where Gudrid cried out," said Skofte. – "Oh, it is, is it?" said Freydis. She went and stood inside the stump, gazing at the spider-strands that quivered in the sunlight like hairs, until, sighing, she closed her eyes. Time passed. Presently she stared down at the darkness she stood in, but still no notion of how to achieve her purpose came to her. Outside, Skofte waited patiently until she remembered him and sent him away. Then she turned her face upward, peeping through that hollow tree-bone around her, and spied the round boles of trees around her rising up into the sky until they ended in spoked wheels of branches in the clouds, and the sunlight marched down them in rings, down, down, until it reached even Freydis in that dark burned trunk filled with dried needles and horrid white moths, and a single bough creaked and clicked somewhere as Freydis stood there with her eyes very big in her pale lost face. – Where was Yggdrasil? – She stared up at those great trees that disappeared in the clouds – and then at last the thought came to her that maybe they were *not* trees, but roots! What if this entire forest comprised the great Tree; what if those wide and branchy boles met above the clouds in a trunk as vast as the world? – As soon as she had thought this, Freydis became certain that she was right. But her pleasure in herself was quickly succeeded by despair, for if this were so how could she possibly destroy these woods that seemed to have no end? And what if the forests of Markland were but other snake-roots of the same Tree? She flung herself down, there inside that dead place, sobbing bitterly.

The Philosophy of Skofte Carrion-Crow

As for Skofte Carrion-Crow, he spied on his mistress as he had done with Gudrid, and thought her mad. He decided to leave her service as soon as he could conveniently do so. Among the ships in Karlsefni's convoy, Bjarni Grimolfsson's was well-ranked in the minds of men. Like Carrion-Crow, Bjarni was an Icelander – a tie to seize upon. Indeed, he was known for his liberality. By experience, Carrion-Crow knew that such men did not pay careful heed to their stores, so that it was easy to steal from them. This suited him well. – "At any rate I have not done so badly with Bastard-Freydis," he said to himself as he went his way home. "She may not have spread her legs for me as I thought she did with all her thralls, but for all her abuse

she has paid me well. And it may be that she will find this gold Tree she
prates about. After all, I found a leaf of gold. So I will not leave her just
yet – not until after I am rich." – It could truthfully be said that other
men did themselves no credit to despise Skofte. Freydis's temper aroused
no more anger in him than a rainstorm. Her very blows were no worse than
hailstones. So, though he was a doleful dog to be sure, Skofte at least never
lay down to whimper under the drizzle of his own ill-luck.

The Way Beneath the Tree

Meanwhile, Freydis whimpered in the hollow stump. But just as the moon is
called "Wheel" by the monsters who serve Queen HEL, for in their country,
which lies in the extremity of the north, the moon seems only to whirl round
and round upon itself like a yellow skull in an eddy; but the Frost-Giants call
it "Speeder," for to them in Jötunheim the wind roars through the mountains
and the black clouds flee across the sky and the very moon tosses and turns
frantically above the clouds (yet it is the same moon in both kingdoms); –
just as the Hell-folk call wood "seawood-of-slopes," for to them in their
lightless realm it is of no more account than any other jetsam at the bottom
of the deep sea; but the Giants call it "firewood," because they must always
be throwing cartloads of fuel on the Wall of Flickering Flames that guards
their castles; – just as Gudrid sang the mild song of Yggdrasil but Freydis
sang the song of Terror's Horse; so in time, when she was calmed from
her despondency, Freydis thought to herself, "I can call these trees roots if
I choose to, or I can call them shoots of *one* root, in which case I can follow
any hole that goes down deep enough." – So that day she wandered through
many a lightning-struck clearing, where the trees were fire-hollowed. Freydis
searched inside them every one. Finding nothing, however, she returned at
last to Gudrid's tree.

It had been burned, and was scaly inside with black shingles. Near the
open top, this tree-well had taken on a greenish color thanks to the mosses
and lichens that stained it and let down their frond-hairs, but where Freydis
was it was dark and cool. Toadstools glistened in the darkness like wet round
sea-rocks. A quilt of twigs lay upon the ground. Through the dead tree's
many shattered windows rolled the green light, louder and more certain than
any hymn she had ever heard in church. This dead stump was hidden in a
hill-hollow, wrapped in a conspiracy of trees, but Gudrid had found it because
she was not the sort of woman who stops short; and of Freydis one had to

say the same. It rose tall and wide like a chimney. It was completely dead and rotten. It had died, Freydis supposed, when Iceland was Christianized.

If then this was the Tree; if Skofte had not misled her; if Gudrid had seen something here; if Blue-Shirt had advised her truly in directing her to follow Gudrid in this matter, how was she to enter it? And how far down must she go? (After all, if this was Yggdrasil, its root descended all the way to HEL.) And what could she do to destroy the Tree when she got there? And could she even serve any purpose by so doing, now that GLOOSKAP had defeated Him? – "Let me recollect," said Freydis to herself. "When I visited Him in Greenland, first I crossed the Frozen Sea, then I followed valleys upward beside a great river, then I called on Him, then I ascended His mountain to the glacier, then I . . . then I . . ." – She sat down and shook her head stupidly. She could not really remember anything except that she had called on Him.

To one side of the stump was a canted boulder. A stunted cypress sapling stood before that rock. Its trunk grew low and snaky against the ground, and moss covered it, so that there was a tunnel of branches between the rock and Gudrid's tree, floored with cool black dirt in which moss grew sparsely; and she saw fat wriggling worms in there when she ducked her head inside, and filth smeared her hair and she felt sick and so knew at once that Blue-Shirt must want her to enter there. Sweating and grimacing and shying away from the worms where she could, she forced her shoulders inside and began to crawl along. The sunlight dappled her at first in her wood-cage, but by the time she brushed against the charred and sodden flank of Gudrid's tree the thicket about her had grown very dense, and it was hard to see. In many places she was forced to lay about her with her axe to clear a way ahead of her; but at last she reached a black and slobbering mouth between two half-burned roots from which blew a draft of cold stale air, and then she was certain that there was her road downward. The entrance to this cave was choked with a great ball of dense-packed twig-bones, all dry and brittle and grey-bleached like trees. Among the twigs grew pale plants with fat, broad-lobed leaves, whose like for unwholesomeness Freydis had never seen before; there was also to be seen much dead white grass, as thick as human hair, in which the black ants swarmed. Among the tree roots was no treasure or battle-gear as there might have been in Norway or Iceland, but only twigs, as numerous and ill to deal with as Skrælings. – Here Freydis was between kingdoms, but she was not yet between worlds. – She swung her axe; she pulled the severed branches aside. She bit her lip; she went on her way. Mold and mud slimed her all over, and the twigs crackled with her every movement. Once she looked behind, and the sky shone astonishingly through the twig-screen like many pale blue jewels;

later she looked again and could see only darkness. Still for a long while she heard birdsongs in the twigs around her. But these died away in time, and then her only companions were horrid spiderwebs, in which there was not even a living spider to scuttle across her face. Freydis wormed her way on her belly. The passage twisted between dripping roots, burrowing into the cool black dirt, scraping between walls of gravel. Now thoughts of things her father had told her flickered in her mind. She was entering his bench-boards. She remembered something about the dog with the bloodstained breast, the horse rushing over the echoing bridge, the high wall of Hell ... Because she did not know when she would first see troll's eyes gleaming at her like treasure-fires, she stopped, she struck spark to tinder, and so lit her candle, which she held at arm's length in front of her. The reflection of the flame glistened in the wet earth, and she crawled down and down until presently earth gave way to cold wet clay around her, and the passage steepened, and she slid down through the slime; she sped down faster and faster – how much easier than in Greenland! – and so she fell into a great cold cavern, and her belly was black with slime.

The Bride of Nothingness

There was a cold dark river, so blue as to be almost black, and Freydis strode along beside it singing to herself, "*I know an ash   called Terror's Horse* . . .", and the words sounded sweeter to her than they ever had before, but they had a hard flat echo. The river was sluggish, and smelled of death. – Freydis Eiriksdaughter was dead! She had always been dead! – But she was brave nonetheless; she was Freydis Fell-Farer. Her way presently steepened; the river *Slíth* became a cataract beside her, and she clambered down a wall of wet and icy stones not unlike the one she had clambered up when she first sought Blue-Shirt; – "the world," she thought, "is mainly weary stone-wastes of one kind or another." She held her candle high to see her way down into that darkness; and the waterfall and the black rocks flickered around her in that feeble light; the ceiling of her world flickered like a mass of snakes, and her heart leaped, but it was only a frieze of Yggdrasil-roots; yet still they flickered and seemed to move, and dank water dripped on her from them like venom-drops, so that she shuddered. But the truth was that this was her third such journey, and Darkness-Horror and Darkness-Terror might strive with each other, but scarcely with her; by now she was a hardened witch. Indeed, after a time she joyed in what and where she was, as she had done in the storm on Blue-Shirt's mountain, and once again the delusion came upon her that she saw her face in every pool, that scores of Freydises walked behind her in her footsteps, that she was legion, and her heart thrilled as she descended with her spirit-army, and she began to march as the hired Vikings did in Constantinople, and she cried out, "Come on, sisters; we'll all kiss Him together!" and in her thoughts she saw Blue-Shirt's cool black serious face, and He was handsome in her sight because she had never seen Him as AMORTORTAK (although she thought she had), and she laughed to see His face swimming there in the darkness; the candle-flame was one of His eyes, and the other – He had no other! He was ODIN the One-Eyed to her now, the bearded Wanderer Whose face was smiling and shadowed and mysterious behind His cowl; He was dead and waiting for her at the bottom of His Tree because Gudrid and the other Christians had buried Him; perhaps He loved her and would come galloping up on His eight-legged horse Sleipnir so that she would not have to walk anymore; He would pull her onto His horse and kiss her, and all her sisters would climb on, too, and sing wind-songs and the *Warlock-Songs* for Him and then He would make her pregnant and she would give birth to a god! – "Come on, sisters!" cried Freydis, and then she stumbled and out went her candle. – Then again He was Blue-Shirt, chilly and grim; and the darkness dripped upon her and smeared her with its *BLACK HANDS* and she screamed.

Freydis's Mother

The reason that Freydis never felt alone anymore was because she *did* have sisters. There were many troll-hags and giantesses and corpses down there, and she had become one of them. – This was not one of those shirts that a person can take off! It tightens and tightens about you; all of its threads are snakes; they sear you and brand you with their venom so that even if through some desperate miracle of strength you were able to burst that horrible garment and you threw it off and crushed the snakes underfoot and pulled the broken snake-heads out of your flesh, you would still be marked by it forever; you would have to flay yourself to be naked . . .

There was an old song that went:

> Elf-Candle will have a daughter
> Before Fenrir takes her.
> The maid will ride her mother's highway
> When all the High Ones are dead.

Who was Freydis's mother? Who gave birth to the giantesses? – Oh, fellow corpses, you know very well!

Jötunheim

Later, when Freydis had followed the black river Slíth to its end at the Stagnant Place that stank of snakes, so that she had twice passed through the wall of flickering flame that encircled Jötunheim, and each time a great black fiend was standing behind the flames; when she came to the high wall called *Strangle-the-Intruder* and threw stones over it so that the wall snapped its jaws and clanged until the dark Watchman came; when she shook her fist at the Watchman so that she would not be scared and screamed, *"Open up, thrall; I'm Blue-Shirt's wife! Where's the Jötun who'd dare to keep me out now?"* so he must scowling open the gate called *Loud-Grating*, made by the sun-blind dwarves; when she had passed by the House of the Giantess with the gates of towering stone; when she had passed the great hall of THRYM, King of the Frost Giants, and THRYM's house-carles, who were as tall and black as mountains, stared at her with dull yellow eyes as wide as mill-ponds; when she had passed the castle of the good giantess Mengloth, who stood sighing and waiting and looking up into the sky, whose clouds were ash-boughs (for Yggdrasil was rooted in this World, too); when she had passed the prison-cave of LOKI, Who stared silently from His nest of chains while the Serpent spat at His eyes and His loving wife Sigyn stood catching the venom in a basin; when she had crossed the kingdom from snow-peak to ice-peak, with the savage Jötun hounds ever growling at her heels, so that she must raise her blue-shining axe against them; when she had followed that black river Slíth down to the wall of flickering flames and saw the great squat Fiend of Niflheim waiting for her in the darkness beyond; when she had crossed through the wall of flames by clinging to the icy riverbank, cutting handholds and footholds with her axe, not daring to go left because there the fire would burn her, not daring to go right because there the river Slíth would freeze her with its black cold-breath, trudging on and on through the steam of nightmares; when she had come at last into the World of Niflheim, where HEL the Concealer was Queen, and the riverbank widened and flattened somewhat so that she fell trembling on a boulder and rested; when she looked back at Jötunheim and saw how now the wall of fire, hidden behind the grim guardian peaks, imparted to them a lovely pink pastel color, and by degrees she began to forget the terrors of that journey, then she forgot everything but the voice of the wind; for in low dead Niflheim the wind is but a mourner, and so is called by the Hell-folk "Whistler," but in Jötunheim they call it "Roarer." It shrieked louder than Freydis ever could; it tumbled rocks; it whined and moaned and sobbed like a monster in pain.

Slab-Land 1987

There was blue light all night, and the birds sang. The ice was thick on the fjord. All through that cold and sunny night I kept coming awake, hearing sounds that I could never recognize, could never place. Very early in the morning there came a noise like something in pain, monotonously droning and sobbing to itself, and at first I thought that it must be some river trying to trick me again into believing in clammy voices that could not hurt me, but the voice became louder, a horrid psychotic Thing's voice whining across that dreary plain of cold stones above the fjord. – "Where am I?" the voice sobbed. "Danny, if you don't fucking tell me where I am, I'm gonna fucking do you know what. I don't fucking care. I don't fucking care!" – Moaning to itself, the voice came closer and closer, and there was no other sound but the sound of the wind far away in the mountains. – Presently my tent was shaken violently as the Thing stumbled against a guy-rope. The voice was abruptly silent for a moment. Then the Thing began to claw at my tent dreamily, fumbling at the netting of the window (which was zipped shut from the inside), scratching at the rain-fly with its fingernails, shoving against me through two fragile thicknesses of nylon already stretched close to breaking, pushing with its hips and chest and knees. It wanted to tear my tent up; it wanted to uproot it, but it was too sick or too feeble. – At last I unzipped my window so that I could look into the Thing's face. "I'm here," I said. – Again the Thing stopped dead for a moment. Then slowly it stumbled back around to the window and peered in with its round, brown, astonished face – an Inuit face.

"Who are you?" the Thing said.

"I'm Bill," I said. "Who are you?"

"Kimberly."

"How old are you?" I said.

"Sixteen. I'm looking for Goodie, but I can't see her."

"If I find her, I'll tell her you're looking for her," I said.

"Thank you very much," she said.

Kimberly went away, and soon was screaming, "I don't fucking care if I

WILLIAM
TANNER
VOLLMANN
BAFFIN ISLAND 1987

die! I don't care!" Her voice echoed dully among the rocks. A little later she was at my front door again, trying to undo the zipper. "Is Goodie in there?" she said. "I want to see Goodie. Please. Goodie's dead."

"There's no one here but me."

"I want to see."

I opened the door, and she fell in, crying and breathing drunk-breath. She lay across my backpack, and her feet were outside. Her upside-down face glowed like copper, and her black eyes blinked slowly. She vomited, sighed, and closed her eyes.

A semicircle of grinning Inuit teenagers stood outside the doorway. "You fuck her?" they said. "You fuck Kimberly?"

"No," I said.

"Why she in there? What you do in there with her?"

"Kimberly wants to sleep," I said.

They laughed. Their eyes shone. They had not decided yet what to do with me.

"All right," I said finally. "Help her go home."

As they dragged her out of the tent she clung to me, so a boy hit her with a board.

Niflheim

That black stream flowed westward from the iron-black mountains of Jötunheim. It was rightfully called Slíth, the Frightful, being so poisonous with cold, so cutting with cold, that it seemed that sharp knives whirled rushing in its eddies, cutting the legs of all who must wade it. In its swirling shallows, between icy black rocks, rushed naked sour corpses, whirling round and round and bleeding; they were unsheltered by grave-earth; they were forgotten by their kinsmen; they lay yellow and disgraced among the dreary ice, and Slíth whirled them in its foaming black pools and the rocks scraped them and tore at them and Slíth's black waterfalls laughed and the boulders sang whirling and whirling in their beds and the corpses spun bleeding; and great black ravens hovered, ripping their bellies when their bellies were uppermost, and otherwise riding upon their shoulders and digging their beaks greedily into their necks and cheeks; their beaks were matted with gory hair; their claws were sticky with flesh. But it was not only ODIN's birds who fed upon the dead, for in that place there also lived Nidhogg the Dragon, whose yellow worm-coils flowed sluggishly between the rocks like a stream of urine beside the black river Slíth; he raised his head high above the mountains, peering all around for the rottenest corpse he could see; he yawned and flickered his black tongue; then he slithered into the river and seized a body from the screaming ravens; he gnawed it with his brown fangs, and the ravens flew like midges around his jaws to catch the drops of corpse-dew that fell when he ground his teeth together with the sound of crunching icebergs; and Nidhogg swallowed and yawned and snatched up another dead man; he bit off a dead woman's frozen breast and swallowed it and the disappointed ravens watched the lump of it working slowly, slowly down into his coils; then Nidhogg screeched suddenly and unfolded his brown-black wings; he fluttered into the icy air like a bat and rose high,

high, high above the mist-clouds and ice-clouds into the blackness of cold
as hard as iron; there he found the root of Yggdrasil and gnawed at it until
the great Tree groaned. – "Well done!" cried Freydis, laughing and laughing
... A drop of spray struck her hand and left a black spot on her palm.

The Changers

In the river Slíth there waded all the mainsworn men, and all the murderous
ones. Now was proven the truth of those words of ODIN the High One:

> Cattle die   and kinsmen die,
>   you yourself soon will die;
>   but one thing   will wither never:
>   the doom over each one dead.

– for there was that misnamed King Dag the Wise, who went to war over
a bird, and must now stand until world's end in that icy stream, searching
numbly from pool to pool for that little feathered corpse; there was King Harald
Greycloak, seeking in death as in life cautiously to cross that sword-stream he
could never cross; there were dead Alric and Eric who had killed each other to
be each other: their wound-blood was frozen on their faces; – there was King
Ingjald the Evil-Worker with his daughter-wife, hairy Aasa (whom Gudrod of
Skaane had called "Wolfling" before she burned him up); they stood clinging
to each other in that torture of cold-knives that was so much worse than
the fire-torture to which they had delivered so many, including themselves;
and the river bled them white. – "Ha, ha!" cried Ingjald; "let us turn into
wolves and have at those corpses!" for he was mad with the pain of ages; but
before he could change himself his daughter did so, and sprang at him with
rending jaws.* They both fell, and a waterfall snatched them up and threw
them out of sight. – There too was old King On who had sacrificed his sons
because he had not dared to die; he shrieked with toothless fear as his bier
bolted down the river; it struck a rock and flung him down upon a bed of
ice-spears; and he screamed because he could feel the ravens swooping near
his blind eyes. – There was Halfdan the Black, who had been untrue in faith
to his son Harald: now the falls were untrue to him, and continually buffeted
him to his knees, so that cold-fire dripped from his hair and burned him (and

* What a mercy that Queen HEL had let her keep her jaws! I have seen Dire Wolf skulls
without any lower jaws; and though they have deep eye-sockets they seem nonetheless to
have no consciousness, because they cannot bite.

his fate was doubly pleasing to the Norn-Sisters since he had died thus in Midgaard also, when the ice he crossed was untrue to him). – There stood grim stout Eric Bloody-Axe, known to men as "Brother-Sinker" because he had killed so many of his own kin; now sunk he too must be, as their corpses rushed down the sword-sharp rapids and struck him in his knees, in his belly, piling up around him and reddening that blue-black water; and though he grimaced and thrust them away, though his wife Gunhild the witch screamed in grief and horror on the bank, in the end he could not stand against his own dead, and toppled at last like a cut tree; the brother-arms fell limply about him as he sank and dragged him down in that poison-cold water and entangled him among the rocks of the riverbed, so that he never rose.* – As for Queen Gunhild, she clapped her hand to her mouth in terror; she looked from side to side; then she lashed together dead men's bones with strips of cloth torn from her dress, so that she had a polestaff; for she loved Eric always and now meant to rescue him; but when she took her first step into the water she shrieked aloud, and her dainty white foot turned black forever with the coldness; and then she fell and was swept down the river to the shore called *Dead-Strand*.

Wearing the Snake-Shirt

On *Dead-Strand* rose the snake-clad Hall of HEL, from whose walls dripped ceaseless drops of venom. Hell-Hall's gate faced the north, for that was the direction of ill omen. It looked out upon the plain called *All-Cold*, where rose the hall of the giant Brimir; it rose high above its many death-mounds, which were open so that Freydis could see the dead men sitting inside and gloating over their treasures by the glare of their own rotting-light; in one of them she saw her father Eirik the Red, who sat admiring himself in a mirror of ice because he wore the Blue Shirt that she had seen in her dream in Greenland, but its patterns were snakes and they slithered on his shoulders and sometimes bit him, at which dead Eirik's numb white fingers fumbled slowly at the Blue Shirt, trying to pull it away from his flesh. – "Father, do you know me?" said Freydis. – "Oh, I know you," he said, "you were the only one who was true to me. My grave is open to your sight." – "Father, tell me the truth! What was the bargain you made with Blue-Shirt?" – As soon as she had said the name, she saw the gloating eagerness come back

---

* The *Eiríksmál* has it that he went to Valhalla, but this is just one of many places where the skalds have surely lied.

into his face, and at once he began caressing the shirt he wore, and the snakes bit his hands and he cried out. – "Father, why should your dead lips not speak to give me wisdom? Tell me what I need to know." – "I know how He lives inside the frost," said the mound-man haltingly. "I know how He once climbed to Aasgaard and was welcomed there because They could not keep Him out, and They named Him 'Future,' at which the Third Norn was jealous because that was her name; I know how He ordered the march of glaciers down the mountains and ODIN nodded His head; I know how He forged seven great chests of ice to keep His frost-seeds in; I saw how He planted His seeds all over the world and ODIN nodded His head; I saw how you received His seed to plant in Wineland beside your brother Thorvald's grave – and yet you want my wisdom?" – Eirik's hands returned to his shirt again, and she let him be. He was like her husband Thorvard now, as he had never been in life, Thorvard who hoarded his Skræling-traded pelts in a long low sea-chest, fitted with metal nailheads as numerous as seeds; at night, since Freydis would not let him touch her anymore, he opened that chest and gloated. – Oh, everything was dead! – Brimir was dead. *All-Cold* was dead. The Niflheim-folk were dead. Even their barley-plants, which the Frost-Giants called "eating," the Hell-men called "hanging" because the ripe ears drooped like the heads of hanged men in the noose. And the wind was called "Whistler," and the snakes hissed bitterly like blood on embers, and all else was silent. – Oh, yes, said Freydis to herself; she loved Him; she loved Him now. Just as in the Saga of the Ynglings the Horse-Goddess, black HEL, took King Dyggvi for Her delight, so Blue-Shirt could take Freydis for His lover if He chose; she wanted Him to; she was so sick to her heart of everything. Her grief was as green as Greenland; it exploded in all directions like a Greenland meadow bounded by low sharp ridges that cut into other meadows that went on and on, dully on and on to the ice; she could smell the lovely little bell-flowers of her grief that tolled so fragrantly in the ice-wind; the sun went round and round, and the moon went round and round, and her grief was still there, and the ice was still there, but above everything stretched the arms of the Ash-Tree, and she could almost feel the warmth of Vinland. How she hated Vinland! She prayed for its black dead decay.

Wearing the Horse-Shirt

Thus came Freydis Eiriksdaughter to the Hall of HEL, which rose as high, cold and windowless as a dream. She had never lost sight of it once she reached *All-Cold*. The closer she came to it, the less she liked it. A great wall of steel girded it round. Its hateful black towers lost themselves in the darkness long before she could see the top of them. – Queen HEL knew that Freydis was here and did not care because She did not care about anything. Shivering, Freydis threaded her way between the death-mounds, blowing on her hands to keep them warm. The bale-fires dazzled her, and she was weary. But at Hell-Hall she might rest. The howes grew hoarier and more numerous, and the ground between them was churned up and littered with splintered wheels and crushed timbers and bits of carven wood, everything being frosty and moldy and pressed flat with the weight of earth; and skeletons were as plentiful as twigs: – Nidhogg had been digging there. – It was very dark and cold and silent. The wind had stopped, and she could no longer hear the roar of the river Slíth. Ahead of her, the great Hell-Gate, from behind whose gratings and lattices streamed blackness, was shut. – Freydis strode up to it and struck it three times with the head of her axe.

Now there was tumult under the ground where the raven-black skulls grinned! – The sentries at Queen HEL's gate were blackish dead mound-men who dwelled in spear-roofed howes beneath the snake-vines; they were *Draugar*, the battle-slain who leap up no matter how many times they were felled. – To the northeast, where *All-Cold* stretched to the borders of Jötunheim, an army of them wound among the hills like an immense dragon; its raised spears were its barbs, and its shields were its scales. At Hell-Hall they lay glaring. – When they could find no giants to fight, they senselessly fought each other in their howes. Their souls had decayed (for the snakes had eaten their hearts); warring was all they could do. Battle-moons clanged against battle-suns.* Nidhogg the Worm followed lustfully after, gnawing at the dead men's arms and legs. – It was the same at the other seven points of the compass. The sound of a stranger's footsteps now sank into their moldy howes; it reached their frozen ears, and then Freydis heard the clatter of spears. At the clang of her axe, the Draugar rushed out to fight her! – oh, they were so skinny and eaten-up: their ribs were their breasts, and their eyes glowed green in their skulls like lanterns. – "May the dogs eat you!" shouted Freydis. "May your dead eyes burst out of their sockets!" – And she hewed off their heads with her axe. (Their blood spattered on her hands and left black burning spots.) – The heads laughed, and laughed, and the Draugar scooped them up and drove them down hard upon their bleeding necks; then they rushed at her twice as ferociously as before. Again and again Freydis hacked

---

* Both common kennings for shields.

at them, sobbing, but they spiraled about her and stabbed at her with coldly glittering sword-play until she called on Him again, gasping for breath; then they sank limply down to the ground, and the steel Hell-Gate flew open of its own accord, with a great grinding noise.

So she entered the Hall of HEL, which was called *Sleet-Cold*, and she stepped over the threshold, which was called *Pit-of-Stumbling*. Snake-poison trickled down the walls; snakes spat upon her from the ceiling, which was domed and grey-glistening like the roof of a corpse's mouth (and a drop of venom burned her left hand and turned it entirely black); snakes dropped down around her neck and shoulders; they slithered up her sleeves and across her forehead; they wrapped themselves round her waist like loathsomely loving arms; they flowed about her as thick as blackest mist, and they had shadows for bones, and Freydis threw up her arms and shrieked. – At this they struck at her and sought to pierce her liver as we know from the *Edda* they had in the case of great King Gunnar: – they desired urgently to dissolve her flesh in the oils and acids of their hate; they longed to tighten and tighten about her until her bones burst; then nothing would separate them from the seat of her being, in which they might refresh themselves as we do with nut-kernels and wolf-hearts; – but because Freydis was still alive she was a mountain of adamant to them; her breast was a marble cliff-wall. Perceiving, therefore, that the nakedness inside her would not now be delivered over to them, they slid miserably down her legs like rain, and she shook them off. – But the shirt she wore maddened the other dead. Themselves being ended, and therefore *placed* and *exposed*, they lusted to strip her bare like them. – "Is she Queen or carline?" they whispered. "How can we know her rank when she walks thus covered?" – So, like the snakes, they determined to rape her. They would see her birthmarks; they would learn if her breast was guilt-stained! Their purpose kindled fire in their cold self-ashes, for they remembered how transformed they had become when Queen HEL's hands undid their life-shirts, and those who died together thrilled to see the greyness overcasting each other's faces as they became at last no more and no less than themselves, which is to say unsteady nothingnesses, now that HEL had put their bright robes away in Her coffers (they thought, they hoped She cherished them when they could not see, but in fact Her coffers were but hungry mindless chests of brass with great teeth that gnawed and gnawed and remained always empty); so now the dead, lacking as they were, said to each other: "What sport it will be to see the life go forth from her! And perhaps our Queen will reward us when we present this woman's shirt to Her!" – So they fell upon her. Sweaty green ogresses with great breasts and huge eyes scratched her face and ripped at her

serk. From the darkness glared naked trolls. They stretched out their arms to
strip her, but she shoved her way past them and strode between the columns
of that dark high hall where the snakes glistened; she seemed almost to be
skating across some hard-frozen lake, so effortless did her way seem to her.
As on Mount Blauserk, she seemed to see her image everywhere: she saw
it in the snake-gleams, she saw it in the monsters' glaring eyes; and cried
out, "You're all me, you witches; you all belong to me!" – And she brushed
aside the trolls like so many mayflies, for the blacker her hands became the
stronger she grew. – As for the dull dead men, she could see herself reflected
in the black workings of their bones; *they* no longer dreamed the Greenland
dream . . . Freydis jeered, "Did you take your shirts off yourself, or did ODIN's
birds do it for you?" – Their hands hung down. – Queen HEL ruled legions
of these skulls; when they knelt before Her they made a yellow pavement of
head-tops. Now they stood aside, being weak low wretches, and watched the
trolls pinch and abuse her. – "You Skrælings!" she shouted at them.★ "You
cowards!" – But they never answered. So she knocked her way through the
trolls, swinging with her silver-shining wound-gasher, cutting off the hands
of those who sought to stop her, and took step by step toward the cold
dark high-seat. – Then she saw a miserable sight that reminded her of the
nightmares of her girlhood at Brattahlid: Against the wall, and facing it, sat ten
thousand rotting women dressed in grey rags, working at dreary embroideries.
Women who had died in sickness were HEL's bondsmaids now, weaving Her
endless tapestries of woe on the creaking clanking looms of that dark place.
– There in fact sat Thjodhild, who had recently died; her features were sharp
and blue, for the ice was heavy on her grave. – Freydis was very surprised to
see her, for she had surely died a devout Christian. – "Mother, what are you
doing here?" she cried. – Thjodhild never turned from her work. "I'm not
your mother," she said, her loom clacking busily; "a troll was your mother."
– Freydis ran to her in a fury and struck her head off with her axe, screaming:
"That's right, you never were my mother; that's why you're here!" Then
she stood nauseous and trembling. The black blood ran down her breast; it
trickled down the handle of her axe and turned her right hand black. – But
Thjodhild groped on the floor for her head and set it back on her shoulders
like a *Draugr*; then she went on with her work as sternly as before.†

★ To the north, on the plain of *All-Cold*, sat the Skrælings, but she never saw them.
These were the lazy men, the untattooed women. It was their fate to wait forever with
bowed heads, eating nothing but butterflies.
† But Thorgunna was not in Hell-Hall, for she was blameless; nor was King Harald
Fairhair there: – he was not a bear; he was not a man; he was not anywhere.

Meanwhile the fiends swarmed upon her with jealous hatred. She grappled with those wild-haired trolls, who gripped her elbows and sought to bite her; she gashed their necks and arms; she smote their heart-ships, their liver-ships,* she cried out that she was *alive*; but they paid no heed, so at last she screamed AMORTORTAK's name at them; and then from somewhere in the dark high-seat ahead of her she heard a low liquid chuckle, and HEL the Concealer said, "Why, don't you know Me, My daughter?" . . . Then she saw HEL's head shining at her like a moon – but it was not the sweet moon of Gudrid's face that the dying Thorstein had seen; no, it was round and icy and brassy, and at first it did not seem to have any jaws, only a mouth of darkness cut into it, illuminated inside by the shining of many bronze fangs that went deeper and deeper back to the darkness of forever, and HEL's eyes were not eyes but shallow craters in Her cold blank head; and She wore a fetter of steel around Her neck that always choked Her so that Her head was canted to one side as if She were lunging; and all around Her was darkness; when She walked through Her hall the dead men nearest Her vanished into darkness until She had passed; but there in the center of Her own darkness HEL's head gleamed so fiercely bright; She towered so high; Her forehead glittered with rays of terror.

She had BLACK HANDS.

Queen Hel Loki's Daughter

Sometimes, when She chose to, Queen HEL took off Her flesh and went naked, Her toothy jaws grinning then no matter how sad She was, and She shook Her skull slowly from side to side and made Her unwilling lovers play tunes on Her ribs. Her breath was worse than the milky stench of the serpents. – "Oh, darling," she said, "sit beside Me and kiss Me; you can take your shirt off now . . ." – The snakes lifted their heads whenever she spoke, and their round eyes glittered like the scales of fish, and their mouths were very black inside. – At other times She had the head of a rotting horse. Her broad teeth went on and on, like a horse's; they were yellow and black. She welcomed dead warriors to Her stinking arms. Freydis too She would kiss, for She was so far dead (and had always been so) as to care nothing for distinctions of sex. – "Come now," She said, beckoning Freydis to Her, and Freydis stepped up to Her high-seat while the trolls laughed, and she knelt before Her and

---

* I.e., their breasts.

could not but smell Her horrible smell, and then Queen HEL bade her rise and stretched out Her *BLACK HANDS* to embrace her, and Her eyes shone cruelly. – Slowly, slowly, Freydis wrapped her arms around Her; she even smiled slightly (such was her resolution) as Queen HEL kissed her full on the mouth. – "Come sit beside Me on the high-seat and I will play with you!" laughed HEL as she fondled Freydis, and Freydis suffered Her to pull her down beside Her and nuzzle her with Her great black head whose eyes were like great green torch-fires; and HEL threw a leg over Freydis's leg and whinnied and nuzzled Freydis's breasts through her shirt with her terrible mouth and sucked her nipples until they bled; and so must Freydis sit, it seemed, until a new dead soul came to *Corpse-Strand.* – "Yes," thought Freydis to herself, "I really must become a Christian so that I do not have to suffer Her again when I am dead!" – It was only then that she saw that white BALDUR sat meekly beside her, bleeding and bleeding from His mistletoe-wound, and smiling sadly at her. At once Freydis became jealous: – she could imagine Queen HEL drawing Her bedclothes around Him and giving Him privileges; she could envision the same with Blue-Shirt. (But then she remembered that HEL *was* Blue-Shirt.)

The New Concubine

Queen HEL was always hungry. She ground Her teeth together so that they clacked, and every moment some blackish troll-carle would rush up to Her high-seat bearing a dish of nice tidbits, such as blood-dripping hands and feet roasted for Her and honey-seasoned to be sweet in Her mouth just as the sunlight was sweet to more fortunate creatures. – All around Her pattered Her familiars; they scuttered softly on mummy-palms; their round eyes were as bright and blank as shields. At the sight of Freydis, they curved down their mouths like sickles in their anguish, and meanwhile the serpents on the walls corkscrewed themselves round and round and prepared to spit at her again, but HEL said, "No, kinsmen, you have no right to treat the child so just yet," and then the familiars stroked their cheeks and whiskers with their paws and purred.

At the foot of Queen HEL's high-seat were many soft skins such as the Skrælings had traded to Thorvard. The dead bears snarled with black square mouths, for their heads were on their pelts, and dead men trod on them unknowing. Baby trolls played on them and peeped out through the great bear-jaws; such was the jollity of Niflheim.

Now Queen HEL brought Freydis into her bed, for the following two reasons: first, to have joy of her, and second, to keep her from learning the one truth that might have saved her from her doom: that some dead aid each other. Queen Gunhild, who had now arrived, would have said to her: "Daughter, wear my shirt and it will help you," and if Freydis had taken it she would have always had witch-help: she could have thrown herself down on icy ground to sleep, wrapping herself in Gunhild's cloak, which would instantly have become a soft warm wolfskin; she could perhaps have conjured with it to prevail against Gudrid, and black Queen HEL did not want that. – HEL's bed-hangings, finer by far than Thorgunna's, silkier than Sigrid the Haughty's, were called *Gleaming-Bale*. They glowed blue with death-fire, and stung and crackled against Freydis's naked skin when HEL drew them over the two of them. – "Oh!" cried HEL. "What a sweet dimple in your freckled belly! How becomingly your hair falls down your shoulders! – I'm in a hurry to eat your heart; I'm going to *rip* your heart from your ribs … Let Me drink more blood from your little paps, and then you may cut My head off with your axe." Her mouth was like a cloud-dripping cliff, like drowned men at the bottom of a river, like moist black earth crawling with worms. Hair grew between Her legs like dead grass.

So HEL took Freydis to Her, riding her like a horse … and then She became *Him*, for She could put Her woman-shirt on and off like Her father LOKI, Who could grow with child from eating a woman's half-burned heart. (For She was Younger Brother.) Seeing Him, Freydis shuddered with fear and love and pleasure as He mounted her; closing her eyes, she saw Gudrid's naked body trampled by grinning horses. And this pleased her exceedingly well.

"Well, now, My jewel-goddess, My necklace-tree," He said to her sarcastically, "what shirt will you wear today? What shirt shall I wear? Or would you rather be naked before Me and let Me bite your breasts again with My frost-teeth?"

Freydis wept; she knelt and kissed His knees. He forced her head down on His chest. – "Ah," He said to her smiling, "I see you drop burning tears on My breast, as dead Helgi's wife Sigrun did. It certainly appears that we shall live out our lot together, you and I."

Freydis Hel's-Daughter

"What was I changed into?" she asked Him. "Sometimes I think I'm different from what I was before, but then I feel the same again. – No, maybe I wasn't changed into anything. But I wanted to be – I *wanted* to be!"

"Everything must lose its shape to become free," said Blue-Shirt. "Is that what you want?"

"No," said Freydis, trembling.

"Well, you are changed forever. Look at your hands! You have no husband but Me; you have no mother save Me; you have no father but Me. Eirik Thorvaldsson is not your father anymore; you must call him 'Wealth-Hiding,' for he is but a greedy troll. Thjodhild Jorund's-daughter you will not see again. As for Thorvard of Gardar, what you call him matters not in the least. You are Mine; you must obey Me. You must be loving and faithful towards Me in all things."

"What must I do?"

"You must plant the frost-seed in the blood of your own kind."

And so she came back to Gudrid's country. The trees grew magnificently high. The beaches there were as soft and white as the best flour.

ASH-FRUIT (VINLAND)

The First Axe-Tale

Though necessity may force you into strife, be not in a hurry to take revenge; first make sure that your effort will succeed and strike where it ought.

Speculum Regale, IV.85

T his story now begins to sprout its crop of war-flowers. The People saw Freydis come crawling out of the black-burned stump of Yggdrasil like a maggot; they saw that she carried her axe with her; then they clamored to Carrying the War-Club to attack her and take her good helm-biter, her wound-gasher, and Carrying the War-Club laughed to hear and shouted, "Yes, yes! Creep close to her, but stay behind the trees so that her Axe-Spirit cannot see you and slay you! Then shoot her in the throat! Ha, ha! His Spear Is Straight will be avenged!" – But Blue-Shirt protected Freydis now that she was wholly His; He sent a mist that deluded the Skrælings and led them away from her, while she returned home, unknowing of her peril. Her eyes glowed in the shadows; her mouth twitched; rays of darkness shone from her *BLACK HANDS*.

Then Carrying the War-Club was enraged, and commanded all the men of the People to gather in a war-party to attack the Jenuaq. – "Kill them all!" he said. "Slaughter the demons; we will burn their ice-hearts!" And the People grinned to hear these words. They painted their bodies red for war and black for death; they put on their finest skins. The women boiled moose-bones; they skimmed off the creamy white marrow-foam and fed it to their men to give them strength for the battle. And the warriors agreed that the attack would take place on the morning after the moon began to wax.

Freydis and Thorvard

"You have black hands!" cried Freydis's husband in excitement. "What does this mean?"

"If you open your mouth so wide the bees will fly in," she said. "Can't you see anything, you fool? Those aren't my hands; those are black silk gloves that Gudrid gave me. Now get out."

And it was seven nights to the waxing of the moon.

Freydis and Gudrid

Now it is to be told that Freydis's longhouse was at as great a distance from Gudrid's as it could be within the palisade; for both women would have it so. They hated each other so much by now that their very breathing, the very sound of their footsteps sickened each other. – One night when she was lying in Karlsefni's arms, Gudrid was sure that she heard Freydis breathing outside. She thought she heard the swish of an upraised axe. Her first thought was for her baby, and she lay there with her heart pounding so hard that it hurt her, while her husband slept unknowing. Then there was a long silence. Slowly her fear became rage, and she lay hoping as much as waiting for Freydis to come creeping in, so that she could have Karlsefni kill her. But still there was nothing. At last Gudrid became drowsy again. Her eyelashes flickered in her sweet, pure face; she sighed and yawned, and slept . . . Gudrid sprang up; she heard Freydis at the door, but when she rushed outside into the fragrant night of Vinland there was nothing. For a long time she stood there in the darkness, breathing heavily. Gudrid's breasts heaved. She smote her forehead in her anger. And she swore to CHRIST that she would find a way to have Freydis disgraced. She heard her little son Snorri crying, and she ran back to him and rocked him and kissed him . . .

And it was six nights to the waxing of the moon.

Womb-Fruit

It is written that Freydis, too, now found herself pregnant – not by her husband, as she well knew, for she permitted him to have no congress with her, but by HEL the Concealer, that is Blauserk, with whom she had lain in Greenland so long ago: – demon-spawn may take a long time to grow inside a woman;

being long-lived, they can easily swell inside her belly for a decade instead of a week before they come clawing their way out of her, leaving her shrieking and dying in her own blood. But Freydis Blue-Shirt did not fear death just yet; although she had become the womb-laid grave of a demon, she knew herself to be well-impregnated.* Night by night she watched her belly swell. And everyone marveled, but said nothing. One night her serk burst, and she grunted in pain and clutched at her white belly with her black, black hands . . . Now the sagas write that in their ale-foamed state the men became quarrelsome that summer, and fought about women. Freydis knew this well. When her serk ripped she stepped forth for all to see, because she no longer cared what she did; it seemed she could not live without strife and raised voices. They looked upon her in the longhouse, and she stood tall with her hair loose like a maiden woman and her head held high, and her big breasts flapped against her big belly and they all drank in her womanhood, until when she was satisfied that she had inflamed them she laughed scornfully and went away. (Thorvard said nothing to her; he had learned at last that he could do nothing.) She was wearing a long blue gown with a white button-stripe falling its length, and a white collar. – When she retired, her men murmured among themselves, talking much about women, and presently they sauntered to Gudrid's longhouse and stood looking Gudrid over and remarking upon her body until Karlsefni drove them roughly away.

And it was five nights to the waxing of the moon.

Gudrid Begins Her Revenge

"Skofte!" cried Gudrid shrilly. "Come here at once, Skofte Carrion-Crow!" – All men looked and laughed and hoped for the sport of a woman-fight, for it was not the custom for one woman to call another's thrall.

The little man came running.

"Skofte, I give you back your witch-leaf that you beguiled me with, you and your wicked mistress! We know what you do; we know what she does! You sought to make me unclean; you sought to make me a demon-friend. I swear to you, I will live no more with filthy witches!" – So saying, Gudrid struck him with her bull-goad; she knocked him to the ground and beat him.

---

* It is peculiar that so little is known of Freydis's descendants, given her famous lineage. The *Flateyjarbók* contents itself with recording a prophecy of Leif's that her progeny would not prosper. "And after that," says the saga, "no one thought anything but ill of her and her family."

– He made no attempt to defend himself, but covered his face and called out to Freydis for protection, which of all the things he had ever done men reckoned most laughable, unmanly and shameful.

Freydis's men gathered round in a circle. They did not attack Gudrid, but stared into her face in silence so that she could read their enmity there. Presently Karlsefni came running from the pasture; when he saw what was happening, he struck his wife across the mouth and dragged her inside. But she only laughed. – In Greenland she had heard of a very cruel way the Skrælings had of catching seals. Leif had seen it. They trapped a cub-seal on the ice and pierced a hole in its flipper, through which they passed a long thong; then they threw it back down the blowhole and stood waiting with their spears. Seeing her baby alive but struggling and threshing at the extremity of its tether, the mother seal came swimming back to its aid, and then the Skrælings killed them both. So now the bond of obligation and honor that Freydis had towards her thrall must soon bring her within striking distance of Gudrid's mercy, which was not quite so generous as her smile.

Everyone knew that Freydis had been inside her longhouse. But she did not open the door; she made not a move to avenge this insult.

Evening came. And it was four nights to the waxing of the moon.

The Hen and the Silver Game

The next night one of Gudrid's hens was found slain, with its blood smeared upon her door. – "Some witch must have done that, not I," said Freydis blandly. – Now, in front of all, Karlsefni brought the two women together and implored them to make peace, "for any day now the Skrælings will attack us," he said, "and we can ill afford to be disunited then." – "I have done nothing," said Freydis icily. "But your wife must pay compensation for the blows she inflicted on my thrall." – "You took it with my hen, you witch," said Gudrid in a low calm voice, and no one liked the way she smiled. – "How much do you want?" said Karlsefni. – "Not less than a half-mark of silver!" screamed Freydis. "You're rich; you could easily pay me that!" – "So be it," said Karlsefni. "But be reminded once again that I am reaching the end of my patience towards you." – Freydis only grinned and held out her palm for the silver, and men said it was a strange sight to see those coins shining like stars in the black night of her hand. – "Give it to me!" cried Thorvard to his wife. "I'll keep it safe." – Looking round her, and seeing the naked hate in the eyes of all but her own men, Freydis saw fit to count

Thorvard as property of at least a little value. So she dropped the coins one by one into his hand (but one she gave to Skofte). Later, when they were in bed, she made Thorvard get them out again, and they played with them like children, ordering them in rows and arrays (and Freydis thought upon how her father Eirik used to sit beside her at the hearth-fire when she was young, saying, "Now, child, this penny is from the mint of Eric Bloody-Axe . . ." – but then she remembered that she was not supposed to think about Eirik anymore). – As for Thorvard, this night of coin-play with his wife was one of the happiest in his life.

But Gudrid sank down weeping; she was as Freydis had been after her dream from GLOOSKAP; she was as a fir-tree stripped of its boughs. And Karlsefni set a guard, to make certain that Freydis could not burn him out.

It was three nights to the waxing of the moon.

The Catechism

The following evening, two of the decoy-men on the headland came to Karlsefni to report that they had seen many skin-boats coming from the south, and they expected that the attack would occur any time now. – "Very good," he said. "Our ships are loaded; Freydis and Gudrid have both drawn blood; we might as well fight." – Later he told Gudrid what the men had said. "But I for one do not intend to be in this country a year from now," he told her. "There is no happiness here." – "So you are ready to let all our labor here be wasted?" said Gudrid. Her eyes were as placid as sunny lakes. – "Well, we've enriched ourselves here," said Karlsefni. "It hasn't been for nothing. We'll be able to buy the best land in Iceland; we'll be sure that our son will be well-taught by priests." – "Let me think on those things," said Gudrid. "I like to think on things before I speak my mind." – "In that you are most unlike Freydis," said her husband easily. "Freydis is another matter for you to consider. If we settle in Iceland, you will never have to see her again."

"I cannot deny that that was cleverly spoken," said Gudrid, rocking the baby.

It was two nights to the waxing of the moon.

Black Hands

The next evening, which was warm and starry and moonless, Freydis beat Skofte until the blood flowed. – "But what have I done, mistress?" men heard

him cry. Freydis did not answer. Later she said it was because he had not
done proper homage to King Blue-Shirt. – "Who is that?" said Thorvard.
– "Ask Gudrid," she said.

The night after that came the moon-horns.

Carrying the War-Club and Freydis

In the morning the skin-boats came up the river in great numbers. Skrælings
and Skrælings leaped out, whirling their long rattle-sticks in counter-sunwise
motions. Their black eyes rolled fearfully in their heads, as if they were
bearsarks. All the Skrælings were howling: "*Kwe! Ya! Kwe! Ya! Kwe! Ya!*",
so that the Norsemen were afraid. So loud was this song that the men on
the headland had no need to summon Karlsefni, for he had already brought
his men and Freydis's men to the fight. Their red shields were aloft; they
hoped to redden their spears. Karlsefni bade them not to fear death, nor to
groan, no matter how wide their wounds gaped – for such was the old law.
Then he blew the war-horn. But to himself he thought that these Skrælings
looked somewhat grim to deal with. – His friend Snorri Thorbrandsson was
there with his son Thorbrand, who had never been blooded; both were brave
and quiet. Bjarni Grimolfsson was there with his men. Karlsefni knew that he
could rely on them; long ago they had all exchanged ring-tokens. Thorvard
of Gardar stood there white-faced and trembling; he had silver hidden about
him, so that if the Skrælings captured him he could ransom his life. As for
his thrall Skofte Carrion-Crow, he arched his back; proudly he wore the
mail that Thorvard had given him. – "Come and fight, you Skrælings!" he
shouted. "I'm as invulnerable as BALDUR!" – And all men laughed to hear
him utter such words. – They strode with swords ready; Karlsefni led them,
and he held his shield cautiously ahead of him.

The People stood waiting and watching the white demons for a moment.
Their spears, their pointed helmets, their red shields daunted the People
somewhat, but they were few in number. The sound of the river was loud
in everyone's ears. Then Carrying the War-Club jumped on a log, and cried:
"See all their axes! We will take the Axe-Spirits now, for this morning dawns
the day of KLUSKAP our Brother, of our Friends the Arrow-Trees, of our
Grandfather the SUN! Now we will walk on ice; now we will creep upon
bears. This day we will kill all the Jenuaq! Now fire your arrows; launch
your flints!"

Now axes were everywhere aloft, and Skrælings fell; and spears rattled and chattered in the air; and the Skrælings launched many volleys of arrows, screaming their hideous cries, and the arrows rattled on the shields of Karlsefni's laughing men like rain. – The Skrælings dashed in close, and sought to pull their knives from their grasp, but Karlsefni's men struck with a will and cut many of them down. They lifted up their glittering axes; they sliced their heads off clean. They laughed when they were spattered with Skræling blood, like the gods laughing at the Fenris-Wolf when the fetter *Glepnir* tightened around him the more he struggled; – oh, yes, everyone laughed except the god TYR, for Fenrir had bitten off His hand.

But ever the Skrælings pressed closer and closer, and presently the Norsemen began to have the worst of it. The Skrælings struck at them with great fury. Still they fought among the high knobby trees: – every wound gladdened HEL. How the corpse-snakes* darted! The Skrælings launched many flints and other missiles, which rained down on the red shields, and when Karlsefni looked round he could see that his men were far from steady. – Suddenly his friend Snorri shouted loudly, and Karlsefni thought that he must have been wounded, but then he saw that Snorri fought much more vigorously and fiercely than before, and his face was wet with tears. Then Karlsefni saw that Snorri's son Thorbrand lay dead on the ground, with a flint point in his forehead. For the first time he began to be alarmed as to how the battle would go. – The Skrælings now launched great stones and boulders from their catapults, so that the ground shook when they landed; as yet the Skrælings had not gotten the proper range, but it was clear that Karlsefni and his men were doomed unless they acted quickly. – "Rush them!" shouted Karlsefni, but before the men could obey, the Skrælings hoisted a dark blue sphere or bladder on a pole and began swinging it round and round, shrieking so fearfully that the men stood paralysed. Karlsefni said later that this sphere was the size of a sheep's stomach. Suddenly the Skrælings let this missile fly; it whizzed over the men's heads like a meteor and fell to the ground with a great crash. Karlsefni's men covered their ears in terror. Then they fled. When the points of their spears tangled in the tree-branches they dropped them and ran on, leaping between roots, and rushing deeper and deeper into the forest. They ran past the palisaded clearing where Freydis and Gudrid waited with the cattle. – "Where are you going, you cowards?" shouted Freydis. – No one paid any attention to her, Thorvard least of all. – As for the Skrælings, they laughed a brazen yelping laugh when they saw her, and called her *Kestijui'skw*.† – "Oh, you'd like me to take my shirt off, would

---

* Kenning for swords.
† Bondsmaid.

you?" shrieked Freydis. "I'll show you, you savage thralls, you Hell-meat!" –
She began to clamber over the wall of the palisade. Gudrid, being Christian,
sought to restrain Freydis from this, for she was pregnant and weaponless,
but Freydis grinned down at her with a HEL-grin and Gudrid looked at her
BLACK HANDS and her own hands fell limply to her sides.

For all her girth of belly, Freydis was very fit and strong. She ran to where
Thorbrand Snorrasson lay dead and snatched up his sword. As the Skrælings
ran towards her, she tore a great rip in her shirt with her hand and pulled
one of her breasts out and began whacking it with the sword, yelling, "Is
that what you want to see, thralls? Ha, ha – have none of you dogs seen
a bitch? Look how I gash myself now with this sword! See the blood, you
thralls? See my BLACK HANDS? See me touching myself with them? You'd
better start running, thralls, or I'm going to touch you with them, too, and
you'll all drop dead. Here I come! *MUSKUNAMU'KSUTI!*"

The Skrælings stopped short. – Freydis glanced over her shoulder to Gudrid.
– "Set the bull on them, you Christian bitch! Hurry!"

Gudrid flung open the gate and prodded the bull. He charged out roaring
and snorting. This was too much even for Carrying the War-Club, and he
called to his warriors to run because the Powers were too strong. Laughing,
Freydis came running after the Skrælings all the way to their skin-boats,
her breast flapping and bleeding, her BLACK HANDS outstretched . . . The
Skrælings rushed into their boats and fled, and Freydis danced among the
dead and dying; such was her strife-lust. Two Norsemen had been killed,
and many Skrælings. One savage lay mortally wounded by the water, run
through with a sword. Freydis kicked him in the mouth. – "Ho, ho!" she
jeered. "Look at him suck his tongue-gravel!"*

Carrying the War-Club and the Axe

But the strangest thing (and perhaps the most significant in this whole Dream)
remains to be mentioned. It has been told that two of Karlsefni's men were
killed. One was Snorri's son Thorbrand, and the other was a man in Bjarni
Grimolfsson's crew named Odd. Odd had had an axe. Seeing it lying there,
sparkling in the sun, Carrying the War-Club rushed to possess it, for here
at last he could achieve his purpose.

---

* Kenning for teeth.

Now there were many names for an axe. Some called it *Shield-Fiend*, and some called it *Helmet-Witch*. Some knew it as *War-Witch*; to others it was *Wound-Wolf*. But Odd's axe had simply been his axe. It was made of good iron. Its blade widened rapidly on both sides, and abruptly flared to make its single jaw, which could bite deep into men's bones. It was decorated with silver and gold. Carrying the War-Club had never handled an axe of its like, for the People had no knowledge of metal. He shouted as he raised it aloft; his warriors laughed for happiness; he cried out the name of KLUSKAP the Invincible, who had vanquished the Jenuaq Power . . . What happened next is told in the *Flateyjarbók*:

> The fighting commenced, and many of the Skrælings were killed. One man stood tall and handsome among them, and Karlsefni reckoned that he must be their Lord. A Skræling had seized Odd's axe, and after studying it he swung it at his companion beside him, who fell dead in a twinkling. The tall man then took hold of the axe, scrutinized it, and at last hurled it a great distance out into the fjord. Then the Skrælings fled with all speed into the wood, and so was this happening concluded.

What could Carrying the War-Club have seen in the axe that made him do what he did? Did he see its metal spirit, its cold blue iron-spirit? – We will never know. And in any case, the entire story might never have happened. *Eirik's Saga*, which bears in many places the stamp of an accountant's steady soul, gives Freydis the sole credit for the victory over Carrying the War-Club and his people, saying of the axe only this:

> The Skrælings discovered Odd, with his axe lying in the dirt beside him. One of them snatched it up and swung it so that it bit deeply into a tree; then each of them in turn essayed the sport. It was clear that they considered the axe a marvelous find, being in awe and wonder at its keenness. But now a Skræling sought to cleave a rock with it, and the blade broke. Thereupon, thinking it worthless because it failed to conquer stone, they cast it down.

So perhaps there was no spirit in the axe after all. *Kespi-a'tuksit*, as the People said: – Here ends this story. But I am convinced that Carrying the War-Club saw the **FACT** of the Axe peering out from its glittering smoothness, a fact that took hold of him and made him kill his enemy, Dreaming of Bad Days, who had always spoken against him; that must have been the case because he had no need to kill him. (Dreaming of Bad Days was gone by now; he had passed beyond the wide lakes; he had crossed the rivers; he had rushed through the empty valleys; he dissolved in the Sky-World; he rotted in the Earth-World.) I fancy that when Carrying the War-Club pulled the axe out of Dreaming of Bad Days's breast and stood looking and looking at his own blue image, across which the red blood trickled, he saw himself grinning a grin of dead horse-teeth; just as Ingjald the Evil-Worker saw himself reflected in his daughter Aasa, so Carrying the War-Club saw himself growing deeper and deeper into death as he looked upon the shimmering surface of that axe like a lake of polished iron whose depths he could never see: – what was *inside* the axe-head? Inside was the thing that watched him; inside was the thing that guarded him and caught him with iron-claw hands and pulled the Ice-Shirt down over his head and shoulders so that he felt cool and superior and needed nothing but to swing his axe so that it whizzed through the air with the speed of a war-arrow and it shone blue and bluer and bluer than the sky and then thudded into some screaming softness . . . – He had not wanted to kill Dreaming of Bad Days. He had sincerely not intended it. Praying to KLUSKAP, he sent the axe spinning through blue sky and down into blue water where it whirled and dimmed and became gold and then green, and it vanished. – And now Carrying the War-Club, like so many others, is out of this saga.

The Victor

Freydis stirred the kettle and set out a fine meal of whale-meat; she washed her hair in a bucket of birchwood. Freydis sat listening by the open door, twisting the thread between her fingers and staring at her distaff. Freydis watched the sun travel across the sky and felt very much alone.

The Accolades

There was no denying (said Karlsefni) that Freydis had showed great courage in battle, laughing at the Screechers as if in the best of humor. For this she was honored (although later she was boastful about her deeds). Just as gulls, no matter how black-seeming in the blue sky, become white against a black cliff, so Freydis's virtues now became manifest to all, for though she was ruthless and greedy no one could call her a coward, and she had saved the Greenlanders in their time of trouble.

Freydis and Gudrid

Gudrid said nothing when she heard Freydis praised. But the blood rushed into her cheeks, so that her face became a scarlet mask.

The Skin-Shirts

The next day, at Freydis's command, her thrall Skofte set out to loot the dead Skrælings. They lay black and swollen in the dreamy forest, where the grass was as lush and tangled as Gudrid's hair; they lay along the river bank. Skofte rolled them over and lifted them up, and they gurgled. – "Oh, you sing a different song today," he said to them mockingly, for he would now say what he liked to these warriors who could not harm him. He stripped off their bloody skin-shirts; he gathered together their scattered arrows and their stone axes, and he lashed his booty into a great bundle and dragged it to Freydis's longhouse. But the choicest items he secreted in the forest for himself, for he was weary with being beaten, and the time was coming when he would serve her no more.

When Gudrid heard that Freydis had pillaged the slain without regard for the rights of others, she spoke to her husband and told him that he must be the one to accuse and punish Freydis. Karlsefni took a drinking-horn and threw it down on the floor so that it smashed. – "No," he said. – But soon enough it turned out as Gudrid willed, and one of Gudrid's men asked her to come to their house.

"Yes, Karlsefni, you be the doomsman to judge me," cried Freydis bitterly, "you are so far above personal loyalties and affections."

Karlsefni stroked his beard. "Do you not think that my men have some right to these skins and stone weapons?"

"*I* was the one who defeated the Skrælings," shouted Freydis, "I and none other!"

"Surely you are right and the rest of us are wrong," smiled Gudrid. "I know that I am wrong; after all, I am only a Christian bitch."

Freydis ignored her. "Karlsefni," she said, "you are the leader here. I feel that I am entitled to all of this treasure. It is for you to decide."

"Everything must be divided equally," said Karlsefni quietly.

Freydis stood looking down at her feet for a moment and breathing heavily. She twisted her hair in her fingers. "Well, Battle-Tree," she said, "well, Treasure-Tree,* I had hoped for fruit to grow from you for my reward; Draupnir's fruit† would have been best, but any would have done. However, it seems instead that you grow only the foliage of words."

She turned on her heel and left Gudrid's house, and so they parted.

The Outlaws

Freydis knew full well that she harmed herself more than Gudrid by her actions. Often now she felt a stabbing in her breast (but it was only her heart); she felt a gashing in her throat (but that was no axe-tooth; it was only her pulse). – Yet just as Thorvard could never stop playing with his masses of amber beads when they were home at Gardar, sifting them through his fingers until they lay in mounds on the table like golden fish-eggs, so Freydis could not stop provoking and revenging herself upon Gudrid. It is written of Queen Gunhild that she once changed herself into a swallow and twittered at Egill Skallagrimsson's window solely out of spite, to distract him from composing a poem. Gudrid was now equally determined to rob Freydis of her every triumph; she wanted to drive Freydis out from among their company. In this she was bound to succeed, because she was Gudrid the Smiler. – So Freydis dreamed happily of a headless woman, of many headless women lying on the floor with blood trickling from their throats and breasts; and their white fingers were clenched and the wind rippled their dresses.

The next day Karlsefni summoned Freydis to meet with his wife. In his presence each of the two women spoke hotly of her own worth, embroidering her stories with gold.

"I am worth far more than this granddaughter of a freed slave," said Freydis. "From my father Eirik I claim all the rights of settlement over Greenland; from my brother Leif I have use of his houses in Vinland."

"Yes, but you are a bastard," said Gudrid. "Anyhow, all the best country in Vinland belongs to me."

Freydis flushed deeply, but said nothing, remembering now that she was forbidden to call Eirik her father anymore.

"She is a wolf as her father was," exclaimed Gudrid, "and she should be hanged on the wolf-tree.‡ At the very least she should be driven out of this place." (This last, of course, was a hint to her husband.)

* Common kennings for a man and a woman, respectively.
† In the *Elder Edda*, Draupnir was a gold ring that gave birth to eight gold rings every night.
‡ Gallows.

At first Karlsefni had tried to tell Freydis gently what tell her he must, for he strove always to be moderate in his behavior, but she began making difficulties as she was accustomed to do, and so quickly exasperated him that he resolved to be short. – "You are a guest on our home-mead," he said. "Your cattle graze in our pastures; your men jostle our men, and you are no longer welcome here. Vinland is a big country; you can take your own land."

Then Freydis railed at him: "*Makings-of-a-Man,*★ they call you, but the man was never made. I saved you all from the Skrælings, and your reply is to outlaw me like a lone wolf! If I shook my tits at you, would you run away, too, you wretch?"

Karlsefni stepped up and slapped her on the cheek so hard that the red print of his hand could be plainly seen. (But then he felt a snaky fear-twist in his guts, knowing at last that she who stood before him was the Queen Sigrid of his nightmares – and somehow she would get her revenge. In suspecting that she would trouble to glut herself on *him*, he continued, of course, to underestimate her.)

Gudrid stood looking on.

Freydis spat on the ground. She wiped her mouth very coolly on the back of her hand. She did not rub her cheek. She fixed her eyes on Karlsefni and said: "Even that you did not do of your own accord, for yonder blonde bitch goaded you to it. – Come now, Thorvard, and stow your pretty pelts on the boat. Come, you men. We'll see how long they last without you. Skofte, claim your gold leaf back from that bitch. – As for you others, if you dare to come in sight of Leif's houses you'll find a bloody welcome, do you hear me?"

"We hear you very well," said Gudrid. But then she smiled so nobly, so winningly. "How have I hurt you, Freydis, that you should treat me this way?" She said this leaning forward, with shining eyes and parted lips.

Freydis and her people set sail that same day, with no more words on either side.

Port-au-Choix, Newfoundland 1987

Wet brown-green grass grew over hummocky ground. The field was empty. There were no markers, no dead Indians even, since the latter had been put in

★ Literal meaning of Karlsefni's name.

the Visitor Center (which was closed). A white fence held back the woodpiles, the little box-houses, the schoolchildren running and shouting at recess. Across the street, powerboats scudded in the grey sea. There was a path across the field, and people rushed across it on their errands.

"Is this the Indian cemetery?" I asked a little freckled boy.

He looked down at the parking lot. He kicked with his shoe-toe. "I dunno," he said. "They used to find bones in it, I think."

Wearing the Wall-Shirt

Wise in measure   should each man be,
but let him not wax too wise:
who looks not forward   to learn his fate
unburdened heart will bear.

ODIN THE HIGH ONE

After being expelled from Gudrid's country, Freydis was harsh and tearless. Her husband strove to comfort her, but she repulsed his attempts, and in time he desisted. All her men still remained with her, excepting only Skofte Carrion-Crow, who had deserted to the woods, but they were discontented. Gudrid's country was much richer than hers, and they had found nothing to plunder even there. – So Freydis was forced to speak to them graciously, promising that they would profit from the journey in the end. – "And I assure you," she said, "that you will soon be able to return to your homes, for this devil-infested country is no good to live in. You will have a share in the grapes and timber that we have gathered together, and any pelts you take for yourselves you may bring back for your own gain. As for the Skrælings, I say again: Do with them whatever you like. Rape them, rob them, or make them your thralls; it's all the same to me." – But after the battle, never a Skræling did they find.

They returned north in Freydis's ship, which she called *Ice-Swift*; they moved their possessions back into Leif's houses. Just as after a storm torn branches float in the water, their leaves still green, so Freydis's plan-remnants continued to flower for a little space. But she had a dream that Gudrid was coming to kill her. Although in her dream she was naked, Freydis rushed out with her axe. She threw a helmet on; her hair streamed down her back. Then she saw Gudrid waiting for her; she saw Gudrid's face, so soft and pure; she knew that if she could strip Gudrid naked she would be safe; she would expose Gudrid's soft white buttocks. But already under Gudrid's gaze her hair was coming alive, rising and coiling and hissing; her head became a net of Hell-vipers that bit her in her face and in her breast; she woke up choking, with a sour taste in her mouth and an ache in her chest . . .

As a blue sky may seem blue-green through a thicket of leaves, so Freydis colored her actions to a greener and richer shade than they were by distributing gifts to her men. Everything was beautiful there in the forest, among the spangles of white and purple flowers. So they settled in and awaited her commands. They wandered again among the trees (although not so far as before the battle with the Skrælings); they lay scratching themselves in Leif's houses. They threw down tanned bear-pelts on their beds as did the Skrælings in their wigwams, but because the longhouses were so moist and noisome the skins quickly became moldy.

The Last Lesson

Blue-Shirt came into her dreams every night. He taught her much witchcraft, both *Galdr* and *Seidh*,* and confirmed her in her evil. But He said that there was still one trick left.

"I would like to see that," said Freydis.

"Here it is," laughed Blue-Shirt, and He struck her full in the face . . .

Helgi and Finnbogi

Now must I tell something of the Icelandic brothers who had accompanied Freydis in hope of gain. – Strange were the marvels of Wineland. It is written that Karlsefni and his men one day discovered a glittering Uniped along the western coast; this creature rushed down from the hills at them when they shouted, and shot arrows at them. – But the two Icelanders were just as strange, for they never did anything, but stayed in their camp with their men except when they were hunting or hewing timber. So the others despised and feared them.

When Freydis had cast them out of Leif's houses, the brothers led their men into the woods and soon raised up a longhouse by a lake. – "Now, tell me, brother," said Helgi, "what plans you have now."

"That is easy," said Finnbogi. "Our foremost purpose must be to enrich ourselves on a par with these others."

"No," said Helgi. "One day a man's highest desire might be for gold. The

* Witch-songs and necromancy.

next day the iron spear-rain might fall, and then gold will be of no use."

"What are you saying?"

"I am saying that our foremost purpose must be our defense while we are here. If Freydis or any of those others come to visit us we must be friendly; we must be more agreeable even than it is manly to be, for we Icelanders are few, and the Greenlanders are many. And we must always keep watch, and stay in our own camp until the ships are loaded. We never should have come here."

Something bad would come soon; of this Helgi and Finnbogi were both aware. It would come from Freydis Eiriksdaughter.

At first the brothers tried to discover the meaning of her actions, but of course there was no more *meaning* in Freydis than there was in glistening water. – "Is this our bargain then?" cried shrill Freydis, clashing her arms together in her anger. – "I don't give in easily," Freydis said. – "Don't try my temper further," said Freydis, smiling through her teeth. "You think your small equalities are satisfactory, do you? I don't need you." – "There are knives in her softest looks," said Helgi; but he thought nonetheless (for we can only know each other's outer shapes) that although Freydis was a loud unpleasant woman she was not impossible to do business with provided that one humbled oneself to her – which few men were willing to do. Helgi sincerely thought that her esteem could be won if he were only patient, as an outlawed Icelander must be with some scowling Norwegian King: – he would greet the King, and the King would return no answer; and he would make friends who were in good standing with the King and they would plead his case, until at last the King would grant him a surly safe-conduct, but still refused to let him serve him at his court; he would compose a great verse in praise of the King, over which the Queen would exclaim in delight, and then the King would nod very faintly to acknowledge him; he would go into the fells to dispatch a family of ogres, and when he returned with their heads in his pouch the King would greet him in a low voice; he would join a battle unasked and perform some high deed, after which the King would smile slightly to see him; he would bring the King great gifts of silver and gold, and then at last the King would clap him on the back and joke with him and acknowledge him as his man. – So Helgi thought his path must be. – But he would not see that it was impossible to conciliate Freydis. He wanted his own murderess to love him. (Thorgunna had made the same mistake with Leif.) – As for Freydis herself, she once thought that whenever she was kind the two brothers should have fallen on their knees and thanked the WHITE CHRIST for this kindness, not that it was anything in itself; but just as the heroism of a coward is more valuable than that of the insouciantly brave, so the kindness that came forth from Freydis's grey and withered heart was so uncommon that it should have been prized like the scent of the angelica-flower – but the brothers did not even notice, and so they were doomed. Now she had better reasons for dooming them. She wore the Ice-Shirt; she wore the Bear-Shirt; she was of the wolfish kind. – Certainly the brothers would be excellent objects of revenge. She would punish them for what Gudrid had done. She would plant the frost-seed in their skulls.

Finnbogi's Luck

One night Finnbogi dreamed that a great woman came to him from the sea. He had seen her before; she was his luck-spirit. The woman said: "My advice to you is to return to Iceland." – He was happy to remember Iceland, where sometimes the stones formed a pavement at the base of the green, green hills. Eyvind Skáldaspillir once made a pretty kenning for the Icelanders, calling them "Eel-Sky Dwellers," and just as it is true and lovely that ice is an eel's sky, so everything in his home country was lovely and true. Waterfalls made silver rainbows between the hills; geysers came up between the flowers. But he replied: "I don't believe that there are any more dangers here than there were at home."

And at this the woman was silent, for that, too, was true.

Every day the brothers and their men felled trees with their axes, striking them not in parallel gashes, as is the case with suicidal neck-wounds, but in scattered cuts, for this was homicide. But there remained so many trees; Wineland was widely wood-clad. And the night pressed tight around them. The darkness of it made the air into a deep dark sea in which they wave-swam, the liquidness of it easing and supporting them at the same time that it stifled them. Bad dreams grew in their hearts like coral. A Death-Kraken moved somewhere inside that dark maze of coral; the brothers could feel the rubbery weight of it upon their chests. They moaned in their berths as the Death-Kraken slithered its arms out of coral-holes and grappled its suckers into their hearts . . .

Reunion

Helgi raised his head alertly. "I hear her," he said.

Presently she came through the trees. They wondered at how fine she looked: for, indeed, she wore a shirt as blue as a lake.

The Second Axe-Tale

I know for certain so much, that you will not get a kingdom if you don't ask for it.

> EARL HAKON, to Gold Harald
> (*ca.* 980)

Dost thou not apprehend that thou art in that condition that, hereafter, there can be neither victory nor defeat for thee?

> KING OLAF, to his prisoner,
> EARL HAKON (*ca.* 1013)

When Gore-Month came, Helgi and Finnbogi proposed that there be games of archery and spear-throwing between the two camps, and Freydis agreed to this, but presently, the tale says, discord crept into their entertainments, and they gave them up. They drilled separately, the members of each house practicing covering themselves with their shields, as if they planned to make war upon each other. Helgi and Finnbogi practiced launching stones with a staff-sling. Men dreamed of blood-sport, slaughter-sport. Then no one from one house visited the other, and so it was for most of the winter.

One rainy night Freydis was in bed with her husband, and when he laid his hand upon her she became as stiff as a corpse. As ever, she refused to open her legs to him, or even to let him touch her. Thorvard asked her what was wrong, but she was silent. – "What is it?" he said. "What is it?" But she would say nothing. She lay beside him, so stiff and wrathful that he was sure that her glaring eyes shone in the dark. He did not attempt to look into her face. – "Freydis, what is it?" he asked her again, almost

out of patience. "Why are you such a bad wife?" – "I'm an excellent wife,"
said Freydis calmly, "but you're a bad husband." And she said that the two
brothers had abused her that day. "But I know you will do nothing about
it." – "It was you who invited them," rejoined Thorvard, for he could think
of nothing else to say. Her story seemed very unlikely to him, and he had
no desire to fight the brothers. – "Naturally, you will do nothing," his wife
repeated bitterly, and she rolled on her side and refused to speak further.
Knowing what she was capable of, Thorvard lay beside her with a pounding
heart. For a long time he was unable to sleep.

Frost-Month passed, and so did Ram's Month. The men lay quarreling
with each other or roamed the woods sullenly; they cursed the ill luck that
had brought them to Vinland and vowed that when they returned home
they would tell everyone not to go there. They talked about raiding Gudrid's
country; they wanted to rape Gudrid and slaughter her animals, but they were
too weak in numbers. If it had been necessary to her purpose, Freydis would
have lain with them one after another, but they were afraid of her; they eyed
her BLACK HANDS with patient terror, like cornered stags. Whenever she
set them a task, they obeyed her. When she spoke to them, they answered
her in low voices. It had always been this way with Freydis's thralls. It no
longer pleased her; she expected it. – The men knew that she lusted to punish
someone. They knew that soon she would decide who deserved death; she
would say, "He is the one!", or, "They are the ones!"; then the men would
rise up and do her bidding; for what else was there to do? Soon they would
leave Vinland, and they would never sail back, never; they would never be
Freydis's men again (and she knew this but did not care because Thorvard's
gold could buy others, could buy *them* again if she willed it); and the men
told over again their stale deeds of murder and rape; being womanless, they
continued to talk of rape more than murder, but always they circled round
Freydis in their speech like nervous birds; they spoke of the women that the
Icelanders had, while Freydis went into the woods by herself every night,
and her belly swelled and swelled and she had now been more than ten
months pregnant but no one dared to speak of it. – The month of Winter's
Wane advanced, and no one gathered cargo for the ship any longer. Soon
the waves of the Greenland Sea would calm themselves to bitterness: then
it would be time to sail home. There had never been any reason for them
to come here.

One morning Freydis got up and dressed before the others had awoken
and she went out into the winter dew. Freydis's dress, it is told, was this: she
wore the pale blue gown that her husband had given her, and on her hand

was a silver ring. But her feet were bare. The path to the brothers' house was overgrown now by reddish thorn-bushes traversed with spiderwebs, there being so few visitors along that way, and bushes seemed to grow two sorts of crops: – the first being ripe red berries, the second, the bees that browsed upon their juices; so that the thorn-bushes were bright with red and yellow. As she went, Freydis shook the bushes with both arms, so that the thorns tore her gown and the bees stung her. The cryings of the gulls rang in her ears.

Finnbogi was lying in the bed farthest from the doorway. He had not slept; he had heard her coming. – "What will you have here, Freydis?" he said.

"I want you to get up and come out with me," she said. "I want to talk to you."

Her voice came flatter than usual to his ears, almost (he supposed) as if she did not want to hear her own words. It would have been very surprising to Freydis had she known his thoughts; she did not doubt herself in the least. She had already decided what she had to do.

"Is everything well with you and your people?" he said.

"Yes, yes," she said impatiently.

He swallowed. It was so unpleasant to him to behold her that he found it hard not to show emotion. But again Freydis did not seem to notice. He looked at her eyes, and the pupils seemed to be tiny black points in the greenish irises; again he felt that she neither saw nor heard him, so that it was strange in the extreme when she said sharply, "Are you coming out or aren't you?"

The house-carles were awake now. They watched her silently. Helgi still slept.

"I will come, Freydis, if that is what you wish," he said.

He smiled entirely too much, she thought. It was not as Gudrid smiled, however; it was the smile of Skofte, or her other thralls who had surrendered.

They went to a felled tree that lay under the house-eaves, and sat on it together. A very mild breeze was blowing. Finnbogi looked around him, and thought again, as he always did, what a lovely country Vinland was, like some treasure of greenness and goodness in the middle of the sea; and wild grapes were growing on the vine by him and he picked one and ate it although it was a little past its season, and Freydis sat so still beside him that he continually forgot that she was there; and a scarlet maple leaf sailed through the air as lightly as a Lappish boat and was stuck in Freydis's hair, and then Freydis said to him, "How do you like it here?"

He looked at her squarely. "I like this land, but not our quarrel. I do not see why it came about."

Freydis smiled. – Oh, how she smiled! Gudrid would have been proud of her. "You are quite right," she said. "But I am afraid that no matter how much we uproot that unseemly blood-tree it will grow again. So let me go away from here, and there will be no quarrel anymore."

"I never expected that from you," he said. "It would be your way to command us to go, but not to go yourself. Are you really finished here?"

"I want to go back to Greenland," she said. "I miss the snow, and the mountains, and I want to see my own people again."

"Well, and what do you want from me?"

"I want your ship, because it is larger than mine, and I have a great deal of cargo. As you are set on staying, you can do with the smaller ship."

Finnbogi was well aware that if he refused to trade with her, she would set her men against his and most likely kill them all. He smiled wearily. "It will be as you wish," he said.

"I see that there is not much stuff in you," she said. "You yield to me without any struggle. Finnbogi, wouldn't you rather match yourself against me than give me a victory without any pleasure?"

"I know not what to say. We are all in your power, Freydis; it is for you to command."

"And your brother, what will he say?"

"He too will do as you wish," he said, clenching his fists.

"Shall we wake him up and hear it from him?" Freydis said, licking her lips.

"I tell you, you will have your way, Freydis!" he said. "Why can't you be satisfied with that? It almost seems that you would rather have your way by force! Do you care so little about what is proper or lucky?"

A kind of dullness had fallen over him, and he did not think or care what he said.

"But you do agree to exchange ships?" she said.

He nodded. "I promise," he said.

"Now, Finnbogi, we are agreeing very well together," said she, "but I have a lust to play the Changing-Game against you. Do you know what that is?"

"I do not like the sound of it," he said. "I will forfeit my stake to you, and declare you the winner as you desire, for you know that we are all Christians here."

"You must never open your mouth to me in such a way," she said, in such a honeyed purring voice that he shrank back from her. "I find it surprising that you do not recall how narrowly you escaped from Leif's houses. Nor do I think that you truly want to forfeit, for the stake is higher than you believe – so I swear by my *BLACK HANDS!* – Yes, look at them! – I am a Changer, Finnbogi. My King is King Blue-Shirt. Have you ever heard tell of Him? Do you know what Power He has given me? The olden Kings could only burn everything, or caper like trained bears. But I can lay waste this entire land with ice. What do you say to that?"

"I say that you are a troll," he said hotly. "You are determined to play with me whether I tell you yea or nay; you will not take what I give freely. Tell me, is Gudrid a witch like you, and am I but a shirt you will wear out in your play against her?"

"No, she is no witch," Freydis replied. "She has never changed herself, and thinks that things are but one way. And so she has lost, even though they call her the Lunde-Sun! And so have you all! For my every word has been a word of Changing; now we shall see what you and I become."

"I do not pretend to understand you, Freydis," he said. "But I wish you joy of our ship, as I am sure that my brother does."

She took his hand. "Sooner than you can believe, I will give you fitting thanks," she said.

As when the sun breaks through the clouds the blue sky becomes a bay among fog-mountains, so Freydis smiled a smile of incomplete radiance. Then they parted, and Finnbogi returned to his bed, while Freydis walked back through the woods barefoot. Once again she forced the bees to sting her. She climbed up into her berth, and the touch of her clammy feet woke her husband.

Thorvard yawned. "Where have you been to now? Why are you so cold and wet?"

She could hear the men stirring and waking; she heard the clank of a shield on the floor.

"Tell me what happened," said Thorvard.

Freydis answered indignantly, "I went to see those brothers to discuss their ship, for I want a larger one, and they took it so ill that they struck and abused me. See, look how my dress is torn! Look how bruised and swollen I am! But it's clear to me that you, you lazy wretch, won't avenge my humiliation, which is your own. I realize now how far away I am from Greenland. I wish I had never come here with you. I tell you now, Thorvard, that if you don't avenge the insult I will divorce you."

She had a snowy face. Pink flowers of anger bloomed in her cheeks. Throwing his belongings violently about, she railed at her husband until no one even pretended to sleep any longer. She called him her thrall. – Thorvard knew that there was nothing to do but to follow her will. When a mountain is sheer and has shoulder-wings you cannot cry to it, seeing its form like yours, its terrible blank face. He roused his men, and they went to the house of the two brothers with ready axes. What they did there was easy, because the inmates were asleep, and Freydis's five extra men were good at the work. Now Helgi and Finnbogi and their men were all dead, but the women were left, and nobody would kill them.

Then Freydis said, "Give me an axe."

The Coming of the Frost*

Now their purpose in Vinland was accomplished. They buried the bodies, and slept, and walked to and fro, and bit by bit the rime-heaviness and ice-weight fell upon them. (There was no thunder-clap; there was no shield-clang.) The earth was stone-grey, the trees bare and grey, the air grey and clammy and cutting-cold in the throat like thorns. The sun came up red, and the forests were already defeated, luridly shining orange and brown like grim monster-woods although of course there were no monsters except the Skrælings who wailed at the bad light and tore their shirts and called and called upon KLUSKAP and upon COOLPUJOT Spring-Maker and especially upon Grandfather SUN, believing that they must have done some evil; but the SUN was a woman again, not their Grandfather anymore, and She fled back to Greenland, rushing round and round again above the snow-fells where She had once lived with Her brother AMORTORTAK and been happy; now She must circle high above Her incest-grave without a hope, just as a ghost must hover and rush at the extremity of its fog-tether, unfree until the last bone, the last rotten rag of its life-shirt has decayed, which takes centuries or longer in cold climates – oh, those mummy-husks glow warm and bright for the naked, like the empty red sun-shell dispensing lurid light to the People in Wineland who denied their chilly future; as for COOLPUJOT, He lay boneless and helpless while KLUSKAP sailed north and south along the fog-strait between Vinland and Markland, searching for His wicked brother, whom He suspected of having returned from Deathland a second time to wreak this evil, but KLUSKAP could find no signs of Him; and KLUSKAP, having lost the battle, could not go down to where He sat in His Man-Shirt or Woman-Shirt, the buttons

---

* "... there shall come that winter which is called the Awful Winter: in that time the snow shall drive from all quarters; frosts shall be great then, and winds sharp; there shall be no virtue in the sun" – *Younger Edda*.

of which were viper-eyes shining like red suns, so at last KLUSKAP paddled His great stone canoe back to Cape Split and returned to Grandmother and Marten, shaking His head. – Marten had thrown many logs on the fire. It was warm and smoky in the wigwam, and filled with the good smell of boiled meat. KLUSKAP yawned; He lay down and wrapped His robe round Himself like a blanket, and Marten squatted in silence looking into the fire, and old Grandmother rocked herself and shook her head and shivered, and tears ran down her cheeks. Outside the wigwam, the high trees spread themselves like bone-fans. Although some leaves remained on them, they grew discolored, going from red to reddish-grey, like Freydis's memories of Gudrid. – How cold everything was! – Along that long low peninsula of grass, snow-patches rose from beneath the tundra like seeping lakes. Ice filmed across the dying eyes of tide-pools and crept up rocky beach-shelves. The streams were poisoned with frost, like the Hell-creek Slíth, and the quick venom they bore changed them to ice. By degrees the water now froze in the large rivers. Between the bare tree-trunks could be seen a dull white shining, and the hills were silhouetted black in the sun. In the air was a white light. – The grape-vines died; the SUN wept cloudy tears; the Unipeds died. (But KLUSKAP, though dream-stained and sorrow-stained, lived, it is said, for another six hundred years. As Vinland grew more chill, so did the People's stories, and He gained the power to blast His enemies with a cold so intense that it put out their campfires and then they fell down frozen and dead.) The wind laughed down from the Greenland snow-fells. – Now there came great famines, as there had been in Greenland and Norway and Iceland, and many of the People had no food to eat but ravens and rats and foxes. The old and the sick they led to the cliff-edge . . . The icebergs came closer; for nine months of the year now the People saw those ominous blue towers of ice at their front door. They learned to wear shirts of thicker skins; they must thatch their wigwams with many more spruce boughs; they must smoke the meat they killed and save what they could of it for the bad days when they would pray to KLUSKAP not for lovers or for holiness-Power, but for food and warmth. Every autumn they had bad dreams; they waited for the frost-months with grim anxiety; when the snow-nights did come the People lay awake waiting for something to happen. – The wind-scream was terrifying. Every winter night they wondered whether the wind would tear their wigwams down. They could hear it coming down from the mountains, piping, whistling, gathering strength from ridge to ridge long before it reached them. When that sound came to their ears, the People braced themselves and called upon Grandfather SUN (Who was not there); the children began to cry. The wind whistled very slowly and terribly.

THE ICE-SHIRT

Then the screaming commenced – how fierce and harsh it was can never be told – and their wigwams began to shake. But life went on in Vinland as it did in Greenland. – The People dressed their babies in swan-skin and soft warm fox-fur. ("*Ehhh!*" cried Christian's Daddy in the kitchen triumphantly. He had just gotten a royal flush. Christian loved his Daddy because when Christian was a little boy his Daddy had left him on an island near Thule for a few days while he went fishing and the ice crept up to the island, and groaned and chuckled in the black sea and came closer and closer and there was nothing that little Christian could do and it crushed his Daddy's boat. – "Never mind," his Daddy said. "It was only a boat. We'll start afresh.") – In the large cities of Vinland, of course, many changes have occurred: – hoarfrost has become whorefrost. Just as New York City becomes a forest of wide golden letters from the air at night, each letter made up of lights, so that from one's window-seat one will certainly see a K, an A, an S, and ever so many L's all underlined and fenced in by night-lines which one must suppose to be freeways; just as the steady texture of the night provides a spurious cleanliness, the lights themselves a spurious elegance; just as the plane continues eastward or westward, and presently the letters are gone and there is nothing but blackness; just as the city-alphabets of meaning, then, give way to emptiness, so the Great Book of Trees in which the Greenlanders had hoped to write, and had indeed written a little, rustled its leaf-pages shut and froze into a Mountain of bluish ice. The King of Vinland wore His blue-black crown of bone.

Skofte Leaves Freydis

When Skofte learned that Freydis had murdered five women in cold blood, then at last he gave up his hopes of using her to find the Tree of Gold and decided to leave her service, for he feared to find out what else she might be capable of. He now went to Bjarni Grimolfsson and asked to be taken on his ship when he sailed for Iceland (for no one pretended any longer that it was safe to stay in Vinland). – "I have heard bad reports of you," said Bjarni. "Men tell me that you steal, that you are lazy, and you have no loyalty in you." – "I assure you that I will work," Skofte cried, sinking to his knees. "You know what Freydis has done. Please save my life and let me come with you." – Bjarni thought for a moment. "Will you work without complaint?" he asked. – "I promise," said Skofte, "never to ask you for anything."

The Frost in Greenland 1987

"In the winter is it very dark?" I asked a Greenlandic woman.
  "Yes," she laughed.
  "How dark?"
  "Like the *BLACK HANDS* sneaking down on my eyes!"

The End

ca. 1010 – *ca.* 1430

> The poor man is wont to complain that this is a cold world, and to cold,
> no less physical than social, we refer directly a great part of our ails.
>
> THOREAU, *Walden* (1854)

And so the Greenlanders, having learned their own limits, returned to their own country, where there remained tracts of farmland between the East Bygd and the West Bygd, and hot-springs ran into fjords where sea-fowl congregated, so that people could catch as many as they liked. Thanks to these springs, the Friars of Saint Thomas would heat their luxurious chambers two centuries later. – Not even then had the terrifying events fully begun; it was not until *ca.* 1430 that we find the bleak statement in Claudius Clavus that the Skrælings "come in a steady stream to Greenland with a strong army, without any doubt from the other side of the North pole." From this time we can probably date the Skræling legend of Ungertok, last of the white demons, for the Skrælings burned the others alive in their church. Ungertok leaped through the window and ran into the fells with his little son under his arm. The Skrælings ran after. Ungertok rushed up and down the green hills; he staggered in the deep green moss, and always the Skrælings came closer and closer. He could not carry his son anymore; he threw him into a lake to save his own life, but the Skrælings were almost upon him. Weeping and gasping, Ungertok ran on. At last they ran him down and killed him: – yes, they stained his blue shirt! – In Berefjord there was a great whirlpool that trapped whales for the settlers' pleasure. On the west shore of Ollum-Lengri Fjord were treasuries of birds' eggs; on the east shore were grassy green plains where cattle could graze. There were many other fjords so long that no one had been to the end of them, and no doubt they too contained their fishes and seals. East of Blue-Shirt was the isle of Karsöe, an excellent hunting-ground for white bears. There was a good deal of snow, naturally, but in those days winter was still worse in Iceland. (No one sailed past Blue-Shirt, due to the perilous whirlpools. "From this point eastward," says Ivar Bardsson, "nothing presents itself to the eye but ice and snow, either by land or by water." (*Unden Is och Sne bade till Land och Vand.*)

The Death of Bjarni Grimolfsson *ca.* 1010

Eirik's Saga says that Bjarni and his men set sail in good order, and they followed the long blue peninsula of Vinland north past Straumfjord, past Marvel-Strand where Gudrid and Karlsefni used to look for stranded whales, and where the Skrælings now shot arrows from the tree-shadows and pierced one of Bjarni's men in the shoulder; past Keel-Ness where Leif repaired his ship so long ago, and presently they were at the end of Vinland, where the seals barked and the seas were high and cold. The men sent up a great shout of joy when that evil land vanished behind a cloud. Bjarni steered into the deep waters of Markland Strait and said that he expected good luck at last. But the ship soon ran afoul of the winds, as had happened to Naddour-Viking, to Thorstein and Leif and Thorgunna and all the rest of us; and he was blown west into the Greenland Sea. The sea-spray froze on the faces of his men, and the black waves threw the ship up and down so that it creaked. – Bjarni watched the horizon anxiously. (As for Skofte Carrion-Crow, he was white with fear.) For a long time there was nothing to be seen, but after many days Bjarni saw a blue spot on the horizon which presently resolved itself into a tower of ice, and he knew that he was in sight of Blauserk, but he was not destined to reach it because the Greenland Sea was maggot-ridden in that season and the maggots ate holes in his ship. So Bjarni's ship began to sink, and Bjarni called everyone on deck to decide who would die and who would live. – "This lifeboat is blubber-tarred, and I have never heard of maggots that could eat through blubber," said Bjarni. "However, it will only hold half of us." – The crew ignored Bjarni's words at first in their panicked life-lust and crowded into the boat, but then it was seen that they were true. – "Even half of us may be too many," said Bjarni. "The boat will sink under the weight of so many. I propose that we draw lots, rather than filling the boat according to rank." – Since Bjarni was the captain, this was considered a very fair and generous offer. So they drew lots, and by chance Bjarni was among those who would depart in the boat. He led them into the boat, and the others, the doomed ones, stood on the deck watching them ready themselves, and suddenly Skofte Carrion-Crow came forward from among them and said, "Bjarni, do you really mean to leave me?" – There was a shout of laughter at the cawing of that selfish and unlucky bird, but Bjarni answered as kindly as he could, "Skofte, that is how it has to be. You can see that there is not room for all." – But Skofte cried desperately, "You promised that no harm would come to me, and now you are abandoning me!" Bjarni had promised Skofte nothing, for Skofte had come with Freydis, but in his panic Skofte did not know what he said. – "What then do you suggest?" said Bjarni. – "I suggest that we change places," said Skofte hurriedly, his eyes full on Bjarni's eyes, and men waited to see what would happen, but Bjarni shook his head and laughed a little and said, "I see that you are so afraid to die that you will do anything. So be it." – Then he got out of the boat, and Skofte Carrion-Crow rushed into his place. – Bjarni and the others who stayed behind were all drowned. But Skofte Carrion-Crow and everyone else in the boat survived. There was much danger and exhausting labor in rowing that little boat across the sea, but it is said that Skofte did more than his part, for he knew better than to trust anyone but himself in the saving of his life. The *Hauksbók* text reports that they landed in Ireland, and there told this tale.

The Tunersuit in their Twilight Years

ca. 1010 – ca. 1050

In the month of Winter's Wane, Freydis and Thorvard returned to their farm in Gardar, which had prospered in their absence. Wood was now becoming scarce in Greenland, and their cargo of tree-trunks fetched a good price. Freydis was still pregnant. She threatened to kill anyone who told what she had done, but rumors about the fate of the two brothers became so insistent that Leif finally tortured some of Freydis's men to find out what had happened. – "I do not have the heart," he said, "to treat my sister as she deserves." For he was wise enough to fear her. As Blue-Shirt had predicted, Freydis was shunned after that, and to some extent, therefore, she grieved and repented, but whenever she felt lonely she could always cheer herself by making her husband give her a belt of silver, a serk lined with velvety *pell*, a strap-cloak with costly borders ... But all her life she was known for her BLACK HANDS. (Of course BLACK HANDS must be endured by those who have everything.) Later she gave birth to a lump of ice.

As for Gudrid and Karlsefni, they sailed to Norway, and the following year to Iceland. Of their departure (some days after that of Bjarni Grimolfsson, whose doom they did not learn for many a year) little is related, from which we know that it was undertaken with gainful success: only failures cry shrilly from the bird-islands of the *Flateyjarbók*. Gudrid's house-men were greatly pleased to be leaving Vinland, for they had shares in the wealth of wood and grape-vines that made the cargo. (As for the booty that they had taken from the Skrælings, those arrows and skin-shirts they reckoned useless at the last, and left them behind.) – Karlsefni, too, was satisfied to be going. He said to his wife, "Soon we will be among civilized folk again!" – "Yes," she said. "Then we shall enrich ourselves indeed." – As she led little Snorri by the hand, and took her last steps upon the soil of Vinland, Gudrid was a little troubled that her heart did not ache, as it had done in the days when she was a girl, and the time had come to leave Iceland. On some nights of that first winter, when people would have thought her praying in that cold drafty farm at Herjolfsness, she had been stretching out her arms to Iceland, longing to touch the soil of home even for a moment; now she scarcely cared that she was going there. – What was the *meaning* of a tree that reached out from its mossy rock with every bud? That it found what it reached for, Gudrid knew from the swelling of those buds into little red birch-fruits, from the unfurling of its leaves; but she could never trust its longed-for One; and so it was with a beloved, with a home, with GOD: – her own embracing arms were there, like Thjodhild's stone church; but these were questionable bridges fading into darkness, no matter how brightly the first terminus might be lit. – The wind ruffled Snorri's blond hair. "Skrælings, Skrælings!" he cried as his mother lifted him onto the ship. But there were no Skrælings; that was only a word that he loved to say, without being certain of its meaning. – Now she herself walked up the ramp, and all the house-thralls saluted her. It was a very fine day, as soft and sweet as honey. Suddenly Gudrid took thought, strangely enough, of poor Thorstein Eiriksson, who had died with his face turned away from her. She remembered his prophecy concerning her. Truly GOD must have spoken through his cold lips, for much of what he predicted had already come to pass. And yet that scarcely made her different. Whatever successes ripened for her, they did so without her sowing. – Yes, Something must be there. Where else could the purple tundra-flowers come from? – Ah, soon she would see them again, even though her father was dead and buried in another land. Was her uncle Thorgeir still alive? Who had Orm and Halldis's land now? And what of her old suitor, Einar Slaveson – which woman had taken him at last? (Of course he might not even be in Iceland anymore; for he had traveled often, as she remembered, to the courts of the Norwegian Kings.) – The trees of Vinland leaf-whispered around her. Soon she would be sailing from this sea of green into the blackish Greenland Sea. Of course, in Stokkaness, where Eirik had given her father land, there had been green trees also (not quite as high as her knee), trees from the edge of the fjord all the way to the top of the hill. – How pleasant the sea-sun was upon her face! There must be Something in that SUN, even though in the days when Thorstein courted her she had sometimes thought it not as real as a single Arctic tree (Gudrid only wanted what was real!) – so she had thought until those same small trees shook in the wind and a cloud returned to its place in front of the poor SUN; then the hillside became a place of trembling despair, and Gudrid knew that the SUN was the most real of all. – Yes, Iceland had been her SUN, but not until she came to Greenland and had to set aside her girlish ways. Her husbands had never been; Vinland had never been. Naturally she felt regret for leaving the kingdom that she and Karlsefni had carved out here. They had made a success, the two of them, but by no means so much as they had hoped. Now their palisade would rot and crumble, like the longhouses within; and greedy green trees would burst up through the ceilings (or would the Skrælings simply burn everything?). But even the thought of her home being eaten by flames scarcely smote her. Vinland had been an unsettled country before, and now it would be again. – But then Freydis and those Icelanders were still here; perhaps they would stay (for no one believed the wild tale that Skofte Carrion-Crow had told). Very pleasing it was to Gudrid to know that soon she would put the Greenland Sea between herself and her greatest enemy (and when she thought of that, Gudrid smiled as she was wont to do, for certainly she had gained the mastery!) She herself was the SUN; she could go where she pleased now and warm herself with her own light. She always had been; nothing could change her. – Grey waves parted insidiously around their ship, and Gudrid thought she saw grey trees, but they were only clouds. – By now the veins stood out on Gudrid's hands, but she was still good-looking. – Karlsefni bought a farm in Glaumby. He was considered a man of the foremost reputation. There he stayed for the remainder of his life, telling the story of WINELAND THE GOOD to all who asked to hear it. His listeners marveled at his luck and courage, and said that they had no wish to journey to such places. After his death, Gudrid and Snorri continued to farm the land until Snorri married; then his mother, remembering the prophecy of Thorstein Eiriksson, made a pilgrimage to Rome and returned to become ordained as a nun. Many prominent people were descended from her. They are all dead now.

Freydis and Thorvard 1944

In the north chapel of the cathedral at Gardar, the grave of a bishop was uncovered by the team of Nørlund and Roussell, the holy skeleton being headless but retaining what was more important – its crozier and its gold ring. At some distance beneath this interment was discovered another from an earlier period, comprising two skeletons – a man's and a woman's. *"This interment, by the way, is peculiar,"* wrote the examination team (1944), *"in that we are presented with a woman's grave in a place so exclusive as the chapel of the cathedral in which afterwards a bishop was laid to rest ... Perhaps this woman's grave, side by side with that of the man, indicates that celibacy was not observed – even officially – in these out-of-the-way parts ..."* – Knowing Freydis's love of exclusivity, I think we need have no doubt that Nørlund and Roussell uncovered the remains of the murderess herself, lying next to her husband, whose very skeleton looks weak-willed and imbecilic in the photo plate, his head sheepishly cocked, his arms bent upward from their pious heart-fold as if to defend himself from his spouse, who lies with her hands crossed grimly in her lap, her skull deformed by grave pressure.

SHEEP SKULL, FLATEY ISLAND
[HALF]

Summer in the Ruins 1987

"What's your favorite thing?" I asked the Greenlanders.

"The summer," they laughed. "Yes! Then we can kill so many animals!"

We ate whaleskin sandwiches for dinner. The blubber was black and white. It tasted like peanut butter. Then we had bread and cheese. My friends slathered their cheese with butter, salami and jam. They put lump after lump of sugar in their tea ("for the cold," they said). – "Eat!" cried Bettina, smiling with every part of her round golden face. "Eat!" – When she was finished she wiped her hands in the moss, but for me she poured water into a basin, because I was her guest.

Henryk stood straight and hatless at the wheel of the boat for hours. His face paled in the frigid wind, but he only smiled. I sprawled at my ease at the bottom of the boat, wearing my parka and gloves and wool hat. When I moved slightly he said, "Are your legs tired?" – "I'm okay," I said. "How about you?" – "Fine," he said very shyly. And every now and then Bettina asked anxiously, "Are you freezing? Are you tired?" The waves in the fjord were bluish-grey. The cliffs were grey and orange.

The mountains rose more and more sheer and enormous. Waterfalls rushed down to the sea between the snowbanks. Everywhere were flocks of birds, black birds and white birds; and I asked if they were good to eat, and the Greenlanders smiled, "Yes, yes, yes!", Bettina looking even more Inuit when she smiled because her high cheekbones showed then.

The Greenlanders camped in big canvas tents staked on a grassy meadow above the fjord, the men grinning happily on the grass as they dumped another knifeful of jam on their buttered bread, poured another heaped spoonful of sugar in their coffee. – "You *hongry?*" they asked me anxiously. – "Halloo!" cried the girls in delight when they saw Henryk coming up the mudbank, his hands full of whale-meat. What a treat it was to see the laughing girls pop long rectangular slabs of blubber into their mouths, talking and giggling as they chewed, then seizing the fat once again between their white teeth and sawing off pieces with their big knives half an inch from their lips! After awhile they made tea, laughing around the primus flame in the big tent, and after tea it was two in the morning with the sun coming up again, and the men slung their rifles over their backs and set out contentedly to hunt sheep. A half-hour later there came three shots. The next morning a sheep hung neatly butchered on a bush, with the skin scraped clean and drying.

The next morning it was the same: tea, cereal, bread and butter and cheese and jam. Later they cooked hot dogs in butter, eating them between slices of buttered bread, and some people drank up a can of sweetened condensed milk. The primus flame burned blue and green. Its steady hiss was very soothing. – "Eat, *Beel!*" they said. "*Beel!*" "*Boof*-a-lo *Beel!*" they teased me. "*Bee*-lee Boy!" – When they talked among themselves their words, though unintelligible to me, were very distinct, because every syllable seemed to begin or end with a hard clean consonant. – From the camp, the fjord seemed to be only a muddy river, for to the west a green tundra ridge cut off any view of the main channel. But over that ridge rose four snowy peaks. – Suddenly Henryk rose to his knees and said, "*Tuttu!*" There were three snow-white reindeer on the ridge, just beneath the third peak. The little boy sat in the grass and slapped mosquitoes off Henryk's back as Henryk looked at the reindeer. – The Greenlanders played games killing the mosquitoes, catching them dramatically in midair, squashing them and throwing them at each other laughing. Then they put sunglasses on their dog and laughed.

Later they went walking. While the women started a fire halfway up the ridge, the men walked to the crest to look for caribou. Above the river, the slope was terraced with granite slabs. (Sometimes the rocks were grown with white lichen-spots like clumps of daisies.) Dwarf birches, their leaves a bright sweet green, grew against a granite shelf carbuncled with quartz. As we ascended, the bushes gave way to moss. It was hot and sunny and windy. Birds sang, as they had done all night, all day. Presently one of the Greenlanders pointed to something. I thought at first that he had seen another caribou. But he was pointing at some rocks a few paces down the slope.

It had once been a house. The stones were still laid out square on one side of the foundation. But the house had fallen in. It was a jumble of rock-slabs grown black and soft with lichen in their thousand years.

"Vikings," one of the Greenlanders said. "Only they built this way."

The house was only rocks now. It was nothing but part of the landscape.

"So they had a farm here," I said, pointing down at the grassy space where the tents were pitched.

"Yes. This was probably a storage building."

"The fjord must have been deeper a thousand years ago," I said. "It's too shallow and muddy for a ship now."

"Yes," the Greenlander said. "Look. In this hole. Bones. Human."

We all peered into the rectangular grave at the edge of the ruin. It too was a room of sorts, being lined with flat stone slabs. I saw some long bones from an arm or a leg, and a cracked skull.

"Maybe he was one of us," the Greenlander said. "Maybe he was an Eskimo.

I think so from the shape of the cranium. This was a reindeer route. Many hunters came here. But I don't know."

"Will you tell the Museum?" I said.

He shook his head. "It's better here."

Gently and unhurriedly, the Greenlanders closed the grave with slabs from the ruins. Later, we found another slab near the fire that the women had made. We put Danish butter on that rock and set it over the flames. When the butter began to melt, we laid reindeer steaks and whale steaks on the stone. The meat was very tender, and cooked quickly. We poured coarse salt on another stone, skewered the cooked meat on our knives, and dragged it through the salt. It was one of the best meals I ever had. Later we lay on the grass listening to the radio, and a beautiful girl lay smiling and picking yellow flowers and singing, "Ai-ya, la-la-la . . ."

L'Anse-aux-Meadows,
Newfoundland 1987

You should go to south Greenland. So beautiful! Trees higher than my
head!

Greenlander (1987)

A t L'Anse-aux-Meadows there are no trees. Or so it seems at first
until you find them, green and almost lush, tucked away behind the ridges.
They are not tall. The trees are so scarce that on the ridgetops they might
be mistaken for men. – The sun in late afternoon best illuminates thoughts
which are melancholy. What takes root on this great cold plain of historical
remembrance, with its snowdrifts and cold hard outcroppings, at which the
sea works sullenly? – Nothing but trees grown bad and grey; and seagulls,
icebergs, half-dead grass. The rest is buried or blown away. – A little to the
south, where Gudrid and Karlsefni once sailed to Marvel Strands, the grass,
now brownish-grey, is pocked with broad shallow lakes to whose margins
still cling snowdrifts on this first day of June, 1987. Then in places the grass
begins to give way to stones. From time to time the waist-high trees and
tuckamores return, as does the grass, shy between ever wider snowdrifts,
but the rocky pavement becomes more and more in evidence, until the
whole of the Great Northern Peninsula seems to be a hard flat road to
Jötunheim. Markland is a blue smudge across the sea, patched with snow;
and ahead there are two blue mountains with snow between. The snow
glows white, even through closed eyes. – Sometimes on a hot dry day in
southern California, shiny water-mirages will appear in the freeway's dark
bends. Here there are cold-mirages in dark white bands on the highway.
The sky is grey, and the grass waves in frigid breezes. – Farther south still,
where Thorvald Eiriksson lies buried at Cross-Ness, grave-robbers and other
archeologists will see a lone blue island, the usual blue island looking cold

in the morose Atlantic, which rubs its slimy hands against the long white slabs of granite in distant Nova Scotia, which is halfway to the equator; dear old Nova Scotia with its grey seas, its white rocks and its white lighthouses. On summer days a quiet breeze blows, and laundry hangs behind the tall narrow-roofed houses with brick chimneys, the houses blue and white and yellow, whose windows gaze upon the blue rivers in the grass, and here and there stands a tall maple tree. Towns have sprung up in windy meadows of camomile and dandelion. The grass is green and sometimes white, as if it were salty from the breath of sea-churches, whose arched windows and tall

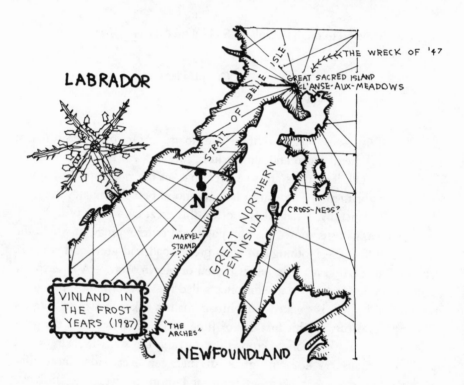

clock-towers guard graveyards – for the traveler in Nova Scotia is certain to pass at least a dozen graveyards a day – to say nothing of those habitations of the living dead, the Indian reservations, with their mean houses set into rainy hillsides, the Skræling boys riding their bikes round and round in the dirt, the Skræling men and women, broad-faced and dark, walking along the road to nowhere – to say nothing of the cheap squat livegraves at Millbrook Reserve with their rickety steps and their warped screen doors; the church built like a red teepee, the craft shop that was closed, and then the highway going on into the drizzle – to say nothing of that great monument to the

Skrælings, the MicMac Mall – to say nothing of the memorializing going on in the very capital, so that, looking out the window of O'Carroll's Restaurant at the view, past the gleaming brass window-bar and between the curtains, whose floral patterns resemble dried mushrooms on velvet, you might hear two businessmen behind you discussing the commercial climate of Halifax, and one finally said, "Well, it's definitely becoming a big city. So is there any street violence here?", and the other said, "Oh, no no no *no*. Although I *did* have an Indian once . . ." – and the other said, "Oh yes yes yes *yes*."

I arrived at closing time. The road to the Visitor Center was already sealed off, so I walked around the barricades. There wasn't a soul in sight as far as the eye could see. The plain was brown and black; the sea was grey. The little parking lot was empty; the Visitor Center on its rise was like a dead space station, and the fishing village half a mile to the north was also still. An iceberg floated in the Atlantic. – A long walkway of elevated planks led from the parking lot onto the tundra. Two birds swooped. As yet I had seen no sign of the ruins. The walkway went up a little rise, where the wind was gusting fiercely, and I saw two grey lakes, the water in each rippling and flowing like a river from the north wind. Could one of these be the place where Helgi and Finnbogi had lived? The lake water was very clear. Close up, it appeared brown. Under the water were reddish stones. In the middle was a sharp boulder like a little islet, against which the water leaped up sharply in wind-whitecaps. The sky was grey and blue and white. A gull-feather lay fluttering; gull-down blew in the wind . . . The rise was soft with moss, hard with rocks pushing urgently through it like tattletale graves. The rocks were orange and black and white with lichens. The tundra was soft. It was brown and green and lichen-white. The springy bushes had tiny leaves. Sitting there, I could finally see the turf house like a brown grass helmet on the plain below, then the white houses of the village, and then, by a dark island, the white iceberg behind everything . . . Just a little off to the left, land-black and snow-white in the mist, was Great Sacred Island, just in front of which (if you look through the binoculars) can be seen the hull of the cargo freighter that was shipwrecked there in 1947. Two men lost their lives, and the others had to wait three days for help, the weather being so stormy. Was *this* the mild Isle of Dew on which Leif landed? Could his half-sister have done so much? Can we? I ask again: – Do we carry our landscapes with us locked in our ice-hearts,* and can we fit them over what

---

* "Most ice islands in the Arctic are small," says the CIA's *Polar Regions Atlas* (1987); "of the more than 100 tabular fragments recorded, only 7 have been large enough to accommodate manned research stations."

was there just as we can clothe ourselves forever in the stiff and crackling cloaks that lie in the churchyard permafrost at Herjolfsness?

Wearing the Ink-Shirt 1235–1988

"You must not strike!" cried Snorri Sturlusson on the night of 22 September 1241 as he hid in his cellar in Iceland, and his assassins hesitated, but their chief repeated, "Strike!", and Snorri repeated, "You must not strike!", and then they killed him; so that later the Norwegian King Hakon could smile and fan himself and say, "If only he had *submitted* himself to Us, he would not have been so severely treated," and in 1262 Norway annexed Iceland, having digested Greenland a year before, and the ice-darkness fell pink and purple upon the sea-islands, and Vinland was lost forever, although its white birch trees still wave in some sea-breeze, black now in the twilight, and the ice came and the ice came and the ice came, and Blue-Shirt laughed in His high-seat on the Greenland snow-fells, and He laughed in snowy Vinland, and the People of KLUSKAP were compelled to add to their language the words *Medooebook'* (hard winter) and *Tegebook'* (cold winter) and so many more; but Snorri had written about the days when Vinland was WINELAND THE GOOD, and a century and a half later, as we know, Jón Finnsson had many stories out of Snorri copied on vellum, and so WINELAND THE GOOD lives on still and the story lives in the faded brown pages of the *Flateyjarbók*.

Here ends the
First Dream

In the Ice

1532 – 1931

Further History of the Greenland
Skrælings 1577 – 1630

The Greenlanders have had to accustom themselves to many new ways,
including self-service stores where they buy most of their necessities.

BERNADINE BAILEY,
Greenland in Pictures (1973)

De la Peyrière, who called them Skrellings and Skreglingers, said that
they consistently arrested progress. They were the reason that Eirik the Red's
colonists had never continued to settle past the Vestrebug. This seems to have
been a disappointment to Peyrière, for at that time Greenland was productive
of unicorn horn, of which he was very fond.

The English sea-captain, Martin Frobisher, after whom Frobisher Bay in
Baffin Island is named, set sail for Greenland in 1577. When the Skrellings
saw his ship, they abandoned their skin tents in a panic. Some hid themselves
among the crags. Others, possibly foreseeing the future, threw themselves
into the sea. Frobisher's party searched the tents. In one of them they found
"a hideous old woman, and a young woman enceinte, with a child, whom
she was holding by the hand. They took them away with them. They took
them by force from the old woman, who howled horribly." – The black
coast-ridge sloped up into the ice as steadily as a knife-blade. The moon
rushed avariciously after the sun, round and round in the sky like the
wheels of that Celestial Clock in which we may be certain that Frobisher
believed; his men stood moodily on the beach with their two prisoners;
the unfastened door-hides of the Skrellingers' tents flapped and flapped, like
KLUSKAP's blanket-door behind which something was never again going to
happen. – Frobisher (whose memory still frowns down, suitably englassed,
from the cliff-walls of various reading-rooms) found the country prone to
earthquakes. He discovered gravel pits filled with gold, of which they took
home three hundred casks.

In 1605 the Danish captain Gotske Lindenau commenced his hobby of collecting Skrellings. When he anchored off the coast, they jumped into their little boats and came to see him. He offered them wine, but they did not like it. They drank some of his whale oil instead. One can easily imagine the scene – the fog, the grinning sailors in their oilskins, the creaking of the lantern, and Captain Lindenau standing in the doorway of his cabin watching the Skrellings as they squat on the deck drinking oil. Perhaps he has already decided which of the savages he wants to bring home. Or perhaps the choice is more of a last-minute impulse, after the trading, where the Skrellings happily part with skins and unicorn horns in exchange for a few penny looking-glasses. In that case, Captain Lindenau would have waited almost until the Skrellings had leaped back into their skin-boats before admitting to himself that he could not bear to part with them. Certainly they would enliven the voyage home. No doubt the King would be pleased to be presented with them. On the fourth day, weighing anchor, he took possession of two. They struggled so vigorously to free themselves that he had to have them bound. The other Skrellings howled and launched stones and arrows across the water, until the Danes fired their cannon and cleared them away.

An English captain whom Lindenau had engaged landed to the west, and after making his own desultory explorations of the stony ground he took four of the savages. One of them caused such a commotion in his rage that they were compelled to beat him to death with musket-butts. (This action, arbitrary as it may now seem, surely had its own divine justice: although the Danes were no longer Vikings, they paid reverence in their own way to Blue-Shirt.) – The remaining Skrellings, I need hardly say, became more tractable immediately.

The King was delighted with the wild men. Unfortunately for Lindenau, he considered the English captain's batch to be better made. – "So I am betrayed," said Lindenau to himself, "and honor, it seems, is but wave-wind and fell-wind!" – But his perseverance was admirable: back he sailed to Greenland. – The Skrellings, alas, were now somewhat harder to approach. Like all dreamers, they hid shyly on their home-cliffs; they drank the mists and hunted for birds' eggs. One of Lindenau's soldiers volunteered to lure them out, but as soon as he got to shore they tore him to pieces. Eventually the Danes tricked them and caught them. One of the prisoners threw himself into the sea in his despair and was drowned.

They were sullen in Denmark, and refused to embrace the Christian faith. Throughout the years of their captivity they were seen worshipping the SUN. When the Spanish Ambassador came, the King amused him by making them perform aquatic exercises in their boats. They maneuvered in so colorful and orderly, so painlessly exotic a fashion, like red-gold carp swimming round and round in a pool, that the Ambassador laughed and clapped his hands, on which shone rings worth more than noblemen's lives. Afterwards he sent them each a sum of money, which they spent on spurs and feathers. Several times nonetheless, being unpersuaded of elementary facts, they tried to escape, which forced the Danes to guard them more severely. The majority, says Peyrière, died of melancholy; and although we may if we choose imagine them in the heaven of the Netsiliks, a place where spirits could play kickball forever with the laughing skull of a walrus, it seems most likely that in death as in life they did not find their way home. (It is not recorded whether the High Bishop permitted them burial in consecrated ground – for so little is known! It cannot even be said for certain why *rigor mortis* is noticed first in the smaller muscles, such as the eyelids; nor can we speculate as to which carven cabinet of the King's library entombed the *Flateyjarbók*.)* – Two of the Skreglingers lived on a dozen years after the rest. The Governor of Kolding set one to pearl-fishing, and he was so successful that the Governor made him continue to dive even among the icebergs, after which he unfortunately died. The last Skrelling thereupon tried again to escape in his little boat. They overtook him between twenty and forty leagues out to sea. They told him that he would infallibly have been lost in the fog and the ice had he persisted, but he did not seem to understand them. When they brought him back to the King's fishponds, he too sickened and died.

"Their coats, made of seal and walrus-skins," says Peyrière, who loves to track the dispositions of property, "their shirts of the intestines of fish, and one of their under-shirts, made of the skins of birds, with their feathers of different colours, are hung for curiosity in the cabinet of M. Vormius . . ."

The sailor Edward Pellham, who with eight companions was abandoned on western Greenland in 1630, never saw them. He asseverated in his pamphlet *Gods Power and Providence* as a matter known to all that of course the country had no permanent inhabitants, Christian or heathen.

---

* Nonetheless, the impression that one bears away from this epoch is one of transcendent order, of the kind achievable only when greed is married to meticulousness. It is written, for instance, that when Iceland fell subject to Denmark, detailed maps were made of the bird-cliffs of the Westman Isles; and none of the islanders could go egg-gathering there without first paying rent to the Danish crown.

Sea-Change of the Demon

It is indeed strange, the manner in which we must begin to think about
the higher world.

C. HOWARD HINTON, MA,
The Fourth Dimension (1906)

As for Blue-Shirt, they called it WHITE-SHIRT by now, for ice
bleaches as it thickens.

The Curse as Landmark 1532

. . . Taking a view of the desolateness of the place, they conceived such a horrour and inward feare in their hearts, as that they resolved rather to returne for England to make satisfaction with their lives for their former faults committed, than there [in Greenland] to remaine, though with assured hope of gaining their pardon.

PELLHAM

In the map of Jacobus Ziegler (Argentorati, 1532), the ocean is full of swirling currents, over which a griffin hovers. Irelandia is a white hatchet-blade; Islandia (that is, Iceland) a white trapezoid (all land is white). Ziegler and his generation seem to have been the first to be apprised of the *extent* of things, because the entire top left quadrant of the map has been cordoned off into whiteness. GRONLANDIA, it says, and INCOGNITA. There is but one landmark, halfway up the coast (longitude 20°, latitude 67°): – a triple mountain overlooking the sea, with the legend HVETSARGH PROMONT. It is White-Shirt. The rest of Greenland is emptily white.

I t is true, of course, that there is no longer a true Greenland or Eskimo culture in West Greenland. But while externally the people incline toward a complete adaption of European ways, there still survives a good deal in the disposition and intimate conduct of the people that is definitely Eskimo. It is a serious reflection upon our natures to say that the rare sweetness of nature, the prevailing sunniness of the Greenlanders was definitely not acquired from European teachers . . .

KENT, entry for 9 October 1931

There is an obvious preference for a clean page of text, unburdened by explanation or any other supplementary matter, although it is easy to see that no text from the past can stand on its own and be enjoyed without misapprehension by the modern reader.

CHARLES ROSEN, "Romantic Originals" (*The New York Review of Books*, Vol. XXXIV, No. 20)

Glossaries

Chronology

Sources

FREYDIS EIRIKSDOTTIR

Glossaries

Note

I have tried to define every term which may not be readily comprehensible. (1) Because this is a novel, not a treatise in linguistics, the words are entered as they appear in the text. For example, in Glossary III I refer to the East Settlement of the lost Greenland colony as the East Bygd. Therefore, the entry is "East Bygd," which is half English and half Icelandic. I have not rendered "east" in Icelandic, since if you know that, presumably you wouldn't need to find the entry at all. (2) Sources for terms are not in any way exhaustive; they merely indicate where I have seen them in my reading. Thus, for instance, it is entirely possible that an *anegiuchak* is known somewhere in Greenland as well as in Alaska, but in Glossary V only the Alaskan origin of this word is indicated. (3) The same word may be spelled a variety of ways in this book (e.g. "Vinland" and "Vineland"; "Eric" and "Eirik"; "*ulo*" and "*ulu*"; "Skrælings," "Skrellings" and "Skrelinges"). Every spelling is taken from a primary source. Rather than be a totalitarian, I have preferred to let the variants stand in all their charm.

Glossaries

Orthographic Notes

NOTE ON MICMAC ORTHOGRAPHY

All Micmac words listed above are from the dictionary of the Rev. Silas T. Rand (1888). The written Micmac language has since been standardized, and Rand's spellings are obsolete. Except as noted below, I have used them in the text only when no others were available. I am very grateful to Ruth Holmes Whitehead of the Nova Scotia Museum for her corrections. I have parenthetically appended the Rand spellings for three reasons: first, because Rand was more phonetical, and his spellings may be of some help in pronunciation; second, because his *Legends*, which employs them, is at the moment the only collection of Micmac tales available in the United States; and third, because I have made Freydis spell KLUSKAP's name after Rand's fashion, in order to conveniently represent her hatred and ignorance. Says Whitehead: "To use Rand's spelling is considered somehow almost insulting, as if it didn't matter *how* one spelled it because it's only Indians" (letter to author, 9 March 1988).

NOTE ON ICELANDIC / NORSE ORTHOGRAPHY

Icelandic (which is basically the same as Old Norse) adds an *r* to the masculine nominative singular. Thus, *Eirik* the Red was actually *Eirikr* the Red. In general, I have found this awkward, and dropped the *r* as my betters have done. However, where leisure and novelty require, as with "Bölverkr," I have not. I am very grateful to Mr. Tom Johnson in the U.C. Berkeley Scandinavian Department for his help here.

NOTE ON GREENLANDIC ORTHOGRAPHY

My friends in Greenland spelled out for me all the words of their language which appear in the text. I would particularly like to thank Mr. Nuka Møller for his corrections and emendations. The old sources which I made use of in writing this book, such as Vahl and Boas, are rarely in accordance with the orthography in sway since 1973, so I have added the New Greenlandic Writing System spellings to the Glossary entries whenever possible.

VINLAND SKRAELING

I
Glossary of Personal Names*

Aasa Ingjaldsdottir Daughter of **King Ingjald the Evil-Worker**. Like him, she loved fires.

King Adils Ottarsson Unable to transform himself as his fathers had, he negotiated with the Lapps and learned how to do so using the hearts of beasts.

Kings Alric and **Eric** Norse brother-Kings who killed each other with their bridles.

AMORTORTAK (lit., "the One who says, 'Ammu-ammu . . .'") A Greenlandic demon with black hands, Whose touch is death. (Modern spelling: *Ammoortortoq*.)

Angangujungoaq Inuit boy in Greenland, kidnapped by the black-armed **Tunersuit**. (Modern spelling: *Anngannguujunnguaq*.)

Aslak of Langadale He and his son Ilugi supported **Thorgest of Breidabolstead** against **Eirik the Red** in the feud of Eirik's bench-boards.

Asvald Leifsson Father of **Thorvald Asvaldsson;** grandfather of **Eirik the Red**.

BALDUR The good Norse god, very fair to look at, with white limbs. Sometimes seen as a prefiguration of CHRIST. Murdered by **LOKI**. (Also spelled BALDR.)

Bjarni Grimolfsson One of the Norse Greenlanders who came to Vinland with **Gudrid Thorbjornsdottir**'s expedition. He captained one of the ships, which went down on the return journey; he was drowned.

Bjarni Herjolfsson A Greenlander. Son of Herjolf Bardarsson, after whom the promontory Herjolfsness was named. Bjarni found Vinland, Markland and Slab-Land when he was blown off-course on his way to Greenland. He may have been the first Norseman to see North America. (But see also **Leif the Lucky.**)

Bjorn the Crusader (Bjarni Einarsson) An Icelander who rescued two Inuit children from drowning in Greenland. The children pledged themselves to him and to his wife, Solveig, but Bjorn sailed off without them, so they killed themselves.

Bláserk Norse name for Blue-Shirt, the great glacier (sometimes rendered in translation as *Blauserk*). See also **Bloserken** and **Mukla Jokel.**

Bloserken Danish name for **Blue-Shirt.** Later called *Huidserken*, White-Shirt.

---

* Norse names are listed by given name, not patronymic. Thus, **Gudrid Thorbjornsdottir** is under G, not *T*.

BÖLVERKR "The Evil-Doer." A name for **ODIN**.

Carrying the War-Club A Micmac chief who sought to kill the Norse settlers in Vinland and take their axes.

Christian Greenland Inuk boy, 1987. He told the tale of **Angangujungoaq**.

COOLPUJOT (lit., says the Rev. S.T. Rand, "Rolled-On-Handspikes") Personification of the seasons. A boneless fellow, whom **KLUSKAP** rolls to the east on a handspike to make spring, and rolls to the west to make autumn. Ruth Holmes Whitehead says: "This definition of who He is, is late. **KLUSKAP** doesn't roll Him in earlier stories. He is only rolled to cut the roots which have sprouted from his down-side, to make medicine. I seriously question Handspikes." So I have substituted a spear for a handspike, and queasily left Him in.

King Dag the Wise Old Norse King who spoke the language of birds. Killed in a battle over his pet sparrow.

Draupnir [*Norse*] A gold ring which gave birth each night to eight gold rings.

Dreaming of Bad Days A Micmac shaman in Vinland who saw danger in the axes of the Norse settlers.

King Egil Onsson Son of **King On.** The first to notice that the royal Changing-blood was getting thin.

Egill Skallagrimsson A brave, greedy, cruel Icelander who also happened to be a skaldic poet of genius. (Modern spelling: *Eigil*.)

Einar An Icelander "with a taste for the ornate." Son of a freed slave. Rejected suitor of **Gudrid Thorbjornsdottir.**

Einar of Laugarbrekka A well-to-do farmer. Maternal grandfather of **Gudrid Thorbjornsdottir.**

Eirik the Red The son of Thorvald Asvaldsson. Born in Jæderen, Norway. Outlawed for manslaughter, he settled in Drangar, Iceland. He married **Thjodhild Jorundsdottir** and moved to Haukadale until he was outlawed from the region for killing his neighbor **Valthjof.** He then moved to Oxen Island in Breidafjord and was soon outlawed from Iceland for three years for killing two sons of **Thorgest of Breidabolstead.** After exploring Greenland, he returned to Iceland briefly at the end of his outlawry to encourage settlement, and then sailed back to Greenland, where he lived out the rest of his life. By Thjodhild Eirik had three sons: **Leif the Lucky, Thorstein** and **Thorvald.** Eirik also had a bastard daughter, **Freydis.**

Elder Brother Ancestor of the **Inuit.**

Emilie Greenland Inuk girl, 1987.

King Eric Bloody-Axe Favorite son of **King Harald Fairhair.** Like his father, he married a Lappish witch, named **Gunhild.** Killed some of his brother-Kings, ostensibly because they were warlocks. Took the throne after his father until he was expelled by his brother **King Hakon the Good.** Ruled a small territory in England under King Athelstan until Athelstan's death; slain in battle in Northumberland *ca.* 954.

Eyjolf of Svin Island A rich Icelander. He supported **Eirik the Red** against **Thorgest of Breidabolstead** in the feud of Eirik's bench-boards.

King Eystein The younger son of King Eystein the Severe, who ruled in Hedemark, in central Norway. After King Sigtryg, the elder son, was killed in a territorial war with **Halfdan the Black,** Eystein became King. He fought four battles against Halfdan, and lost them all. In the end he sued for peace; Halfdan let him retain half of Hedemark.

Eyvind Kellda Norwegian warlock put to death by **King Olaf Trygvesson.**

Eyvind Skáldaspillar An Icelander; skaldic poet.

Fenrir The great Wolf (**LOKI**'s offspring) who will devour King **ODIN** at the end of the world. According to the *Prose Edda*, the river Ván flows from his slobber as he howls in his fetter *Glepnir*, waiting to revenge himself for his captivity. (NOTE: *Fenrir*, but *the Fenris-Wolf.*)

FREY Norse god of fertility. Usually depicted seated, with an immense erect penis.

Freydis Eiriksdottir Bastard daughter of **Eirik the Red.** Mother unknown. Married to a rich man of little character, **Thorvard of Gardar.** In one of the sagas she is mentioned as being pregnant, but her issue is never mentioned. Sailed to Vinland to enrich herself. Saved the Norse colonists there from a Skræling attack, frightening the Skrælings by whacking her bare breasts with a sword. At about the same time she murdered two Icelandic colonists, **Helgi** and **Finnbogi,** and all their establishment, reputedly killing their women herself with an axe.

FREYJA Norse goddess of fertility and beauty. Not known for Her chastity. She has long golden hair, and is so lovely to look upon that fine and costly things are often named after Her. When She cries, She weeps tears of gold.

FRIGG A Norse fertility goddess. In function the distinction between Her and **FREYJA** is not clear. FRIGG was **ODIN**'s wife. Of Her the *Heimskringla* says only: "It happened once when Odin had gone to a great distance . . . that his two brothers took it upon themselves to divide his estate, but both of them took his wife Frigg to themselves. Odin soon after returned home, and took his wife back."

Gauthild A princess from Gotland. Wife of **King Ingjald the Evil-Worker.**

Gautvid Foster-brother of **Ingjald the Evil-Worker.**

GLOOSKAP Freydis Eiriksdottir's name for **KLUSKAP.** See the Note on Micmac Orthography immediately preceding these Glossaries.

Grimhild Wife of **Thorstein the Black.** She was a Norse Greenlander who died of the plague. Another saga calls her Sigrid and gives her a less unpleasant character, but the same fate.

Grjotgaard A henchman of **King Harald Greyskin.**

Gudrid Thorbjornsdottir Her father was **Thorbjorn Vifilsson,** who was descended from an ex-slave; her mother was **Hallveig Einarsdottir.** Gudrid was very beautiful, and married frequently. Her first marriage (which may be apocryphal) was to another Icelander, **Thorir.** They were shipwrecked, and rescued by **Leif the Lucky,** soon after which Thorir died and Gudrid married Leif's younger brother, **Thorstein Eiriksson.** (Another account has Gudrid coming to Greenland with her father, unmarried until she met Thorstein.) After Thorstein's death, Gudrid married an Icelander, **Thorfinn Karlsefni,** and went with him to Vinland. There her son, **Snorri Karlsefnisson,** was born. Later Gudrid and Karlsefni returned to Iceland and farmed until Karlsefni's death. Gudrid made a pilgrimage to Rome and became a nun.

Gudrod King of Skaane   Husband of **Aasa Ingjaldsdottir.**

King Gudrod the Hunter   Son of **King Halfdan the Mild.** Father of **King Halfdan the Black.**

Queen Gunhild Ossur-Tote's-Daughter   A Lappish witch, the wife of **King Eric Bloody-Axe.** Her father was a warlock in Halogaland. (But a note in Appendix I of the *Heimskringla* says that she "was in fact a daughter of King Gorm of Denmark, a fact mentioned only in the *Historia Norwegiæ* . . . The transformation of her origin in the Icelandic sources must depend on the evil reputation she enjoyed there. The fostering of Harald Greycloak by King Harald Gormsson and the support the sons of Eric had from Denmark . . . are easily understandable . . .") She bore her husband eight children: Gamle, Guttorm, **King Harald Greyskin,** Ragnfrid, Ragnhild, Erling, Gudrod and Sigurd Sleva. She, Eric and her brood were all Christianized in England, where they fled after being expelled by **King Hakon the Good.** After Bloody-Axe was killed, Gunhild used her sons to kill King Hakon and conquer Norway. She had the title of "King-Mother" only a brief time, however, being exiled in the end, and outliving all her sons, who died various violent deaths.

Gyda King-Eric's-Daughter   The beautiful girl who inspired **King Harald Fairhair** to conquer all Norway.

King Hakon the Good   Son of **King Harald Fairhair.** Expelled his half-brother **King Eric Bloody-Axe** from the throne (AD 934?) and ruled until he was killed by Bloody-Axe's sons (961?).

King Hakon Jarl the Great   Succeeded to the throne of Norway after King **Harald Greyskin,** AD 965(?). Succeeded by **King Olaf Trygvesson** in 995(?).

King Halfdan the Black   So called for his black hair. King in Norway. Married **Ragnhild,** the daughter of King Harald Goldbeard. He lost his Yule-feast to the magic of the Lapps. Died crossing treacherous ice. Father of **King Harald Fairhair,** whom he denied the inheritance of the Bear-Shirt.

King Halfdan the Mild   Grandson of **King Halfdan Whiteleg.**

King Halfdan Whiteleg   Successor to **King Olaf Tree-Feller. Halfdan the Black** came six Kings after him.

Halldis   Pagan foster-mother of **Gudrid Thorbjornsdottir.** Married to **Orm.** Taught Gudrid witchcraft-songs. Accompanied her to Greenland, but died on the voyage.

Hallveig Einarsdottir Mother of **Gudrid Thorbjornsdottir; wife of Thorbjorn Vifilsson.** Thorbjorn's brother **Thorgeir** married her sister.

King Harald Fairhair A friend to Lapps. Unified Norway under him by reducing other Kings to Earls. (Those who fled him settled new lands to the west, including Iceland.) Married **Gyda Ericsdaughter,** Ragnhild the Mighty, who bore him his favorite son **Eric Bloody-Axe,** Swanhild, from whom **King Olaf Trygvesson** was descended, Aashild, the Lappish witch **Snæfrid,** and doubtless many others. By his serving-maid Tora Mosterstang he fathered **King Hakon the Good.**

King Harald Grænske The father of **King Olaf the Saint,** of Norway. Was intimate with **Sigrid the Haughty,** but not intimate enough to marry her.

King Harald Greyskin (Greycloak) Third son of **King Eric Bloody-Axe.** Ruled Norway after he killed **King Hakon the Good** (*ca.* 961). Killed in a sea battle some four years later. In his time the kingdom was very divided.

King Harald Redbeard Father of Princess Aasa, wife of **King Gudrod the Hunter;** killed by Gudrod when he refused to give Aasa to him of his own will.

HEIMDALL The watchman-god of Valhalla. Prayed to by sailors, navigators, etc.

HEL "The Concealer." (But others say "The Bright," because Niflheim was the radiant land of the elves until the dead came.) Norse goddess of the Underworld, **LOKI**'s daughter. **ODIN** cast Her down into Niflheim when She was born. Black and hideous; sometimes called "the Horse-Goddess."

Helga Wife of **Thorkel,** the farmer at Herjolfsness.

Helgi and **Finnbogi** Two Icelandic brothers who accompanied **Freydis Eiriksdottir** to Vinland in their own ship. Freydis seems to have coveted their larger vessel, and murdered them in cold blood, even though they agreed to exchange with her.

Herlaug and **Rollaug** Two brother-Kings in Norway at the time of **King Harald Fairhair.** Herlaug chose to die a King, and committed suicide; Rollaug preferred to live an Earl, and swore fealty to Harald.

His Spear Is Straight A Micmac warrior. Killed by the Norse Greenlanders for stealing weapons.

King Ingjald the Evil-Worker Last of the **Yngling** Kings. (See Glossary II.) He was fed a wolf's heart to become brave, and became vicious. His children were **Olaf Tree-Feller** and **Aasa,** who burned herself alive with her father.

Ivar Bardsson In 1349 he wrote a report to the Bishop at Gardar, reporting that the Western Settlement of Greenland (West Bygd) was deserted. (Variants: *Bardarson, Bardson,* etc.)

Ivar Vidfavne Nephew of Gudrod King of Skaane, who married **Aasa Ingjaldsdottir.** Aasa enticed Gudrod to murder his brother Halfdan, Ivar's father. In his good time, Ivar avenged himself upon Aasa and her father, **King Ingjald the Evil-Worker.**

Thorfinn Karlsefni An Icelandic trader, whose name means "Makings of a Man." He made **Eirik the Red** happy when he gave him ale-malt for a Yule or Christmas feast. Last husband of **Gudrid Thorbjornsdottir.** He and Gudrid and various other Greenlanders attempted to colonize Vinland. The venture failed, because Norse provocations incensed the native population and made it impossible to stay there. By Gudrid he had a son, **Snorri Karlsefnisson.**

KEWKW In some Micmac myths, the Power of earthquakes. (S.T. Rand: KUHKWA.)

Kimberly Baffinland Inuk girl, 1987.

KISU'LKW "He Makes Us." A Person or Power among the Micmac.

KLUSKAP A powerful Person Who appears in some Micmac legends. Not a god. ("Calling Him a god," says Ruth Holmes Whitehead, "is like saying seriously that Lumberjacks worshipped Paul Bunyan and his ox.") (Rand's obsolete spelling – and Freydis's – is GLOOSKAP.)

Leif the Lucky (Leif Eiriksson) Eldest son of Eirik the Red and **Thjodhild Jorundsdottir.** The sagas are in dispute as to whether it was he or **Bjarni Herjolfsson** who first sighted Vinland. In any event, he seems to have explored there, and also to have brought a priest to Greenland at the urging of the Norwegian King, **Olaf Trygvesson.** He was called "the Lucky" because of the wealth he brought from Vinland, and also because he rescued **Gudrid Thorbjornsdottir** from a shipwreck (and thereby became entitled to driftage?). Whether or not he married is unknown, but he had a liaison in the Hebrides with a witch named **Thorgunna,** who bore him a son named **Thorgils.**

LOKI The Norse trickster-god. In the *Edda* He sometimes helps, sometimes harms the gods with His cunning, but steadily becomes more wicked. Married to a Jötun woman, Sigun, by whom His sons were Vali, Nari and Narthi. On the Jötun Angrbotha He begat **HEL** the Concealer, the Serpent of Midgaard, and the wolf **Fenrir.** (LOKI is also hermaphroditic; He once became a mare, seduced a stallion, and so bore **ODIN's** eight-legged horse **Sleipnir.**) He tricked another god into killing **BALDUR** the Good with a sprig of mistletoe, and prevented his resurrection. Punished by being chained to a rock beneath a snake that spits poison into His eyes. His name means "The Ender," for He will help to bring about the end of the world.

Margethe Greenland Inuk girl, 1987. **Christian's** girl-friend.

Marten A thrall of **KLUSKAP**.

Naddour-Viking An accidental discoverer of Iceland. His ship was blown off course.

Nidhogg The Norse dragon of **Niflheim,** who devours corpses and gnaws at the root of **Yggdrasil.**

NIKSKAM "Our Grandfather." (Micmac word for GOD.)

Norns The three sisters who weave Norse men's fates. Their names are Past, Present and Future. Their bower is by the **Well of Weird.**

ODIN King of the Norse Gods. He paid one of His eyes to gain the wisdom of runes. One kenning for the sun is "ODIN's eye." His weapon is the spear. He is a shape-changer, and the patron god of hanged men. In His hall **Valhalla** He gathers together the most valiant of the battle-slain in preparation for the day of the **Fenris-Wolf.** His two black crows are called Hugin and Munin (Thought and Memory); they circle the world and tell Him everything.

King Olaf the Saint (Haraldsson) King of Norway AD 1015?–1030. Completed Olaf Trygvesson's work. Considered more holy than he. A martyr, like most of the old Norse Kings. He was revered when he was safely dead.

King Olaf Tree-Feller Son of **King Ingjald the Evil-Worker.** Disbelieved that men could transform themselves without the Bear-Shirt.

King Olaf Trygvesson (now more correctly spelled "Trygvason." Perhaps the nineteenth-century translators used the former spelling in order to make the pronunciation closer. In any event, I have preferred it, in order to appall and annoy) King of Norway AD 995?–1000. The grandson of **King Harald Fairhair.** Probably bore a special grudge against **Queen Gunhild,** because she sought to destroy him when he was a child, and because her son Gudrod killed his father, King Trygve Olafsson. A zealous Christianizer who tortured or killed those who would not convert: during his reign Norway, Iceland, the Faroes, the Shetlands, the Orkneys and possibly Greenland became nominally Christian. Some accounts have him commanding **Leif Eiriksson** to bring the True Faith to Greenland. He sought the hand of **Queen Sigrid** of Sweden, but the engagement was broken off. Died in battle, leaping into the water with his shield above his head, and never rising again.

King On Swedish King who sacrificed all but one of his sons to **ODIN** to prolong his life. (Variant: *Aun.*)

King Onund Road-Builder Father of **King Ingjald the Evil-Worker.**

Orm Foster-father of **Gudrid Thorbjornsdottir.** Married to **Halldis.** When pressed by **Einar,** a suitor for Gudrid's hand, he interceded with her father, but was rewarded by having Gudrid taken from his care. Accompanied her to Greenland, but died on the voyage.

King Ottar Egilsson The first of the **Yngling** Kings to have trouble changing himself into a bear.

Ragnhild Harald Goldbeard's Daughter Wife of **Halfdan the Black;** mother of **King Harald Fairhair.**

Ragnhild the Mighty One of **King Harald Fairhair**'s wives.

Seth Pilsk the Thin He explored **Slab-Land,** and was almost drowned for his pains.

THE SHINING ONE Hebridean deity (Celtic?), about Whom little is known.

Queen Sigrid the Haughty A Swedish Queen who burnt up all her lesser suitor-Kings. The mother of King Olaf of Sweden. She was engaged to **King Olaf Trygvesson,** but they quarreled over religion, she being pagan. She later married **King Swend Forkbeard** of Denmark and goaded him into attacking her ex-fiancé.

Skofte Carrion-Crow Thrall to **Freydis Eiriksdottir**. He helped her find **Yggdrasil** in Vinland.

Slayer-Styr Thorgrimsson A strong man. He supported **Eirik the Red** against **Thorgest of Breidabolstead** in the feud of Eirik's bench-boards, and sought a favorable verdict with **Snorri the Priest** at the Thorsness **Thing** (see Glossary V).

Slepnir **ODIN**'s horse (see **LOKI**). (Variant: *Sleipnir*.)

Snæfrid (Snowfrid) **Svasesdottir** A Lappish witch who enchanted **King Harald Fairhair**. He married her and had four sons by her. When she died, the bewitchment remained so strong that for three years he thought her still living.

Snorri Karlsefnisson The first white born in Vinland. Son of **Gudrid** and **Karlsefni**.

Snorri Sturlusson Author of the *Heimskringla* and many other great works. An Icelander. Born 1178. He was very greedy and ambitious, and met his deserved fate when agents of the Norwegian King, the current Hakon, murdered him in his cellar in 1241.

Snorri the Priest He officiated at the Thorsness **Thing**, where a decision was to be made as to whether or not **Eirik the Red** should be outlawed for killing two sons of **Thorgest of Breidabolstead**.

Snorri Thorbrandsson A friend of **Thorfinn Karlsefni**, whom he accompanied to Vinland. His son Thorbrand Snorasson was slain by Skrælings: Karlsefni's son Snorri was perhaps named in his honor.

Solveig Wife of **Bjorn the Crusader**.

Spirit Woman Ancestor of the **Inuit**.

King Swegde Norse King who sought **ODIN** and was trapped in a rock.

King Swend Forkbeard King of Denmark. Married **Queen Sigrid the Haughty**. He was a great warrior in England. The famous Canute was his son.

Thjodhild Jorundsdottir Wife of **Eirik the Red**. Daughter of a woman named Thorbjorg Ship-Breast. She bore Eirik three sons, **Leif, Thorstein** and **Thorvald**, and accompanied him to Greenland, where she lived out her life with him. She became a Christian even though Eirik did not, and refused to have sexual relations with him until he should convert. Thjodhild's church was discovered in Greenland in the 1960s.

Thorbjorg Ship-Breast Mother of **Thjodhild Jorundsdottir,** who married **Eirik the Red**. After her husband Jorund Ulfsson died, she married **Thorbjorn of Haukadale**.

Thorbjorg the Prophetess An old clairvoyant at Herjolfsness who foretold the end of a famine in Greenland, and promised a bright future for **Gudrid Thorbjornsdottir**.

Thorbjorn of Haukadale Foster-father of **Thjodhild Jorundsdottir,** who married **Eirik the Red**. It would have been Thorbjorn's responsibility to decide on Eirik's suitability as a match for Thjodhild.

Thorbjorn Vifilsson Son of a freed slave named **Vifil.** His wife's name was **Hallveig Einarsdottir.** Supported the cause of **Eirik the Red** against **Thorgest of Breidabolstead.** He tended to live beyond his means, and was forced in the end to leave Iceland for Greenland with his daughter, the famous **Gudrid.**

Thorbrand of Alptafjord His sons supported **Eirik the Red** against **Thorgest of Breidabolstead** in the feud of Eirik's bench-boards.

Thorgeir of Hitardale He supported **Thorgest of Breidabolstead** against **Eirik the Red** in the feud of Eirik's bench-boards.

Thorgeir Vifilsson Brother of **Thorbjorn Vifilsson.**

Thorgest "the Yeller" of Breidabolstead He held some bench-boards in keeping for **Eirik the Red,** but when Eirik wanted them back, Thorgest refused. Eirik attacked him and killed two of his sons. For this, Eirik was outlawed for three years, and went to Greenland. At the end of that time Eirik returned to Iceland and had another battle with Thorgest, which again he lost; after this they were reconciled.

Thorgils Leifsson Bastard son of **Leif the Lucky** by the witch **Thorgunna.** Supposed to have been a very pale and uncanny person, whose coming to Greenland might have coincided with an outbreak of disease. Nonetheless, Leif duly acknowledged him.

Thorgunna A Hebridean witch who had an affair with **Leif Eiriksson** (Leif the Lucky). Leif tired of her, and she thought to pursue him to Greenland, but was blown to Iceland, where she died. Her corpse haunted the country for a time. Her son **Thorgils** later came to Greenland.

Thorir First husband of **Gudrid Thorbjornsdottir.** A sea-captain. He may never have existed, as he is mentioned in only one of the sagas, in an anecdote which contradicts another.

Thorkel A farmer at Herjolfsness, who guested **Gudrid Thorbjornsdottir** and her father when they first came to Greenland.

Thorolf A farmer in Frodis-Water, Iceland. Husband of the covetous **Thurid;** host of the Hebridean witch **Thorgunna.**

Thorstein Eiriksson The second son of **Thjodhild Jorundsdottir** and **Eirik the Red.** An unlucky man who tried to reach Vinland but was blown hither and thither by unfavorable winds. He married **Gudrid Thorbjornsdottir** in Greenland and died of a plague shortly thereafter. His corpse prophesied a glorious future for Gudrid.

Thorstein the Black A Greenland householder in the Western Settlement who provided **Thorstein Eiriksson** and his wife **Gudrid Thorbjornsdottir** with lodging. After his wife **Grimhild** and Gudrid's husband both died of the plague, he seems to have fallen in love with Gudrid, but she did not marry him.

Thorvald Asvaldsson Father of **Eirik the Red.**

Thorvald Eiriksson Third and last son of **Thjodhild Jorundsdottir** and **Eirik the Red.** He sailed to Vinland, attacked a settlement of Micmac or Beothuk

Indians (Skrælings) unprovoked, and was killed in the succeeding battle. His men buried him there, at a place they called Cross-Ness.

Thorvard of Gardar One of the richest men in Greenland during the early settlement times. He married **Freydis Eiriksdottir** and accompanied her to Vinland, where he got rich cheating the Skrælings at trade. He and his wife eventually returned to Greenland, where nothing more is written of them.

THRYM In the Norse myths, a great Frost-Giant; King of **Jötunheim.**

Thurid A woman from Frodis-Water, Iceland, who asked the witch **Thorgunna** to dwell with her because she coveted her clothes.

Earl Torbrand Henchman of **King Harald Greycloak.**

Ungertok Inuit name for the last of the Norse Greenlanders, who was slain by the Inuit as told in one of their legends.

Valthjof Neighbor of **Eirik the Red** at Haukadale. They had a dispute that culminated in landslides. Eirik killed Valthjof, and also his kinsmen Eyjolf Saur and Hrafn the Dueller. He was outlawed from Haukadale.

Vifil A British captive brought to Iceland by the matriarch Aud the Deep-Minded. Aud freed Vifil from slavery and gave him land. He had two sons, **Thorbjorn** and **Thorgeir.** Thorbjorn was the father of **Gudrid.**

YGG "Terror." Name for **ODIN.**

YMIR "Roarer." According to the Norse myths, the great giant from whose corpse the world was made.

Younger Brother Ancestor of the **Inuit.**

II
Glossary of Dynasties, Races and Monsters

Bearsark [*Norse*] A **Kvedulf**, a man capable of supernatural strength in battle when the bear-fit came upon him. Berserkers may have eaten the death-cap mushroom to bring on their fits. (*Sark* = shirt.)

Beothuk [?] An Indian culture that once inhabited Nova Scotia. The Beothuk resisted assimilation and were exterminated by British Canadians in the nineteenth century. Several different types of Skrælings are described in the *Vinland Sagas*, and it seems likely that the Norse at least glimpsed Beothuk people in Vinland.

Berserker [*Norse*] See **Bearsark**.

Booöineeskwa [*Micmac*] Witch.

Draugar (sing. **Draugr**) [*Norse*] Undead warriors who fight fiercely and leap up from the ground no matter how many times they are slain. (More generally, says Mr. Tom Johnson, any revenant.)

Eskimo [?*Indian*] Foreigners' name for the **Inuit**. The literal meaning is "eater of raw meat." Many Inuit now consider it derogatory.

Greenlandic Colloq. for the Kalaallisut language spoken in Greenland. See also **Inuktitut**; and the Note on Greenlandic Orthography immediately preceding these Glossaries.

Halfsstramb [*Norse*] Sea-monster, sometimes described as manlike, elsewhere as octopoid.

Inuit (sing. **Inuk**) [*Greenlandic, Alaskan, Canadian and Soviet Inuktitut*] "The people" – the natives of Arctic Canada, Greenland and Alaska; the Eskimos' term for themselves. (See also **Eskimo**.) Robert McGhee says that "the Eskimo populations of West Alaska, South Alaska and Siberia speak other related Eskimo languages and do not think of themselves as *inuit*." But I have heard this both ways.

Inuktitut [*Inuktitut*] The language of the **Inuit**. Greenlandic is a dialect of Inuktitut. (Mr. Nuka Møller, who is more precise than I, adds the following: "A dialect of *Iñupik*, which is a scientific term for the Eastern 'Eskimo' language which covers Inupiaq (*Alaskan*), Inuvialuptun (*Western Canadian 'Eskimo'*), then Inuktitut, which is Eastern Canadian 'Eskimo', and Kalaallisut (*Greenlandic*). The western 'Eskimo' language has the branches Yupik (*Southern Alaskan–Siberian*) and Aluutiq (*Aleutian Islands*) . . . [But] 'Inuktitut' will be understood throughout . . . the Inuit world as 'the Inuit language.'") See the Note on Greenlandic Orthography immediately preceding these Glossaries.

Jenuaq (sing. **Jenu**) [*Micmac*]   Northmen, or northern demons, according to the Rev. S.T. Rand (who spells it *Chenoo*). In one of the Micmac legends in his compilation, they have hearts of solid ice. But Ruth Holmes Whitehead, who knows more, says: "It does NOT mean 'Northern Devil' . . . A Jenu is a human who has become transformed (probably by fat deprivation in winter). These people become psychotic and eat and kill other humans. They can be cured by drinking fat and being thawed out."

Jipijka'maq [*Micmac*]   Race of horned serpents.

Kvedulfr [*Norse*]   "Wolf of evening"; a berserker.

Marguguers [*Norse*]   Mermaids.

Micmac [*French*; from a misunderstanding of the word *nikmaq* used in greeting, meaning "my kin-friends"]   An Algonkian culture once widespread in Maine, Nova Scotia, Quebec Province and environs. Still in existence. Also called *Souriquois* by the French. Like many Indian tribes, they called themselves "the People" – in their language, *Lnu'k*. Quite likely it was the Micmac whom Norse Greenlanders encountered at the beginning of the eleventh century. See the Note on Micmac Orthography immediately preceding these Glossaries.

Netsiliks [*Anglicized Inuktitut*]   Actually, the Netsilingmiut, or Seal People. These Inuit lived in Arctic Canada, between Pelly and Dolphin and Union Strait. They wintered on the frozen sea, hunting for seals.

Norse   A culture that dominated Scandinavia, Iceland, parts of Greenland and much of the British Isles during early medieval times. One thinks of Vikings when the Norse are mentioned; most Norse, however, were traders and farmers. The people (at least as described in their sagas) seem to have been brave, fatalistic, ruthless and highly regardful of their honor. See the Note on Norse Orthography immediately preceding these Glossaries.

Qivittoq [*Greenlandic*; pronounced "hrevitoq"]   "A man who went to the mountains to live alone, usually because of women or other factors that made it impossible to live in Inuit society. Much feared . . . and believed to have magic powers. There are stories about people having met religious *qivittut* (plur.) with Bibles and psalm books. But mostly they were believed to be bad people who came either to steal food or seek revenge by scaring people. Some of them were believed to have the ability to transform themselves [in]to animals. They were perfect 'boogie-men' to us Greenlandic kids." – Nuka Møller.

Skrælings [*Icelandic*]   Generic term used by the Norsemen to describe the **Inuit** of Greenland and also the Red Indians of Vinland. It meant something like "dried-up savage wretches." (Jacqueline Simpson (1964) proposed two variant meanings: "Screechers" and "Flinchers.") In the map of Sigurdur Stefansson (1590) there is an explanatory note on the Skrælings: "These people are so named from their aridity, being dried up both by heat and by cold."

Tornaq [*Greenlandic*]   Assistant spirit. (Modern spelling: *Toornaq*.)

Troll [*Norse*]   Everyone knows what a troll is. But I cannot resist quoting the definition of H. Rider Haggard: "an Able-Bodied Goblin."

Tunersuit [*Greenlandic*]   Legendary race of evil giants with black hands who fought the **Inuit.** Possibly Northmen; possibly some other native tribe. (Robert McGhee in his *Canadian Arctic Prehistory* (1978) mentions a mythology of *gentle* giants, the Tunit, who were dispossessed by the Thule Inuit. He equates them with the Dorset Inuit.) In *Seven Dreams* I have assumed that they were in fact Norse.

Viking [*Norse*]   A Scandinavian sea-raider or pirate.

Ynglings [*Norse*]   The first dynasty of Norse rulers, descended from the god FREY. Their saga says: "Frey was called by another name, Ygnve; and this name was considered long after as a name of honor, so that his descendants have since been called Ynglings." In this volume, the following Yngling Kings appear: **King Dag the Wise, King Swegde, Kings Alric** and **Eric, King On, King Egil, King Ottar, King Adils, King Onund Road-Builder** and **King Ingjald the Evil-Worker**, after whom the kingship fell from their race.

III
Glossary of Places*

Aasgaard The world of the Norse gods, ruled by ODIN. Also known as *Asaheim*. In the *Heimskringla*, Snorri identified it with Asia.

Blauserk (Bláserk) Blue-Shirt, the great glacier in Greenland used as a landmark by Eirik the Red in sailing west from **Snæfellsness.** See also **Bloserken** and **Mukla Jokel.**

Bloserken [*Danish*] Blue-Shirt. Later called *Huidserken*, White-Shirt, when the ice changed color (or when the chroniclers got confused).

Brattahlid Steep-Slope. The hall of Eirik the Red in Greenland. (Variations: *Brattalid, Brattelid*, etc.) The Inuit name for this place is *Qagssiarssuk*.

Breidabolstead A farm on the Icelandic mainland south of Breidafjord, where there lived a man named Thorgest ("the Yeller" or "the Old"). Thorgest refused to return Eirik the Red's bench-boards, which caused a dispute between them.

Breidafjord "Broad-Firth." The widest fjord in Iceland, on the western side. The isle of Flatey, where the *Flateyjarbók* was written, lies here, as does Öxney (Oxen) Island, where Eirik the Red lived after being outlawed from Haukadale. (Haukadale is on the mainland, but very close; so is **Breidabolstead.**) The bird-islands where Eirik hid from Thorgest are in Breidafjord. It was from here that Eirik sailed to Greenland, with Snæfellsness on his left; it was to Breidafjord that his eldest son's concubine, Thorgunna, came to die.

Cross-Ness Place in Vinland where Eirik the Red's son Thorvald was buried after a battle with Skrælings.

Dimunar Two hills close together. Eirik the Red hid from his enemy Thorgest in Dimunarsbay, on an island in **Breidafjord.**

Drontheim Modern Trondheim (Norway).

East Bygd; West Bygd The East and West Settlements of the lost Greenland colony. Oddly, both of these are on the western coast of Greenland, the East Bygd coming first and south, in the more fertile area, and the West Bygd (where Nuuk, the capital, is now) being to the north of it. Both sets of ruins are in sheltered networks of fjords, where the coast is not nearly as bleak as between them.

---

* Unless otherwise stated, all place-names in this Glossary are Norse.

Eiriksfjord **Brattahlid** was located here. (Inuit equivalent: *Tunugoliarfik*.)

Eiriks Holms "Eirik's Isle." Small isle explored by Eirik the Red, near where he eventually settled in the **East Bygd**.

Estland "East Land." This could have been any of the petty kingdoms east of Sweden.

Finnmark Lapland.

Gardar The site of Freydis Eiriksdottir's farm, in the **East Bygd**. Her husband Thorvard was from there. Gardar was at the inner extremity of Einarsfjord. The Inuit name for the place was **Igaliko** or *Igaliku*, meaning "the deserted cooking-place."

Ginnunga Gap The primeval abyss in which the world was created when ice and fire met. Sometimes thought to be Davis Strait (between Greenland and Baffin Island). In the Norse myths it lay between **Muspelheim** to the south and **Niflheim** to the north, which realms supplied the fire and the ice, respectively. From the heat-droplets thus generated came the first being, **Ymir,** an evil Frost-Giant. In some accounts, Ginnunga Gap was thought to be a channel which led out from the land to the great world-circling Ocean-Sea.

Gotland A large province in ancient Sweden. Now divided into East and West Gotland.

Great Blueland Africa, so called because the Africans were considered "blue men."

Great Swithiod Russia. (Swithiod the Lesser was Sweden.)

Haukadale District of relatively lush farmland in Iceland, near **Breidafjord**. Eirik the Red got land there when he married Thjodhild Jorundsdottir, but he was outlawed from it when he killed his neighbor Valthjof.

Helluland "Slab-Land" or "Flint-Land." Between Greenland and Markland. Probably Baffin Island.

Herjolfsness Promontory in south Greenland, at the extremity of the **East Bygd,** where ships often stopped to trade. Bjarni Herjolfsson, perhaps the first discoverer of Vinland, lived there; the place was named after his father, who was the first Norse settler. Gudrid Thorbjornsdottir and her father were guested there by a farmer called Thorkel.

Holm [*Icelandic*] Island.

Huidserken See **Blauserk.**

Igaliko [*Greenlandic*] "The deserted cooking-place." Sardonic Inuit place-name for Gardar, where Freydis and Thorvard used to live in a mansion, and later there stood a Norse cathedral. (Modern spelling: *Igaliku*.)

Jæderen Birthplace of Eirik the Red, in Norway.

Jökull [*Icelandic*] Glacier (as in *Snæfellsjökull, Mykla Jökull*).

Jötunheim The kingdom of the Frost Giants (Jötuns). Thought to be an icy land in the distant north, connecting Greenland to Norway.

Kapasillit Small village in Greenland, just across the fjord from **Nuuk.**

Mafshaak [*Canadian Inuktitut*] A hole in the ice, treacherously concealed by snowdrifts.

Markland "Forest-Land" or "Wood-Land." The Greenlanders continued to visit it for timber after the route to Vinland was abandoned. Between **Helluland** and **Vinland**. Possibly Newfoundland or Nova Scotia, but most plausibly (to me) Labrador.

Midgaard "Middle-World." Of the nine Norse worlds, this one is the most important to us, for we dwell on it. It is encircled by the Mare Oceanum, in which dwells LOKI's child, the Serpent of Midgaard, a great horror so long that it must swallow its own tail. To the north lie **Jötunheim** and **Niflheim;** to the south lie **Muspelheim** and **Aasgaard** (Asaheim; Asia); the location of the other worlds, and even some of their names, is conjectural.

Mukla Jokel The Great Mountain: Eirik the Red's name for **Blue-Shirt;** now known as Gunnbjorn's Peak (12,500 ft). (It has alternatively been suggested that Blue-Shirt was the glacier peak of Ingolsfjeld. However, I prefer the notion of Gunnbjorn's Peak, that being the highest in all Greenland. This commanding mountain was not climbed until 1935.) The spelling used here, by the way, is probably an old translator's error, so I have religiously kept it. (Variant: *Mykla Jökull.*)

Muspelheim The Kingdom of Fire, which in Norse mythology lay southward of **Ginnunga Gap.** Muspelheim's sparks became the stars. One of the signs of the world's end will be when LOKI appears upon the sea, piloting a skiff crewed by men from Muspelheim.

Niflheim The Kingdom of Ice, which in Norse mythology lay northward of **Ginnunga Gap.** The realm of the dead, ruled by the goddess HEL.

Nuuk Capital city of Greenland. (Danish name: *Godthaab.*)

Ostrebug; Vestrebug [*Danish*; ?mistranslated] The East and West Settlements of the lost Greenland colony. (Variants: *Ostreby; Vestreby.*)

Slab-Land Helluland (also translated "Flint-Land"). Between Greenland and **Markland.** Probably Baffin Island.

Slíth "The Frightful." The stream of poisonous cold that flows between **Jötunheim** and **Hel.**

Snæfellsness (Snowfells Ness) A glacier-topped volcano in Iceland at the western extremity of the peninsula that comprises the southern boundary of **Breidafjord.** Eirik the Red sailed west using Snæfellsness as a landmark behind him, and **Blue-Shirt** in Greenland as a landmark ahead. The glacier itself was called **Snæfellsjökull.**

Upsal or **Uppsala** Old Norse kingdom in Sweden. The god FREY is supposed to have built a great temple there shortly after ODIN died. King On ruled there and sacrificed nine of his sons to ODIN in the sacred grove there; King Ingjald the Evil-Worker was fed the wolf's-heart there. Human sacrifice was abolished in Upsal sometime between AD 860 and 1060.

Valhalla [*Norse*] The hall of ODIN, where slain warriors would be received. There the dead men would do battle in tournaments by day; at night they would be feasted, their mead-cups filled by lovely maidens. At the end of the world they would defend ODIN valiantly, if hopelessly, against the brood of LOKI.

Vanaheim [*Norse*] "The country of the Don River people was called Vanaland, or Vanaheim," says Snorri in the *Heimskringla*; "and that river divides the three parts of the world, of which the easternmost part is called Asia and the west Europe." The Vanaheim people had a war with ODIN's folk in **Aasgaard** (Asia) and finally made a truce with them. Snorri claims that the god FREY was from Vanaheim. When King Swegde was seeking ODIN he took a wife from Vanaheim named Vana. The country seems to have been fertile in witches.

Vinland "Vine-Land" or "Wine-Land." North America. The Norse thought of it as a promontory, and I have imagined it as being the Great Northern Peninsula of Newfoundland.

Well of Weird The pool whose water nourishes the roots of sacred **Yggdrasil**. All knowledge comes to him who drinks deep of it. ODIN gave up an eye for one taste of it.

Yggdrasil [*Norse*; literally, "Terror's Horse," because YGG (ODIN) hanged Himself from it] The great World-Tree of myth. It supports the universe. Humankind lives beneath one of its nine roots.

IV
Glossary of Texts

Eddas The meaning of the word "Edda" is conjectural. There are two of these compilations of lore (although the copies contain some different material). They are variously known as Elder and Younger, or Poetic and Prose, or Sæmund's and Snorri's after their collectors. The Snorri of the latter is indeed Snorri Sturlusson, the author of the **Heimskringla**. Aside from some ballads, the Eddas are our main source for Norse mythology.

Flateyjarbók "The Book of Flatey." Vellum compilation of various Norse sagas, histories and myths, written for Jón Finnsson in 1382. See the introductory textual note for further details. (NOTE: The *Flateyjarbók* contains *Grænlendinga Saga* but not *Eirik's Saga*. In this novel I have sometimes pretended that it does, that the *Flateyjarbók* is a sort of celestial Macropedia that contains everything we know about Vinland and the Norse Greenlanders. As it stands, the range of material in the *Flateyjarbók* is impressive enough.)

Heimskringla "The World-Circle." The great history of the Norse Kings written by Snorri Sturlusson in 1235. Not identical in content with the *Flateyjarbók*, although there is a good deal of overlap – as in, for instance, the *Greater Saga of Olaf Trygvesson*, which includes *Grænlendinga Saga*.

Kenning A phrase taken from story and popular allusion to characterize something. Thus, the ocean might be called "swan-field," and a ship could be called "ski of the swan-field." I have used and invented many kennings in *The Ice-Shirt*. R. Harbison calls them "certainly more stimulating to current readers than [to] the first hearers."

Landnámabók The Icelandic Book of Settlements. A chronicle of who colonized which districts of Iceland.

Vinland Sagas This appellation most often refers to *Grænlendinga Saga* and *Eirik's Saga*. The story that they tell, of the attempted colonization of Vinland, is not exactly consistent from text to text. For instance, *Grænlendinga Saga* describes how Freydis murdered Helgi and Finnbogi with all their entourage; *Eirik's Saga* mentions these events not at all, but tells instead how Freydis saved the colony by whacking her breasts with the flat of her sword, thus throwing the attacking Skrælings into terror. I feel somewhat abashed that I have thought to harmonize all these glorious contradictions, but hopefully I missed a few.

V
General Glossary

A-mo! A-mo! [*Greenlandic*]   The cry of the demon AMORTORTAK. The meaning is conjectural.

Anegiuchak [*Alaskan Inuktitut*]   A sunken dwelling of a square shape, sometimes cut in the ice and sometimes in sod.

Angákok; Angágkoq [*Greenlandic*]   Shaman.

Āoobŭlogeâk′ [*Micmac*]   The wind goes down with the sun. (Rand's orthography.)

Appa [*Greenlandic*]   Edible sea-bird (probably guillemot).

Arnap angutinup [*Greenlandic*]   A woman's sex appeal to men. (The all-purpose word is *pilerinartoq*.)

Bonder (sing. **Bonder** or **Bonde**) [*Norse*]   Freeholders of land. In the *Heimskringla*, for instance, Harald Fairhair's concubine Gyda is described as being "brought up as a foster child in the house of a great bonde in Valders." Thorgunna's body was laid out for the night in the house of a bonder in Iceland, there being no inns at the time. In old Norway the bonder were often at odds with their Kings; many of them rose up against King Olaf Trygvesson when he set out to impose Christianity upon the land.

Carle (fem. **Carline**) [*Norse*]   Thrall.

Drumlin   A hill of glacial deposit drift.

Ell [*Norse*]   Unit of measurement. About eighteen inches. (NOTE: Not to be confused with English, Scottish or Flemish ells.)

E'pit [*Micmac*]   Woman. (S.T. Rand: *Abit.*)

Esker   A glacial stream deposit.

Fey [*Norse*]   Subject to supernatural presentiments or precognitions. A fey person might see his own double, as Gudrid did; he might see the future, as Thorbjorg the Prophetess did; most commonly he sensed the approach of his own or another's death.

Frilla [*Norse*]   "Concubine," said the Victorian translators. But a modern scholar says, "Whore."

Galdr [*Norse*]   Singing-witchcraft. It was this that Gudrid would have been taught by her foster-mother Halldis. (Variant: *Guldr.*)

Goi! [*Greenlandic*]   An invocation of an Inuit shaman.

Holm [*Icelandic*]   Island.

Holmgang [*Icelandic*]   A duel to the death, usually fought upon a small island. The combat area was marked off by birch rods.

Hús-freyja [*Norse*]   Housewife.

Inuk [*Greenlandic, Alaskan, Canadian and Soviet Inuktitut*]   The singular of **Inuit** (literally, "the people" – what Eskimos call themselves).

Inukhuit [*Canadian Inuktitut*]   Stone "scarecrows" in the likenesses of men, built to frighten caribou.

Inuktitut [*Inuktitut*]   The language of the Inuit. Greenlandic is a dialect of Inuktitut.

Jarl [*Norse*]   Earl. (The Victorian translations of the *Heimskringla* which call King Hakon "King Hakon Jarl" do so, as do I, to distinguish him from King Hakon the Good before him, but there is no such oxymoron of titles in the original.)

Ji'nm [*Micmac*]   Man. (S.T. Rand: *Cheenum*.)

Kamiks [*Greenlandic*]   "An English adaptation of *Kamik*, the singular for skin-boots (*Kamiit* in plural)." – Nuka Møller.

Kĕskooskwá [*Micmac*]   To creep upon bears. (Only Rand's orthography available.)

Kespi-a'tuksit [*Micmac*]   Here ends this story. (S.T. Rand: *Kĕspĕadooksit*.)

Kestijui'skw [*Micmac*]   Bondmaid. (S.T. Rand: *Kestejooeesqua*.)

Knarr [*Norse*]   Small open boat, in which the Northmen often traveled great distances.

Kŭskimtŭlnàkŭnuhkwŏde [*Micmac*]   To have a hundred feet; to be a centipede (first conjugation). (Only Rand's orthography available.)

Kvedulfr [*Norse*]   "Wolf of evening"; a berserker.

Kwe! [*Micmac*]   "Greetings!" (S.T. Rand: *Kwa!*)

Lmu'ji'jmanaqsi [*Micmac*]   Willow tree. (Literally, "Little Dog Bush": willows are an introduced species anyhow in the Canadian Maritimes; where Rand got this from is a mystery.) (S.T. Rand: *Ŭlŭmoojejŭmânŏkse*.)

Mafshaak [*Canadian Inuktitut*]   A hole in the ice, treacherously concealed by snowdrifts.

Maktāwāākwā [*Micmac*]   Blackness.

Maktokŏkŭnŭmăse [*Micmac*]   To paint something of one's own black.

Medooebook' [*Micmac*]   Hard winter.

Melasól [*Icelandic*]   Variety of Arctic poppy with yellow milksap and yellow flowers.

Mimtŭgopkatpŭsăsik [*Micmac*]   War-Club. (Only Rand's orthography available.)

Mooskōbe [*Micmac*]   Womb. (Only Rand's orthography available.)

Muskunamu'k [*Micmac*]   Blue. Literally, "It is in kind with the sky." (S.T. Rand: *Mooskoonanamóok*.) Micmac is a holophrastic language.★ Hence the next three entries:

★ S.T. Rand points out in his dictionary (p. iv) that "the conjugation of a single Micmac verb would make a large book. It would have to contain about *fifteen thousand* forms."

- **Muskunamu'ksuti** [*Micmac*]   Blueness. (S.T. Rand: *Mooskoonamooksoode.*)
- **Muskunamu'kwesik** [*Micmac*]   Bluish. (S.T. Rand: *Mooskoonamoogwasik.*)
- **Muskunik** [*Micmac*]   Blue cloth. (S.T. Rand: *Mooskoonek.*)

Nanoq [*Greenlandic*]   Polar bear; ice-bear.

Örer [*Norse*]   An eighth-ounce, as in "twelve örers of silver," the minimum customary bride-price at the time when Eirik the Red married Thjodhild.

Pell [*Norse*]   Costly velvet-like lining for garments.

Puisi [*Greenlandic*]   Seal.

Puoin (plur. **Puoninaq**) [*Micmac*]   Witch or warlock; shaman. (A synonym is *Puoini'skq*, which the more phonetic if less fashionable Rand spells *Boooineskwa.*)

Qajaasat [*Greenlandic*]   Medicinal herb known to the Greenland Inuit (*Ledum Groenlandicum*).

Qangattarsa! [*Greenlandic*]   Let us fly up!

Sark; Serk [*Norse*]   Shirt.

Sava [*Greenlandic*]   Sheep.

Seid [*Norse*]   Necromancy.

Skald (also **Scald**) [*Norse*]   A poet. Skalds tended to choose as their subjects contemporary events, the exploits of heroes, etc. In ordinary circumstances they could be counted on to eulogize the Kings to which they were attached. Skalds recited their work at public gatherings. Skaldic verse followed a rigid pattern of stresses, alliteration, etc., and the use of kennings. In the *Heimskringla* Snorri Sturlusson relied on skaldic verse as sources for his history of the Norse Kings. He wrote well in the skaldic manner himself, as exemplified in the *Prose Edda*.

Skóbrodar [*Norse*]   Spikes fastened to the shoe-soles for travel on ice.

Stefánssol [*Icelandic*]   Variety of Arctic poppy with white milksap and white or pinkish flowers.

Steindórssól [*Icelandic*]   Variety of Arctic poppy with white milksap and yellow flowers.

Tegebook' [*Micmac*]   Cold winter.

Thing [*Icelandic*]   Civil meeting in Iceland, when proclamations were heard and men brought suit. In the tenth century, the Thing (or Althing, as it was also known) convened on the tenth Thor's Day of summer.

Tuckamore [*Newfoundlandic*]   Stunted, wind-twisted tree.

Tuttu [*Greenlandic*]   Reindeer.

Ŭlněgŭn [*Micmac*]   Blue broadcloth. (Post-Contact, of course.)

Ulu; Ulo [*Greenlandic, Inuktitut*]   Woman's slate knife.

Unaak [*Alaskan Inuktitut*]   A long spiked pole used for testing the thickness of the ice.

Weapontake [*Norse*]   In the annual **Thing** of medieval Iceland, when lawsuits were decided, weapons were prohibited until the assembly dispersed, which time was thus called *weapontake*.

Wŏbálŭse [*Micmac*]   To whiten oneself.

A Chronology of the
First Age of Vinland

Note

Many of the earlier dates in this Chronology are so provisional as to be only slightly better than useless. In particular, the reigns of the Norse Kings seem to have worm-holes in their significant digits. The Icelanders recorded them differently in their Annals than the Danes or the Norwegians, for they added an intercalary week to their calendar. Many of the dates in the *Heimskringla* are speculative; still more so are the dates proposed by archeologists. Various scholarly works on the Vikings written in the past hundred years often clash about dates; so I have interpolated here as best as I could, always devoutly hoping to provide you with knowledge adequate to the demands of any cocktail party.

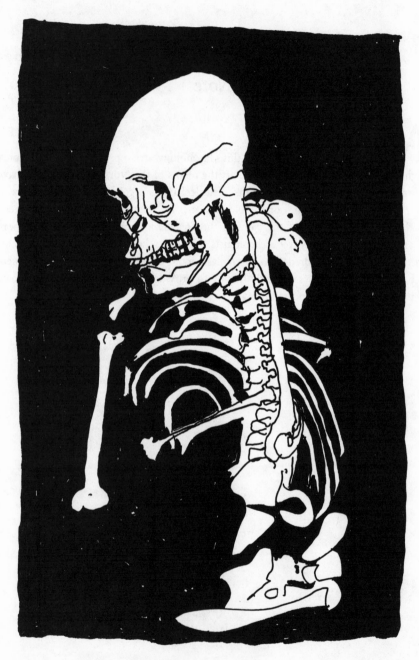

SKELETON OF A WOMAN
FROM AN ANCIENT ICELANDIC GRAVE

The Age of the Ice-Shirt

??	Elder Brother and Younger Brother begin the Inuit race.	
??	The Sun and the Moon go into the sky.	
30,000 BC		Siberian hunters cross the Bering Strait land-bridge to the northern Yukon.
??	KLUSKAP helps the Micmac in Vinland.	
??10,000 BC		Bering Strait land-bridge submerged.
?2000 BC		Arctic Small Tool culture present in Alaska, Canada, Greenland.
?2000 BC		Independence I culture present in northern Greenland, Ellesmere Island, Devon Island, Cornwallis Island. "The overwhelming picture," writes an anthropologist, "is one of meagreness . . ."
?	ODIN leaves Aasgard (Asia?) and leads the gods to settle in Scandinavia.	
?1700 BC		Pre-Dorset culture present in Low Arctic.
??	Demon AMORTORTAK invoked by north Greenland Inuit.	
?1000–?500 BC		Independence II culture supplants Independence I.
?500 BC–AD 1000		Dorset culture dominates the Arctic.

?150	FREY begins the Yngling Dynasty.
?200	King Swegde, grandson of FREY and ruler of Sweden, seeks ODIN; tricked into entering enchanted rock.
?300	King Dag the Wise, who speaks the language of birds, dies in battle over a sparrow.
?400	Kings Alric and Eric kill each other with their bridles.
?500	King On prolongs his life by sacrificing nine of his sons to ODIN.
?650	King Ingjald eats a roasted wolf's heart and becomes wicked. End of the Yngling Dynasty.

?775		Irish anchorites begin living in the Faroe Islands.
793		First accurately dated Viking raid on Lindisfarne.
795		Vikings raid the Hebrides.
?800		Vikings conquer the Faroes.
?820	King Halfdan the Black takes his dead father's kingdom in Agder.	
?835–96		Viking raids on England.
845		Vikings plunder Hamburg, conquer Paris.
?850	King Harald Fairhair born.	
??		The Viking Naddour sights Iceland.
?860	Harald befriends a Lapp and succeeds Halfdan.	
?874		Ingolf settles Iceland.
?890	Harald crushes his last enemies in the Battle of Hafrsfjord and becomes supreme in Norway.	
?900		Ulf Crow's son Gunnbjorn sights the skerries off east Greenland.

?900–?1200		Thule Inuit migrate east from Alaska, eventually reaching Greenland. ("To the archeologist, spending his nights alone on the gravel floor of a windblown tent, the excavation of a Thule winter house is an exercise in envy.")
?900	Harald marries a Lappish witch, Snæfrid; believes her living for three years after her death.	
?910	Harald's favorite son, Eric Bloody-Axe comes of age at twelve and marries the Lappish witch Gunhild.	
?915		Aud the Deep-Minded settles in Iceland; gives land to her ex-slave Vifil.
??	Thorbjorn Vifilsson born in Iceland.	
?930	Harald dies. Succeeded by Eric Bloody-Axe.	Althing begun in Iceland.
		All good farmland claimed in Iceland.
930–1030		Saga Age in Iceland.
?934	Hakon the Good expells Eric and Gunhild from Norway. They emigrate to England to rule under King Athelstan.	
939	Athelstan dies. Eric no longer welcome in England.	
?945	Eirik the Red born in Jæderen, Norway.	
?954	Eric slain in Northumberland. Gunhild escapes to Denmark with her sons.	
?960		Denmark becomes a Christian country.

?961	Eric's sons kill King Hakon the Good. The eldest, King Harald Greyskin, takes the throne of Norway.	
?963	Eirik the Red is outlawed and sails to Iceland.	
??	Gudrid Thorbjornsdottir born in Iceland.	
?965		In Norway, King Harald Greyskin is slain in a sea battle with Gold Harald. Succeeded by Hakon Jarl the Great.
?970	Eirik the Red marries Thjodhild Jorundsdottir; moves from Drangar to Haukadale.	
?975		Terrible famine in Iceland, in which people eat ravens and foxes and kill the old.
??	Leif, Thorstein and Thorvald born to Eirik and Thjodhild.	
?978	Eirik is outlawed from Haukadale.	
??	Gudrid marries Thorir.	
?980	Eirik's bastard daughter Freydis born.	
?981	Eirik is outlawed from all Iceland for three years.	
?981–3	Eirik explores Greenland.	
?985	Eirik settles Greenland. East Bygd established.	
?986	Bjarni Herjolfsson sights Vinland.	
?995	West Bygd established.	In Norway, King Olaf Trygvesson succeeds King Hakon Jarl the Great.
?997		King Olaf sends Thangbrand the missionary to Iceland.

?999	Leif Eiriksson seduces Thorgunna the witch in the Hebrides.	
??	Freydis Eiriksdottir marries Thorvard of Gardar.	
1000	Thorgunna sails to Frodis-Water in Iceland and dies. Her ghost haunts the country.	Iceland becomes a Christian country. Greenland becomes a Christian country.
	Leif discovers Vinland, rescues Gudrid and Thorir from a shipwreck.	King Eirik Jarl succeeds King Olaf by the royal expedient of killing him.
?1002–3	Thorvald explores Vinland and dies in battle with Micmac Indians.	
?1004	Gudrid marries Thorstein.	
?1005	Thorstein dies.	
?1006	Gudrid marries the Icelander Thorfinn Karlsefni.	
??	Eirik the Red dies.	
?1007	Gudrid and Freydis sail to Vinland with their husbands and followers. Accompanying Freydis are the Icelandic brothers, Helgi and Finnbogi.	
?1008	Battles between the settlers and Micmac Indians.	
?1009	Freydis murders the brothers.	
?1010	Afraid of Indians, the settlers return to Greenland. Death of Bjarni Grimolfsson in the Greenland Sea.	
?1014		In Ireland, 7,000 Vikings slain at battle of Clontarf.
?1015–30		In Norway, King Olaf the Saint succeeds King Eirik Jarl.
1032		Icelanders pass a law mandating banishment for witchcraft.

??	In Greenland, Inuit boy, Angangujungoaq, kidnapped by blond, blue-eyed giants.	
1060		In Sweden, sacrificial hanging abolished at Grove of Uppsala. (Some sources date this 200 years earlier.)
?1100		Sweden becomes a Christian country.
		Landnamabók (Book of Settlements) written in Iceland.
?1127		Islendingabók (Book of Icelanders) written in Iceland.
?1178	Snorri Sturlusson born.	
?1190	Grænlendinga Saga written.	
?1200	Commencement of Little Ice Age. Climate in Greenland begins to deteriorate.	
1235	Snorri completes the Heimskringla.	
1241	Snorri murdered by agents of the Norwegian King Hakon.	
?1260	Eirik's Saga written.	
1261		Norway annexes Greenland.
1262		Norway annexes Iceland.
1286		Norway cedes Hebrides and Isle of Man to Scotland.
1345	In Greenland, Inuit destroy the West Bygd.	
1347		Last recorded visit of Greenlanders to Markland.
1380		Iceland falls under Danish rule.
1382–95	Flateyjarbók codex written for Jón Finsson in Flatey, Iceland.	
1385	Bjorn the Crusader (Bjarni Einarsson) saves two Greenland Inuit children from drowning on a skerry; when he sails for Iceland without them, they kill themselves.	

1389	Inuit attack the East Bygd, killing eighteen and enslaving two.	
1400		Nicolò Zeno visits the monasteries of Greenland, reports the Norsemen firmly in control.
1410	Last ship from Greenland to Iceland.	
1468–9		Norway mortgages Orkneys, Shetlands to Scotland.
1492		Columbus discovers Vinland.
?1500	The Norse are now extinct in Greenland.	
?1540		Jon the Greenlander, a whaler, discovers the frozen corpse of a Norseman in Greenland.
1576		First voyage of Martin Frobisher to the Arctic.
1577		On his second voyage, Frobisher visits the Greenland Inuit.
1587		John Davis sails to the Arctic in hopes of finding a Northwest Passage.
?1600		Modern Inuit culture present in the Arctic.
1605		Captain Gotske Lindenau begins kidnapping Inuit.
1615		William Baffin searches for a Northwest Passage.
1721		The Danish missionary Hans Egede sets sail for Greenland to convert the Norsemen. Finding none, he turns to the Inuit instead. AMORTORTAK's influence begins to wane.
1801		Althing abolished in Iceland.

1894		Rev. Silas T. Rand's compilation of Micmac legends published. Rand reports that knowledge of KLUSKAP has almost died out.
1944	Danish report published of a woman's skeleton found beneath the ruins of a cathedral in Gardar, Greenland.	Iceland seizes independence from Denmark.
1960		Dr. Helge Ingstadt discovers Viking ruins at L'Anse-aux-Meadows, Newfoundland.
1977		Greenland gains home rule.
1984	Seth Pilsk the Thin explores Baffin Island.	
1987	William the Blind explores Iceland, Greenland and Baffin Island.	

Sources

And a few notes

Note

I t may be of interest to the reader to know what use I have made of my sources. My aim in *Seven Dreams* has been to create a "Symbolic History" – that is to say, an account of origins and metamorphoses which is often untrue based on the literal facts as we know them, but whose untruths further a deeper sense of truth. – Did the Norsemen, for instance, really come to the New World bearing ice in their hearts? – Well, of course they did not. But if we look upon the Vinland episode as a precursor of the infamies there, of course they did. In this Dream I have done several things which, narrowly speaking, are unjustified – which is to say that I consider them perfectly in order. To begin with, I have conflated the accounts of the Vinland voyages in the *Tale of the Greenlanders* and *Eirik's Saga*. There are many contradictions in these two sources, so many as to baffle the most ingenious interpreters. My conflation is no more satisfactory than the rest, from a literal standpoint. – Too bad. – Secondly, having been born in an age of continental drift, I have played tricks with the location of Vinland. The sagas say that Vinland had no frost, but there is frost there now; so for my fabulous Vinland Paradise-that-was I selected Nova Scotia; for my corrupted present-day Vinland I used the Great Northern Peninsula of Newfoundland. In fact, given the number of voyages, and the vagueness of the accounts, it is perfectly possible that both of these places *were* Vinland. – For similar reasons, in describing the Greenland that Freydis saw I used the harsh region of Auyuttuq, in Baffin Island (Slab-Land); while the Greenland of the Skrælings, the real Greenlanders, was always Greenland. Landscapes are as we see them, and what was hell for the Norsemen was a happy heaven-haven for the Skrælings. Here one walks the proverbial tightrope, on one side of which lies slavish literalism; on the other, self-indulgence. Given these dangers, it seemed wise to have this source list, so as to provide those who desire with easy means of corroborating or refuting my imagined versions of things, to monitor my originality, and to give leads to primary sources and other useful texts for interested non-specialists such as myself. I have tried to do this as fully as seemed practical. For two explanatory cases of my method, see the extended notes under "Wearing the Bear-Shirt", pages 390–91 below. – All quotations, excerpts and epigraphs in the text, by the way, are genuine.

The Ice-Shirt

ICE-TEXT: *THE BOOK OF FLATEY*

page 7 For equation of AMORTORTAK with Gunnbjorn's Peak, see Bernardine Bailey, *Greenland in Pictures* (New York: Sterling Publishing Co., Oak Tree Press, 1973), p. 2; and with Ingolfsfjeld, Magnus Magnusson and Hermann Pálsson, introduction to *The Vinland Sagas* (New York: Penguin Books, 1965), p. 17.

page 7 ". . . those to whom truth is more important than beauty" – As Paul B. Du Chaillu remarks, "The spade has developed the history of Scandinavia" (*The Viking Age* [New York: Scribner, 1889], p. 2).

page 9 For names of Icelandic flowers, see Askell Löve, *Flora of Iceland* (Reykjavík: Almenna Bokafelagid, 1983), pp. 206–7, 194, 158, 198.

THE ICE-SHIRT

page 14 Professor of Maps epigraph – R.A. Skelton, Thomas E. Marston and George D. Painter, *The Vinland Map and the Tartar Relation* (New Haven: Yale, 1965), p. 171.

page 14 Wainwright Eskimo epigraph – Richard K. Nelson, *Hunters of the Northern Ice* (Chicago: The University of Chicago Press, 1969), p. 129.

WEARING THE BEAR-SHIRT

page 17 Greenland epigraph – Jan Welzl, *The Quest for Polar Treasures*, trans. M. and R. Weatherall (London: Allen & Unwin, 1933), p. 269.

page 17 Thord Kolbeinsson – Snorri Sturlusson, *Heimskringla*, Part One: *The Olaf Sagas*, vol. 1, trans. Samuel Laing (1844), rev. Jacqueline Simpson, MA (London: Dent, Everyman, 1964), 1.XXIII.

page 18 King Dag – Snorri Sturlusson, *Heimskringla*, Part Two: *Sagas of the Norse Kings*, trans. Samuel Laing (1844), rev. Peter Foote, MA (London: Dent, Everyman, 1975), 1.XXI, pp. 19–20.

page 19 Alric and Eric – ibid., 1.XXIII, pp. 21–2.

page 19 King On – ibid., 1.XXIX, pp. 25–6. In some translations, King On becomes King Aun.

page 22 King Ingjald the Evil-Worker – ibid., 1.XXXVII–XLIV, pp. 31–7.

page 22　In my account of these events I have been relatively conservative and literal. In the *Heimskringla* appear a few lines about the war-games between Ingjald and Alf:

> One year there was a great assembly of people at Upsal, and King Yngvar had also come there with his sons. Alf, King Yngvar's son, and Ingjald, King Onund's son, were there – both about six years old. They amused themselves with child's play, in which each should be leading on his army. In their play Ingjald found himself not as strong as Alf, and was so vexed that he almost cried. His foster-brother Gautvid came up, led him to his foster-father Svipdag the Blind, and told him how ill it appeared that he was weaker and less manly than Alf, King Yngvar's son. Svipdag replied that it was a great shame. The day after Svipdag took the heart of a wolf, roasted it on a stick, and gave it to the king's son Ingjald to eat, and from that time he became a most ferocious person, and of the worst disposition.

This of course is the foundation for the whole story, upon which I have built. The suggestion that Ingjald's father despises him, the hunting of the wolf's heart by Gautvid, and Ingjald's ravishment of his bride are all "interpolated," the first and last because they make emotional sense and the other to color the story. The burning of the Kings in Upsal and the alliance between King Granmar and King Hjorvard-Viking are described in the *Heimskringla* in much more detail than I have given (but, as always with these old sources, *sans* any detailed exposition of feeling and motive; and I have of course manufactured as many details as I omitted). The *Heimskringla* mentions that Gautvid and Svipdag the Blind were killed in Ingjald's war on those Kings; I have used that bare fact to construct the scene of their end, with Ingjald's abandonment of them, and their own last words. There is no assessment of either of their characters in the *Heimskringla*, but it seems to me that I have taken no impermissible liberties here, since we do know that Svipdag gave Ingjald the wolf's heart, and he thus takes on a pimpish character; as for Gautvid, once I made the decision to send him off to get the wolf's heart, he became brave, and had to end bravely. Of Ingjald's daughter Aasa the *Heimskringla* says only that "she was like her father in disposition," but her return to her father after murdering her husband, and her resolution with her father to die in flames, made it clear to me that the relationship was claustrophobically abnormal; hence my "interpolation" of the incest, and of the indestructible wolf's hearts beating in the coals.

page 29　King Halfdan the Black – ibid., 2.V–IX, pp. 46–50.

page 29　King Harald Fairhair – ibid., 2.VII–VIII, pp. 48–9; 3.I–XLV, pp. 51–82.

page 30　My life of King Harald Fairhair is based on the little we know from the *Heimskringla*. Almost nothing is given about his early life. The whole idea of the Bear-Shirt (and, for that matter, the Blue-Shirt, the Ice-Shirt, etc.) is an imagined one. The point of Harald is that he was a unifier and consolidator; therefore, if the wars of petty chieftains prior to his reign can be represented as bear-wars, Harald's war, and therefore his character, must be represented as something else, something that brings the bears to an end. Most likely such a person, not being a bear, would feel inadequate in a world of bears. Hence the bad feeling between Harald and his father (and in fact Snorri says that "he was much beloved by his mother, but less so by his father"); hence, therefore, the father's decision to hide the Bear-Shirt, and Harald's fruitless search for it in later life (with the suggestions of impotence); hence also Harald's dream of the bears as a boy (and by using that device I can also introduce other real bear-Kings). As for the disappearing Yule-feast, that, and young Harald's flight with the Lapp, are mentioned in the *Heimskringla*, but the journey itself, the magician's tricks, Lapland and the reappearance of the feast are all "interpolated." That Gyda refuses to be Harald's concubine until he conquers Norway is given in the original; her reason, that she suspects him of being emasculate, un-beared, is a logical supposition based on the Bear-Shirt mythology I have constructed. The tale of Herlaug and Rollaug is expanded and more prettily told than the original, but in essence it differs from it very little. I have made the Flight of the Earls into a single apocryphal incident, when actually, of course, it was a number of episodes over a long period of emigration. It was already stylized in the *Heimskringla*, and many other accounts of individual settlements are given in various sagas listed below. The death-scene of King Harald is once again totally invented as was required to put paid to my era of the Bear-Shirt.

page 33   Lapland – From various nineteenth-century memoirs of travel.

page 37   King Herlaug and King Rollaug – *Heimskringla*, Part Two: *Sagas of the Norse Kings*, 3.VIII, p. 55.

page 39   For more details on the settlement of the islands, see *Orkneyingja Saga*, *Færeyingja Saga*, the beginning of *Laxdæla Saga*, and *Landnamabók*. In his book *Ancient Emigrants: A History of the Norse Settlement of Scotland* (Oxford: Clarendon Press, 1929), A.W. Brøgger writes (pp. 5–6): "The Norwegian emigration to the Shetlands, Orkneys, and Hebrides covered, broadly speaking, two generations, between 780 and 850, when the great period of early settlements [in Norway] to all intents and purposes ended. During the same period an important contingent also crossed to Man and Ireland. This first wave . . . was quickly followed by another, to the Faroes and Iceland. This period fell in the reign of King Harald the Fairhaired, between the years 870 and 930."

page 41   "Then King Harald sailed southwards . . ." – *Sagas of the Norse Kings*, 3.XXII, p. 66.

page 44   There is, of course, nothing to suggest that the real King Harald became a resigned or impotent King once he had achieved his end. I have felt free to change his character to suit me.

page 45   Eric Bloody-Axe and the witch Gunhild – *Sagas of the Norse Kings*, 3.XXXIV, pp. 74–5. Gunhild appears in *Njal's Saga* as a nymphomaniac whose jealousy and witchcraft helps bring about the burning alive of Njal and his family.

THE ICE-SHIRT

page 45   Quoted summation of King Eric Bloody-Axe – ibid., 3.XLVI, p. 83.

page 45   Eilif Grisly – Ari the Learned, *The Book of the Settlements of Iceland* (*ca.* 1110?), trans. Rev. T. Ellwood, MA, Rector of Torver (Kendal: T. Wilson, 1898), p. 74.

page 46   "the great Macrobius" – That is to say, Ambrosius Theodosius Macrobius (*fl.* AD 399–422); cf. his *Commentary on the Dream of Scipio.*

page 47   *Speculum Regale* on glacier-breath – *The King's Mirror* [*Speculum Regale*]/ *Konungs Skuggsjá,* trans. Laurence Marcellus Larson (New York: The American-Scandinavian Foundation, 1917), part XX (p. 153). Henceforth, passages from this work will be sourced directly in the text wherever possible, with the part appearing in Roman numerals, followed by a period, followed by the page number in Arabic.

page 48   The Ice-Mountain in the Swedish forest – Actually Mount Shasta, California, in April 1987.

page 49   *Kvaeði af Loga i Vallarahlið* epigraph – Adapted from Jacqueline Simpson, trans., *The Northmen Talk: A Choice of Tales from Iceland* (Madison: University of Wisconsin Press, 1965), p. 277 ("Logi of Vallarahlid").

page 49   The careers of Gunhild and her sons – *Heimskringla*, Part Two: *Sagas of the Norse Kings,* 4.I–V, pp. 84–8; X, pp. 90–91; XX, pp. 98–9; XXII–XXVI, pp. 100–103; XXVIII–XXXII, pp. 104–11; and 5.I–V, pp. 112–17; 6.I–XIII, pp. 118–26. I have tampered slightly with the facts as Snorri presents them.

page 51   Eirik the Red, his family, supporters and descendants – *Grænlendinga Saga* (*ca.* 1190) and *Eirik's Saga* (*ca.* 1260). Generally I have preferred the versions in Magnus Magnusson and Hermann Pálsson, trans., *The Vinland Sagas* (New York: Penguin Books, 1965). *Grænlendinga Saga* also appears in the *Heimskringla*, Part One, vol. 1, sec. 3, as *The Tale of the Greenlanders* (pp. 100–116).

page 56   The Vinland Sagas say only that Eirik and his father were outlawed "because of some killings."

page 56   Footnote on the advent of King Olaf Trygvesson – Before Olaf came King Hakon Jarl, but he plays little role in this story.

page 56   Eyvind Kellda's death – *Heimskringla*, Part One: *Olaf Sagas,* LXX (pp. 59–60).

WEARING THE BLUE SHIRT

page 57   *Heimskringla* epigraph – *Olaf Sagas,* v.i, 3.LXVII.

page 60   Floxi from Sodor, on Snæfellsness – *The Book of the Settlements of Iceland,* pp. 4–5.

page 62   The marriage of Eirik and Thjodhild – Here I must quote another source which sheds light on the customs of the country: "There are no singles bars in Iceland," says an article called "The Visitor's Reykjavík" in the tourist monthly *Around Reykjavík* (8 June–8 July 1987), "but a single man can go everywhere,

and so can unescorted ladies, and they do, mainly in groups of two or three."
One must be in front of the Europa Diskotek at midnight to apprehend it: –
all these blond young men in suits getting out of taxis and going round to the
entrance to stand in the fog and rain, waiting for other Icelanders to leave so
that they could enter (although there were many other things they could have
done, such as ordering a *hamborgarar* on a sesame seed bun, or maybe even an
Eskimóa flipp!), and they stayed and stayed while the music roared and the lights
winked steadily behind the blinds and cars splashed down the streets past the
cubical white buildings in the white fog, and the blond men were silent.

page 68 "The world holds nothing that can be had without a struggle" – Words
of ODIN the High One.

page 73 Epigraph on an axe and blue clothes – *Hrafnkel's Saga and Other Stories*,
trans. Hermann Pálsson (Baltimore: Penguin Books, 1970), p. 42.

page 73 Footnote on blue shirts – Footnote in ibid., p. 25.

page 75 Details on the Thing at Thorsness – William Morris and Eirikr Magnússon,
trans., *The Story of the Ere-Dwellers* (*Eyrbyggja Saga*) (London: Bernard Quaritch,
1892), p. 54.

page 79 Footnote on Thorolf Butter – *The Book of the Settlements of Iceland*, p. 5.
The same source gives an account of how Iceland got its present name: "The bay
so abounded in fish, that by reason of the catch thereof they gave no heed to the
gathering in of hay, so that all the live-stock perished in the winter. The following
spring was rather cold; then Floki went up to the top of a high mountain and
discovered north, beyond the mountain, a firth full of drift-ice; therefore they
called the land 'Iceland,' and so it has been called since then."

page 79 "The Land is wonderfull mountainous" – Edward Pellham, 1631 (see
citation for "Further History of the Greenland Skrælings", page 401 below).

page 81 "no Skrælings then to harry anybody" – Quite likely because the Dorset
culture had died out and the Thule culture had not arrived on the scene (see
Chronology). However, even then the Norse had discovered native artifacts. Cf.
Ari the Learned, *Islendingabók* (*The Book of the Icelanders*), vol. 1, trans. Halldór
Hermannsson (Ithaca, New York: Cornell University Library, 1930), p. 65.

page 82 Narrative of Ivar Bardsson – Bound with the Zeno ms. (cf. epigraph
for *Seven Dreams*) in a facing translation entitled *The Voyages of the Venetian
Brothers . . .*, trans. Richard Henry Major, FSA (London: Printed for the Hakluyt
Society, MDCCCLXXIII). The report of silver mines and white bears and the
sailing directions also come from the Bardsson ms.

page 82 Extinction of the Norsemen in Greenland – It is important to realize here
that no one is sure exactly what happened. Many sources insist that the Thule
Inuit had nothing to do with it, although their reasonings are as specious as those
of the dogmatists on the other side. See, for instance, Martina Magenau Jacobs
and James B. Richardson III, editors, *Arctic Life: Challenge to Survive* (Pittsburgh:
The Board of Trustees, Carnegie Institute, 1983), pp. 86–91.

THE HERMAPHRODITE

page 85   This chapter was inspired by a Nunivak Eskimo tale which appears as
"The Origin of Nunivak Island" in John Bierhorst, ed., *The Red Swan: Myths
and Tales of the American Indians* (New York: Farrar, Straus and Giroux, 1976).
According to Bierhorst, the tale was collected by Edward S. Curtis in his *The
North American Indian* (1907–30), vol. 20. The Spirit Woman gives birth at the
end to dogs or wolves, who give birth to humans.

page 87ff.   Various seal-hunting and ice-walking techniques – Richard K. Nelson,
Hunters of the Northern Ice (Chicago: University of Chicago Press, 1969).

page 90   The woman leaping and flying – Actually, a rehearsal at the San Francisco
Ballet as choreographed by Mr. Alan Scofield (1987).

page 93   Spring and summer – Greenland and Baffin Island, spring–summer 1987.

page 100   Dr. Bruce disturbing the ivory gulls – From R. N. Rudnose Brown, DSc,
*A Naturalist at the Poles: The Life, Work and Voyages of Dr. W.S. Bruce, the Polar
Explorer* (London: Seeley, Service & Co., 1923), p. 74.

BROTHERS AND SISTERS

page 102   Epigraph – Anthony Fiala, *Fighting the Polar Ice* (New York: Doubleday,
1906), p. 294.

THE MOON AND THE SUN

page 107   This chapter is based on a quarter-page account of an eastern Greenland
Eskimo myth in M. Vahl *et al.*, ed., *Greenland*, vol. ii (Copenhagen: A Reitzell,
1928). Boas gives a very similar Baffin Island tradition in his book *The Central
Eskimo* (1888), repr. Bison Books (Lincoln, Nebraska, 1964), pp. 189–90. A shorter
version still (provenance: Tuglik, Igloolik area, 1922) appears in Robert McGhee,
Canadian Arctic Prehistory (New York: Van Nostrand Reinhold Co. / National
Museum of Man, National Museums of Canada, 1978), p. 1.

page 107   Justina epigraph – *Rockwell Kent's Greenland Journal* (New York: Ivan
Obolensky, 1962), entry for the Saturday before Christmas, 1931.

page 107   Spoiled Eskimo girls epigraph – Martin Lindsay (Royal Scots Fusiliers),
Those Greenland Days (London: Blackwood, 1932), p. 117.

page 109   Hinton footnote – C. Howard Hinton, MA, *The Fourth Dimension* (London:
Swan Sonnenschein & Co., 1906), p. 74. I have been told, rightly or wrongly I do
not know, that this book has driven several mathematicians mad.

WEARING THE WHITE-SHIRT

page 112   The tale of Bjorn the Crusader and the Skræling children is mentioned
in Vahl and elsewhere, but I have not been able to find the original source.

DRESSMAKERS' PATTERNS

page 128   Welzl epigraph – *The Quest for Polar Treasures*, p. 243.

GUDRID THE FAIR

page 131   Gudrun (wife of Orm Lyrgia), called the Lunde-Sun – *The Olaf Sagas*, vol. 1, 1.LIII (p. 47).
page 136   Gudrid and the Prophetess – *Eirik's Saga*, pp. 81–3. All citations of this saga refer to the translation given in Magnusson and Pálsson's *The Vinland Sagas* (listed above).
page 138   There were two kinds of witchcraft known to the Norse: *Guldr*, or singing-sorcery such as Thorbjorg the Prophetess practices, and *Seid*, or necromancy, taught by the goddess FREYJA. Almost nothing is now known of either.
page 143   Thorgunna and Leif – *Eirik's Saga*, pp. 84–5. No description of Thorgunna is given here, but in the *Erbyggja Saga* a vivid picture is drawn of her in later life. It is there that her weird death and its aftermath are recorded. I have drawn the young Thorgunna from a redhead of my acquaintance; the old Thorgunna is modeled after a redheaded corpse at the hospital.

THE LAND OF THE COUNTERFEITERS

page 153   Skelton–Marston–Painter epigraph – *The Vinland Map and the Tartar Relation*, p. 197.
page 157   Grimhild and Thorstein as zombies – "Some authors have concluded that the macabre description of the deaths of Thorstein and Sigrid [Grimhild is called Sigrid in *Eirik's Saga*] are the results of the vivid and superstition-ridden imaginations of the saga writers; but this is probably not the case," says Farley Mowat in his book *Westviking: The Ancient Norse in Greenland and North America* (Toronto: McClelland and Stewart, 1965), pp. 176–7. "There are a number of diseases which could have produced the effects recorded in the saga. Epidemic cerebro-spinal meningitis and typhus fever are two of them. Victims of both these diseases have been known to sink into a penultimate coma, which, to any observer except a trained physician, seems like death . . . Whatever the disease may have been, that long dark winter in Lysufjord when people sickened and died in the cold, crowded and filthy sod-walled houses must have represented an eternity in hell to Gudrid and to the rest who survived it."

FREYDIS EIRIKSDAUGHTER

page 162   Epigraph – Edward Pellham, 1631 (see citation for "Further History of the Greenland Skrælings", page 401 below).

page 162   Effects of the wolf's heart – *Heimskringla*, Part Two, pp. 32–3. (Already cited for Ingjald the Evil-Worker.)

page 166   King Swegde and the dwarf – ibid., 1.xv, p. 16.

page 166   Freydis and the Skrælings – It is actually unlikely that Freydis would have seen any Inuit, since even as late as the mid-thirteenth century the Greenland priest Halldór thought it news to write to the priest Arnold that some trees had been found cut with small axes, presumably by Skrælings.

page 166   Dwarfish Norsemen – Vahl *et al.*, p. 414.

page 169   Day-Spring in Jötunheim epigraph – Adapted from "Fjölsvinnsmál" in *The Elder or Poetic Edda, Commonly Known as Sæmund's Edda*, Part I: *The Mythological Poems*, trans. Olive Bray (London: Viking Club Translation Series, vol. ii, 1908), p. 163. (NOTE: As I use several translations of the Edda, the translator of each version is always indicated in these Source Notes [e.g., Bray, *The Elder or Poetic Edda*]. Some phrases in this section are indebted to the *Speculum Regale*.)

page 184   Blue-Shirt's fortifications – Partially inspired by a description of medieval defenses in the *Speculum Regale*.

page 185   Words of ODIN the High One – Adapted from "Hávamál" in Bray, *The Elder or Poetic Edda*, p. 61.

page 188   Lindsay epigraph – p. 129.

SHIPS AND COFFINS

page 189   Butler epigraph – Samuel Butler, *Erewhon* (1872) (New York: Lancer/ Magnum, 1968), pp. 260–1.

page 189   Welzl epigraph – op. cit., p. 51.

page 189   King Harald Fairhair and Snæfrid – *Heimskringla*, Part Two, 3.xxv, pp. 69–70.

page 195   Story of Queen Sigrid the Haughty – Appears in various places in the Saga of King Olaf Trygvesson.

THE VOYAGE TO VINLAND

page 206   An excellent reference on the plants of Baffin Island is A. E. Porsild, *Illustrated Flora of the Canadian Arctic Archipelago*, 2nd ed. (1964).

page 213   The description of the country is based on a journey through western Newfoundland, from Port-au-Basques in the south to L'Anse-aux-Meadows at the tip of the Great Northern Peninsula.

WINELAND THE GOOD

page 215   The description of the country here is based on a journey through southern Nova Scotia. The more dismal northerly descriptions of Vinland were written in the Cape Breton Highlands. Freydis's visit to the Person KLUSKAP took place near Cape Split.

page 216   Joyful trees – *Speculum Regale*, V.90.

page 219   ODIN footnote – Bray, *Poetic Edda*, p. 73.

page 221   King Olaf Trygvesson's skill at diving – *Laxdœla Saga* (*ca.* 1245), trans. Magnus Magnusson and Hermann Pálsson (Baltimore: Penguin, 1969), ch. 40 (pp. 144–5).

page 222   The longest dive of King Olaf Trygvesson – *Heimskringla*, Part One: *Olaf Sagas*, vol. 1, 1.CXIX–CXXII (pp. 95–8).

WEARING THE ICE-SHIRT

page 226   Tears of Killer-Glum – *The Saga of Viga Glum*, trans. Alan Boucher (Reykjavík: Icelandic Review Saga Series, 1986), p. 34.

page 227   Vinland treescape – Muir Woods, on Mount Tamalpais, California, 1981–8.

page 229   AM 73846 *'Okunnur listamathur* – Arni Magnusson Institute, Reykjavík.

SKINS FOR MILK

page 232   Alternative identification of the Skrælings – Mowat suggests (op. cit., Appendix H, pp. 372–83: "The Vanished Dorsets") that at least some of the Skrælings might well have been not Micmac or Beothuk, but Dorset Eskimos, in which case the Norse identification of Greenland Skrælings with Vinland Skrælings would have been highly justifiable. Because there is also evidence on the other side, I have preferred to imagine that the two kinds of Skrælings were very different, that the main point they held in common was the Norsemen's sweeping inclusion of them into a single inferior race.

page 243   Micmac words – Rev. Silas Tertius Rand, DD, DCL, LLD, *Dictionary of the Language of the Micmac Indians, who reside in Nova Scotia, New Brunswick, Prince Edward Island, Cape Breton and Newfoundland* (Halifax: Nova Scotia Printing Co., 1888). Rand was a missionary among the Micmac, and did a great deal to preserve their stories and language. This *Dictionary* is only the smaller, English–Micmac portion of the record; Rand notes sadly, but without surprise, that the government refused to pay for the printing of the Micmac–English part. – The Reverend was an admirable man, for he wrote (p. iii): "A dictionary is defective which omits a single word."

page 243   Footnote on the word "Micmac" – Ruth Holmes Whitehead and Harold McGee, *The Micmac: How Their Ancestors Lived Five Hundred Years Ago* (Halifax: Nimbus Publishing Ltd., 1983), p. 1. I have also made use of this book (p. 7) in my discussion of Plant Persons, in this section and the next.

page 243   The *Jenuaq* – It is interesting to learn that (in Rand, at least) these demons were supposed to kill with their terrible voices. But Ruth Holmes Whitehead, Assistant Curator in History at the Nova Scotia Museum, says that the word *Jenu* "does NOT mean 'Northern Devil, Demon or men.' A *Jenu* is a human who has been transformed (probably by fat deprivation in winter). These people become psychotic and kill and eat other humans. They can be cured by drinking fat and being thawed out" (letter to the author, 29 March 1988). The resemblance to berserkers is interesting.

page 245   Footnote on the tallness of the Beothuk – Mowat, op. cit., p. 460.

page 245   Power (and Micmac metaphysical culture generally) – An informative and most prettily written essay is Ruth Holmes Whitehead's "I Have Lived Here Since the World Began: Atlantic Coast Artistic Traditions" in comp., *The Spirit Sings: Artistic Traditions of Canada's First Peoples* (Toronto: McClelland and Stewart / Glenbow Museum, 1987).

page 245   Dreaming of Bad Days on the derivation of Porcupine People – Actually the Micmac were called Porcupine People because of their skilled quillwork with porcupine.

page 245   Panthers – though so-called in many sources, were probably cougars.

page 247   Freydis and the moose nose – "Give her a moose's nose," advised Whitehead (letter to the author, 15 April 1988): "This is a great delicacy, and would be 'a delicate mark of respect to the late crone,' to quote Marie Conway Demler, the famous S.C. novelist."

page 249   The other Gudrid – "The woman who came to the door of Gudrid's hut was said to have had large, light-colored eyes and chestnut-colored hair, and to have worn something which resembled a black Norse kirtle," says Mowat (op. cit., pp. 459–60). ". . . The only authentic portraits of Beothuk Indians which we possess are of two women, Mary March (Demasduit) and Shanawdithit, who were captured and brought to St. John's in the early part of the nineteenth century. By far the most salient feature of both women according to their portraits, which were drawn from life, is their remarkably large, wide eyes . . . As for the chestnut-colored hair, it was normal practice for the Beothuks to dress their hair with powdered red ochre mixed with fat . . . The kirtle is also indicative of Beothuks." But Whitehead says categorically: "She is NOT a native american of any sort. She is a Norse "fetch," a doppelganger . . . There are not two Beothuk portraits. There is only the one miniature on ivory of Demasduwit, painted by Lady Hamilton, which was the basis for all other copies . . . Ingeborg Marshall has done some great detective work to show this is the case . . . The kirtle is NOT indicative of the Beothuk . . . And half the world's population has large eyes" (letter to the author, 9 March 1988). So, as so often, I have felt free to do as I pleased.

AMORTORTAK AND KLUSKAP

page 255   Butler epigraph – op. cit., ch. 25 (p. 287).

page 257   In describing Micmac clothing, birchbark work, woodwork and quillwork, I have made use of Whitehead's *Elitekey: Micmac Material Culture from 1600 AD to the Present* (Halifax: The Nova Scotia Museum, 1980).

page 259   Landscape seen by the travelers – Memories of New Hampshire around Lake Winnipesauke, 1967–73.

page 260   "The Four Wishes" is based on a Micmac tale (originally collected by Rand) appearing in Ella Elizabeth Clark, *Indian Legends of Canada* (Toronto: McClelland & Stewart Ltd., 1960), pp. 34–6, "Glooscap and his four visitors." I have conflated this tale with the tale of KLUSKAP, KEWKW and COOLPUJOT (Rand, pp. 232–7).

page 262   Dragons seen by the travelers – Actually *jipijka'maq*, or horned serpents.

GIANTS AND TREES

page 278   Vala epigraph – "Völuspa" in Bray, *The Elder or Poetic Edda*, pp. 277–9.

page 279   Karlsefni's plan – *Grænlendinga Saga*, ch. 7 (p. 66).

page 280   The two songs of Yggdrasil – Based on "Voluspá," stanza 19 in Lee M. Hollander, trans., *The Poetic Edda*, 2nd ed., rev. (Austin: University of Texas Press, 1962), p. 4. Gudrid's song is nearest Hollander's translation.

page 282   The trees that rose into the clouds – Redwoods near Gualalla, California.

page 283   The road to HEL – cf. Hilda Roderick Ellis, *The Road to Hel: A Study of the Conception of the Dead in Old Norse Literature* (Cambridge, 1943).

page 286   The dead ODIN – For Snorri the gods were gods because they were the founders of Sweden. Near the beginning of the *Heimskringla* he says (*Sagas of the Norse Kings*, p. 14): "In his time all the gods died, and blood-sacrifices were made for them."

page 286   The song of Elf Candle – Adapted from the Lay of Vafthrudnir (*ca.* 1200), in Paul B. Taylor and W.H. Auden, trans., *The Elder Edda: A Selection* (New York: Random House, 1967), p. 44.

page 287   The topography and inhabitants of Jötunheim – From the *Elder Edda*, especially "Fjolsvinnsmál," "Vafthruthnismál," "Thrymsvitha," "Skírnismál." Many of the translated names in this section (such as "Strangle-the-Intruder") come from the Hollander version. Location of Jötunheim – *Heimskringla*, Part Two: *Sagas of the Norse Kings*, 1.V.

page 287   The cave of LOKI – The *Edda* does not locate it anywhere in particular, so I felt myself at liberty to put it here.

page 291   The words of ODIN the High One – "Hávamál" in Hollander, *The Poetic Edda*, p. 24 (stanza 77). I have modernized the language of this stanza a little.

page 292   Kenning for Eric Bloody-Axe – E. O. G. Turville-Petre, ed. and trans., *Scaldic Poetry* (Oxford: Clarendon, 1976), p. 22. This is a wonderful anthology and is highly recommended. The introductory essay is of considerable interest to those who want to know more about kennings and such. In *Seven Dreams* I have used three or four kennings taken from this book. (Another excellent source of kennings is Part III of the *Younger Edda* of Snorri, which is cited below.)

page 293   Miscellaneous description of HEL's hall, howes, etc. – From photographs
in Aslak Liestøl, redigert, *Osebergfunnet* (Oslo: utgitt av Universitetets Oldsak-
samling, n.d.); Snorri Sturlusson, *The Prose Edda*, trans. with intro. by Arthur
Gilchrist Brodeur, PhD (New York: American–Scandinavian Foundation, 1916),
especially part I, sec. XXXIV (p. 42). (NOTE: Also known as the *Younger Edda,
Snorra Edda*, etc.); Lee M. Hollander, ed., *Old Norse Poems: The Most Important
Non-Skaldic Verse Not Included in the Poetic Edda* (New York: Columbia University
Press, 1936). Cf. especially "The Lay of Eric," "The Song of the Valkyries,"
"The Curse of Busla," "The Sun Song."

page 297   The Queen's forehead that "glittered with rays of terror" – Here I have
borrowed from Turville-Petre's splendid translation of Egill's *Arinbjarnar Kviða*
on Eric Bloody-Axe (op. cit., p. 5): "That moonlight of / Eric's eyelashes / was
not safe / nor fearless to look on / when the forehead moon of the ruler, / glittering
like a serpent, / gleamed with its rays of terror."

THE FIRST AXE-TALE

page 303   Footnote on Freydis's descendants – *Grænlendinga Saga*, IX, p. 70.

page 306   The Skrælings' flints – "Flint doesn't occur here," says Whitehead (letter
to the author, 15 April 1988). "Chert does, which is a relative of flint . . . The
saga translations use 'flint,' because that's what they knew from European lithic
tools."

page 309   Axe citation from the *Flateyjarbók* – Adapted from *Grænlendinga Saga*, VII,
p. 67.

page 309   Axe citation from *Eirik's Saga* – Adapted from XI, p. 100.

page 312   "the foliage of words" – This phrase too was borrowed from the great
Egill Skallagrimsson.

WEARING THE WALL-SHIRT

page 315   ODIN epigraph – "Hávamál" in Bray, *The Elder or Poetic Edda*, p. 77.

page 315   Note on Freydis's return to Leif's houses – The sagas say nothing about
her leaving Karlsefni. However, *Eirik's Saga* and *Grænlendinga Saga* say contradictory things about who was with whom, as I have noted elsewhere. Leif's houses
may well have been at the L'Anse-aux-Meadows site. And there is evidence of
travel south of this place, and then of a return, for, as Whitehead says, referencing
Birgitta Wallace: "This . . . Norse site has been found to contain fragments of
butternut . . . , both wood and nuts. This tree does not grow and never did grow
north of northern New Brunswick and the Gulf of St. Lawrence" (letter to
the author, 9 March 1988).

page 316   The Uniped – *Eirik's Saga*, XII, pp. 101–2.

The Second Axe-Tale

page 319   Hakon to Gold Harald epigraph – *Heimskringla*, Part One: *Olaf Sagas*, vol. i, 1.VIII, p. 10.

page 319   Olaf to Hakon epigraph – ibid., 3.XXVIII, p. 136.

page 324   *Younger Edda* footnote – Snorri Sturlusson, *The Prose Edda*, 1.LI (p. 77).

The End

page 328   Thoreau epigraph – *The Illustrated Walden, with Photographs from the Gleason Collection*, text edited by J. Lyndon Shanley (Princeton: Princeton University Press, 1973), p. 13.

page 333   Report of the forensic examination team – "The Medieval Norsemen at Gardar: Anthropological Investigation by K. Bröste and K. Fischer-Møller, with Dental Notes and a Chapter on the Dentition by P.O. Pedersen" (1944), in *Meddeleser om Grønland*, vol. 67, p. 5.

L'Anse-aux-Meadows, Newfoundland

page 339   Footnote on manned ice islands – Central Intelligence Agency, *Polar Regions Atlas* (1978), p. 13.

Further History of the Greenland Skrælings

page 343   Self-serving epigraph – Bernadine Bailey, *Greenland in Pictures* (New York: Sterling Publishing Company, 1973), p. 38.

page 343   De la Peyrière – Bound with Zeno ms.

page 345   Pamphlet of Edward Pellham – The full title was *Gods Power and Providence; Shewn, IN THE MIRACVLOVS Preservation and Deliverance of eight Englishmen, left by mischance in Green-land, Anno 1636, nine moneths and twelve dayes* (London: R.Y./John Partridge, 1631).

Sea-Change of the Demon

page 346   Epigraph – Hinton, *The Fourth Dimension*, p. 61 or 62.

page 346   Findings which will seem irrelevant only to the vulgar appear in M. Maurette, C. Hammer, D. E. Brownlee, N. Reeh, H. H. Thomsen, "Placers of Cosmic Dust in the Blue Ice Lakes of Greenland," *Scientific American*, 22 August 1986: "A concentration process occurring in the melt zone of the Greenland ice cap has produced the richest known deposits of cosmic dust on the surface of the earth . . . With modest field efforts it seems possible to collect hundreds of grams of millimeter-sized cosmic particles. The bulk of such a collection of millions of particles would consist of material from comets and asteroids although presumably there would also be trace components from the moon, Mars, and possible other sources." It is with the other sources that we are concerned.

Acknowledgements

Grateful acknowledgement is made of a 1987 grant from the Ludwig Vogelstein Foundation of Brooklyn, New York. This award was of substantial assistance to me during my travels in Nova Scotia, Newfoundland, Iceland, Greenland and Baffin-Land.

CANADA

I would especially like to thank Ruth Holmes Whitehead, Assistant Curator of the Nova Scotia Museum, for providing me with so much valuable information on the Micmac and Beothuk (which is sourced in the appropriate places of *The Ice-Shirt*). Mme. Whitehead challenged me to improve the Vinland Skræling sections, and thanks to her guidance and suggestions they did improve; I appreciate it. (Of course any errors are my own.) – My appreciation also to the service personnel at Auyuittuq National Park (Baffin Island), Gros Morne National Park (Newfoundland), Kejimkujik National Park (Nova Scotia), L'Anse-aux-Meadows National Historic Park (Newfoundland), and Cape Breton Highlands National Park (Nova Scotia), for their courteous and knowledgeable assistance with plant identification, local history, etc., etc. I would like to thank Mr. Dennis Stossell of Atmospheric Environmental Services in Winnipeg for his kind advice and assistance. And I much appreciate Mr. Farley Mowat's words of encouragement. It would certainly be ungracious of me not to express my gratitude to Jean Claude Alavoine, Clovis Cornet, Hemé Mequignon, Michel Amiotte, Jean-Luc Berenguer, José Trigueros and Jan Piskore, for their kindness to me on Baffin Island.

ISLAND (ICELAND)

In Iceland I would like to thank Mr. Eythor Benediktsson, the schoolmaster of Stykkishólmur, for pointing out to me several of Eirik the Red's haunts, and for answering my questions. I would like to thank the Arni Magnusson Institute in Reykjavík for allowing me to visit its collection of saga manuscripts during off-hours. (I must also credit the Institute with a shining honesty not to be met with in more average institutions, for when I asked if I could send a letter containing further questions, I was told, "You are welcome. Please go ahead. But don't expect an answer. Icelanders are proverbially lazy." And I never did get an answer.) Mr. Scott Swanson gloried in the scenery with me and bought me some of the best dinners I ever had in my life.

KALAALLIT NUNAAT (GREENLAND)

In Nuuk, Greenland I want to thank Holger and Kristina Thomassen, Jorn Larsen and Najaaraaq, Bettina and Henrik Skifte, Jens Emil Binzer and Lisbeth for a debt of hospitality I can never repay. I would also like to thank the Kalaallit Nunaata Katersugaasiviat (Grønlands Landsmuseum) for permitting me to handle and study a seal skull and a polar bear skull. I am more grateful than I can say to Nuka Møller for his corrections.

NORWAY

This was the one country significant to *The Ice-Shirt* that I was not able to visit. I am all the more grateful, therefore, to Helen Jakubowski, who lived there, for checking my mythic and hearsay topography for errors.

UNITED STATES

My gratitude to Mr. Bradford Morrow, who caught a number of errors and fizzled phrases in the proofs. I would like to thank Professor Eric O. Johannesson, Professor at Berkeley's Scandinavian Department, for his encouragement and introductions. His colleague, Professor Carol Clover, author (with Professor John Lindlow) of *Old Norse-Icelandic Literature: A Critical Guide* (Ithaca: Cornell University Press, 1985), was very helpful in answering many textual questions. Mr. Tom Johnson, a graduate student in the Department, was very helpful in the matter of Old Norse orthography. (Any errors remaining in this respect are my own.) – Mr. Christopher A. Shaw, Assistant Curator at the George C. Page Museum in Los Angeles, very kindly allowed me to study and sketch some fossil predator skulls recovered from the La Brea Tar Pits (Dire Wolf and Sabertooth Cat). Particularly nice was the latter (Smilodon; cat. # 2001–2, Pit 67, delta-11, $14^1/2$ feet). – In Fresno, California, my friend and former teacher Dr. John Mawby gave me some helpful suggestions that enabled me to better prepare for sketching Arctic plants. In Long Beach, California, Jacob and Janis Dickinson assisted my Greenland researches in many directions; their help and friendship is warmly appreciated. In Berkeley, California, Mr. Seth Pilsk drew the map of Baffin Island which appears in *The Ice-Shirt*. The illustrations on the map were done by Mr. Charles Browning, and the calligraphy by Ms. Cheela Smith. In San Francisco, Mr. Paul Foster very kindly read and commented upon several drafts of the manuscript. Mr. Jock Sturges, the ballet photographer, and Mr. Alan Scofield, the dance choreographer, permitted me to witness much beauty of form and movement, which I have noted in the appropriate parts of the Sources section. Ms. Andrea Juno, co-editor of *RE/search* magazine, served as a model for the form of the young Thorgunna in *The Ice-Shirt*. A redheaded corpse at a hospital very obligingly rounded out the picture. Last, but far from least, I would like to thank the transvestites "Miss J." and "Miss Giddings" for a complete presentation on man-to-woman transformations, on which I based a scene in *The Ice-Shirt*.

Water stains noted 1-2-05

11/04